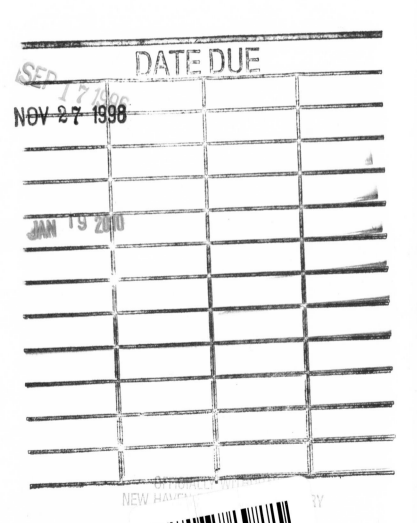

Allende:

A Novel

Allende:

A Novel

Fernando Alegría

Translated by Frank Janney

Stanford University Press

Stanford, California   1993

Allende: A Novel was originally
published in Spanish in 1989 under
the title *Allende: Mi vecino el
presidente*, © 1989 by Editorial
Planeta Chilena S.A. The present
edition has been revised by
the author.
Stanford University Press, Stanford,
California. © 1993 by the Board of
Trustees of the Leland Stanford
Junior University. Printed in the
United States of America.
CIP data appear at the end of
the book.
Partial translation of Neruda's "Sad
Song to Bore Anyone" courtesy of
John Felstiner.
Photographs courtesy of Marcelo
Montecino and the Fundación
Salvador Allende: p. 1, Allende in
military service; p. 125, Allende;
p. 143, Allende and Fernando Alegría
at a campaign meeting; p. 200, Allende
and Pablo Neruda; p. 213, the
Allendes with their grandchildren;
p. 219, Allende and José Tohá; p. 221,
Allende and his nanny, Mama Rosa;
p. 254, Allende at his inauguration,
escorted by General Pinochet; p. 271,
Luis Corvalán and leaders,
in exile in Bulgaria;
p. 273, Allende, Corvalán, and Carlos
Altamirano; p. 287, mourners at
Allende's funeral.

Foreword

In history there is often fiction, and in fiction sometimes much history. Occasionally the two collide, then merge, enriching and refining each other. Nowhere is this more apparent than in Latin America, and Fernando Alegría's *Allende: A Novel* is a prime example.

Salvador Allende's 65 years encompassed tumultuous decades of Chile's recent past. Most of what transpired during those years has been written about at length. There are many interpretations of Allende's chapter in history, but never before has a Chilean political leader been the subject of a book such as this one.

I see four principal reasons for this. First, Allende was both a product of his times and a man who helped shape them. Second, his truncated presidency and death occurred during an epoch when prose fiction became the primary vehicle by which Latin America's past(s) and present(s) were being critically examined by intellectuals. History, in short, was being written in fictive form, revised in ways appropriate to a region where the frontiers separating fact from fiction shift constantly and are not at all the same as those obtaining in Europe or North America. Third, Allende's life and death were epic in their ingredients, at the very least romantic. And fourth, Allende never had a chance to write and publish his own memoirs.

The 1973 putsch that dismantled Allende's *vía chilena al socialismo* is still fresh in the minds of Chileans and North Americans. Long after memories of the Brazilian coup of 1964 and allegations of U.S. complicity have begun to fade, North Americans still remember what happened in Chile on that bloody Tuesday, September 11, 1973. This is probably the most compelling reason why Allende's life and times will continue to influence the way foreigners think about Chile. Allende's face, his posture, his personality, his gestures, his grit, and his foibles are better known to foreigners than those of any other twentieth-century Chilean.

What a novel may lack in fidelity to historical detail it can compensate for in insights and impressions. The closer a novelist is to history, or the closer the past is to the present, the easier for history and literature to come together felicitously. Some might think this confluence detracts from historical perspective. I prefer to think of it as a sharpening of overall perspective on writer, subject, and the times of each. Reliance on fictionally historical (as opposed to historically fictional) material in so many works of the past few years is no coincidence. Latin America's "new novel" of the late twentieth century is a phenomenon of historical proportion, a major force of historical revisionism.

There is an intense relationship, probably more so than at any other time in the history of Latin America, between the recent period and its literature. Never before have alternative narrative forms—surrealism, stream of consciousness, intertextuality, internal monologue, magic realism—composed so rich a mix. In Latin America pasts do not become presents as they do elsewhere. The passing of time is more an eddy than a flow, more spiral than linear. What strikes the foreigner as bizarre is often commonplace; the outrageous is tolerable, the unreal real. Presents blur with futures, only to become presents and then pasts again.

In this book we see history and literature become literally inseparable because of the intensity of political conflict. One of Allende's political confreres is Pablo Neruda. In 1945 they both run for the Senate: Neruda is elected in the north, Allende in the south; the Left closes in on the center.

Other collisions and mergings of fiction and history dot these pages. In one place Allende is compared to García Márquez's Colonel Aureliano Buendía. Carlos Ibáñez's lamentation on the death of Arturo Alessandri is as poignant as though his old nemesis, the Lion, had been a real *patriarca*. Imagined and remembered political dialogues as intense as some in Carlos Fuentes's *Hydra Head* or Mario Vargas Llosa's *Conversation in the Cathedral* both inform and tease. Historical figures are woven into fictive backgrounds much as they are in Alejo Carpentier's *Concierto barroco* and Tomás Eloy Martínez's *Perón Novel*. Fictional history is as lyrically and evocatively portrayed as in Vargas Llosa's *Real Life of Alejandro Mayta* and Fuentes's *Old Gringo*. Alegría's intimate sketches of rural Chile are as passionate as those by the great names from the country's literary past. They are as representative of the Latin American experience as those offered in Guillermo Cabrera Infante's *View of Dawn in the Tropics*.

Most of the significant themes of the new novel are indeed here: authoritarianism versus libertarianism, military-civilian relations, relationships between men and women, depictions of urban and rural life, history and the search for national identity, the recent politics of oppression, adumbrations of the future. Through the efforts of the new novelists, such themes have become paths to historical revisionism. Important in the life and times of Salvador Allende, they all fuse in Alegría's book, giving *Allende: A Novel* a place of its own in Chilean and Latin American letters.

Allende: A Novel is vintage Alegría, faithfully rendered in Frank Janney's translation. It is a logical extension of *Recabarren* (1938); *Lautaro* (1943); Alegría's memoir, *Una especie de memoria* (1983); and *Chilean Spring* (1980), the fictional diary of a young Chilean photographer who was killed after the 1973 coup. (For a comprehensive discussion of Alegría's works, see Alegría and Juan Armando Epple's *Nos reconoce el tiempo y silba su tonada* [1987], which includes a bibliography of works by and about Alegría. See also Epple's edited *Para una fundación imaginaria de Chile: La obra literaria de Fernando Alegría* [1987].)

From the Chilean literary "Generation of 1938"—a critical year in Chile's political and historical evolution—comes Fernando Alegría, one of a number of writers who constitute the country's richest concentration of political-literary talent between the "Generation of 1842" and that since 1973. Chronicler and essayist in the manner of nineteenth-century Portugal's José Maria Eça de Queiroz; Salvador Allende's own cultural attaché in Washington; novelist and poet of Chile and Latin America, whose works are widely read not only in Spanish but in Portuguese, English, French, Bulgarian, Romanian, and Russian; scholar known to generations of students through his critical texts on poetry and prose, Alegría now takes us with him to a place where fiction and history collide and merge, to a time when the new novel is revealed as Latin America's greatest literary movement since *modernismo*.

Frederick M. Nunn

Preface

I don't remember exactly when and where I met Salvador Allende. It must have been in the thirties, at a time when students and workers were engaged in an intense struggle to unseat the oligarchy that had been ruling Chile since the nineteenth century. When I met Allende he was one of the leaders of this movement as president of the Students' Center of the School of Medicine at the University of Chile.

His relatives called him Chicho. I never knew why. Some people, not too friendly, preferred to call him Pije, a somewhat derogatory term reserved in Chile for men too fastidious about dressing. The truth is that Allende always dressed well and acted courteously firm. In difficult, threatening situations he could throw a well-aimed punch, in spite of his nearsightedness. Most of the time, though, he was kind and gentle. He was a ladies' man, willing to risk anything to gain a woman's favor. He also enjoyed practical jokes and disguises. All of this made Allende vulnerable, a strangely naive realist.

Our friendship was long and solid. I campaigned for him in the presidential elections of 1958, 1964, and 1970 (in 1964 together with Pablo Neruda). Hortensia Bussi, his wife, was a fellow student of mine at the University of Chile. I frequently visited the Allende home on Guardia Vieja in Santiago.

In 1971 President Allende asked if I would be interested in writing his biography for a publisher in Barcelona. I accepted and began a series of conversations with him. The last one took place in September 1973, days before his government was overthrown by a military coup. On September 11 I was going to be a guest for luncheon at La Moneda. That morning, at 5:00, I received a call alerting me to the fact that the coup had begun.

My book provides a reinterpretation of Chilean history in the twentieth century, specifically the efforts of a medical doctor to accomplish a peaceful socialist revolution. Allende was forced to confront a formidable opposition both from within and from without the country. As the leader of the second largest political party in Chile, he faced a well-organized, financially powerful Chilean oligarchy with strong links to the United States and Europe.

At the time that he was democratically elected president of Chile, it became obvious that Allende was offering Latin America a new democratic road toward liberation from economic injustice, foreign intervention by multinational companies, and state terrorism by military forces. Allende's socialist regime was doomed from the start. He was sabotaged by local political bosses and isolated by international economic interests. His own party drew away from him. At the end, Allende was a lonely fighter desperately struggling for a lost cause. He tried to bring about a coalition with the Christian Democrats, but failed.

In Samuel Chavkin's *Storm over Chile* (1985), I have been quoted as saying, "In my opinion Allende will not emerge in history as a revolutionary fighter, although he died fighting as a revolutionary." Now I would add that in telling the story of this respectable rebel, a liberal in the traditional sense of the word, I realize that he did not have the time to learn the martial arts he needed to defend the cause of freedom and democracy for which he died.

Allende did help the Chilean middle class and working class reach a measure of political and financial power. He did offer Latin American nations a way to find a well-balanced modus vivendi with the United States.

I consider this a conclusive biography of Allende. I have written it after working with him and representing him as cultural counselor at the Chilean embassy in Washington, D.C., home of Ambassador Orlando Letelier. I believe that my book reveals the inner struggle among the Popular Unity parties and leaders, together with the clandestine actions of agents plotting the overthrow of Allende's government; it tells the facts about the memorable battle of La Moneda and the death of Salvador Allende.

Why a novel? Writing about a personal friend who also happens to be a historical figure has induced me to go beyond simple circumstances: there are moods I must describe and interpret, words that I can hear which perhaps were not said, rumors, events that I did not witness and yet I feel I know how they happened. All this has become a hidden world that calls for a novelist, not just a reporter.

To friends such as Tencha Bussi de Allende, Hugo Miranda, Galo Gómez, Edgardo Enríquez, Carlos Briones, Hernán Santa Cruz, Mireya Latorre, Moy de Tohá, Isabel M. Letelier, Osvaldo Puccio Huidobro, Louis M. Rodríguez, Jorge Ruffinelli, Jaime Concha, Frederick M. Nunn, and George Vasquez, I say, *gracias, muchas gracias*, and to my editor, Karen Brown Davison, *gracias, mil.*

F.A.

Contents

Part I

1   The Coup: First Movement   3

2   The Man Who Would Be President   12

3   It Must Be the Students Who Are
    Keeping Us Awake   24

4   The Fall Off the Horse   31

5   Five Days That Shook Chile   43

6   In Troubled Waters   48

7   The Red Colonel   60

8   From the Jailhouse to the Senate   65

9   The Ghosts of Caldera   73

10   1938: Spring   78

11   Kill Them All!   87

12   Skyquake   92

13   Punta Arenas Is a City Carved in Stone
     by the Wind   100

14   The Proletariat's Banner   111

Part II

1   The Victory Train   127

2   The Man with the Beard   147

3   The March   152

xiii

Contents

4   It's No Better the Third Time Around   155

5   Tati and the Nephews   162

6   Waves   172

7   The Angelic Smile of Ho Chi Minh   179

8   "Habemus Candidatus," Said Condorito   187

9   "El Pueblo Unido Jamás Será Vencido"   203

10   Bye, Bye, Guardia Vieja   223

11   Allende in New York   241

12   The Butcher's Thumb   251

13   The Bull by the Horns   262

Postscript: After the Coup   289

Chronology: 1920–1989   293

Notes   297

Selected Bibliography   301

The Coup:
First Movement

Valparaíso at dawn was suspended in a wispy but tenacious fog. The city looked like a busy international port with all the usual ship and small craft movement, dock cranes, trucks and carts loading and unloading. But the commercial bustle was only a specter. The people who lived down by the docks knew that the port was a machine with the power cut off. It keeps on working for a while out of sheer momentum, but then loses steam, coughs, sputters, and finally comes to rest, surrendering at last to a state of total collapse.

The year? 1973. Although it was the weather and not the year which counted more on that morning. Between the patches of fog, the cruisers, destroyers, and frigates appeared, sliding noiselessly through the troughs in the heavy sea, their flags still furled in the darkness. Heavily armed men disembarked and quickly mobilized. The command had been given. While the hills around the port remained deep in sleep and only a few lights still winked in the workers' barrios, the marines occupied the public buildings, the plazas, the local political headquarters, universities, industries. Without a shot. Sliding across pavement shiny with dew, beating on the great doors of a fort with rifle butts, breaking off locks, cutting chains. Later, the jails would spring to life, the trucks fill with workers and students, and the cargo holds of freighters transform into instant torture chambers, rocking on the thick seas.

September 11, 1973: the military coup against the government of Salvador Allende was beginning. No explosions or sirens yet. Just the tapping of Morse code and the static of shortwave radios. Lights, signals, countersignals.

The skies close in over the barrios of Santiago. The old mansion on Tomás Moro Avenue in the suburban foothills of the Andes is still asleep when the telephone rings. President Allende sits on the edge of the bed and answers. The voice seems familiar, but the words are garbled. He turns on his reading light.

"Repeat," he says. "Repeat." And then, "Where is Minister Letelier? All right. Where is General Pinochet? It can't be. Keep calling him. Yes, we're going. Yes, yes, to La Moneda, immediately. It's not necessary, the guard unit has already been reinforced. Four cars. Exactly. Let them put their weapons in the pickup. We're leaving."

As if in a dream comes a clamoring, a banging of weapons, racing footsteps on the second floor. The guards load their rifles. Commands issue from the garden. Motors are warming up.

Allende gets up, puts on a robe, takes a few steps toward the window and draws open the curtains. The dark, snow-covered sierra. The pool reflects the shadows of the paulownia trees. The president's slow movements convey a vague sense of weariness and anguish. He is awakening from a bad dream, and the first notion to enter his head is that the end is looming near. Faces pass next to him, like mobiles, in the dark bedroom. One of them stops to look at him but quickly fades away, and in its place appears a luminous mirror. He showers, shaves, and without hurrying chooses his clothes. He will wear a magenta turtleneck and dark gray pants. In the breast pocket of his tweed jacket, a red silk handkerchief. There's no time to talk with Tencha. He'll call her later from the palace.

The caravan of blue Fiats streams out. In the scruffy barrios the clouds are lower and the light more uncertain. The September flags of Chilean independence and the red ones of the Popular Unity alliance shake off the morning dew. The thick smoke from bonfires curls upward, and the smell of burned bread comes from the wooden houses. Numbed faces look to the sky. Sparking braziers burn near the irrigation ditches.

The heavy traffic on the riverside boulevard hasn't started yet. The bus and truck companies are on strike. Business won't open today, or tomorrow, or ever. All of Santiago is paralyzed. Men, women, and children wait in their homes. Dark cars go by with smooth-looking men from the Fatherland and Freedom party at the wheel, mobilizing to take their combat stations.

"Turn on the radio," says Allende. "No, no music."

"That's all there is, compañero."

The same melody, the same "Seventh Infantry March." Then at once, an adolescent voice that warbles the spine-chilling pap of "Lili Marlene," as warlike and passionate in bed as in the trenches of the world. And now an official decree.

"A decree? A decree from the Junta? What Junta?" Allende chews on his white moustache. Smooth voices come on the air to persuade the people to remain calm.

Allende, without a hat, leaning back into the seat of the Fiat, says something about Puerto Montt but doesn't finish the sentence.

"Valparaíso has fallen," the driver says.

Allende continues to repeat names.

"Yes," he insists, "Minister Letelier, General Prats, Pinochet. Call the Defense Ministry."

He consults his wristwatch. The Fiats and the pickup maneuver like fighter planes, changing positions on the road, weaving a lightning pattern, sirens blowing.

The first camouflaged tanks appear. Allende observes them and asks if anyone can identify them. They're already very close to La Moneda. A group of reporters and photographers comes toward the Fiat. Allende gets out quickly and looks around. He walks toward the corner of Morandé Street and questions a police officer. The reporters record the conversation. "Of course," Allende says, "the guard doesn't surrender. You, señorita, you want to spice it up, put it in then: 'The guard doesn't surrender, for shit's sake.' No, of course not, the words aren't mine, Napoleon said them."

The gigantic palace guards present arms. Allende salutes and enters La Moneda without further delay.

"We brought 23 armed men," he goes on saying to his political adviser. "In the pickup are two 30-caliber machine guns, three bazookas. The navy has risen against us, the fleet has sailed back to port. We knew it all the time, Operation Unitas was only a joke. The yanquis already have aerial support over the Andes. Central Telephone Service! I can think of a better name for the bastards, they're coordinating the coup. How do you like that?"

From his office the president observes the empty plaza, the tower of the Social Security building.

Suddenly, absentmindedly, he rises from his desk, goes to the balcony and opens the French doors. He grasps the iron railing with one hand and waves with a smile to a group of shouting workers below. His private phone rings and he answers it. A reedy voice speaks to him in the name of the Junta. "Yes, sir," it insists, "the members of the Junta are offering a plane to you and your family. Of course for you, your family, and whomever else you wish to accompany you."

Down below, the plaza has filled with tanks.

"As I said," the voice repeats, "resign and leave, or leave and resign, the alternative is simple. La Moneda will be bombed."

Allende remembers the voice and the words. He heard them years ago. Thirty-two years ago? And he remembers the response: "Traitors don't know what a man of honor is. Dead is the only way you'll get me out of here." Don Pedro Aguirre Cerda was the speaker.

Allende is standing near the desk, firm and defiant. He hangs up the phone. A helicopter hovers, draws close to the Ministry of Finance building and spits machine-gun rounds. The plaza explodes in crossfire.

He has a machine gun in his hand and has put on a helmet.

"It's time to shoot," he says.

On June 26, 1908, six months after the massacre of Santa María de Iquique, Salvador Allende is born in Santiago. He will grow up in Valparaíso, the city of wind and fog, of cable cars, of hills and valleys red with clay, green with aspen and fig trees, golden with poppies.

His father, Salvador Allende Castro, was a lawyer and a notary. In those early years he was moving up through the ranks of a civil service career. His mother, Doña Laura Gossens Uribe, was an accountant. She planted the seeds of liberal education in the family, a talent perhaps passed on by her French ancestors. Six children were born to this marriage, of which four survived: Alfredo, a lawyer like his father; Inés, married to Dr. Eduardo Grove Vallejo, a naval physician and the mayor of Viña del Mar during the government of Pedro Aguirre Cerda; Laura, the youngest, married to Gastón Pascal Lyon, a four-term representative from Santiago; and Salvador.

The great figure in this solid, middle-class Chilean family was the paternal grandfather, Ramón Allende Padín, founder in 1871 of the country's first secular school, Partido Radical's representative in Congress and Grand Master of the Chilean masonic orders. An imposing man, with flaming red mustache, sideburns, and hair, straightforward and easygoing in his dealings, he was known in the hills surrounding the port city as the Red Man, not because of his politics, which were liberal but certainly not revolutionary, but in homage to his exuberance and his blazing physical appearance. The image of the grandfather inspired Salvador when years later he became initiated to the mysterious labyrinths of the outskirts of Valparaíso, with its narrow streets, workers' security cooperatives, and shops where long-haired cobblers discussed the doctrines of Bakunin and Tolstoy and talked about the adventures of Recabarren in the pampas.

Dr. Allende Padín died in poverty, having given away everything during his life, and his family received the support of the Chilean masonic orders: two houses, one to accommodate the widow and her sons, and the other to provide a modest rent. It was in the former that the father of Salvador Allende was raised.

Following the path of Salvador Allende Castro's career, the family moved to Tacna, where young Salvador completed primary school. This move, and subsequent ones, signified a pilgrimage to the Chilean frontier. Tacna was in Chilean territory, but it was the subject of contention in international courts. The wounds of a war that had divided families, fanned patriotic fires on both sides of the border with Peru, and produced a vast restructuring of wealth were not yet healed. A single company, the Andes Copper Company, owned the most important Chilean copper mines, including El Teniente and Chuquicamata, the largest open pit mine in the world.

The workers protested the monopoly of foreign consortiums and the regimen of economic slavery that the company stores and co-ops imposed through forced debt and scrip payments. They denounced, above all, the aggressive and brutal support that the armed forces gave to foreign companies, maintaining a virtual state of war with the workers' communities and organizations.

Long columns of miners marched across the pampas waving their red flags. At sunset the workers would light torches, cry out their slogans in the desert, and enter the towns as night fell. Mounted on a bench, Recabarren would speak and call to organize and unite, to defy the government and its rear guard of fraudulent bosses.

Parades filled the streets, then troops would appear. A bugle call, shouts of "fire," gunshots. Armed with chains and clubs, plainclothesmen would attack the workers' union buildings, break up the printing presses, burn the files, books, and newspapers. The leaders would end up in jail.

This was the northern Chile that Allende knew in his youth. From Tacna, the family transferred to Iquique. He wouldn't forget the marches through the pampas, the revolutionary torches, the meetings of the Socialist Workers' party in the Iquique plaza, the military abuses, the strikes, the resistance.

A notary job in Valdivia brought the Allende family back south. From the Peruvian border, they traveled to the region that separates the Central Valley from the southern extremes.

Land of lakes and volcanoes, of woods and oceans, *patria vieja* of larger-than-life traditions.

By the end of World War I, Valdivia is one of the most flourishing centers of German colonization in the south of Chile. O these earthy German gentlemen farmers who dream and sing of their new world utopia before crackling fires of hawthorn and cinnamon wood, and toast it with fiery shots of homemade booze!

Cowboys, loggers, contractors, shipbuilders, industrialists, merchants; in half a century they have turned the unruly, inhospitable country to the south into an exclusive society, firm and resilient. A rough-hewn frontier world, yet one of poetic beauty, where the winter rains blur the outlines of smoking pine cabins along the riverbanks, the lakeshores, and the tumbling sea.

Four years will be the length of their stay in the south. The Allende house in Valdivia will become the meeting place for lawyers, doctors, professors—radical masons all. They come with family, and while the grown-ups discuss, the young girls and boys sail their boats along distant and isolated channels in the Calle-Calle River: mysterious names of places, a cove where the river widens and the boats enter, nodding along between dark *boldo* forests suddenly illuminated by the light flames of the copihue flowers.

Salvador's sisters are pretty high-school girls. Salvador is a thin, clean-cut boy, with dark chestnut hair and an expression both distant and alert, an inquisitive look accentuated by glasses. He rides bareback, galloping through the forests over moss-covered logs and tangled vines. He returns home at dusk to the stone and wood house with the fragrant laurel wood smoke curling up from its chimney. Tired and hungry, he glances at the guests who are still talking next to the hearth, and he seeks out his mother in the living room, with its heavy furniture. He is absorbed for a moment in studying that beautiful, stern woman, and she returns his look with a distant smile.

His parents decide to go back to Valparaíso to build a stronger base for the family. Salvador is a young man filled with questions, intrigued by the country that unfolds before him framed by hostile frontiers. He is torn between the seductive world of fiction and the more clear-cut satisfactions of the family calling in the sciences.

Valparaíso is a merry-go-round illuminating Salvador's youth.

In 1918 the police burned down the local headquarters of the Workers' Federation in Magallanes. At that moment a new leader appeared on the scene, with a silver tongue and brilliant histrionic powers; a man of the newly wealthy middle class, who sang to the masses from the balconies of Chilean history in alluring slogans. "Beloved rabble," he would say, "hatred engenders nothing, only love produces." Then he would cajole them to rebel against the rural aristocracy, not by bearing arms, but rather by the simple expedient of voting for him for president. His name was Arturo Alessandri Palma, and he came to power to the tune of "Cielito lindo" in 1920.

Some years later, political polarization in Chile reached its limit. In 1924 a group of army officers strode into the Senate and banged their swords loudly against the floor, chanting a chorus of slogans that demanded a new order for the country. This seemingly trivial incident became the rallying point for a revolt that in one way or another rocks Chile to this day. The immediate consequence in 1924 was the overthrow of Alessandri and the takeover by a military junta that governed for a few months, only to be replaced by even shorter-lived governments. That is, until a colonel put his name on a barracks revolt of historic dimensions.

September 11, 1924. Allende would never forget this date.

The streets of Santiago are wrapped in a strange light this time of year. Springtime hides behind the snowy mountains, lighting up the high cliffs. Yet there is an uncertainty surrounding those buds that are to burst forth with new life. It is expressed by the Santiaguinos, who stay wrapped in heavy clothes even after the first long sunsets reappear and the sultry breezes of spring begin to blow. The streets and plazas start to fill with people, the pace quickens, an afternoon greeting becomes a promise of things undefined. Brass bands appear in the plazas. Young people talk of parties. At last, nights become generous, people stroll and chat until dawn.

But all at once a long military convoy rumbles by. It is the first sound of a coup brewing: coattailed civilians with bowler hats and walking sticks are fleeing the presidential chambers, while generals and colonels strike their favorite pose for photographers and resign themselves to ruling the nation. President Alessandri has considered his situation and, after listening to the counsel of his ministers, decides that the armed forces have the winning cards. He leaves the palace at midnight and seeks refuge in the American embassy.

On September 11 a military junta under the leadership of General Luis Altamirano takes over the government. In the previous months the ultra Right had been planning an uprising. They accused Alessandri of stirring up Marxist unrest.

Alessandri had proposed progressive social legislation for workers and government employees, the creation of a central bank, the institutionalization of federal income tax collection, and drastic means to fortify the executive branch. The conservatives, fearful of losing their privileges, tried then to plot with the armed forces to overthrow the president. But as the civilians conspired in secret cells, the men in uniform put their backs to the task, made their coup, and seized the day.

Then came the troop movements, and the vehicles disappearing down remote alleys carrying the crafty gentlemen away from the ruins of the fallen regime.

In Valparaíso, Allende would not forget this image. This was the way the country was done and undone: the people scattering out across the pampas, men of power opening and closing the doors of palaces and army barracks, manipulating another shred of history. This 11th of September faced him like a curtain obscuring the spring that he and his friends had just welcomed in. It gave him a strange sensation of familiarity. The day was lost and there was barely a trace of it: a weak sun suspended in time behind the snowy sierras.

The Man
Who Would Be President

In those years in Santiago, it was the names themselves—with or without the coat of arms—which
stood guard over that fountain of patrician social life and national history comprised by Dieciocho Street, República Avenue,
and the park surrounding La Moneda. During the September parties celebrating the birth of the nation, the Beaumont carriages
carrying the president and his ministers would pass before those
stately white and gray stucco residences. Sparks from the hooves
of pawing horses flew within the amber glow of bronze lamps in
the vast courtyards insulating the mansions from street traffic.

Among those houses Ramón Allende Castro's, on España Avenue, was not out of place, although it did not belong to the tight
circle of the criollo aristocracy. It was a mansion worthy of a don
with a high rank in the masonic orders. Don Ramón was politically cautious. He disliked assemblies, preferring back-room lob-
bying during moments of strife between the executive and parliament. In December 1924 don Ramón called a secret gathering.
Curling his blond mustache between his fingers, he announced
with a smile, "History is talking to us through the lips of the man
who has been, and will be again, our president. This will be a discreet, restricted meeting, señores, we don't want any upstarts or
opportunists in our midst. A little family gathering, that's all, just
to hear and weigh the man's words and get to know him better.
As if we didn't know him!"

When the guest list was almost assembled, don Ramón
thought about his brother, the notary from Valparaíso, and especially about his favorite nephew, Salvador, who was already
preparing to study medicine in Santiago.

"I'm keen to have Salvador," he said. "No matter how much

he may want to be a doctor, I can tell you he is the politician in the family. He has the eye and the nose for it. I insist. He must come."

Salvador felt the pull of the secret meeting and came to the house on España Avenue. The festive air of the occasion would not deceive him. No one would make a mistake. After the usual family matters, they would eventually arrive at the inevitable questions. Who was climbing the little ladder that led to the presidential heavens? Who was following behind him toward leadership of the party? Who was advancing from dome to dome to the serene heights of those maestros of the masonic orders?

For a young man like Salvador, those questions were better left unexplored. He was reserved, not out of timidity before the magnates of his uncle's circle, but rather out of an instinctive mistrust of this cardboard palace where the big shots played at being national patriarchs. Salvador concentrated on his studies. He read political literature but was more concerned with his grades and gaining entrance to the School of Medicine.

He would hike from one hill of Valparaíso to another, absorbing the image of the port that seems always adrift, never at anchor. He would leave his house atop Alegre Hill, with its glass-covered hallways and library with big leather chairs, and try to lose himself in the rocky alleyways and dirt paths, the little shops and bars, where dry shavings absorbed the spillings from casks and mugs.

Salvador, since school days, had had a friend at the base of the hills. More than a friend, a master—a master cobbler, tall and thin, with a deep bass voice, dark and feverish eyes, reddish spots on his prominent cheeks. His name was Juan Demarchi, an Italian immigrant and an inveterate chess player. Salvador was his disciple. Bent over his workbench, juggling nails, tacks, and shoe lasts, his hammer singing with each blow, Demarchi would speak endlessly of the dreams of the Spanish anarchists and the bombs of the Italians.

Why were the Chilean anarchists all shoemakers? Why theorists and never terrorists in fact?

"Not so fast," answered the maestro. "Don't jump to conclusions or underestimate things. Not all cobblers are anarchists, nor are all anarchists theorists."

He would grow quiet as though tallying up the bombs he had tossed and the presidents and monarchs he had decapitated. He would dream. Then he would remove a tack held between his lips and exclaim, "Organization!" He would hammer away with fast little blows and spit out another tack. "Insurrection!" He sighed, and between his bony fingers a shoe revolved, its leather tongue hanging out.

"Pablo Iglesias could take over in Madrid whenever he wanted to. Knock off Parliament. Easy. But he doesn't get excited. That's not the way with the rule-by-none folk. And the Basques? You're asking me about the Basques? The conservative ones came to Chile and became vintners. Big bucks. The revolutionaries stayed over there. The bad thing is that their revolution is terrorist and Catholic. They don't get along with the Russians. In Chile," he hammers furiously, "anarchy is the gospel of Bilbao and Santiago Arcos. Put all of don Recas's miners together with Bilbao's astronomers, Pope Julius's *metafísicos*, Dr. Cange's sociologists, and Admiral Latorre's sailors, and you'll have the republic of Yasnaya Polyana, the red sky and the black star of the rule-by-none."

Then he would reach beneath the workbench with his dark claws, pull out an even darker jar, and take a swallow as long and sonorous as the wind through the almond groves of Valparaíso. He would hammer away again, but now with the air of a visionary.

How to tell this prophet that his uncle had invited the man who would be president? The maestro would give his sick little laugh, like the bark of an asthmatic dog. "President," he would say, "to preside over pure shit."

Salvador would walk around the shop for a moment, pick up a heel or tongue, or a last with the acrid odor of horsehair, then straighten the thick tortoiseshell frames of his glasses, leaf through the maestro's pamphlets, the tired yellow pages of Bakunin, Kropotkin, Lafargue, Malatesta. He would seem to read attentively and then say abruptly, "I'm going riding, and I'll come back tonight. Do you think the socialists were wrong to support the war?"

"If you can, bring a little of your daddy's red wine," responded the maestro. "About the socialists, I don't know. The anarchists are never wrong. And if they should be wrong, there's no hope whatsoever. They'll have already thrown the bomb."

From his room in the big house on España Avenue, Salvador could witness the arrival of the dignitaries. They came in black shiny carriages drawn by spirited teams of horses with rubber shoes, or in old black Fords, or on foot, steadying themselves with stout walking sticks. Severe, reticent gentlemen dressed in dark suits and with carefully trimmed silver-flecked sideburns; señoras in bird-like hats, with wraps over their summer dresses. Gesturing madly, they would disappear behind the screens of chiseled glass. One could anticipate the embraces and the back thumping. Who among them was the historic personage? It couldn't be that little fellow with the bird's neck and slicked-back hair, who looked up at his peers as though they were buildings; nor could it be that young gentleman, tall and elegant, who greeted people as he admired himself in the reflections of the windowpanes; still less likely was that army officer, stiff and mustachioed, with a timid smile and measuring look. Salvador had his doubts too about the mature man of tired demeanor who spoke through clenched teeth, without moving his lips. He was now being saluted by the younger officer, who stood at attention.

That one reminds me more of a barracks bully than a president, Salvador decided.

The house had sprouted wings on that summer Sunday, with maids floating by carrying wicker baskets, and the servants their hemp bags; there were sprigs of sweet basil and rosemary, there was squash and roasted corn, and just now, the sweet piquant fragrance of corn pies in crusts baked until golden, served in smooth, brightly colored clay dishes. The Allende feast was like an open window, a daybreak of shellfish, the breath of meadow valleys and parks bathed in the golden wine of sunshine, noonday at the soup cauldron, with a sun made of corn for a centerpiece and the crackling of baked sugar, cooked beneath the light touch of celery stalks and watercress, all contained in the atmosphere of velvety wines that linger on the palate, of celery brandy in the afternoon breezes.

On the long tablecloth the guests saw a forest of glass and silver. At the heavy hour of desserts, they were signaling to each other with starched linen napkins, like abandoned sailors. A servant dressed in a short white jacket, insecure and swaying, smiled sleepily as he washed out the glasses and gave a goodnight kiss to the wine bottles.

Later, the scenario changed: the señoras were in the garden with the retreating sun as a backdrop, the young gentlemen now gesturing among Salvador's sisters, the patriarchs speaking slowly and heavily in the hallway next to the orange trees and avocados. The secret council had started.

And the one who seemed least predisposed to shine was the one talking: the little old man with the squinty eyes and mouth of a rodent, hair plastered to his scalp, pointed ears. His hairy fingers toyed with the watch chain that crossed his vest.

"Scrip money," he was saying, "scares off real capital. Don't you see? Our industries are fictitious, they're a burden to the people. Agriculture? Our landowners live in Santiago; they are ignorant, indolent, and rapacious."

It was a great national siesta that the little old man wished to interrupt. Beneath his voice came the buzzing of flies, the drone of a country nodding off with indigestion.

This gentleman would not raise his voice. In his hands he held the map of the crisis of the twenties and now he unfolded it, dampened as it was in lemon-scented water. This little doctor once had sent open letters to President Pedro Montt and to Barros Borgoño, but the old dignitaries were at that time "doing the continent." Among the graybeards of the period, Dr. Cange was known as eccentric and of questionable taste.

"We live off loans, we are buying time, and time is measured in bankruptcies. The yanquis are charging us interest that our grandchildren and great-grandchildren will be paying off . . ."

The response came from stomachs and intestines. "Yes, sir!" the country judge exclaimed, slapping his knee, and the professor next to him took his own pulse after each shot of cognac.

Salvador, at a discreet distance, leaning back in his chair, looking at the scene from top to bottom, like a person with myopia, said nothing; he wouldn't have dared, but he observed his uncle waiting for him to make himself heard. Why doesn't this old muskrat hold his tongue? he thought.

The señoras were having refreshments in the arboretum. Salvador's sister Inés, tall and svelte, was walking among the trees on the arm of her caballero. A smile lit up the blue eyes of her sister Laurita for an instant before her chestnut hair obscured it.

Then, just as Salvador would have liked to tell his uncle that the conversation was losing interest and that if the old man didn't hush the whole crowd would take a siesta, the smooth powerful voice of the army officer rang out. He leaned slightly against his rattan chair, and his sentences were cut somewhat short with a bit of a southern purr. His tone suggested paternal benevolence, but with a slightly mocking edge.

"If the farmers like scrip," he said, "it's because we live with an invisible currency. Ours is a country of financial sorcerers. Our farmers aren't ignorant, doctor; their science consists in sowing debts and paying them with little colored pieces of paper. No one loses, no one wins. Nitrate, my good doctor, has no future, only a past. They've already squandered it. Now they'll clean out the copper, too. Just give them time."

"The country?"

"It's got a name, doctor, a name and capital to burn."

"The people?"

The colonel looked at him kindly.

"Since when have the *rotos* counted? A clever Chilean invented the survival economy. 'Our people don't have a life, they're just alive,' as Pancho Encina once said."

Salvador thought, "Ah, here's the rooster," and looked up at his uncle. Don Ramón listened and rocked in his chair, wrapped in the smoke of his Havana cigar. The talk acquired a new rhythm. It was as though the colonel had come to change ways rather than laws; he wanted to shake things up, rather than educate; to lead, not to convince. Was this the colonel who had ordered his comrades-in-arms to the Senate to strike the floor with their sabers? The colonel with long arms, a horseman's legs, and a mysterious Central American wife?

Salvador began to recognize him little by little. The Allendes and the Ibáñezes had known each other in Iquique when Salvador's father was employed there as a notary, and Ibáñez, who held the rank of prefect, was in charge of the local police force. Now he began to understand. That afternoon, his uncle had set up a chessboard to play a match with kings, knights, towers, and bishops, but without queens or pawns. Years ago, in the shadows of a loft, next to the garden, fading away like an equestrian monument against the mountains, the colonel had mustered his own pawns and prepared the attack, while Salvador, his brother and sisters—still very young—observed the maneuvers from a little watchtower improvised on top of the chicken coop on the second patio of their house. The prefect was passing muster in front of his troops, dressed in tropical uniform, taking long steps, rigid and silent. The sun hit the hard sand under the feet of his men. A bugle had sounded. The palm trees of Iquique, immobile, withstood the noonday blast. The men mounted their horses and a sad carrousel began to twirl in the sand. The ground was pierced by shards of light. The big bass drum drove the horses wild, and between the tails with their ribbons of green and white, the children could see that in the little tower of the house was a lady with very white skin and red hair, in a vaporous robe, waving a lace handkerchief, as if bidding adieu to her paramour and his troops, or as if shooing away the blue flies that came from the desert or the stables.

Yes, he was the major, the colonel, the prefect, Carlos Ibáñez del Campo, svelte and dignified, with black hair cut like a Prussian; his wife was Rosita Quiroz, virgin of San Miguel de El Salvador, made wealthy on indigo and henequen, a beauty transplanted from jungles of ceiba trees and flaming flowers to the dry sadness of the sands of Atacama.

Salvador owed his being sent to study at the National Institute of Santiago to the wisdom of Ibáñez. He also owed him the fact that he was able to surprise his parents years later by serving with the cavalry regiment of Viña del Mar; Ibáñez was a consummate riding master.

One day, however, this tall, well-mannered man appeared on the national scene with his deceivingly smooth air and a reputation based on action; he was the only Chilean military leader in those years who had actually fought in a war, a foreign one it is true, and in a tropical country, but with bullets, cannon fire, charges, retreats, and casualties, and he had won it. And by the same token, he was the only military leader who, instead of strutting about delivering harangues, really acted. While the others discussed and appointed commissions, he would mount his horse and, squeezing flanks with spurs, make the leap.

The white-jacketed waiter, with bloodshot eyes but partially revived, entered at that moment and bent down next to don Ramón, whispering something in his ear. Don Ramón stood up and said, "Señores, let's retire to the library. Doña Inés Echeverría has arrived."

All rose and mutely followed their host. In the well-lit library, doña Inés was waiting, leaning slightly against the mantelpiece, her blond hair floating as though tossed by an invisible wind. Her shawl seemed to fall from her shoulder, and her attitude was at once dominating and guileless, like the figurehead of a drifting ship. She smiled with just a touch of disdain, but on taking don Ramón's hand, she seemed to relax, closed her eyes for a moment, and—haughty all the while—opened her lips as though on the point of singing or announcing the end of just one more world, the dying moments of an unconfessed passion. From then on, doña Inés would be queen; and from his altar across the ocean, pensive, distant, and condescending, don Arturo Alessandri, the Lion of Tarapacá, the man she had come to venerate, would shine forth even in his absence.

Salvador had drawn near, offering her a chair next to don Ramón. She smiled at him, holding on to his arm and saying gracias with an otherworldly accent, as though it were a word she had invented at that moment and just for him. The gathering was hers, the guests her retinue. With cool elegance, she took a sheaf of papers and began to read, although in truth she was singing, impassioned now, impetuous, yet with wisely distributed and dramatically effective pauses. Her uplifted hand directed a choir of deputies, senators, generals, and writers, a turn-of-the-century coterie, laced with cognac and the smoke of Havana cigars. The name of Alessandri emanated as though from a warm, sad cello, nostalgic and presidential. She read from a recent letter written abroad by don Arturo, inspired by a scene in the Grevin Museum: " 'I contemplated the sight of Napoleon there, in the fullness of youth, with all of the splendor of a sun as it rises. . . . In the fullness of love, Josephine next to him, listening to a symphony, caressing silently this superior being, future ruler of the world, king and master of her sentiments and entire person. . . . My thoughts, like a lightning bolt, flew over there, far away, toward that little patch of distant land, lost between the majesty of the ocean and the cordillera. . . . Dearly beloved lady, my friend . . .' "

At this point doña Inés squeezed her finely embroidered handkerchief between her fingers and fell into silence with a wounded, hurricane-ravaged heart.

Salvador imagined her crinkling up don Arturo's enormously wide necktie, and had to restrain a laugh. What a pair the country has bestowed upon us! The palace hasn't seen such a show since the famous tenor of the Alianza Liberal Party flew the coop!

"Is it true," he asked his uncle, "that don Arturo's grandfather came to Chile from Italy with a company of puppeteers and tenors?"

Don Ramón looked at him astonishedly, and with forefinger to lips, he bade his nephew be silent.

Doña Inés kept reading, pausing to observe her audience, looking for that martial man of order who would convulse the country, opening the paths of Alameda Park to the passage of the prodigal president. Her eyes fell on the taciturn figure of Colonel Ibáñez, who was massaging his knuckles while he listened and looked at his boots.

"The country," said doña Inés, "awaits action. It awaits it from you, colonel, so that my land can once again be young and beautiful."

The colonel raised his eyes and, adjusting the metallic frames of his glasses, regarded her at length. With amused irony, he assented.

"Doña Inés," he responded, "the Alameda is open. All that's lacking is to erect the bleachers so that the country may receive don Arturo."

And he smiled, admiring his own aplomb.

The summer revealed itself in all its exuberance through the large window, and the sound of voices celebrating the warm solitude of an abandoned Santiago floated up from España Avenue. No one stays in the city, nothing happens in these lazy months. Not even barracks revolts? Not even barracks revolts. Nothing. Politics are out on break. Pudgy senators buy brightly colored little shovels and buckets for their children and mobilize their wives, and for three months Chile rests belly up on the sand and sleeps like a log. Ah, but the regiments stay behind! It is true, the regiments stay, but the massive doors of the military are nevertheless shut. The privates on guard duty are like happy sleepwalkers watching the lovesick students wandering by.

> *"What could that noise be*
> *coming from over there?"*

"It's not the students, my dear friend," says doña Inés, looking at don Ramón with her eyes half shut, "it's the colonels; only they know the other face of summer, the steady drum that heralds in the fall for us.

"You, Salvador," she says, suddenly turning around, "you are already old enough for the military, isn't that so? Of course it's your turn," she adds, without waiting for a reply. "I'll bet you think like I do, that the barracks don't die with the summer, ah?"

"The barracks never close, doña Inés," he replies. "For them there are no seasons at all. I'm going to join the cavalry regiment of Viña del Mar in January."

"See what I mean? Isn't that just what I was saying?"

And the beautiful lady remained pensive. "It must be odd to have never been in a barracks and arrive just in time for a coup."

Much later, past midnight, when all the guests had left, Salvador discreetly entered the library, where he had seen his uncle smoking and gently swirling the last drops of cognac in his bell-like glass. On seeing him, don Ramón asked, "Did you like the man?"

"The old man's wires are frayed."

"I don't mean the doctor. I'm talking about the man who wants to be president."

"Don Arturo," said Salvador, wrinkling his brow.

Don Ramón lifted his glass as though he were going to toast. "It looks like you didn't even see him," the uncle said.

Salvador remained thoughtful and looked at his uncle. Touching the end of his nose, he asked, "The colonel?"

"Of course, man, and who else would it be?"

"He didn't seem to show any ambitions, he only talked about don Arturo and his admiration for him. Besides, he doesn't have the makings of a ruler."

"But he's all right with a sword in his hand. That's what is needed, a strong hand."

"A strong hand," Salvador repeated. "And if he overdoes it?"

"Ah, that's what Alessandri the Lion is for," said don Ramón, "so that he doesn't overdo it."

That night Salvador lay wrapped in the dense vapors of the secret council and entered restlessly into a profound slumber.

Astonished, he discovered that they were all wrong: in his dream the man who wanted to be president was he himself, not the soldier or the Lion, but rather an adolescent Salvador, cuddled in the arms of the all-powerful Iris, dizzied by perfumes and the smoke of Havana cigars. And in the living room of his uncle's mansion, all of a sudden, the deer on the national coat of arms fell prey to the talons of the condor, and above both creatures shone the sovereign image of a clever colonel waving a broom for a sword.

It Must Be the Students
Who Are Keeping Us Awake

The little country, stretched out between the snow-covered mountains and a blue ocean of prehistoric pulse, all of a sudden caught fire, like a revolutionary's torch. From Santiago, where there was no government except a headless junta, the politicians and the military were sending off telegrams north and south. Special troop commanders were dispatched to apply war measures against defenseless crowds.

From the courts of Europe former president Alessandri returned via Argentinian ocean liner, smiling and at ease, savoring generous wines, kissing hands, inscribing his tortuous signature on ladies' fans, articles of fine leather, and even souvenir menus recalling extravagant dinners. Always surrounded by dark coats and shiny domes, he basked in the praise of fiery female patriots and was guarded by odd-looking civilians who kept their uniforms hidden in the closet. With glass raised on high to the Statue of Liberty, who reciprocated with her plastic torch, Alessandri came a-flying, coattails floating behind. Deep diving over from the Eiffel Tower with his retinue of peers—señores all, members of the Club de la Unión—dishing out money to oust the colonel—*who do they think they are?*—don Arturo forged down boulevards and avenues, from Paris to Buenos Aires, Buenos Aires to Rio, to Montevideo, to Valparaíso, to Santiago, striding through leafy parks, patrician, august, a lion among lions, yet humble, kissing the ring of Pope Pius XI to seal the eternal separation of church and state, kissing Mr. Coolidge's ring to bury the conflict with Peru and to invalidate the plebiscite of Tacna and Arica. Moving on, somewhat slow and hunched over, with an unrelenting facial tic but a wide smile on his lips, most recently dressed in a black MacFarlan cape, he would greet onlookers with a tip of his bowler. He looked a bit sad, yet elegant in his way, right down to those patent leather shoes and black silk socks. Arriving at the Mapocho Station like some sluggish night train, Alessandri hit all the bells and whistles, as the whole country applauded from new bleachers thrown up on both sides of the Alameda. It was a warm day in April beneath the pepper trees laced with streamers and smelling of dead seed. Covered with dust, dragging his feet on the road like a wanderer off course, his derby sitting back on his crown, enormously tired, surrounded by shouting and laughing men, women, and children who jumped from the bleachers, the Lion of Tarapacá submerged himself in the dusty Alameda de las Delicias until finally he entered La Moneda, seeking in the Red Room a chair to rest his weary bones in, and Colonel Ibáñez wordlessly took him by the arm and sat him down on the tricolored presidential chair.

The house with the white facade and the turquoise green cornices, floating up Alegre Hill, looked as though it had been plucked by fate from a shipwreck in a typhoon. Fate, or whoever put it there in defiance of the laws of nature, perhaps thought that a great swelling of the rivers would someday reach it, and with flags unfurled in the breeze, a visionary captain would set sail in it once more, down below, through the open bay of Valparaíso. But this was Viña del Mar territory, where the discreet manner of the local folk bore the stamp of two Protestant churches of English origin and this sort of fantasy would not have been condoned. Salvador was fond of the house, and now alone, packing his bag and putting his books aside for storage before going off to the military, he knew that he would miss it. From his room he could see the fig trees of the neighborhood and beyond them the eucalyptus and pines studding the hills.

That morning Salvador decided to take his leave of maestro Demarchi. Armed with some beautiful wine from his father's cellar, he arrived at the shop, greeted the maestro, and gave a sparing account of his next moves. The anarchist listened to him with his cobbler's tacks firmly gripped between his lips, and then, without looking at him, delivered an opinion.

"It's good you're going into the service. That's the way it should be, not like the rich kids from your neighborhood who weasel out of it with fifty pesos. You've got to go with the people and live through the tough times. And you know what's waiting for you. They'll try to get a rise out of you at every turn—especially you. Don't kid yourself. But remember, you're going in with a sacred duty"—here he adopted a sermon-like tone—"and to complete a mission: organize and agitate, as a revolutionary sowing the seeds of a new, classless society. A revolutionary, my young man, not a green recruit. And if they catch you in the act, hold fast and look 'em in the eye."

Salvador was not listening to him; he was looking around and taking in the smell of the shop, thinking what a long time would pass before he would return to it, maybe never to see the maestro again. Once his military service was over, he would go to Santiago and start at the university, not one cloistered in tradition, but more like the one Gorky had evoked in a difficult and mysterious era, the street university, with student assemblies for revolutionary recruits.

Outside, just a few steps from the shop, a barrel organ blasted its music of whistles and groans, kisses and cherries, with a rhythm of nocturnal anticipation, a wordless song open to the hills without an answering echo from the sea, lost below in the distant noise of cranes and tugboat sirens.

By now the maestro was skirting the theme of Rosa Luxemburg in the martial courts of the czarist officers, whom he described with baggy pants and gigantic muskets doing target practice.

"It will be your lot to serve in tough times, Allende my friend, very tough. And you guys will serve as henchmen. The Lion has come back, yes, but Ibáñez will trim his mane right quick. They'll send you out into the street, Salvador, and don't forget, when you're prancing around with your horse and looking down your lance, don't forget that the ones running out from under you are your brothers. Think it over—twice."

Useless words. Behind him they would scatter in the wind. He would go down the hill with great long strides, breathing deeply, using as his guide the lights of the street lamps, which signaled the flatlands around Viña del Mar.

It was an Allende tradition to do military service. He simply did not question that. And there was more to it: behind the Allende name was military history of the epic variety. The red, impulsive Ramón Allende Padín had been director of medical services during the Pacific War. When the war started he was a senator. He resigned immediately and enlisted in the celebrated Seventh Line Division. He died at forty, and his funeral was the occasion of national mourning. Among the pallbearers were don José Manuel Balmaceda and don Ramón Barros Luco. The farewell was delivered by Enrique MacIver, known as the Golden Tongue. "El rojo" Allende was the founder of the first maternity hospital in Santiago and president of the Sanitation Department and the Department of Public Education.

Other Allendes shone brightly in the history of Chile: a great grandfather, Ramón Allende Garcés, and his brothers Gregorio and José María, fought in the War of Independence. Gregorio Allende commanded O'Higgins's personal guard and marched into exile with him in 1823. Ramón and José María fought together with Manuel Rodríguez in the Hussars of Death regiment. There were as many Ramóns and Salvadors of patriotic lineage among the Allendes as José Arcadios in the García Márquez fables about the famous Buendías.

In 1925 Allende is a vigorous man of 17. He wears thick glasses and dresses with care. He has a reputation as a student for being somewhat of a grind, yet he is a swimming and decathlon star.

Allende the soldier would like to get a handle on the political crisis by canvassing his comrades-in-arms, but in those days such activity would smack of subversion. He would save his questions for his visits home. Now it is his father, open to the concerns of the young soldier, who gives him his ear, even while demonstrating reluctance at seeing his son commit himself politically.

"You can't be a soldier and promote revolution," his father says to him. "Your duty is to take orders and pipe down. You'll have plenty of time for politics when you're a medical student."

During that year family relations between the Allendes and the Groves became more intimate. Dr. Eduardo Grove had married Salvador's younger sister, Inés, and the Grove mansion had become a frequent scene of family get-togethers. Salvador hung about with the doctor's brother Marmaduque, a red colonel and inspired conspirator. Colonel Marmaduque Grove mistrusted Ibáñez and stated that behind the mask of patriotism were the fangs of a tiger, adding that one could see the claws when he massaged his knuckles.

"That man is trigger-happy," he would tell Salvador, "and under his poncho, you can spot the cudgel of a true cop."

Grove, then, was inclined to support Alessandri, a conspirator like himself, a man of action and a master of the art of political intrigue and populist coddling.

Listening to the colonel, Salvador learned to sympathize with Alessandri. And his father had always felt a bond of affection for the Lion, stopping to visit him in his trips to the capital.

There he was, Allende, the raw recruit: thin and bony with large powerful hands made stronger in the daily handling of tough, spirited horses. At dawn he would spend hours cleaning harnesses and saddles, shining leather, combing manes, tying roses to mares' tails, a sleepy recruit waiting for a bugle call, smelling the aroma of coffee, dreading the hour of bareback trotting, the races without reins where he would hold on and guide the horse with his knees, taking aim with a lance. Then maybe a fall, followed by a jump, and again the reckless galloping, while thoughts would come into his head of tomorrow's shouting crowds, marching and running along Playa Ancha, those same people who only yesterday were singing "Cielito lindo" and today demanded the Lion's mustache.

The year 1925 will pass quickly and violently.

On October 12 Ibáñez tossed out Alessandri. Then he called general elections for the presidency. Two candidates run: don Emiliano Figueroa Larraín, a seasoned flashy type, cigar smoker, and collector of erotica, and in the opposing corner, Dr. José Santos Salas, a person of questionable reputation about whom astonishing things were being said—"The employees of the Ministry of Public Health and Social Welfare, among others, said that Dr. Salas was fond of hosting get-togethers in his office of the military hospital where he practiced, and would invite soldiers there—privates and sergeants—with whom he would dance, lacking señoras to accompany him, in these improvised little after-dinner soirees." Emiliano Figueroa triumphed with a great majority of votes.

Months went by, ministries rose and fell, and finally Colonel Ibáñez began discarding his adversaries one by one, isolating the new president and pitting him against the Supreme Court. Bored with the foppish idyll of Figueroa's term, Ibáñez finally deposed him. Don Emiliano was profoundly grateful. He resigned on March 4, 1927.

Having ascended to power with the one-half of the tricolored sash that was his spoils as vice-president, Ibáñez revealed his involvement in a cult hitherto concealed from public view: he was a devout worshipper of Benito Mussolini. Following the example of the black-shirted baldpate, Ibáñez reorganized the local police and founded the Carabineers, dictated a Mussolinian Labor Code, and created some new low-income housing following the model of the Dopolavoro of his master, Il Duce.

When the moment arrived Ibáñez decided to institutionalize, and he called for new presidential elections. He had established a strong political base. Facing a single rival, he was elected by a greater than absolute majority, something unheard of in Chile:

Ibáñez obtained 98 percent of the national vote. Once in power he governed with an iron hand, eliminating the opposition by means of banishment and prison. Colonel Grove marched out in fashionable exile, assigned as military attaché to the courts of Europe.

All of a sudden the back and side doors of the Chilean economy were opened: the British companies departed and enter Anaconda, ITT, and a fake Chilean Electric Company, made in the USA, with a 99-year lease. U.S. investments, which in 1913 had added up to $15 million, jumped to $729 million in 1930. Ibáñez made use of his unlimited powers, appointing a puppet Congress without elections. Ruling at his leisure in a kind of parliamentary limbo, he began to amass a monstrous external debt. The dictatorship of the pensive, executive colonel began full blast.

The students, with Salvador Allende in the lead, are the first to rise up.

The Fall
Off the Horse

Santiago, with its schools spread out through diverse neighborhoods, was a university city of transients, in spirit and body. They were literally everywhere, stopping in plazas and parks, soda fountains and cafes, marking time between strikes and graduate studies, at the ready but grinding for exams, while the smoke from their debates spiraled up toward the pages of history.

In those years students went from school to school, hanging on to yellow trolleys and buses called "góndolas," laden with books and pamphlets, hatless, wrapped in scarves, shouting and laughing, pockets filled with chalk for writing their memoirs on the walls. Colonel Ibáñez despised them, but the Federation of Chilean Workers (FOCH) made them a place in the revolutionary vanguard. Their leaders appeared under the guiding spirit of the University Reformers of Córdoba. "Autonomy!" they shouted. "The university defends its domain. Let no one violate it!"

From the rooftops came the police thugs, swinging left and right, roughing up the kids in preparation for the campaign that followed. Some of the students—the boldest, in law and medicine, led by Salvador Allende—would take cover on the rooftops of the Law School or on the towers of Santa Lucía Hill and take feeble shots with pistols more like peashooters than weapons. A bugle would sound and then, galloping through the Alameda, the mounted police would appear. The students would run, leaping over newsstands and benches, taking refuge behind statues, flinging volleys of rocks until finally, beating a timely retreat, they would enter the administration building, slamming the gigantic colonial doors behind them. Once inside, they would holler down from the balconies, "Autonomy!"

The police waited patiently, calming their pawing horses, which decorated the streets with steaming dung. A captain with a little blond mustache and furrowed brow raised his saber and shouted, spurring his prancing horse. All of a sudden the cannon shot of noon was heard. Everyone looked at watches and set them, attackers and attacked alike, and then the troops retired to the barracks with a short, rhythmic trot. Students, strikers, police, and spectators all went home. It was lunchtime. The battle would resume at dusk, at the vermouth and cinema hour.

In those moments, when the provinces and their young leaders cried out against the centralism of the capital city, a whole revolutionary generation bound to change the face of Chilean society was raising its head.

The young people came from north and south. They had read Marx and Engels, had grown up in the aftermath of the October Revolution. Fraternizing with Peruvian socialists, they read Mariátegui's essays as their bible. They claimed political and economic power and came to Santiago sweeping away the traditional university barriers, finding the roads to government jobs and the narrow paths into the hermetic cloisters of military and naval command centers.

A long-beaked student of French literature strode the corridors of the old house on Cummings Street, where the Pedagogical Institute operated. The young man with long, slow strides, shrouded in a cape too long for him, was Pablo Neruda, who had just published his *Twenty Poems of Love* and was writing the first part of *Residence on Earth*. His first literary salvos were fired from *Claridad*, a review he published with Pablo de Rokha, Raúl Silva Castro and Eugenio González, all revolutionary writers at the time. In the university assemblies and street gatherings, other young men, arrogant and aggressive, would speak out with grandiloquent gestures: Pedro León Ugalde, Juan Pradenas Muñoz,

Carlos Alberto Martínez. Among them Pradenas stood out because of his stature, his huge Stetson, and his wide shoulders and hamlike fists. When he waxed forth in Congress, the rickety benches would shake and ripples would form on the surface of the parliamentarians' morning refreshments.

In that exuberant period of wild and woolly caucuses, Salvador Allende arrived at the University of Chile and registered in the School of Medicine, the most politically progressive and belligerent of the schools. It occupied an old building on Independencia Avenue, near the city limits of Santiago. Just a few blocks away, carts and wagons would pass by at dawn, bringing in vegetables from neighboring farms. Field-workers and street toughs settled their differences in the bushes of Centenario Park. Unidentified bodies were picked up later to be exhibited on the tables and in the glass cases of the morgue.

On one side of the School of Medicine was the restaurant-bar End of Sorrows. From its back rooms you looked straight onto the vast public cemetery, which beckoned patrons with its great portals open in ambivalent greeting.

Allende was well received: he was coming from the port city with the lean, hard look acquired in the cavalry, and at the same time with something of that trim elegance that associated him with Viña del Mar. He spoke with vigor and enthusiasm, in short, clear, and well-thought-out sentences. He wasn't a facile orator out for dramatic effect; he propelled the university's mandate directly into the bitter political duel at the national level. But the leftist groups that took him in were divided. Under the influence of Allende and his fellow students at the School of Medicine, the young communists and socialists closed ranks in a tight, disciplined, activist formation called Group Avance.

As the nation's political crisis deepened, hastily printed flyers, calling for assemblies and denouncing the repressive measures of the government, floated over the barrios surrounding the university. Students would gather in the main auditorium, with its cavernous acoustics. Spontaneous orators hung from the highest gallery, speaking out of turn. Only the brigades of the student federation could shut them up, dislodging them from their perches. In such a forum, there was no room for lofty theoreticians, scholarly zealots, or superpatriots. The arena was strictly for the impassioned expression of barkers, baritones, and tenors with hair-raising gestures, masters of the long, modulated phrase wadded with repetition and framed in an abrupt, apocalyptic finale. Allende learned from them, and once in the street was bold enough to improve on their style, exchanging the strident note for the concise statement, direct and vibrant.

The dictatorship of Ibáñez pushed the Left toward a violent confrontation. The workers and the students chose the weapon that either makes or breaks a revolutionary movement: the general strike. The action started in the provinces and flowed in toward the big urban centers. It was getting more and more difficult to avoid the internal strife within the Group Avance. Squaring off against its communist nucleus, a Trotskyite resistance group appeared. Debates overflowed the university classrooms, continuing in the local headquarters of the Federation of Chilean Students, in bars and at hot dog counters. For Allende they lasted all night at his boardinghouse on Recoleta Street.

Salvador came to the revolutionary movement through his consciousness of a class inequality typical in Chile and exacerbated in Santiago. The oligarchy marked its fiefdom with absolute arrogance. The "big house" of which Orrego Luco wrote was also the closed house, where those of crusted lineage would fortify themselves, wielding their nontransferable stamp of power as they governed banks and industry from boards stacked with members of the familiar circle. The middle class chafed under the scorn, sometimes expressed openly, but usually indirectly, of this untitled aristocracy.

A seismic shake-up in the Chilean class system was brewing. First came the nitrate-mining crisis and the world depression of the 1930's, which together swept away the classist defense barriers of the oligarchy. The great families had to close off their second and third patios, retreating to inhospitable country houses, there to spend limitless "vacations," mortgaging themselves to the hilt, depositing their European luxuries in ever-larger and dustier steamer trunks. These nouveaux poor began to constitute a new class, called the *medio pelo*. A barometer of the period, many of them would descend to the misery of the boardinghouse in old neighborhoods, or with luck hang on to their no-man's-land in the country.

Recollecting those years, Allende once said, "I began to frequent the barrios and the countryside, because I wanted to be like my grandfather, Dr. Ramón Allende Padín. I wanted to study medicine to be able to serve the workers and the needy."

His father no longer had the means to pay for Salvador's studies, so Salvador became a teaching assistant in the university's Pathology Department, while also working shifts at the local emergency room and at the psychiatric hospital. He also taught night school.

He brought a new dimension to university politics, seeking a combination of grass-roots action and ideological bonds with workers; he and his friends worked to ally progressive elements of the middle class with the revolutionary workers' vanguard. The students responded to his call. He was elected president of the student body of the School of Medicine in 1927 and in 1930 vice-president of the Federation of Chilean Students. In 1929 Salvador joined the Chilean freemasonry.

During this period, the most repressive of times under the Ibáñez dictatorship, Allende was already well known in the meetings where the student federation was preparing for the general strike. His name was starting to become even better known in the secret files of the government political intelligence service. At the conclusion of a meeting in front of the Law School, after a speech to a group of students and workers, Allende was sequestered by agents of the secret police.

With the increasing economic disaster of the thirties, panic took hold of the Chilean people. As merchants folded shop, estates were mortgaged, and banks closed their baroque doors, this country—"a model among nations of civic virtue and moderation," in the parlance of the times—entered into an arena of political turbulence that would mark it for the rest of the century. The era of paternal presidents and big shots who handled the country's business at the Club de la Unión was gone forever.

Ibáñez ties his horse up in the Patio of the Orange Trees and strides into La Moneda. Chile falls, in the end, into the trap of the old style Latin American *caudillismo*.

The leading actors play out some of their parts abroad, in scenarios combining the theatrical mise-en-scène of Alessandri with the backdrop of adventures, barracks revolts, and conspiracies so favored by Colonel Marmaduque Grove.

In May 1929 Grove is already in Buenos Aires giving the last strokes to his grand plans for a coup that will be known as the "waggish landing of the Red Plane." The preparations took over a year. On September 20, 1930, Grove left Buenos Aires in a Fokker Trimotor, intending to overthrow Ibáñez. With him was a strange crew. The pilot was an American named Edward Orville, from Oklahoma, specially hired by the would-be revolutionaries. After a pit stop just east of the Andes, he aimed his craft toward Concepción and eventually landed, not at the regiment where he was supposed to arrive, but in the middle of the municipal racetrack during the last lap of the main race. They had made it over the mountains sucking air from rubber bags, pitching and turning like a lost kite.

The country was greatly amused by this event, and newspeople given to exaggeration stated that the revolutionaries had brought Halley's comet into the race. Left to their own devices by the denizens of the horse world, Grove and his people took a taxi downtown. The general on duty, alerted of the danger, was seen getting on and off trains that took him fleeing toward San Rosendo and then hurtling back to Concepción with the hope that the coup had by then failed. Grove and the rest of the founding fathers of the failed new order-to-be, pale, dizzy, disheveled, landed in jail and were sent later to the brig at Talcahuano.

The tale is told that Grove, facing the judge who would sentence him, shouted, "Listen, Vigorena, my friend, it's a simple matter: the death penalty and nothing less. You don't need to spend time heating up the old brain on it."

Vigorena, smiling with satisfaction, agreed, and right there on the spot condemned Grove to be executed. But Ibáñez, on hearing the verdict, exclaimed, "No! How did you get such an idea to shoot Grove? You've only got to send that fool to Easter Island to keep him from sticking his nose in things!"

Straight to Easter Island the aerial revolutionaries went. They didn't stay long, however. One day the Valencia, a pretty sloop, appeared with her sails and her larder well filled, having been provisioned in Tahiti by representatives of Alessandri and his Parisian cronies. At dawn, under the dispassionate gaze of the great stone icons, the fugitives slipped between the rocks and into a canoe that took them to the Valencia. Sometime later they disembarked in Papeete.

Salvador Allende, leader of the Federation of Chilean Students, commented to Eugenio Matte Hurtado, enlightened evangelist of socialism, that if such attempts at revolution existed on the fringe it wasn't exactly by spontaneous combustion, but rather because the country was ripe for a change in the system itself and not just in the present regime.

"Socialist revolutions," responded Matte, "happen when the people have their own party and their own program, and not until then. What we are witnessing is merely the bumbling antics of rash fools. Chile is waiting for a genuine cataclysm, one that will be heralded by the slogans of the new state, the workers' republic."

Santiago became filled with revolutionary conclaves; they would take place in private homes or in social clubs or in casinos. People lunched and dined in order to plot. Orators forgot their speeches, raised their glasses, and remained motionless waiting for the call of history.

Political programs were spread out on the table in a gamut of fascinating colors: from red Soviets coming to Chilean soil, to the foundation of a celestial blue City of God beneath the wings of

Christian Socialism, to the paper-white stages of union legalization, university reform, and eventually the takeover of country properties and a naval insurrection.

But one could hear voices that were out of tune with the chorus, haughty and shrill voices that demanded action instead of castles in the air, voices that seemed to come from streets as far-removed from the wealthy enclaves of Santiago as from the stock exchange or the tree-lined avenues of Congress.

"It is the students," Oscar Cifuentes said, "who are coming . . ."

The students who came down from their pulpits to visit the homes of politicians, to yank their chains a bit, to shake them up: Oscar Schnake, with his long, dark hair, tall, thin, and tough; Eugenio González Rojas, even taller, pale and dressed in black, deep and quiet, a philosophical orator capable of sad lyricism, a popular novelist to boot.

"Where do they come from?" asked Luis Barriga Errázuriz.

"They want to make revolution," said Alfredo Lagarrigue Rengifo.

"Yes, but they're overdoing it."

"They want to throw 'The Horse' right out of the palace."

"And not the rider?"

"Well, both of them. And they won't stop at that. They want to keep striking."

So well coordinated were the forces of conspiracy that the dictator began to teeter. His fall was a natural phenomenon. He went down under his own weight: the ruin of the national economy; the general strike organized by the Federation of Chilean Students; the assault, commanded by Allende, on the University of Chile; plus a big shove—the last and most decisive one—by the conservatives of the Club de la Unión, who put their heads and wallets together to get arms to the students.

There was fighting in the streets. The police had defended Ibáñez desperately. But suddenly they disappeared and went back to their barracks, locking the doors. Those who didn't flee in time were strung up in the Central Station and Mapocho barrios. The army retired and kept a prudent distance. Ibáñez, terrified, called a council of national leaders. No one showed up. Months before, he had sent his minister of finance, Pablo Ramírez, to Paris, with the purpose of obtaining new loans to save the government from bankruptcy. The forces in exile, led by Alessandri, sabotaged that effort.

One July afternoon the medical students called a meeting. Tempers were boiling over, and from the cemetery came the rumble of a confrontation between the police and the schoolteachers. At dusk the students invaded the Independencia Avenue area and reached the grand plaza and the portals of the public cemetery.

The demonstrators were surrounded by infantry with machine guns; behind them loomed the growing shadow of the cavalry, blending in the dark with the arches and walkways. The speakers followed one another, competing in their fiery denunciations of the military government. The afternoon was going out with the melancholy brilliance of Chilean winter sunsets; from the cloudy sky came a cold mist that wrapped around the horses and the mass of police cloaked in heavy ponchos. The street reflected the yellow light of the street lamps. From inside the cemetery the students began hurling rocks over the wall.

Next to the platform Allende awaited his turn to speak. Drawn up and stiff, looking over the heads of the crowd, he felt the afternoon wind in his face. More than the cold, he registered the silent, morbid threat of the horsemen and the lethal mixture of fear and anger in the front ranks of the police. Placing one foot on the step of the platform, he felt his leg start to tremble, and he had to make an effort to calm himself and face the crowd. In a measured, powerful voice, he told the story of an obscure teacher who had defied the powers of the dictatorship during his union's strike. Allende described the hours of terror, the ordeal at secret police headquarters, the torture chamber, the punching, the electric shocks, and then death itself.

"The dictator cannot silence the voice of this dead man," he said. "His rebellious cry will keep ringing in our ears as a call to battle and sacrifice. Compañeros in education, comrades of the

Federation of Students, fellow students, the hour to demand our due from the dictatorship has arrived! Nothing will stop us. We are the people of Chile, and in our hands belongs the flag of popular democracy!"

In the midst of vivas and applause, over the shouts of the multitude massing toward the portals, the first shots could be heard, muffled bursts like big raindrops from a flash storm in the growing darkness. Then came the downpour, the stampede of workers and students and the galloping of the cavalry, the blows struck with sabers and clubs. A command rang out and a bugle sounded a charge.

The disturbance was short-lived. Night fell. The demonstrators retired when a rumor began to circulate in the plaza: *They killed a student.* Who is he? There he is stretched out near the gate. Allende and his comrades kneeled next to the corpse. They killed Jaime Pinto Riesco. He was hit in the face.

The students marched down Independencia Avenue, toward the center of the city and the Alameda. Mysteriously, the police had faded away. From the big balconies of the Club de la Unión, gentlemen in dark suits, smoking thick Havanas, were in agreement, nodding their heads.

"And yes, he is falling! He will fall!"

Allende observed the faces around him. He looked at the dead man. The wound on his face, above his left eye, grew larger. It seemed to reflect the growing darkness around the mass of horsemen in Nazi-brown mourning clothes, who kept shouting without voices.

The focal points of resistance spread, and the center of the city became an open battlefield.

The dictatorship was crumbling. Shut up in the palace, Ibáñez, now a general, received only those closest to him. "I am tired," he repeated, "tired and sick. I can't keep on fighting." His ministers studied him, carefully observing his gestures, the yellowish shadows around the eyes, the weak tone of his voice, which had already lost the barracks-room edge once capable of inspiring fear.

"Your supporters are battling in the streets, your excellency," a minister said.

"Poor fellows," the general commented, "they should fall out, go home, and leave me in peace. As for me," he added, looking strangely at one of his finance ministers, "I'm going into exile."

The minister assented in silence and began adding figures in his head, trying to imagine how many hours the general really had left.

Then the general felt a strong pang, clasped his hand to his abdomen and called for help. His ministers accompanied him to the bedroom. In the shadows of the room, heavily curtained in red plush, he began to murmur.

"You handle the car situation, and make sure everything's ready for tomorrow, Sunday. We'll leave early. Tell Ventura Maturana. We'll go across the trans-Andean route to Mendoza. I've already spoken with my man in Buenos Aires and he'll be waiting. You, sir, will see to it that my wife is not bothered here. My father-in-law should be advised, and she'll stay with him. You know, the house across the street from La Moneda. Everything must be expedited with care. No surprises or snafus. Got it?"

The finance minister thought to himself that the general was giving instructions just like a housewife managing her weekly expenses and duties. And if there's violence? This man has no idea of the *rotos* who are after him like hunting dogs. He has no idea how many cops died in the barrios today. Who'll answer for their lives?

"Have them get my gray overcoat and black hat. Pack my big suitcase, right, that one, the one I always take to the hot springs. We'll have breakfast in Los Andes. Call ahead, hombre, so they'll have my royal jelly waiting. In that black briefcase over there on top of the chest of drawers are all my papers."

He gave a melancholy smile and added, "That's where my new passport and the necessary funds are. Don't let me forget to bring my gun."

Indeed, more than a passport and a civilian overcoat, he needed weapons, a poncho, and a mule. Because that's how he would cross over the cordillera on July 26, 1931: first by car, then on foot, and finally by mule.

In Santiago, the people hit the streets in improvised parades, waving flags and shouting slogans in chorus. Cars went by with honking horns. Bells were pealing. The doors and balconies of the Club de la Unión were wide open for the volley of corks from bottles of champagne.

At dusk the jails were opened too, and the cells emptied. The wind from the mountains swept down to clean the dungeons. The prisoners came out rubbing their hands and pulling up their collars. They looked up at the reddened sky and hurried off into the night.

Salvador Allende emerged in the same manner and headed for a meeting that would have a decisive effect on his political life; the ranks of the Left at the university were splitting, and from that division would come the first map of a Chilean road toward socialism. With great strides he went to the local headquarters of the Group Avance.

Five Days
That Shook Chile

September 1, 1931. The chalk white, bony hands
of Vice-president Manuel Trucco clutch a trem-
bling piece of paper bearing a terse message: the navy has revolted
and a Soviet regime has been implanted under the direct command of the noncommissioned stewards of the armored ship Admiral Latorre and a revolutionary committee that includes representatives of the Communist party. The message adds that the
officers of the Latorre are being held on board under arrest. While
the rumor of a naval rebellion buzzed about Santiago, the insurgents had already swung into action, making contact with all of
the country's naval units and forming revolutionary committees
in Valparaíso, Quintero, and Talcahuano. The operation on
board the Latorre, the flagship of the Chilean fleet, was presided
over by petty officer Ernesto González, a primary-school teacher
and navy volunteer.

The sailors sent the government an ultimatum with a 48-hour
deadline.

As the city of Santiago awoke on September 2, war
clouds brooded overhead. Troops were mobilizing along the road
to Valparaíso. In the streets policemen resurfaced for the first time
since Ibáñez's fall, armed to the teeth and wearing the dark green
caps that had replaced the helmets of the dictatorship era. Groups
of improvised militia streamed by, looking for all the world like
an after-hours vaudeville act, to the obvious amusement of pass-
ersby. The purpose of the marches was to intimidate workers who

had joined the general strike. From the sidewalks, hidden behind parked cars, students hurled bags of water at the militiamen.

Several squadrons of planes flew toward the coastal sierras. There were rumors that the Aviation Academy of El Bosque was hurrying to join the sailors' revolt. Radios broadcast a blow-by-blow account of fighting in Talcahuano.

A manifesto was beamed from the Admiral Latorre's transmitter to the whole populace: "We declare before the country that at this very moment, in view of the unpatriotic intransigence of the government, and upon considering that the only cure for the national political crisis is a change in the very structure of society, the crews of our battleships have decided to join with the people in their revolutionary aspirations. We have asked a group representing the Federation of Chilean Workers and the Communist party to weigh anchor and sail with us. The struggle in which the government has locked us all has become a social revolution."

On the afternoon of September 5, government forces attacked the port city of Talcahuano. The sailors and workers fell back toward the hillsides. Beneath the cold drizzle of the late afternoon, they returned fire. On the bay the destroyer Riveros had been hit hard, and with its boilers aflame it weakly retreated to Quiriquina Island. All of a sudden a new center of resistance materialized near the naval munitions yard, where 400 workers fought to stop the advancing soldiers. Night had already fallen when the firing ceased. The army took a large number of prisoners and continued its attack against the diehards.

On Sunday, September 6, the revolutionary flotilla anchored off Coquimbo was bombed by government planes. Meanwhile, other army regiments took over the Naval School of Communications and the airbase of Quintero. The insurrection was failing.

The sunsets were becoming longer. Salvador walked along Recoleta Street and passed the bridge skirting Forestal Park. The almond and peach trees were already in flower. The medical student was filled with impatience and an urgent need to act. He felt that night that the city had changed. People moved hurriedly through the streets. Something in the evening air was demanding a decision from him.

In the Group Avance the political lines were being drawn and territories defined. Manuel Fuentes, looking up, squinted at the bulb that hung from the ceiling. In a lisping voice, he announced that the naval revolt had been intended to push the workers toward a communist-backed revolt. Rojitas, smoothly oriental in appearance, stabbed the air with a cigarette butt and cut Allende off before he could speak, shouting through clenched teeth, his eyes nearly shut: "Consequently, our *compañero* here should not, cannot, come round to propose fancy little reformist solutions hatched over cocktails at a seaside resort. The realities of the present have overtaken him, they are zinging over his head, and it would be advisable and certainly convenient that he awake from his dream and depart from the scene."

He drew a half circle in the air with his cigarette butt, and Allende felt that it had been drawn around his neck.

The independents were against the wall. Allende saw a break coming in the form of a crushing defeat.

"The real basis of the revolt was clear and concrete from the start," said Allende. "The navy rose up in arms to defend its right to live in dignity within the bourgeois society of our country: its salaries were cut by an arbitrary decision of the government that protects the treasure chests of the oligarchy at the expense of the people. It wasn't a show of demagoguery on the part of the rebels, just a struggle for basic needs. The sailors reacted to the abusive policies of the government just as the workers do when their salary becomes a pittance and their right to speak is crushed. The Federation of Chilean Workers declared a general strike. If that spark of protest and action had caught fire in our urban centers, in the seaports, in the mines, in the countryside, Chile would be a socialist republic today. The masses hit the streets and were ready to fight. The truth is that there was nobody prepared to shoulder the burden of leading the movement at the crucial moment."

The students were intrigued by the historic event emerging before their eyes, but it was important to weigh the facts and not jump to conclusions. A group led by law students wanted to take a drastic position. It proposed a manifesto that, in terse and dogmatic language, would endorse a Soviet state in Chile. Allende, and with him a growing group of independents, opposed the proposal.

"There's an effort afoot to misrepresent this authentic grassroots movement and transform it into a parade of symbols with no connection to our own workers," said Allende. "What's needed here is to strengthen the base of the movement through a leadership free from all outside meddling. What's needed is an alliance of socialist groups to support the workers with a political program framed in a language suited to the economic reality that we live with here in Chile. We need a party embracing freedom of action within the lines of revolutionary behavior and Marxist thought—a party that not only responds to the demands of workers but also anticipates them and orients them."

The debates in the university would always be extremist—intellectual, but also heated with the fire of street battles. Short-tempered harangues reverberated through the night in the smoky halls. Young professors spoke, forgetful historians, speedy lawyers; trippy psychiatrists spoke, defrocked priests, worn-out medics; wasted artists spoke with hands in pockets, pacing heavily in slow waltz-time, clamping cigarettes between their teeth until the yellow nicotine flowed.

Allende leaned back and smoothed his hair, observing coolly. He exuded self-confidence as he fixed a pathologist's gaze on his interlocutor and refused to accept what he disparagingly called "asininities." He would be heard and would impose himself. But, facing him, the team of banderilleros leapt into the air and with implacable aim raised their fists and placed their barbs, delivering the unappealable sentence.

". . . And given the origins of the political crisis to which the sailors responded with their drastic action, and given the need to cement the first decrees of the Revolutionary Government composed of the naval forces and the workers in a decisive manner, supporting the Soviets, we hereby proceed to expel the following . . ."

Expel whom? Not Allende, who struck camp and left those windbags leaking air into the night. Later on he would recall that the phonies who had tossed him out of the Group Avance on that afternoon would end up selling out to the party of opportunism.

The reaction to the subversive acts of the naval forces was fierce.

The Council of War requested the death penalty for Ernesto González, navy clerk; Victor Villalobos, gunner; Luis Pérez Sierra, seaman first class; Victorino Zapata, sergeant; Lautaro Silva, steward; and Juan Bravo, seaman first class. Life imprisonment was requested for Manuel Astica and Augusto Zagal.

The sentences were communicated by telephone to the minister of war, who relayed them to Vice-president Trucco for his seal of approval. But the latter was "doing the town" and thus unavailable, so the matter had to be postponed. The cabinet convened in La Moneda, where the sentence was discussed until 3:00 A.M. Unable to reach an agreement, the minister of foreign affairs, Luis Izquierdo, proclaimed, as he looked at his watch, "Señores, I must advise you that we are smack into the 18th of September, our national holiday, and that it would be by any account unacceptable to condemn anyone to death on such an occasion."

A short time after the revolt, the government decreed a pardon for "all persons sentenced for crimes of a political nature."

In Troubled Waters

In October 1931 the citizenry elected a new president, Juan Esteban Montero, in a free and peaceful voting process. He had not yet occupied the presidential chair when the nation's patriarchs took to the streets demanding his head.

Then on Christmas night, as the Montero government was just becoming established, a revolt exploded at the port of Copiapó. A group of workers assaulted the barracks of the Esmeralda regiment and fought with some success for a few hours. But after recovering from the initial shock, the soldiers repulsed the attack and scored eight casualties. The action didn't end there. An attempted revolution in Vallenar followed fast on the heels of the Esmeralda attack. The two actions seemed to have been strategically orchestrated. What started as a skirmish ended up as a pitched battle. After getting the situation in hand, the Vallenar police killed 23 insurgents.

President Montero began to lose his benevolent smile. Lightning riots flashed in Santiago. In response to the massacre at Vallenar, the Federation of Chilean Students called a general strike that lasted for two days. The students hit the streets with red flags raised on high.

Allende withdrew from the fray in order to prepare for his final exams at the School of Medicine. The brief incarcerations that he had undergone under the Ibáñez dictatorship had interrupted his studies. But now he studied hard in the isolation of his boardinghouse. His pals missed him when it came time for fun—Allende had not been one to pass up an all-nighter. His reputation as a showman came partly from his special talent for disguises, one of which was the Groucho look.

In March 1932 he passed his boards and went to Valparaíso to write his dissertation on mental health and delinquency. His father was seriously ill from diabetes and had to be hospitalized. The money that his mother earned was not enough to pay family expenses, and Salvador felt pressure to finish his thesis and get a job.

A general atmosphere of bankruptcy pervaded Chile after the crash of 1929, and the misery of the nitrate and copper workers had at last spread to the middle class. Heads of families lost their positions, businesses closed, university students quit their studies, and small industrialists and farmers clamored for more credit. "Moratorium" was the catchword in banks and government offices. It seemed to be christening an era.

The Allendes were reduced to a proud but uneasy state of poverty. While Salvador made the rounds of offices and hospitals looking for work, his socialist friends needed his support in the struggle for power among the groups in Santiago that had decided to overthrow Montero. The capital was a wasps' nest of conspirators: Alessandri was manipulating his agents in the professions and the military; Ibáñez was preparing his men to infiltrate Alessandri's ranks; and the Federation of Chilean Workers was recovering from the blows received in Copiapó and Vallenar. Those were the circumstances in which Salvador met the Metro-Goldwyn-Mayer lion.

The man whom Allende saw approaching him on Ahumada Street was short and round without being fat; the general impression he gave had something to do with his clothing. He somehow seemed to float inside his suit without overflowing, like a well-filled balloon. His tiny feet, encased in patent-leather shoes, stepped out in the style of some forgotten period. He wore no hat, and his dark hair shone with brilliantine. Upon seeing Salvador standing in front of El Naturista, the man flashed a smile of feigned surprise and came toward him with his hand extended. Salvador took it somewhat hesitantly and smiled in turn, looking him up and down.

They went in the restaurant and sat at a corner table far from the noon customers—office workers and students who lingered on after their meals, chatting and gesturing. Salvador's host was Carlos Dávila, and it had been his idea to come to El Naturista. Salvador had heard Dávila's name but had never met him. It seemed that he was a regular, because all the waitresses gave him warm hellos.

"My call must have come as a surprise," Dávila said. "The fact is we have a lot of friends in common. Everyone speaks highly of you. They say you have a great future . . ." He let his voice trail off to create the impression that a highly significant word had remained trapped between his teeth.

Salvador said nothing.

"People like . . . Núñez Morgado, Dr. Cifuentes . . . and our old Colonel Grove, who thinks the world of you, thinks you have it in you to be a leader."

He took out a pair of glasses with thick tortoiseshell frames and placed them on his nose as he brandished the menu like a ship's captain who has lost direction. First he opened it backwards, then he turned it around, making little clucking noises with his tongue.

"What do you say we tell them to leave us alone here so we can talk? What do you say? They've got spinach molded to look like a lamb chop, first class. And the beans . . . Oh, man! Famous. And the peaches, don't even talk about it. If our people would learn how to eat like they should, instead of stuffing themselves with pork and bread . . . With the coast we have . . . Can you imagine? Did you know that the Japanese never get cancer? And why not, eh? Because they eat fish all the time. Think of the iodine, the seaweed."

Salvador made an impatient gesture, and the man signaled the waitress with a little clicking sound.

"Listen, sweetheart . . . Bring me the usual, and for the doctor . . ."

"The same thing," said Salvador, noticing the girl's Germanic look.

El Naturista had a reputation in those days as a bit of a Nazi cell, mixed in with disciples of the new guru, the Elqui Christ, reporters from the magazine *Topaze*, Rosicrucians, and leaders of the boy scout scene in the metropolitan area.

As they ate Salvador observed the man cautiously. His gestures were calm and his gaze was cold and measuring. There was something vaguely foreign about him. He had a strange inflection, accentuating oddly the d's and s's. The r's came flattened and whistling from behind his teeth.

Dávila had been editor of *Hoy*, a new antigovernment weekly. He surely was interested in learning which way the students and the dozens of socialist groups were leaning politically. Just as he started talking about a plan to save the nation, a kind of Chilean Christ-figure appeared at the threshold of the dining room—a man with a wide forehead, a clear yet somewhat surprised look, and a soft, chestnut-colored beard. He approached as though he were the Lord upon the waters, with long, winged strides, his arms moving gracefully. He stood next to their table and greeted them from on high.

It was Ismael Valdés, the owner of El Naturista, a pragmatic moralist, philosopher of the nation's middle ground, and author of bold editorial pieces that hung from the restaurant's windowsills for the edification and enjoyment of the pedestrians along Ahumada Street.

"Pleased to meet you," he said to Salvador, without looking at him. He was watching Dávila's impassive face. Fixing his clear gaze on that dark forehead, he said, "And you? What plots are you hatching now?"

Dávila did not return his gaze, but smiled.

"What a man, this don Ismael. I am an orderly soul."

"You learned all about order from the yanquis, Dávila. That's the bad part. It's not good to forget your own roots, you know. It's not good at all for Chileans to turn into gringos. Their hair falls out, they get very pale, and since they're dark to begin with, it gives them a leaden cast, as if they hadn't washed for a while. They start talking slow and careful, hot potato in the mouth, for all the world like sanctimonious, oracular monkeys. Let's get Chilean, my friend, enough gringoisms, back to the earth and the ways of the old folks. If you want to do some conspiring, better come work for me. I have jobs for everyone. You'll get a bath of Chilenism and a brand-new passport. Did you see my editorial on the window? The economy . . ."

"The economy of this country," Dávila interrupted, "should be planned immediately, restructured according to modern, dynamic canons. We need a plan . . ."

"The gringo in you never dies," Valdés said. "You even got plans to take siestas. Ibáñez made a mistake sending you to Washington as his ambassador. Our country knows only one economy—the earthquake. Who the hell needs plans for that? We build, it falls, we build again."

And his laughter erupted from the gut, in gentle, dreamlike convulsions. He took his leave and went toward the kitchen.

"That longhair's a nutcake," said Dávila. After a moment he added cryptically, "González von Marées has formed his party. Did you know?"

"Speaking of nutcakes?" asked Salvador. He was still intrigued by the invitation the man had dropped. What did he want? What in the world was on his mind?

Dávila handled his spoon and fork with expertise, simultaneously devouring two enormous peaches with sauce.

He munched away with his cheeks inflated like a squirrel's until only the pits were left. Ah, said Salvador suddenly to himself. Now I remember! He thought of squirrels he had seen in the movies. Little by little, the image of this man came into focus—the puckered lips, the black, smooth hair, the slightly alarmed expression in the eyes—and became a banker in a checkered jacket with a neatly folded handkerchief in his breast pocket, approaching a gigantic mahogany desk from the rear of a luxurious office. He was looking out at Salvador from the screen of the Metro Theater. Salvador could see him sitting on one cheek on the edge of the desk, speaking smoothly in a dehydrated Spanish, something to the effect that a new epoch in the history of humanity was arriving, the eighth wonder of the world: talking movies. Then the head of the Metro-Goldwyn-Mayer lion emerged through the ring, gave two resounding roars, and shook its mane ceremoniously. The man returned to the screen but was now facing a bank teller. Speaking all the while he was writing a check. You could hear the pen scratching. "You can even hear the pen!" a spectator cried out. The man detached the check. "D'ya hear how you could hear the check?" In fact, it sounded like a guillotine falling. The man counted his bills and you could hear the new paper crinkling between his fingers. He walked off, and you could hear the lock mechanism of the door turning and the squeaking of his new shoes on the parquet floor. "Holy shit, you can hear everything!" The theater audience buzzed in excitement, applauding Carlos Dávila, Chilean ambassador to the United States, who had just introduced the lion, roars and all, to humanity.

This was Dávila, who lost his position when the Ibáñez dictatorship fell, and who returned penniless to remake his life in Chile.

"A plan," Dávila kept saying, forgetting about the bearded Valdés, "like that paradigm of plans invented by the Bolsheviks. For that sort of thing they are great, you know, especially for five-year plans. Do you know what this country needs to eliminate poverty?"

"Tell me."

"It needs an economic structure based on state enterprise: we'll create a national agricorporation, a national mining operation, a national industries company, a state transportation system, a state commerce corporation . . ."

"That's what I read in *La Opinión* this morning."

"Ah, you read my article! That's it, my friend. The state, supreme maker and watchdog of the nation, must meet face-to-face the needs of this long-suffering people."

With that he deposited the glistening pits of the sacrificed fruit neatly onto his spoon and popped two more large peaches into his mouth, swelling his cheeks to accommodate them.

Salvador looked in an obvious manner at his watch.

"Don't worry, my friend," said Dávila. "We'll have a cup of boldo tea and we're off. You have to wash down the lunch."

A Carbonated Spring Water Plan for the Public Flatulence, thought Salvador, smiling. Then he asked, "Are you referring to the presidential elections of '38?"

"No," responded Dávila. "How'd you get that idea? I'm addressing the few men of action left in this country. We have to move now, without delay. Look, Allende, you're a young leader with recognized talent and a future. No, let's not kid around. Everyone says it. Eugenio Matte, the other day in a very private meeting, said it too. We all think you have the stuff to do . . ."

"Nothing," Salvador cut in. "But if you are interested in knowing what I think, here it goes. The conspiracies and barracks revolts of leaders—with or without parties—have little appeal for me. And none when men in uniform are involved. Señor Von Marées is dressing up his goons with uniforms. The government dolls up the republican militia and has them march around flexing their muscles in the backyards of regimental headquarters . . ."

"Ah, no! But now we're not talking about some chicken-feed backyard number. Now, my young friend, we're going to change the system and not only the president, we're going to have a social revolution—s-o-c-i-a-l," he repeated, staring at Salvador, "a social revolution, and nothing less."

"And who were you saying was going to accomplish it?"

"The people. Yes, compañerito, the people with their leaders up in front."

Allende sized him up in a glance.

"Matte and Grove," added Dávila after a long pause, observing the effect that these two names produced.

After a moment he continued, insisting, "Who would defend a government that doesn't govern and is a mere tool of the oligarchy? The armed forces are with us."

"With you?" Allende asked coldly.

"Well, with the movement, which, by the way, it's clear enough I should orient and . . . lead, of course."

Allende folded his napkin calmly, stood up adjusting his glasses, and responded, "Señor Dávila, the Metro-Goldwyn-Mayer lion is calling, in the roaring Hollywood jungle. It suits you better. Say hi to the lion for me."

And he left.

      Colonel Marmaduque Grove, dressed in blue with a gray fedora hat in his hand, got up from his chair and, looking steadily at his interlocutor, exclaimed, "You can take my resignation, Mr. Minister, and stick it wherever you want. As for me, I'm not signing a goddamn thing. I'm nobody's patsy. They'll find me at home if they need me."

With doors slamming, he stormed out of Defense Minister Urrutia Manzano's office and joined his brother Jorge, who was waiting in the corridor. They flew down the stairs, directly to the colonel's office, and began emptying the drawers of his desk.

"They can't hand this bullshit to me after serving with absolute loyalty, a deaf ear to all conspirators. Why just yesterday, yesterday, Commandant Lagos stopped me in the street and, in front of everyone, asked for my support because they're going to throw out Montero. See what I mean? I'm the last person they could call on, but now I'm being paid off by the brass under suspicion of disloyalty. But how could they have approached me with such a thing, and in the street? Montero is the most honorable president this country has had in a century. Why would I want him out? And why do they want him out? Where does Dávila get the notion?"

"They want to put the Lion in again, Duque. Don't you see?"

"Don Arturo again. They've lost their minds."

They gathered all the documents and walked to the car. When they were about to pull away from the curb, a man ran up to them with a frenzied look on his face. He handed an envelope through the window to Grove.

"Colonel, colonel," he said, "don't go off without this, the ministry sent it to you."

"I'll read it on the way," the colonel said drily as he took the envelope.

Off they went.

"Who was that?"

"Ramón Vergara."

"Want me to read you the letter?"

"It's not necessary. I know what it is. They're promoting Vergara to commander in chief."

"They're taking your job?"

The colonel began whistling between his teeth.

"They sawed off the limb I was on. They'll be sorry."

"What will you do, Duque?"

"I'm going to kick the shit out of them."

Later, at home, Marmaduque got a call. The voice was familiar.

"Yes, my colonel, here in San Bernardo. You have plenty of time."

Grove was doubtful.

"And what do you need me for?"

"You are indispensable. You've got to come join us now."

The voice spouted names of military brass. ". . . And Señor Dávila will be there."

"And what has he to do with us? It's a mistake. Disinvite him."

"It can't be done, my colonel. We're already in with him. Don Eugenio Matte will be here too."

"Ah!"

The name of Matte inspired his confidence.

"OK. I'm heading over."

At 9:00 Grove was at El Bosque. Matte, Eugenio González, Schnake, Fernando Celis, and Lieutenant Carlos Charlín arrived a little later. From that point on events progressed rapidly.

On June 3, near midnight, the commander Ramón Vergara, appointment in hand, arrived at the Aviation Academy of El Bosque. A committee of young officers received him but responded angrily to the orders that he began to issue immediately, in a nervous voice. Vergara took out his pistol and began firing. He was quickly disarmed and shut up in one of the rooms of the Officer's Club.

Without even realizing it, Colonel Marmaduque Grove had suddenly become the leader of the new revolution.

The news spread quickly throughout Santiago. Warplanes buzzed La Moneda, dropping leaflets heralding the revolt.

Late at night the commander of the Buin regiment arrived at the palace and declared before the astonished generals that his men had joined the revolt against the regime. The Cazadores regiment had also risen. Panic took root in the palace. The president brought his ministers together and offered to resign. They decided first to call a caucus of the venerable patriarchs. The crème de la crème of the armchair politicians in the Club de la Unión all answered the call and entered La Moneda solemnly, as though they were attending the funeral of Juan Esteban Montero himself.

The president observed them assembled in the Red Room and, with a sad smile, delivered a speech that was neither new nor apt to be discarded from the future repertoire for such occasions: "I have gathered you here, señores, at a grave moment. Commodore Grove of the air force has been charged with conspiracy and relieved of his command. He no longer accepts the authority of his superiors, and he has subverted the entire Aviation Academy with his rebellious attitude. The necessary measures have been taken. Armed forces of the Infantry School were dispatched to subdue Grove, but these forces have also revolted and thrown in their lot with the insurgents. Several regiments have been brought in from the provinces. All have taken the same crooked path. There is not a single loyal soldier the government can count on, nor any supporting body to help maintain it in power. Faced with this situation I have called you together so that I might hear your opinions."

All of the civic eloquence of the national patriarchs could not save Montero's government. Something more powerful was needed: the invincible secret weapon, the right word, and the personal influence that could move the country—don Arturo's of course. And Alessandri the Lion sallied forth with stormy countenance, swaddled in a greatcoat and brandishing his staff, packing a brand-new British pistol, his Italian hat pulled down over one eye. He was received in San Bernardo by Grove himself and his company of rebels. On seeing Grove Alessandri strode up to him with open arms. "Greetings to my colonel, my friend, in this decisive hour in the destiny of the nation," he exclaimed. They held their embrace in silence for a moment while Grove prepared himself to be regaled by an eloquent harangue.

There are many versions of what Alessandri actually said on this occasion. It must have been brilliant and wise. Historians say that upon taking his leave, after declaring his conciliatory mission a failure because Grove and his followers refused to obey Montero's orders, Alessandri took his old friend by the arm and whispered in his ear, "Don't give up, colonel!"

And Grove didn't give up. That same afternoon the revolutionary committee met in La Cisterna and named the members of the new ruling junta: Eugenio Matte, Arturo Puga, a retired general, and Carlos Dávila. Colonel Grove was, without a doubt, the leader behind the junta, and he reserved for himself the title of minister of national defense.

There were moments of high drama at the El Bosque airbase. The insurgents were divided: some troops had remained loyal to Grove, while others followed Commandant Pedro Lagos, a supporter of Ibáñez. Militant socialists, armed to the teeth, waited for the order to advance on the city in buses and trucks parked on the base. At 7:30 on June 4, junta members Eugenio Matte, Carlos Dávila, and Ministers Cifuentes and Schnake arrived at La Moneda by taxi. Marmaduque Grove, his brother Jorge, and Carlos Charlín arrived in a private car. The revolutionaries who came to take over the palace were unarmed . . .

A hundred people were in the Red Room when Grove entered. Montero looked at him and said, "I'm listening."

Grove addressed President Montero in a strong, serene voice.

"As commander in chief of the three branches of the armed forces, I have made the decision to depose the government you preside over and to establish in Chile a socialist republic. I now proceed to take command of the nation, in the name of this new republic, for the Chilean people, with the Chilean people."

The president called his second-in-command, General Vergara, and with him at attention at his side, said, "General Vergara has assured me that the army no longer recognizes the authority of the government. Faced with these circumstances, I can no longer combat the insurrection, as was my purpose and my duty. I therefore retire under such coercion."

He left immediately, without bidding farewell to anyone, followed by his ministers.

All of a sudden Grove was alone facing the big presidential chair. He was confused, and for an instant, he felt the temptation. He looked around. His comrades-in-arms were staring at him, some smiling encouragingly, others going pale. Grove realized that one of his hands was still raised, like a shadow of his salute to the departing president. He felt uncomfortable. As though I were a monument, he thought. He relaxed his muscles, and after the tension had left his body, he exclaimed in a dry cavernous voice: "Cheers, compañeros, the socialist revolution has triumphed! Long live the Socialist Republic of the Workers!"

A chorus of strong, energetic voices answered his words, and Marmaduque Grove, now free of all doubts, took his seat.

The Red Colonel

What moved Allende to support Grove with such conviction, to go the last mile for him and his new republic? In a 1932 photo published in the dailies of Santiago, Grove appears in civilian clothes with his fedora perched on the center of his head, his smile intense and enigmatic. He is accompanied by the young Salvador Allende, wearing a Stetson and a tightly fitting four-button jacket with a white handkerchief in the breast pocket. Something binds them together, yet they seem apart. For Grove this young militant and university leader represented a freshly minted political reality; he clearly was well outside the menagerie of political bosses so typical in those days.

Governments had fallen like pages off calendars and caudillos had gone into exile only to return, months and even years later, waving brand-new flags with their winning colors. The people had seen them pass through the Alameda de las Delicias, sometimes on wagons wearing the tricolored sash across their chests, and sometimes among the shadows, fearful of conspiratorial ghosts.

What land did they rule? Surely not the north, with all its misery; nor the coal mines of the south, where the workers dug buried in the depths of the sea; nor the barrios of Santiago and Valparaíso, where the unemployed waited in line for their turn at the cemetery. Grove and Matte faced their sad little band and suddenly realized that they had come to the palace virtually alone. Allende brought them the new faces of Chileans in search of a party with revolutionary action on the agenda.

In twelve days the group of stalwart aviators, illuminati, and civilian revolutionaries tried to re-create a country, to transform a socioeconomic structure that only appeared to be a solidly democratic state, while in reality it was a pawn in the hands of a crusty, landed oligarchy, politically conservative and paternalistic to a fault.

Decrees from the new government shot forth from La Moneda like rockets: disband the self-appointed Congress inherited from Ibáñez's time; establish the dole; guarantee university autonomy backed by student-faculty commissions; create government-owned monopolies of iodine, oil, phosphorus, and sugar; decree a state monopoly on foreign exports; nationalize nitrate and copper mines.

In response to such emancipatory and revolutionary voices, U.S. and English warships menacingly approach the coast of Chile.

The government team of young economists denounced the situation in Chile after the worldwide crisis of 1930: 626 landowners possessed 14.5 million hectares; multinational companies, particularly those of U.S. origin, were in control of all the major mining enterprises, the banks, the insurance industry, the public utilities, and foreign trade. The country needed 500,000 houses built. As many as 400,000 children lacked schools to attend. The infant mortality rate was appalling: 262 children of every 1,000 died. Tuberculosis and typhus, in epidemic proportions, were devastating the country.

During the early days of the revolt, the central administration building of the university had been taken over by ultra-leftist groups.

Grove, feeling the pressure, decided to eliminate Dávila. But the latter surprised him by resigning from the junta after exactly eight days. The commander in chief of the army called a meeting of the high brass, including members of the air force and police officers. They demanded that Grove include the armed forces in his government. Grove responded by saying that Dávila was going abroad on a special mission and that Rolando Merino Reyes would replace him in the junta.

On June 14, in private council, Grove and Matte discussed the possibility of arming the populace. Matte was in favor of arming a popular militia at once. Grove didn't agree; that would only provoke the army.

On June 16, at midnight, a group of officers led by Merino Benítez arrives unexpectedly at La Moneda. Buin's troops take over the Ministry of Defense. Grove runs toward La Moneda, and when he finds himself surrounded by armed men intent upon arresting him, he escapes and shuts himself off in one of the palace rooms. He grabs a phone and dials a radio station that puts him on the air. He begins haranguing the nation: "Arms! Arms for the people!"

His call is relentless, but it's not clear who is to provide all of those rifles, grenades, and mortars. His enemies fall on him and drag him to a waiting car; on the way they pick up Matte and Dr. Cifuentes, the minister of public health, and send them under guard to Valparaíso, where a frigate waits to convey them to Easter Island.

Thus the flags of the short-lived Socialist Republic of Chile were ripped down during a cold winter's night in Santiago. The shouts of Marmaduque Grove chase their own echo in the frozen solitude of a deserted plaza. The street lamps light the shadowy way to another exile. The soldiers salute the passing procession of vehicles. "There goes Colonel Grove," they say. They are not aware that he is under arrest and heading for exile.

The socialist republic has lasted a total of twelve days. Yet for a brief moment, Chilean men and women had been able to entertain a certain illusion when they regarded their palace: that Chile was finally theirs, that a new life had begun.

The next day Allende was winding up a fiery speech to a large crowd when he was taken by the arm and rushed to a green truck. In the back of the truck were his brothers. The truck lurched forward with its sirens screaming. The men were jailed separately, incommunicado.

The front pages were filled with news of the latest barracks revolt. "Junta of National Hope," said the headlines. "Grove and

Matte to Easter Island." "Dávila in Command." "Juan Antonio Ríos, Minister of the Interior." "Allende Jailed." The same old story. The Chilean people were used to it: a colonel impatient for his turn rises with the mist of dawn and makes his little move. If not in person, with a suitable ghost. Today was Commandant Lagos's turn, and Dávila manipulated him with sleight of hand, invoking arts newly learned in Washington. He began by designating a military tribunal, "since it is a question," he would say, "of crimes against the state. These things must be done under protection of the law." The court martial committee convened in Valparaíso and declared the Allende brothers innocent. They were set free. Within a few hours the junta revoked the decision and the three headed off to jail again.

Allende learned that his father's condition had worsened and that he was near death. One leg had been amputated and the other was gangrenous. The military judge authorized the Allende brothers to visit their father.

"I was able to speak with him for a few minutes," said Salvador later, "and he told us that all he was leaving us was a clean record, nothing of material value. The next day he died. At his funeral I promised to devote myself to social justice, a promise I have kept."

And then it occurred to General Ibáñez to return secretly from Argentina. Once more the cat-and-mouse game commenced. From the airport Ibáñez went directly to his father-in-law's house facing La Moneda. The country, properly apprised of the general's every move despite the clandestine nature of his arrival, interpreted this as a sign that he was preparing to cross the street and take over. Alessandri, amid uncertainty and fear, took refuge in the Spanish embassy. Ricardo Baeza, a fiery writer and the ambassador at that time, received him regally and prepared himself for the next round.

Ibáñez took a step backward. Surrounded by friends and supporters who were happy to spend hours mulling over sweet old times with him, the general weighed his possibilities. "After all," he said, "I'm too close to La Moneda. Consequently, it behooves me to move tonight, señores." "Where, my general?" "To Barilo-che," he responded, and then remained silent. He had made a mis-take; it would have been better to stay in Buenos Aires, where he could winter far away from the cold that filtered through the heat-less houses.

Alessandri ventured forth from his asylum, and with his hands behind his back and the ever-present hat over his eye, he began visiting the conservative circles and the military officers' clubs.

On September 12, 1932, a grand forum of military top brass presented Carlos Dávila with a resignation letter, which the Metro-Goldwyn-Mayer lion hastened to sign. His mandate con-cluded, he wavered for a moment, looking around him. No one paid any attention to him now. He got up from the presidential chair, removed his tricolored sash, and left the Red Room. He walked to his office, put on his coat and hat, and went down the stairs to the door opening onto Morandé Street. He lit a cigarette, raised the collar of his overcoat, and hailed a cab. "Where to?" the driver asked. And the ex-president realized that he had no-where to go. The taxi pulled away from the curb and, with its weary passenger, disappeared from history.

It had been a good show, it can't be denied. But this time the cameramen fooled him: for his star performance, the cameras were without film—they were shooting blank, and the big screen never reflected a single image.

Chapter Eight

From the Jailhouse
to the Senate

And who were these men, who would they be in a few years?

For a young professional like Allende, who responded to the political challenges of the moment with the instincts and conscience of an activist, they were cards in the hand, cards that one played with expediency, win or lose. But for the masses they were rootless images, icons from nowhere, without rhyme or reason to their movements in and out of the thick-walled colonial mansion called La Moneda. They were the bookkeepers, the groundskeepers, and to some extent the men who ruled the destiny of human life, which occasionally became an offering to the thirsty desert or the lonely ocean's depths.

Arturo Alessandri had a background that his enemies were eager to draw attention to: it was said that his grandfather had been an ambitious Italian puppeteer. The truth is that he could well have been a grand-opera impresario, revitalizing the municipal theater of Valparaíso, a social gadfly during the times when wealthy port dwellers traveled to London by steamer and returned puffing on pipes, making courtly bows, and taking crumpets with their Bombay tea. In any case his grandfather was not a politician; and when Alessandri did speak about his ancestors, they suddenly became filthy rich hacendados, owners of great estates with pieds-à-terre in Santiago, leading a pack of cronies in the Club de la Unión.

Allende learned from Alessandri the disciplined and dynamic style associated with the political profession in Chile. Become a university student leader in order to become a congressman; then become a senator in order to become a cabinet member who succeeds in strengthening the executive; and finally, if you've handled the job in such a way as to make it a work of art, why then become a presidential candidate. Once you gain the respect and support of the armed forces, then and only then, you manage to become president of the republic. How many yearn to accomplish that and never make it? The big prize is delivered by the hand of God, but with some luck and uncommon vision, your own hand comes into play too.

Once having attained the presidency, Alessandri would be, until the day he died, the oracle of the nation, its divine messenger, rescuer of the shipwrecked economy, peace-pipe smoker, and curfew caller in moments of crisis. Those who intended to follow his example failed: Ibáñez, because of his blind faith in the sword; Grove, because his brain was wired to the roaring airplane motors and his kind heart beat at the sound of naive, sentimental, socialist slogans. The others were just understudies, eager to accommodate, smiling and calculating. Some also-rans managed to get their foot into La Moneda and got fat in the grand halls and orange-tree patios. All they desired was to hold on to the presidency for six years. The people elected them, allowed them to do their trickery, and let time pass until they were forgotten and relegated to the dusty attic of national history.

Allende confided to his friends his intention to dedicate himself to politics. Full time? And give up the medical profession? Isn't it too soon? The fact is that even with his medical degree and the support of his professors Allende could not get a position in either the public or the private sector, nor was he able to start a practice in Valparaíso. He applied for an open slot in the municipal hospital. They didn't give it to him. He insisted, presenting his case four times. No one else had applied for the job. Still they didn't give it to him! A chalk circle was being drawn around the revolutionary young doctor.

Finally, Dr. Eduardo Grove, his brother-in-law and an influential physician in Viña del Mar, gave him an office in his own clinic. Allende began to receive patients, mostly friends who came from the Valparaíso hills. They would complain a bit about this and that, but mostly they came to talk politics. Allende wrote them prescriptions. They had no money. Allende gave them medicine anyway. Eventually he had to take a position at the morgue as an assistant pathologist. He began writing an article on the organization of public health.

It was then that Salvador started to detect some ripples on the surface of the murky political waters, discussing them only with those close to him.

Recent years had deeply marked him and his friends: they found themselves without an alternative to the traps awaiting them. Chile was on the very edge of a violent crisis. Barracks revolts, strikes, and the disappearance of political leaders threatened to crack the facade of civic order so shrewdly fabricated by the old "liberal" alliances of landowners and their political toadies.

"Chile will have its civil war in the twentieth century," cautioned those in the know. "No it won't," said others. Who was wrong?

Can a state that knows no economy other than that of the international bank loan, and no balance books other than those written in red, stay in power? Printing money is government sport for a time: the economic boom is printed on gaily colored bills. Like bumper stickers? Not quite. They're called pesos. And the future of the country is measured in zeros. To the right or left side of the decimal point?

No one knows for sure what the National Treasury really is. Some think of it as a big, armored piggy bank, others conceive of it spatially, as a bank vault, still others see it as a building with no address. All, however, work for that enigma, live and breathe it, ride it for all it's worth, and go down with it, too. Ibáñez fell when the people realized that the National Treasury didn't exist. Patriots conspired and suffered exile, all in search of the Treasury. When Dávila disappeared, people went around saying that he had heisted it to Miami.

A hawklike general suddenly proclaimed hoarsely that he

knew where the Treasury was. No one believed him. Another general called from the northern provinces and warned him to evacuate La Moneda. "If you don't leave," he advised, "we will leave the country with the Treasury and a nice chunk of land that goes with it." General Blanche resigned. A wise and kind man, don Abraham Oyanedel, became the first magistrate for a fleeting moment. He called for general elections. Five candidates ran, one in absentia because he was at that moment incarcerated on Easter Island. Arturo Alessandri won, again. The man on Easter Island, Marmaduque Grove, provided a surprise: he came in second and swung a majority in Santiago and Valparaíso. His comrade, Eugenio Matte, was elected senator with a big majority in Santiago, and Hugo Grove became senator for Valparaíso.

A calm and dignified Alessandri declared, "Chile is on the edge of a civil war. We must save the country. We are going to reorganize the national economy and reestablish the constitutional order."

When the president began putting his plans into action, Allende was unexpectedly granted a podium from which to pass judgment upon them, anticipating the congressional proceedings of 1933–34. In Valparaíso socialist groups were gathering to settle on a common platform, a preliminary step to the foundation of the Socialist party of Chile. Allende chose this occasion to air a political balance sheet of the state of the nation since Montero's fall.

"Alessandri," he said, "is at a decisive moment in his political career. The little two-step he danced between the Left and the Right, in and out of the presidency, into the anti-Montero conspiracy and the coup against Dávila, is winding down. There's no more dance floor. If you look carefully, you will observe that we have lived out a cycle in Chile that could only lead to the closed door we are now facing. The civil utopia of 1920 gave us progressive legislation and dictatorial governments. The worldwide bankruptcy of 1929 coincided here with the surrender of the country to the economic machine of the United States through massive loans and that sad Trojan mule, the Chilean Nitrate Company. As you know, that company was just a whore working for pimps determined to sell our nitrate mines at a low price, for a big kickback. Don Arturo squeezed every drop out of his leftist performance in 1920. Today the alternative is quite simple: with his old utopian pantomimes outdated and stripped of popular support, he can only govern with his right hand. We are attending the grand finale of a brilliant career in sleight-of-hand wizardry: the Lion of Tarapacá is roaring these days in defense of those he once labeled 'the gilded swine.' Now he is the president of the oligarchy. Alessandri commands forces committed to the destruction of every single attempt at economic and political liberation by the working classes."

With these words Allende finally told don Arturo the score. In a single year Alessandri's government had crushed a railroad strike with hot lead flying; it had massacred protesting peasants in Ranquil; and as dawn was breaking—the usual hour for muggings—it had sent a bunch of thugs to do a hatchet job on the printing press and offices of the daily *La Opinión*.

As a well-orchestrated reaction against the "red menace" that the influential daily *El Mercurio* had been vociferously denouncing, an armed group suddenly appeared on the scene calling itself the republican militia. Ready for combat, its ranks marched up and down the streets of Santiago. Simultaneously, the pathetic hordes of the Nazi party, led by González von Marées, made their debut in grotesque, and sometimes bloody, street skirmishes. The president, stopping on the corner of Teatinos Street, observed the parade of the militia and cracked jokes as he watched his old, pot-bellied buddies stuffed into blowsy blue overalls, marching stiffly in formation, right hands pointing at their little peaked caps in salute.

After the meeting marking the founding of the Socialist party of Valparaíso, Allende, the party's new regional secretary, went with a group of friends to eat at Crazy Victor's on Alegre Hill. They drank an amiable red wine punch with the fresh bouquet of those fat Chilean strawberries redolent of the windy Valparaíso. In Santiago, on Sunday, April 19, 1933, the party was born, with the image of Grove in the background and Matte's defiant figure in the foreground. Oscar Schnake was elected secretary general. The records of the proceedings were signed by representatives of the New Public Action, the Revolutionary Socialist Action, the Socialist Order, and the Marxist Socialist party.

The good old days of bribes, political booby traps, booze-filled conventions, and corny parades were coming to an end. One era was on the way out while another was coming in, the combination foreshadowing tough, armed encounters. The response to Alessandri's rightist, law-and-order government was an ironclad and disciplined opposition of popular parties and workers' organizations. The two most influential political forces were on a collision course on shifting, treacherous ground.

Eugenio Matte Hurtado died on January 11, 1934. Grove, after being persecuted and jailed by Alessandri's government, replaced him in the Senate.

"Our generation," Allende said, "grew up without a roof over our heads, scarred by the elements and by government abuses. We wanted to change things, but we didn't know how. The young people curse the country and leave. Some go away without knowing why. Professors go, students go, artists and athletes leave. They all want to conquer the world but they won't find a world to be conquered. Those of us who were born with the century, and with World War I and the greatest revolutions in history, don't even know yet where we are destined to make a revolution. How many years have to go by before we realize that such a world is within reach of our very hands, that we have been going around in circles, within a single city block, believing all the while that we are defying the world order? That's how I perceive my lot and that of my party. Unhappy and defiant, you look me in the eye and tell me you're leaving the country and the rest can go to hell. Me, I weave my skein and weave it tight. I follow the only paths that I seem to know by heart. The path of the underdog, but not the quiet variety. All of a sudden fellow party members see me for

what I'm worth. The old farts are saying that I'm no longer re-
deemable. Fighting times are ahead of us. The Nazis are goose-
stepping around, the militia is presenting arms with rifles made
of broomsticks, the Catholic kids from the Falange movement are
haranguing the multitudes with their arms stretched out like a
cross.

"There will always be cops hiding in their green cages around
the corner from us; there will always be young peasant draftees,
disguised as soldiers, trembling beneath their cooking-pot helmets; always some nervous lard-ass with a pistol in his hand, fixing his decorations and shouting, *Charge!*

"Parks fill with smoke and explosions celebrate another miserable new year. The thirties came in with a political message,
with an act of repression, a bloody street scuffle. And throughout
all this, each day I'm drawn more into the oven. I can't step back.
I don't know how to step back. We were born under the sign of
Claridad. We were witnesses of the Chaco War. Eventually we
will follow the betrayal of Spain step by step and tie ourselves to
the destiny of the Spanish people by our own umbilical cord. We
will hear Neruda sing a song against four generals and Roberto
Parada sing the chorus:

> *Para la noche buena*
> *para la noche buena*
> *mamita mía, mamita mía*
> *serán colgados, serán colgados . . .*

"If all that has held us together, what bound them, the generation of 1920? They got their message and didn't hesitate. They
brought out the rifles they had kept on their old wooden shelves
and set the sights. They held their fire. There was time. They called
elections and presidents followed one another calmly, like melons
ripening in the summer sun, and the same with the senators, representatives, cabinet members, and judges. Years of roll calls and
choruses followed. The colonels and generals came and went with
the falling leaves of democratic peace. What's more, Chile had a
cardinal, Monsignor Caro, a good and humble priest, and when

he died he handed the miter to Monsignor Henríquez, a worthy successor dressed in a poncho from Temuco and plain cotton cloth, one who would never turn his back on the people.

"That is how it was."

Visionary, doctor to the poor, editor of the *Chilean Medical Bulletin*, director of the medical association, founder of the *Journal of Social Medicine of Valparaíso*, Allende will emerge from his early years a socialist leader: he has been a cell chief and regional secretary of Aconcagua for the Socialist party. Now, after protesting state terrorism in 1935, he is jailed and then exiled to Caldera, a mining port in the north.

Chapter Nine

The Ghosts of Caldera

The banished politician makes news in the Chilean boondocks, where, far from world events, people have neither watches nor current dailies to consult, only the yellowed copies of the past. There the people keenly sense the contours, the peaks and valleys of history, its silences and nostalgias. A fat sun hits Caldera straight on, glancing off adobe walls and rooftops; mingling with the dust, this sun takes on a reddish hue, smells of copper, and seems to take wing. The neighbors, hoping for a miraculous dawn, have to be content with the crowing of a rooster, followed by the sound of conveyor belts, cranes, and freight trains.

Allende is not exactly banished into solitude, but rather to a mining center, where the miners live in ghostly barrios. The name of the single street that makes up the town has been lost, and the doors have forgotten their numbers. The ocean announces that somewhere is a world where unknown people wait for letters, reports, and wealth from this dot on the map.

If the one who arrives on the docks is a doctor, fantasies are awakened; if it is a young doctor, anxieties. If the doctor is Allende, whose fame as an orator and popular leader has preceded him, there is a certain flurry of activity in the houses. Coming out to greet him from the local club are the judge, a schoolteacher, a druggist. The captain of the police unit does not come out because it wouldn't look good; he prefers to wait for the exile to present himself, sign in, and receive instructions.

The exile has arrived by train, alone, with a suitcase and a satchel. He doesn't have to ask where to go, because they already have a room for him in the only boardinghouse in town. In his room there's a bed, a night table, a chair, and a desk. There's a shelf with a pottery jug on it, a basin, soap, and washcloth. The window opens onto the street. The smoke from the chimneys of Copiapó hangs over the surrounding hills.

Allende makes it known that he has not come to rest and that he will not take patients in his room, but that he will make house calls; he says that if the sick have the wherewithal, let them pay, if not, it doesn't matter.

In the plaza is a monument to Juan Godoy, the discoverer of copper, and a bench occupied by three lifetime retirees. A priest walks out of the church at dusk and, cutting across the plaza, goes down a nameless cross street. He can't go far. Where that street ends, the town ends. The priest is impatient, the flock does not believe in him. They say he is an anarchist. In fact, he is not, but he subscribes to and collects the magazine *Topaze*.

Allende establishes a routine, sending notes to the copper miners' union headquarters. He wishes to start a socialist group in Caldera.

The day after his arrival, a judge comes to meet him. Juan Antonio Díaz Cliff is a gentle, sad fellow, tall and thin, with a dark complexion and distant green eyes. He is a Catholic, and a Christian socialist by persuasion. He comes to bring greetings, he says, in the name of the youth that does not exist here—they are all in the mines—and in the name of those who want social justice for the town. In the name of those who want the expulsion of yanqui imperialists, the closing of the bars and whorehouses, and the granting of a seaport to Bolivia.

He walks out with Allende. They go to visit the police captain, a heavyset man with a deep voice, who blows his nose and surprises Allende with a prepared speech.

"Up here, Señor Allende," Captain Oscar González says, "we are a patriotic people, peaceful, and hardworking. In spite of what is rumored, good manners are the rule here. We greet you respectfully and with an open mind. Sow goodwill, and we will respond in kind. And since it is our way, even with affection. Being who you are, it is not necessary for you to sign this book every day. Sundays is enough. After mass." He ends his discourse with an explosive laugh like a breaking dam.

"Being who you are . . . ," Allende thinks. Later he discovers that the captain has been thinking about his grandfather Dr. Ramón Allende, the Red Allende, and that he was in effect saying, "You may be a socialist, but you're a mason, too, and that's the important thing."

Alejandro de la Barra was the schoolteacher—an older but youthful man who was even taller and thinner, if that were possible, and more distant than the judge. At parties the teacher strummed heavily on a guitar and sang in a deep bass voice the "Song of the Pampa" by Francisco Pezoa. "Doctor Allende," he said, "the north was made by God for the poor, but Mr. North stole it for the gringos; Recabarren recovered it for Chile."

Allende improvised a sickroom in the school, where he vaccinated the entire town. "Come and get baptized," the teacher said jokingly. "It's free, and may God spare us from eternal life." A special area was set aside for women, and Allende taught them how to care for themselves during pregnancy and birth.

"Someday," de la Barra would say, "you will be the president that Recabarren was not able to be, and you will save our children; you'll give them the milk that is as white as our mountains, the iron that is as blue as our ocean, and the intelligence that is as red as our working class."

"I owe de la Barra the love of childhood," Allende would say years later, "learned in the depths of my exile. These dictators don't know what gifts they hand us when they banish us to the four corners of the earth. We learn there that solitude, abandonment, hopelessness do not really exist, because the folks who live in the most isolated places live for solidarity. And they get our revolutionary faith in return."

The druggist was Juan Alsina, called San Juan, perhaps because he had no life line on his right palm and because people saw the martyr's look in his face. He had been a democrat in the days of Artemio Gutiérrez, but now was a communist. He placed his laboratory and pharmacy at Allende's service, but maintained the exclusive right to set bones, an important job in a mining town.

The months Allende spent in Caldera were not exactly gravy, yet they were rich in friendships and the exchange of ideas. All would return from the day's work thirsty, and the judge would pull chairs out on the street and set out glasses and a bottle of *pisco* from Elqui. The afternoon would slowly wane as the analysis of national problems began in earnest. Nothing interrupted these seminars. Sometimes Captain González would pass by with his assistant, greet the students with a touch of his cap and the blowing of his nose, his eyelids blinking away.

Allende brought a satchelful of news to the town. Back in 1934 Ranquil had been a mere police-blotter item in the dailies of the north. Little was known in Caldera about the massacre, which the Alessandri government had hidden behind a smoke screen. Allende reported to his friends in Caldera the details that Congressman Carlos Alberto Martínez had revealed in a speech before the Chamber of Deputies. During the Ibáñez rule there had been an attempt to repair the desperate condition of the colonists in Alto Bío-Bío through a series of emergency measures. About ten thousand workers were moved to lands in the sierras in the vain hope that gold extraction operations could be established there. When winter hit, the hunger-driven workers carried out a suicidal raid on the storerooms of local ranchers. Repulsed by gunfire, the rioters killed landowners and foremen. The government, now headed by Alessandri, mobilized the police, and the uprising was crushed quickly. Pradenas Muñoz decried before the Senate the fact that of the 500 prisoners taken in the fray, only 23 had arrived in Temuco alive. The rest had been killed en route. *La Opinión* denounced the massacre in screaming headlines. Within several days, security agents of the government assaulted the printing press and offices of the paper.

Alessandri would suppress uprisings without hesitation and then, without blinking, issue a decree of amnesty to wash away the sins of the guilty, leaving only a few faint stains.

The news traveled through the grapevine of the north: in Caldera a secret cell of the Socialist party was in operation, and Salvador Allende, the exile, was instructing and stirring up groups of copper miners. "Delegates" without credentials began appearing left and right, disciples eager to learn, messengers of revolutionary groups in Copiapó.

The discussions expanded in scope, and there was need for a larger arena. The principal of Caldera's high school, Fernando Ortiz Letelier, gave Allende the use of an ample classroom, where the seminars on national politics took place. The armed forces—that is to say, Captain González and his orderly—looked the other way. Interviewed by the correspondent for *El Mercurio* in Copiapó, the captain declared, "Doctor Allende gives medical services to the people of Caldera, who are grateful for this gesture of great patriotism. We all leave each other alone out here and get along just fine."

In those long work sessions, Allende spelled out the changes of strategy being initiated in Santiago and Valparaíso: the formation of a popular front with the goal of contesting the presidential elections of 1938 from the broad base of a solidly unified working class and vast sectors of the middle class.

From this idea Allende gleaned the germ of a political plan that would serve as a counterpoint to Alessandri's utopian republic of 1920, and also to the monolithic and isolationist dogmas of the extreme Left. "We have the parties to put this plan into practice," said Allende, "and the civic traditions that will protect and ensure its survival; we have the maturity and political wisdom of a people well grounded in parliamentary experience."

Allende spent six months in Caldera, months of tireless professional labor and partisan political activity. By the time he was allowed to return to Valparaíso, the country, caught up in the suppression of antigovernment revolts, was facing a moment of truth.

1938: Spring

Alessandri opens his arms wide in an attitude of astonishment that cannot mask a deeper concern. He has been saying all along that Chile is the great exception in Latin America because of its long-standing faith in a strong state based on laws. It is the other countries that hack themselves to pieces in brawls between bosses and uniformed toughs. He has preached a kind of authoritarian democracy, or government by the superior. In other words, the landowners and the bankers together were to preside, with the support of an obedient middle class and the saintly service of the workers and peasants as a base. The armed forces provide the guarantee of order in such a picture, and they have been, and will continue to be, rewarded for their service. Chile, he believes, is a quiet country, used to a dreamy climate and memories of a golden age. "Let's not allow anyone to rock the boat," says the patriarch. "Let us govern, we who know how. The middle class, with its pretensions, is happy to be admitted to the foyer of the big house; with its obvious merits and taste for work, just give it time, for one day it will grow roots and become upper class. Let no one be impatient for this day to come." But the fact is, the *rotos* and the army get impatient and start to raise hell. "At such a cost, señores!" But it's too late. It's time to use a heavy hand and put them all in their place.

By 1936 the Alessandri government has become a sort of legalized dictatorship that defends itself by declaring a state of siege and by demanding constitutional guarantees for its existence. Few know that coiled underfoot is a move to implant a genuine dictatorship. The man behind the scheme is Gustavo Ross, a pale, bald economist, an international financier who complied solicitously when the president conferred upon him the position of minister of finance. He recommended the resumption of payments on the foreign debt and lent his support to the Nitrate and Iodine Sales Corporation; he placed a 2 percent tax on retail sales, increased the rents in the public sector, and raised the salaries of government employees. He pushed for road construction, hospitals, stadiums, and founded a bank to finance low-income housing. Until one day he surprised even his close friends and the president himself: he proposed, with a straight face and in a dignified manner—albeit with a slight smile on his thin lips—the installation of a corporativist regime, following the model of Mussolini and Salazar. An out-and-out dictatorship.

Was it the mirage of an arrogant old man who lay dreaming of fresh republics waiting for despots?

The president woke up on February 28, 1936, to the acrid smell of gunpowder coming from the direction of the barracks. He grabbed the phone and decreed jail terms and banishment for the conspirators. The innocent fell with the sinners. Most of the military participants in the aborted coup were retired, their names never made public.

Alessandri was playing one of his best cards: he drew the attention of the populace to a dubious danger. With the grand gesture of a chef who lifts the lid from a casserole, he exposed the civilian conspirators, pointing his finger at Ibáñez.

Ross came out of the fray even stronger than before. His name was a magnet for those who were preparing the political scene for the 1938 presidential elections.

The slogans of the Popular Front spread, causing curious reactions. Some said the politicians had finally hit the nail on the head. There was an evangelical fervor in the air, and the proletariat and the bourgeoisie lay down together like the lamb and the lion. All of a sudden everyone wanted to join the parade, but few knew why or where it was heading. In the nuclei of the revolutionary cells, where the militants cocked their ears toward ancient prophets, young illuminati would leap to their feet to announce bizarre conclusions: "Yes," they exclaimed, as though they had been reborn, "it's the hour of the Alliance for Liberation. Prestes did it in Brazil, why not Ibáñez in Chile?"

It was also a time for purges: when one rebel was kicked out of a party, he would drag a whole flock of wild and woolly Ibáñez followers with him. "A big fist," the government leaders would recommend, "to crush the flowering germ of Ibáñismo."

A diminutive and elegant man, with an upper-class name and the air of a roué, stood up one day in the Chamber of Deputies and, without making a fuss, laid out the program of the Popular Front. He was Justiniano Sotomayor. Among other things, he said, "Our aspiration is to come to power constitutionally. Let us not forget that the Popular Front is the response to the deep crisis the country is passing through, which is not, as some believe, of a political nature. It is, rather, a social dilemma."

He cited some alarming statistics: in 1936 German imports reached 100 million gold pesos. The United States exported 12 million pesos worth of goods to Chile.

In the outskirts of the city, around Bellavista and Recoleta, Matta Avenue and El Tropezón, one didn't hear such discourse. Instead, one saw the broad strokes of graffiti artists, who painted the preamble for bloody battles between Nazis and Marxists, as the carabineros looked on from a distance. The gangs would approach each other on the dark sidewalks, armed with paintbrushes and buckets of paint, chains and brass knuckles. In the gentle light of the streetlamps, they would go at each other, the deafening noise of their encounter spreading far beyond. Until someone pulled a gun and shot. In a swirl of dead leaves, the wounded man convulsed and fell. The carabineros closed in. The graffiti artists dragged the fallen man away. Then there was nobody. Until the break of dawn, when they would begin their task again. Dripping letters emerged from their frenzied strokes. Sometimes the drops were blood.

What was going on, why such encounters?

The strategy of the Popular Front transformed the traditional makeup of Chilean politics and was the first phenomenon actually to affect the social crisis that Chile had been in since the end of the nineteenth century. Politicians like Alessandri and Ibáñez felt that the country of cataclysms and fly-by-night solutions, hidden between the mountain ranges and the sea, archipelagoes and volcanoes, was also a part of the world and of a civilization about to explode into pieces.

It had always been said that Chileans were a people of education and political maturity, with a civic, libertarian spirit and great stamina. But what was not clear was the origin of those qualities: from where, through what struggles and processes, had this political experience come? The ruling class prided itself on its mercantile and financial arts, on its masterly handling of the economy; it never spoke of the disasters of the agri-economy, nor of its lack of interest in entering into the industrial revolution. It governed conservatively in a country where even the conservatives had forgotten what it was they were supposed to be conserving.

Young tribunes, clothes cut in England, echoing Maritain, boldly gesturing like Primo de Rivera, wanted to shake Chile, to integrate the country into a program of Christian socialism. The blue-collar workers, however, had not learned their political lessons in classrooms or in the cloistered offices of the government: they learned in the broken-down nitrate mines, in ghost towns, in jails and concentration camps.

Now, all of a sudden, the precise nature of the Chilean political crisis was being defined, in order to strike a trail toward genuine change, away from the order of the illusionists. This was what Salvador Allende grasped at that critical moment, and this is how he explained his specific brand of activism: "The Popular Front is not going to bring revolutionary change to Chile," he said. "Its platform grows out of the roots of our social crisis, and its slogan is, 'Bread, a roof over your head, and a coat on your back.' A humanitarian slogan, not a revolutionary one. We're joining this coalition in order to form the Left wing of the capitalist system."

Alessandri sensed the dangers of this new Left as it advanced. He applied pressure without hesitation. He had to contend with general elections on March 7, 1937, and the roll of the dice gave him quite a huge surprise. Face-to-face with the patriarchs who intended to assure the government of a landslide conservative victory, a new reformist guard raised its head: a group of youths split from the Conservative party and founded the Falange Nacional party. They elected four representatives, Eduardo Frei, for Iquique; Manuel José Irarrázaval, for Illapel; Fernando Durán, for Valparaíso; and Manuel Garretón, for Santiago.

Gustavo Ross's bribing and coercive tactics were to no avail. His failure to influence events led to his resignation from the cabinet. The country celebrated his departure, and Alessandri had to reshuffle the ministerial deck. Among the new faces he chose a 27-year-old, an eloquent Catholic, calm and sure of himself, named Bernardo Leighton. With his dark looks and ironic, skeptical smile, he seemed to foretell the Lion's departure.

The socialists and communists brought a team of fierce polemicists to Congress. Elías Lafertte, who had been persecuted under the Alessandri government and was living out his exile in Mexico, was elected senator for the northern provinces.

And Allende? Among the Marxist leaders, Allende was referred to as an ace-in-the-hole that could dramatically alter the game. They tested his mettle, having him run for representative in Valparaíso and Quillota.

In that, his first electoral campaign, Allende displayed the style that would mark all his campaigns. With his retinue of followers, he covered every corner of the port and combed the hills. He didn't turn up his nose at a single plaza, theater, or promising street corner. He took to the soapbox everywhere, conversing, cajoling, inspiring; those who followed him asked him to rest, but Allende left them behind and walked on with new followers, men and women of the port city—railroad workers, stevedores, students, hospital workers, and friends. His reputation as a leader grew among the youth of the port. He was seen as a dedicated, untarnished militant who kept promises; he was also a visionary and exciting orator who got to the heart of the issues. At 29 years of age, Allende was elected by a great majority, and his name jumped to the front page of the political chronicles. His record of exile and prison terms lent him a certain aura.

He felt that he was emerging from a year of premonitions and entering a year of grave decisions. 1936 had brought promises, 1937, triumph and greater responsibilities. 1938 would be the crucial one.

During a stretch of beautiful sunny days in April 1938, the Popular Front held its presidential campaign convention. In January the Partido Radical had decided to rally around Pedro Aguirre Cerda. A quiet man, he looked like a poor farmer and spoke like a schoolteacher. Aguirre Cerda stood with the unified Left.

"The only way to have a decent, egalitarian system is by spreading and fortifying democracy. The radical Left, both generous and idealistic, faced with the ever-increasing egotism of the governing parties, cordially accepts an alliance with the workers," said Aguirre Cerda.

The verbal battles at the convention were highly charged, and the voting ended in a locking of horns that few had expected: socialists versus communists.

The electoral process was itself somewhat complex. Convention rules stipulated that the winner had to receive two-thirds of the votes. Obviously, the Partido Radical and the Socialist party, once united, could bring a common candidate to power if they could agree on a name. It was soon clear, however, that such an agreement was not in the cards. The radicals would accept no compromises, and the socialists would not back down either. The latter had come into the fray with Marmaduque Grove in the cockpit, and they were determined to back him to the bitter end. But the magical balancing act that would guarantee victory was in the communists' repertoire.

The convention got under way on April 14, the anniversary of the Spanish republic, in an appropriate setting—Caupolicán Arena, which, in addition to the occasional political event, had seen many a boxing and wrestling match. After the inauguration the convention moved to the assembly hall of the Senate.

The voting started on Friday the fifteenth. The ensuing discord developed mechanically, as a matter of course. The radicals voted for Aguirre Cerda and the socialists for Grove; the communists voted for Lafertte and the democrats for Pradenas Muñoz. What started as a political struggle turned into a fuming melee by the second day.

Santiago, always slow paced and quiet at summer's end, followed the ups and downs of the convention in a sporting mode. Bets were made, people of every stripe jammed through the doors of Congress to applaud or hoot the delegates. While the Catholic elites of the city went to their accustomed pews in the cathedral, and large family groups in their Sunday best strolled the paths of the Plaza de Armas, the last meeting of the Popular Front's convention began. There would be no further opportunities. The curtain was about to fall.

Marmaduque Grove, ashen and grave but with his customary military bearing, strode up to the podium, faced the 1,200 delegates before him, and publicly withdrew his candidacy. After an awkward silence he announced the Socialist party's support for don Pedro Aguirre Cerda. The true populist—Grove himself—was being sacrificed, the man loved by workers and students, a man beyond the world of scheming politics, the perennial exile, the prisoner who went from jail to the Senate. When Grove stopped speaking, Congress turned into a free-for-all, shouts and insults flying about the room.

Don Pedro was elected unanimously. But a great fissure split the Marxist parties. That afternoon don Pedro invited all the delegates to the Lucerne, a teahouse. When Lafertte stood up to speak for his party, the socialists shouted him down. Don Pedro observed this calmly, his brow furrowed and a yellowed cigarette burning in his hand.

In a frenzied moment González Videla leaped onto a table, tore off his jacket, rolled up his sleeves, and challenged all those threatening Lafertte to fight. Lafertte, wide-eyed and pale, moved his chair to the side and walked toward the door. A group of communist delegates followed him.

Allende analyzed the conflict in its historical context: "When we founded the Socialist party, the Communist party already existed. On analyzing the situation, we thought there was room for a party that, although having a similar doctrinal and philosophical position to the communists and sharing a Marxist approach to history, would be free of international links. This didn't mean, however, that we would ignore the internationalist dimension of the proletariat. A party based on similar ideas was needed, but with a wider vision, and tactics suited to Chile's problems."

Before the new congressional sessions were to start on May 21, 1938, Alessandri got his coterie of Draculas together and exorted them to sharpen their teeth. "Work up something sweet, boys," he told them, "let's make a little history." And they didn't disappoint him.

When he stepped down from the carriage, with the tricolor sash across his chest and his top hat in hand, Alessandri detected a movement of fleeing shadows in the gardens of Congress. He looked sideways at Waldo Palma, his chief of police and top heavy. Palma gave him a wink and smile. As Alessandri ascended the steps leading to the entrance of the building, a tremendous explosion rocked the ground and a thick column of black smoke spiraled upward. A blackened palm tree folded like an old umbrella. Alessandri, imperturbable, looked straight ahead and entered the assembly hall. After dusting off his coat, he lifted his head and was about to begin his speech before the full Congress and the diplomatic corps, when a high-pitched voice shouted, "Mr. President, may I have the floor?" Alessandri paid no attention. The intruder insisted, got to his feet, gesticulating. Bodyguards and secret police fell on the man. A cavernous voice from the underworld said, "Get him out of here," and the men dragged Congressman González Videla out by his feet. The howling continued as his head bounced along the floor and down the steps of Congress.

Alessandri, still under control but making eye contact with Waldo Palma, arranged his papers for the presidential message and prepared to read. He had just opened his mouth when another representative stood up, walked down the row past his colleagues, and once in the middle of the aisle, took out a pistol and began firing. It was González von Marées, pale as a ghost. He shot with his eyes closed, and instead of hitting Alessandri he blew the national coat of arms to smithereens; another bullet nearly creased the bonnet of the papal nuncio. The others came to rest in the venerable clock above the podium.

The whole country was moved—more to laughter than tears—by the events in Congress. "The Great Little González Brothers Act," people would say. They laughed at the photos of González Videla being carried off with one leg in the air, shoeless, his shirttails flying and a shock of hair covering his face. Some months later, when the Nazis had renewed their armed assaults on the Popular Front, and the minister of the interior was having it out with the communists and the Federation of Chilean Students, an act of violence took place in Santiago that was unique in the history of Chile. Unique because of its ferocity and its bloody and dramatic political consequences.

A group of Nazis, commanded by González von Marées, assaulted the administration building of the University of Chile and the Social Security building. Their purpose was to provoke a rebellion and overthrow the government.

Chapter Eleven

Kill Them All!

The execution of the Nazis, defeated in battle by the carabineros, occurred on a stairway. Some of those men, from remote provinces, had never seen a stairway like that one. To them it seemed endless, and so indeed it turned out to be. They hadn't known exactly how many floors were in the building. Perhaps ten, they thought. But they discovered that there were at least seven, because after they had killed the carabinero guarding the entrance door, they made their way up to the seventh floor, herding the employees of the bursar's office before them. It was lunch break, and the secretaries and clerks had left their offices for cafeterias and restaurants. And so it was on the seventh floor that the Nazis took their stand, erecting barricades, shooting their guns, and establishing the foundation for the state they had dreamed of. But they never found out for sure how many floors there were.

The first hour went by quickly. After stacking furniture and taking firing positions, there was nothing to do but wait. Down below, way down below, near La Moneda, could be heard police sirens, shouts, scattered shots.

They kept on waiting. The carabineros went up to the sixth floor and shouted garbled orders. The voices of the officers were tough and dry, those of the rank and file, singsong. A lot of wasted shots were fired. At about 3:00 the stairway began to be real. The rest of the building seemed to disappear, floor by floor, window by window. Then the doors, the elevators, the ceiling, nothing could be seen. Only the stairway and the landings were left. A geometric shape rigorously defined, like a silo of yellow light that was turning gray, later becoming suspended in a long, narrow vacuum like the space a rock plummets through down into a well. The stairs no longer had an end to them.

87

At about 4:00, maybe a little before, a crowd started to climb up from the first floor, making noise as it went. From above could be heard the sound of commands, scurryings about, the sound of heavy objects hitting the ground. No shots. Then the rapid movements ceased. Suddenly a Nazi appeared on the landing of the seventh floor, on the edge of the barricade; he was very pale, and blood was running down his chin. He was unarmed. He shouted, "We are lost, they'll kill us all, we'd better go down." The Nazis formed a quick council and made a decision. They took their hostages out of the room where they had been held, and falling in behind them, they began to descend the stairs. On the sixth floor they met groups of fellow Nazis with their hands held high, who had fought and surrendered at the university's administration building.

With their hands raised above their heads, they had been paraded down Arturo Prat Street, later down Bandera Street, and finally down Morandé. The crowds, cordoned off by the police, observed in silence. When they passed the side door of La Moneda, General Arriagada, rifle in hand, gave orders to a tall, fat lieutenant colonel, slightly stooped as though he had a chronic hearing problem. The latter transmitted the order to his troops, and the prisoners, instead of continuing down Morandé Street, entered the Social Security building.

There was a hubbub in the main hallway. The carabineros were running back and forth in opposite directions, carrying orders and counterorders. The only clear message was that if the carabineros didn't finish off the Nazis by 4:00 the army would start bombing. A gentleman in a white jacket and thick glasses was smoking nervously, and in a carefully measured, quiet voice, he offered cots for the wounded. There was no response until a prefect said, "Doctor, there won't be any wounded here." The gentleman left.

President Alessandri went down to the Morandé door of the palace, listened to General Arriagada's report, expressed his opinion, and retired to his office.

At 4:00 General Arriagada got bored.

"Tell Major González to go to hell," he said to a carabinero, "and to get this over with."

The Nazis, divided into groups so that they would fit on the landings of the stairs, started to come down. They were greeted by bullets.

"Come on, boys, do your duty!" said a lieutenant who had loosened his belt and opened his jacket in order to fire more comfortably.

The Nazis fell, and once on the floor, they were shot again. By 6:00 all were dead.

But they weren't all dead.

At dusk Raúl Marín, a conservative patriarch, accompanied by a priest, appeared in the hallway and requested permission to go through the building. At the sound of the prayers of the priest, who was moving slowly through the corpses, four Nazis hidden under the bodies of their comrades spoke up. There was no way to finish them off before witnesses. Those living corpses narrated the events later, in proceedings that the government was forced to initiate.

And González von Marées? With his right hand held high, and the other on his waist, he declared, "It is not my intention to diminish the gravity of what has happened, and I am resigned to suffer the punishment that I legally deserve. I ask only that my compatriots not judge me too harshly and that they realize that the terrible guilt hanging over me at this moment has not been the result of unbridled ambition but rather the fatal consequence of a regime that has whipped the desperation of a people into a frenzy."

And with the word "frenzy," he disappeared from history.

Alessandri had moved quickly. As the Nazis attacked the university and the Social Security building, he locked Ibáñez and von Marées in jail. Then he confronted a vehement opposition that immediately accused him of ordering the massacre of the Nazis. For a country in the grip of collective terror, the presidential election was a purgative ritual. With Alessandri out because the Chilean constitution does not allow a president to run for re-election, the contest was between Aguirre Cerda and Ross, the former winning by only four thousand votes. Don Pedro went immediately to the radio station of the influential daily *El Mercurio*. Calmly, he gave voice to the hopes of the people: "It is necessary to create an environment of reconciliation, to relegate to history the details of the tragedy in the Social Security building. We must turn the investigation over to the civil courts and move on."

On December 25, in a solemn session of Congress, Alessandri removed the presidential sash and raised it in the air to place it on don Pedro. The latter, small and thin, felt that it would hang down to the ground. He received it with an ironic smile.

Later, don Pedro celebrated with a party that broadcast to all the nature of his government: he opened the doors of the palace and, shoulder to shoulder with the people, drank the red wine of the land, happy but discreet in his behavior. At his side radical freemasons, socialists, communists, democrats, labor leaders, and small businessmen celebrated together.

In the Patio of the Orange Trees, the names of potential ministers and ambassadors were once again being shuffled. Don Pedro, looking out from his balcony, measuring time and space, blew on the ash of his cigarette, which flew out over the heads of the sorcerers.

"We have a big job ahead," the president said, never imagining that even as he spoke the country's innards were roiling and that a month later a ferocious earthquake would ravage the south of Chile. It would level the cities of Chillán and Concepción, undo towns and villages, and jumble up rivers with the salt waters of the ocean. Don Pedro, instead of starting on the programs of the Popular Front would have to remake Chile, putting an orderly façade over its unruly geography.

From the start there were no misunderstandings or doubts in the relationship between don Pedro and Allende. The president valued Allende's talents as an activist and organizer and recognized his instinctive ability to transform popular disturbances into solid electoral campaigns. He recognized Allende's natural genius for directing from within an organization, rather than imposing hierarchical structures from without. Don Pedro wished to bring him into his cabinet, but the Socialist party needed Allende for the Senate.

Years later, recalling his life as a young politician and parliamentarian, Allende accurately evoked the image of don Pedro: "Look, that's don Pedro in this photo. A man of great human qualities, very generous. His direct contact with the people led him into ever more progressive positions. He began as a middle-of-the-road politician, but because he was able to respond to the affection of the people, little by little he became a man of conviction. He never stopped being a constitutionalist and never wanted to be anything else."

When I think about don Pedro, I think about winter: you could feel the glacial weather of the Chilean south in his dark, wind-cured face, a grayish frost on his mustache. He would smoke with the lit end of the cigarette toward his palm, as country folk do to keep their hand warm. With a knotted scarf around his neck and a cap pulled down over his eyes, he looked as though he foresaw a winter all his own. He would say, "We have to fill Chile's potholes, and put the Mapocho River back in its bed; it fools around too much, and it plays a crooked game with the poor." Those holes were solitude and poverty, and he described them to Allende because he wanted him in his cabinet. "There's time, don Pedro," Allende responded. But don Pedro knew that his days were numbered.

Chapter Twelve

Skyquake

On the night of the earthquake, Salvador was attending a meeting at the freemasons' headquarters in an old building noted for its stairways, banisters, spacious halls, and parquet floors. At the first shock, Salvador gripped the sides of his chair and sprang to his feet. By the second, third, and all the rest, he was running madly through patios, hallways, and rooms, without stopping until he found himself safe out in the street, face-to-face with the shaking Santa Lucía Hill. Traffic had stopped, and the devout visitors of the San Francisco Church were on their knees in the middle of the avenue, beating their chests and begging for mercy.

After his initial panic had subsided, Salvador walked to the entrance of the Santa Lucía Theater. The marquee had crashed to the ground in pieces. In the crowd he noticed a colleague and his wife. They introduced him to a young woman whom Salvador seemed to recognize. He kept looking at her. She smiled back, amused at his ruffled state, his unbuttoned collar, his glasses a bit off center.

"Earthquakes always mean panic in Chile," as Tencha recalls later, "and people hit the streets to save themselves from the falling debris in the buildings. We went outside too. That's when I bumped into this young man, an ex-senator, who was the minister of public health in the Popular Front government of President Pedro Aguirre Cerda, one of the most beloved leaders of the Chilean people. As minister of public health, Salvador was often on the road to Chillán, to bring emergency aid to the people there. One of the things that most attracted me to Salvador was the way he spoke with such great warmth of the people shaken by the earthquake."

"Doctor Allende," his friend said, "this is Tencha Bussi."

Salvador fixed his tie and, adjusting his glasses, suggested coffee. People were still running, and ambulance and fire engine sirens were keening full blast. Allende and friends ducked into a little spot on Tenderini Street. The lights were on but the place was empty. Someone in shirtsleeves was fiddling with a radio dial, producing deafening static. They called him over.

"This is a catastrophe," pronounced the man, "a tremendous tragedy. All of the radio stations in the south are out. There's no communication, telephones, nothing. I'm listening to a ham operator here."

The espresso machine had broken, and the floor was covered with hot water. Standing next to the radio, they all listened in silence. The ham operator spoke of fallen buildings in Concepción, the university in ruins, the bridge across the Bío-Bío broken in half, the municipal theater in Chillán collapsing, leaving no survivors.

The friends decided to leave, but Salvador asked Tencha to stay with him awhile. The man finally appeared with the coffee. Through the plate glass window they could see the summer sky over Santiago, loaded with stars, hanging low over the mountains, a sky like a park decoration gently rocking in the breezes. On Santa Lucía Hill the street lamps winked against the faded red of the terraces. A typical night in that corner of Santiago, but now the hills released an intense aroma of herbs and wet earth.

Tencha had said, "But how can it be that a socialist leader is going around to masonic lodges? Masons are history by now. What does it mean to be a mason now? Philanthropy?"

"No, social justice."

"A bourgeois fraternity . . . Rotary, Lions, Kiwanis . . ."

Then Allende spoke about his family, his grandfather, the Red Man. He told her about the help his grandmother had received at the death of Allende Padín and the debt that Salvador and his brothers would never forget.

That night Tencha made some observations that left an impression on Salvador. "This independence of judgment was a part of our relationship," she says. "Salvador always appreciated my expressing myself freely even when my ideas contradicted his."

Later, Allende said that he would organize a relief train and travel south.

The month went by quickly. Salvador directed the operation of field hospitals, health clinics, and the distribution of food and clothing in the areas affected by the earthquake.

When Salvador came back to the Ministry of Public Health, he and Tencha continued seeing each other every day.

Time went by. Salvador and Tencha began living together, in apartment 26 at 191 Victoria Subercaseaux Street, facing Santa Lucía Hill.

Who was Tencha? Salvador knew that she was from Valparaíso, the daughter of a merchant seaman of Italian origin and a Chilean mother; knew that she studied geography and history at the University of Chile and also library science. Tencha had an air of quiet self-assurance, a gentle smile, and big eyes with a violet glow that would lighten her face. She seemed older than she really was. At the university she was on the sidelines. Her beauty intimidated the students. Salvador was intrigued by her distant air.

Their decision to live together did not really surprise their socialist friends. Among them there was talk of Tencha's having had a love affair before she met Salvador, but no questions were asked. Salvador and Tencha settled quietly into a life of study and work.

The fall arrived, with its short afternoons and sunsets spilling over the terraces and the bronzes of Santa Lucía and the National Library. Salvador and Tencha revised some manuscripts that he was preparing to send to the printer. The hours went by. The aroma of coffee. The cries of street vendors mixed with the pipes of the organ-grinder. Night approached. Salvador was making plans to travel south in the winter.

The streets around Santa Lucía are a bit like a sad, romantic merry-go-round. Salvador and Tencha wanted to be with old friends. They went out and the air grew colder; soon winter would start, and Santiago would be the city surrounded by snowy mountains.

Some friends began to insist that they marry. "Not because of what people say, you know, but because you've got to think about your political career and Tencha's future." In their apartment, filled to the brim with books, paintings, and magazines, Tencha and Salvador would listen with a smile, agreeing to everything. What could all that fuss have mattered to them? However, they finally accepted the idea, just as they could have not accepted it, without attributing any particular importance to the change. One day they went from the house of the best man, Hernán Santa Cruz, to the Marriage License Bureau, and got married. No bells, no sermons. The party that followed was more intimate than usual. As their neighbor, the poet Vicente Huidobro said, "It was a skyquake."

Other things were happening, too. The reconstruction of the south of Chile was a titanic operation; the government of Aguirre Cerda pitched in with all of its resources and without losing sight of the objectives of the Popular Front. To generate electricity the government tapped the power of the torrential rivers that spring from the Andes and flow into the ocean in the short space of a few kilometers. The hydraulic capacities of the country were channeled through new plants: Sauzal, Abanico, Pilmaiquén, Los Cipreses. Allende responded to the calls of the president and was one of the executives who mapped the plans for CORFO, a development corporation controlled by the government to find an economic strategy for solving the crisis inherited from the Alessandri administration. Allende agreed with don Pedro on the need for a state economy. He was aware of the ramifications of the increase in the population, such as the growth in demand for goods. Don Pedro founded the National Health Service, which placed medical care within reach of three million people. He promoted laws for the protection of working women and children. Among them was a law giving women financial support from the government after the fifth month of pregnancy. He also established aid councils for the schools to administer free breakfasts to children.

And then what should have been expected finally happened. Taking advantage of the state of emergency in the south, and the economic difficulties of the government as it faced reconstruction costs, a small but rapid opposition developed. With an ear cocked toward any hint of a conspiracy or a coup that would help them, this group decided to have a go at the Aguirre Cerda government. It was a short, harum-scarum adventure. When the alarm sounded, 50,000 workers set off toward the Alameda and, together with the armed socialist militia, surrounded La Moneda in defense of the Popular Front.

Allende went to La Moneda with a group of leftist leaders. Don Pedro received a telephone call from General Ariosto Herrera's assistant. Years later Allende would remember don Pedro's response: "The army has risen," said the assistant. "You are out of office. The general asks you to surrender, leave the palace, head for the airport, and fly to the Latin American country of your choice. The general guarantees you immunity under this option."

"Tell the general," Aguirre Cerda replied calmly, "that the president of the republic does not submit to traitors and does not intend to leave the palace. I advise the general, before it's too late, to take advantage of the aforementioned airplane and leave the country."

It is 1939: Madrid and Barcelona have fallen, and the heroic resistance of republican Spain comes to an end. World War II begins. The Stalin-Hitler pact puzzles and divides the membership of the Popular Front. The tacit alliance between communists and socialists is in trouble. Allende appears as the leader of a powerful and unified segment of the Chilean Left, but he is having trouble getting a hearing.

Salvador and Tencha together add the final touches to *Society and Medicine in Chile*, a book that will have a decisive effect on Salvador's professional career. The book is published, well reviewed, and receives the Van Buren prize at the end of the year. Salvador gives the first copy to Tencha, dedicated, "To Tencha, comrade and friend, with deep affection."

Another summer is beginning, but before Santiago starts to

get sleepy, it throws a party. The students hit the streets, the old trees shake in the breeze. Forestal Park celebrates, and the road to Valparaíso and Viña del Mar sparkles.

The couple lives some happy days in that corner of Santiago which has always attracted dreamers and visionaries, near Santa Lucía Hill, where the earthquake brought them together. Among cinnamon trees, araucarias, and acacias, they are near the homes of lifelong friends and leaders in the social struggle: Hernán Santa Cruz, Carlos Briones, Manuel Mandujano, and Víctor Jaque. The moment will come when several writers who are part of a grand, romantic literary tradition will also take up residence in the neighborhood, all busy in the midst of a joyful bohemia. Among them is Benjamín Subercaseaux, at that time writing *Chile: A Geographical Extravaganza* on wide sheets green as ferns, and Pedro de la Barra, dreaming about his own "theater of the world."

In 1940 Salvador travels to Peru with Jaque and Mandujano to meet with Haya de la Torre and other leaders of APRA, a coalition of anti-imperialist, pro-Indian political forces.

On January 10, 1941, Carmen Paz is born, the Allendes' first daughter. Salvador celebrates until the lights burn out.

Don Pedro, living a few blocks away, is suffering from tuberculosis and calls Salvador to him for the last time.

Chile had not yet known an era of democratic peace and political well-being, contrary to what the historians are fond of saying.

The earthquake that shook don Pedro was the prelude to a cyclone, a military uprising named Ariosto Herrera. The ministers, with Allende in the lead, applied poultices left and right with the firm hand of a country doctor. But just as the task got under way, don Pedro Aguirre, small, dark-skinned, and handsome, turned to skin and bones, until finally there was nothing left of the man. He died on November 25, 1941, of what was called in those times a "galloping" tuberculosis.

Foreseeing his fate, don Pedro had begun to keep his distance from La Moneda, naming Jerónimo Méndez Arancibia minister of the interior; the office of vice-president of the republic was immediately conferred upon him.

Two weeks after the death of Aguirre Cerda, Allende traveled to the United States to represent Chile in a meeting of the Panamerican Association of Public Health. He was in New York and Washington for ten days. His speech before the group contained a tough message: he delivered statistics describing the impoverished living conditions of Chilean workers and their families, denounced the exploitation of women and children, and accused imperialist enterprises of fleecing the country of its natural resources. He returned to Chile at the end of December, Tencha recalls, "with an armful of presents for Carmen Paz."

And now what? Alessandri, Ibáñez, one more time?

A rather unusual call came from the provinces of Chile. Accustomed to controlling the political life of the nation from Santiago—and mainly for its benefit—the old leaders were suddenly confronted by new generations of politicians who angrily demanded to be heard. Tired of knocking on La Moneda's doors, they flung them wide. From Ñuble came a presidential candidate, a well-established country gentleman, minister of the interior under Dávila, a discreet and aloof professional, tall and quiet, with gray hair and the eyes of an owl. His name was Juan Antonio Ríos. In opposition to him, from La Serena, came a razzle-dazzle lawyer, a high-energy man fond of dancing and fancy speeches: Gabriel González Videla, the peripatetic congressman who had once dared to threaten Alessandri, only to be ignominiously thrown out of Congress by the Lion's bloodthirsty henchmen. They fought for the vacant presidency with familiar weapons—ministerial manipulation, straw votes, and great ambition. Groups of young revolutionaries agitating for decentralization—also from the provinces—sounded an alarm. Allende realized that neither Ríos nor González Videla would be the man to break away from the bureaucratic tradition of the old political sharks.

Ríos, a leader from the murky waters of the Partido Radical, defeated González Videla and became the candidate of the Left. The presidential campaign was brief and decisive. Speaking for the old forces of the Popular Front, and counting on the support of a large group of Alessandri's followers, Ríos won a handy victory. He assumed the presidency and appointed a cabinet composed of radicals, liberals, socialists, and democrats.

In April 1942, Allende resigned his position as minister of public health. A sizable rift was growing in the Socialist party. One faction wanted to keep up the alliance with Ríos's party and go on collecting their fat rewards. Allende and his followers pushed for more-radical changes in the country. Meanwhile, the minister of the interior, Arturo Olavarría, showing his true colors, shut the doors of the communist daily *El Siglo*.

The Allendes were in a holding pattern, the party absorbing Salvador's time. Tencha had a job substitute teaching, first in the European School and later in the School for Girls #1. Eventually, she took a permanent position as librarian in the Statistics Bureau. One fine day Salvador got a call from the government. He was being offered a position as director of social services. It was not a bureaucratic job, but rather a chance to cement the reforms that he had initiated as minister of public health.

"I've been a minister in a reformist government for more than two years," Allende said. "I believe I have done my best as a militant socialist in that position. When the government asked me to organize an exhibit showing the wretched condition in which the workers and their families lived, I placed it in front of the fat cats at the Club de la Unión, right across from their elegant dining room. The whole population of Santiago filed past. But the government of the Popular Front never took wing. Like a big red balloon, it hovered over one and another barrio, floating over ports and mines, country and city, but without gaining altitude. What's wrong, compañeros? Where did we fail?"

At the beginning of 1943, the ninth congress of the Socialist party convened. Allende was elected secretary general.

On September 8, a second daughter was born to the Allendes, Beatriz, "La Tati."

Chapter Thirteen

Punta Arenas
Is a City Carved in Stone
by the Wind

Carved by the wind, a city white or gray, like a sea-gull, living off thin, glacial air, hovering over the transparent waters of straits that mark the only discernible limits in a world where things seem to have no fixed borders. Colors are not really colors, just shades of the wind. Things dissolve and change appearance; at certain times of day, the coirón grass of the pampa becomes a choppy green ocean and later a smooth stone surface, a sky, or a snowfield. The city is anchored up high, and its deep-sea appearance is a surprise at each step. The wind cleans and smooths it, courting it in a timeless ritual. Chileans from other regions who go to work there sometimes do so as though they were serving a prison sentence. They come and go, but they don't quit Punta Arenas completely. The borders of the city are never fixed, not with that wind and those snows. People leave, ships, buses, trucks leave; actually, they just lose themselves in seas and pampas that draw out the Punta Arenas mirage.

At the age of 37, Salvador Allende was chosen by his party to run for senator from Valdivia, Osorno, Llanquihue, Chiloé, Aysén, and Magallanes. Candidate from the Ends of the Earth. The elections took place in March 1945. Earlier that year, January 18, the Allendes had their third child, Isabel.

In those days Salvador had a solid appearance; he dressed in a big, fleece-lined leather coat, sweater, corduroy pants, and thick-soled boots. He went bareheaded with a blue cap in his pocket. He would go from town to town without stopping over in any of them. His comrades who had organized the campaign knew where the votes were and where they were not. They scheduled no visits to ranch owners, those who smiled from their big log houses—clinking their glasses of *pisco* and warming themselves next to fires—as they watched the candidate walk by. They didn't consider Allende a threat. Their feudal society would survive his speeches and his utopian promises. "Field workers? No sir, don't make me laugh. You mean tenants, our people. They're like our own sons. Sometimes you have to be a little tough on them, but they'll always tow the line. My grandfather cleared the land and made it what it is." Woods, grandfathers, men and women, bridges, train tracks, and telegraph poles, all planted on the land, to stay for good. "Legal entanglements came later, but at that time just the rubber stamps and a retaining fee were enough. The boundaries used to shift around, but today they're settled."

Allende went further south, to the hinterlands of the country, to Tierra del Fuego and the big estates, to the meat-packing companies, where the workers weren't peons or tenant-farmers, but union members. That's where the votes were. He spoke to them.

"Comrades of Laguna Blanca. To the polls! Comrades from Entreviento, workers from Bahía Catalina. To the polls! Workers from Gente Grande, Río Tranquilo, Fortuna, Río de Oro, Vicuña de Tres Cerrillos and Penitente, from Tres Pasos and Puerto Consuelo! To the polls, you mule drivers from Angostura and San Gregorio!"

What was Allende saying? He was speaking to those empty expanses of Aysén and Tierra del Fuego about a new, privately owned kind of solitude: those lands, touched by icy seas, beneath the wings of migrant birds, have owners like gods. These gods have their parishioners, but are themselves invisible until judgment day. No one really lives in their paneled houses, no one strolls down their halls of stained-glass windows, nothing stirs the black weather vanes, and the vertical iron rods in the grillwork of their gates are like lances left by the ghosts of conquistadores centuries ago. Allende addresses a hardened proletariat—men and women with strange accents, forgotten Indians, European refugees of wars and revolutions, Argentinians from prisons and unnamed lakes, fishermen from Chiloé lost at canal crossings. This is a multitude caught and held by the era of frozen lamb for international export. Nothing is alien to them: neither the letters from Engels to Marx, nor the polemics of Proudhon, nor the unionism of the Spanish Marxist Iglesias, nor the coronation of the king of the Araucanians, nor the Amazonic weddings in the City of the Caesars.

The hidden doors of the meat-packing houses open and shut, and workers without name or number go in and out, leaving no more trace than that of their boot prints frozen in the mud. Sometimes they come and simply sit in the snow, with frost on their eyebrows and mustaches, rocked by the wind. They identify Salvador by his voice and his slogans. He wants cooperatives where there are feudal estates, and he speaks about redistributing the land and unionizing the field workers, bringing them into the modern world, putting up walls and roofs for them, replacing their huts of stone and sheepskin. He talks about flying in helicopters with nourishment and vitamins, and about moving their winters closer to the hearth of a continent.

Salvador was elected senator. Pablo Neruda was also elected, by other latitudes and solitudes; the poet became the senator from the desert, and he campaigned for the nationalization of the copper and nitrate mines.

Neruda and Allende brought an international level of discourse to their campaigns that was rare in Chile. World War II was coming to an end, in a scenario no longer identified by indiscriminate bombings and sinking fleets, but rather by the apocalyptic blast that rained death on Japan, a magical parasol intended to hide the disappearance of humanity. The nations, before the eyes of the world, in the stage box of an opera house in San Francisco, signed a declaration of repentance and put multicolored flags on it. Truman's representative signed with a skull and crossbones.

Allende introduced a piece of legislation before the Senate that would ratify the United Nations' charter, but only under protest, because of the participation of the Argentinian and Spanish military dictatorships.

President Ríos decided that the moment to visit the United States had arrived. He got on the plane conscious that he was taking a trip to a world beyond. A deadly sickness was consuming him. He went through the North American cities silent and undetected, waving to the shades of Hiroshima in the empty streets. He left his friend Alfredo Duhalde, vice-president of Chile, in charge in Santiago.

Ríos returned without a sound, went home and to bed. His colleagues begged him not to leave Duhalde in La Moneda, but rather Alfredo Rosende, a peaceful and moderate man. On his deathbed Ríos declined to accept. On January 28, 1946, the police, following Duhalde's orders, routed a Socialist party gathering with gunfire.

Ríos never knew what happened. He died in June 1946, and the country had to elect a new president halfway through his term.

Allende had affirmed his solidarity with the Socialist party, which in those days ran the danger of breaking apart in a tangle of opportunism and betrayals. A firm hand was needed, and a revolutionary strategy capable of fast action. Allende jumped in without hesitation. But new paths contained sudden surprises.

Who could have predicted in 1946 the temptations that Truman would dangle in front of a jumpy, loud-mouthed rodent, hungry with ambition? Neither Allende nor Neruda. No one was warned. The nation fell into the trap.

The Right, worried by its recent setbacks, looked for firmer footing. "Let's cut our losses and get back on our feet," they said. What did that mean? "Come on, can't you see? A different Alessandri—don Fernando."

Within the Conservative party old-timers observed and analyzed the political situation, and one spring morning white smoke came out of the chimney of the Club de la Unión: the name spelled by the smoke was Eduardo Cruz Coke, a scholarly physician, an orator with a cavernous voice and the gestures of an apostle.

The Left was united behind González Videla, while the Right

was divided: the Conservative party supported Cruz Coke, and the Liberal party supported Fernando Alessandri.

The Left couldn't lose. Or could it?

The winner was "the people call him Gabriel."

González Videla appeared to have won. He had a plurality, followed by Alessandri and Cruz Coke.

El Mercurio piped up, "A dark horse takes the day: González Videla has 40 percent of the votes, with 60 percent of the population against him."

The election would be decided by a vote in Congress. And the well-known games began. "If Fernando Alessandri gives his votes to Cruz Coke, Mickey Mouse Videla is lost, the communists will back off, and the country is saved," a daily proclaimed.

But a maneuver from the palace produced a strategic cut of the deck, and Congress's vote took place under a radical leftist cabinet. The triumph of González Videla was assured.

What led this newly minted politician to renege on his promises and commitments and turn on the communists whose votes had brought him to the presidency? He went after Neruda like a bloodhound and opened a concentration camp where he sent hundreds of communists, including leaders such as Volodia Teitelboim. He declared solemnly that World War III was on its way "in about three months," and that Chile should take the front ranks in the struggle against the Soviet Union.

In 1946 he had brought the Communist party into the governmental fold by giving it three cabinet positions. But surprised by its show of strength in municipal elections, he decided to haul in the reins. He pushed the comrades out of the government, named a cabinet with Center-to-Right affiliations, and requested extraordinary powers.

He shouted, "I won't allow the Communist party, with its demagoguery, to be the exclusive voice of the working class!"

He appointed an admiral to his cabinet to oversee in-house security; he appointed a general to take over the Ministry of Defense. He had an old philosophy teacher brought in to regiment education, and a managerial type to protect the Treasury.

On the floor of the Senate, Neruda delivered a "J'accuse" that put the country in a state of alarm.

A furious González Videla persuaded Congress to pass a special law that gave him dictatorial authority. Full of enthusiasm, he pushed through another law for the "defense of democracy," baptized by the people as the Damned Bill, the purpose of which was to deprive communist militants of their civil rights, thus eliminating them from the electoral register and the public administration.

"The legislative project under discussion," Cruz Coke declared in the Senate, "is not only diametrically opposed to what was agreed to by the executive committee of the Conservative party, but also to everything that we are, as a democratic country with a Christian tradition. By focusing on the sole objective of repression and using it, not as an instrument of anticommunist activity, but rather as a dangerous weapon against *all* political rights, the government is creating a police state that will suppress all opposition. It is quite simply unconstitutional."

Allende, explaining his negative vote in Congress, stated, "A wave of indignation and protest is moving the ranks of the workers and employees. Gross errors are being committed. An atmosphere of moral insanity reigns that will bring tragic days to the republic."

The struggle between the government and the Communist party was no longer simply a war of words. It had become a war of pent-up emotions and sordid schemes that lasted for years.

"Salvador stayed looking out the window, his mind far away. I would open the blinds every morning, just enough so that he could see the leaves of the ferns like giant wings, the lace of the cinnamon tree, the stone stairs, the little paths that snake their way to the high plaza and the watchtowers of Santa Lucía Hill.

"Sometimes he would look at me with a melancholy smile during his meditations. He had recently taken a trip to Peru and had had an interview with the Aprista leaders. But he didn't have his heart in that business. He felt that Haya de la Torre's movement was a sleepy affair, a confederacy of fog-bound idols, rocked from time to time by the eloquent lullabies of lawyers and notaries who sang of revolution by the descendants of the Incas.

" 'There are masses of Indians trickling down from the sierras,' Salvador would say, 'and it seems as if they can't make it into the city. They stay among the debris and the rocks on the hillsides. Yet they somehow set the tone and shape the content of the Aprista struggle. I wish I had known Mariátegui, a man on fire with intellectual passion, spouting oracles from a wheelchair. I can understand how my compañeros feel about the Indo-American dream of revolution—but it's a dream that's spawned great novels and poems without really changing Peruvian society.'

"Salvador had traveled to Peru for several reasons, but he was particularly attracted by the meaningful struggle engaged in by Haya de la Torre and his followers.

" 'For example, how could I forget Betancourt at the time of his exile in Chile? He was my neighbor in Santiago and compañero in daily political powwows, sharp and vitriolic behind his big glasses. A pipe smoker, as you know. Pipe smokers have invented a ritual to keep from throwing away their secrets too quickly or easily. They fill their pipes and then toy with the tobacco using odd little tweezers; then they light it. They look at the tiny embers and take clever little puffs, sending smoke signals into the air. Finally, when you think they're really going to smoke the thing in earnest, they take it out of their mouths and stare at you. It has just been a smoke screen that has somehow intrigued you but left you in limbo. Betancourt would carry out the ritual while looking at you with a little smile in his eyes.

" 'But his people never dealt the coup de grace necessary to create a revolutionary government, never could check the principal weapon of imperialism—its capacity to exploit its underground empires in our mines and in our countryside. Betancourt and Haya sang with a lovely voice, but at the moment of truth, when the tough decisions had to be made, they couldn't squeeze a note out. In Chile we always wanted to respond to their progressive campaigns with a big support movement reflecting socialist solidarity. We called a meeting after the foundation of our party. They came and spoke. They sang.'

"In this little room that served as his study, sitting room, and drawing room for shared seclusion, I heard Salvador speak about González Videla as though the poor man, instead of being president of Chile, had been just another worn-down public figure in the annals of a doddering nation losing its direction.

"'For me,' he said, 'the face of a traitor suggests something, maybe a great deal, of the misguided hero, as old Borges described in his famous story. But González Videla,' he added, shaking his head, 'seemed to forget that he should enter the national vacuum as a hero and not just as a screwball. By sticking to his ways, he multiplied his problems, and then he tried to do the impossible—become the absolute villain. González Videla never doubted the role he should play in the postwar years and the cold terror initiated by Truman. But those perfect villains don't last on the Chilean stage. Half-baked tyrants, yes, but rotten to the core, no. Our tyrants, in general, succumb to the temptation of ending their performances as nice guys instead of monsters; they get friendly and make cooing noises. They give medals to children, kiss beauty queens, and forget to watch their backs. That temptation ends up dragging them into a state of bathos. González Videla cemented the unity of a persecuted people. He, who hated us so much, made possible the victory of socialism. The victory? That's what I'm saying. When? It won't be in '52. Even though it began in '38. Maybe in '58. I'll keep working at it.'

"I kept coming back to the little saga of our national dictatorships.

"'Ibáñez was a wrong-headed dictator,' said Salvador. 'He was born with the vocation and the temptation of a ruler. He didn't know how to distinguish between one and the other. That's why as a dictator he could never last beyond the cannon shot of noon.

He was what you might call an unenlightened ruler. He could lead a cavalry school but not a country. It's true, he had no doubts about his place in society. That's why he got the great support that he often held. In contrast, González Videla betrayed the insecurity of a special class of Chileans: he didn't know if he should sit at the end of the big table or at the head of the one in the kitchen. He was a man of considerable courage, you know—quick as a snake and slippery as a fish. He was always ready for a fistfight, but often he didn't know why or against whom. He swam in life's waters, as uncommunicative as a fish, without taking the trouble to understand anyone or even having an interest in doing so. I believe he was surprised to know that presidents do become part of history, a history to which he was totally indifferent. It occurred to him to pick a fight with Pablo Neruda! Can you imagine? Neruda, of course, whittled him down to a toothpick.'

"Looking back on these things now, it's clear that Salvador had found his path, and it was just a question of time before he would transform that path into one of those wide revolutionary avenues that ran through his speeches. To clear the way and sweep aside the opportunists and traitors was the job at hand. He picked a rocky path that was going to cost him some great disillusionments. But there was no thought of turning back. In him you could sense a quiet, undefinable force. I liked to look at his hands. They made gesture after gesture and then became still in front of you, waiting. His silence made his hands seem to talk. We sensed the fragrant shadows beneath the trees of Santa Lucía. We looked at each other and the senatorial discourse slowly vanished. Salvador rose and reached for two whiskey glasses, creating a glow of indirect light between my sofa and his slow and steady steps. Then I rose to shut the window. From outside came the murmur of soft rain. The huge, ancient night had fallen."

"I'm especially interested in the presidential campaign of 1952, Salvador's first," Tencha said to me, "because there you could see the inner change in him, a change that would mark him for the rest of his life. That campaign was the most revolutionary and truly heroic; it was a test in which Salvador showed he had the stuff to be a popular fighter and not just a leader in the polls."

I kept thinking about these words, which intrigued me. You see, everything in the world has been said about Allende: that he was a reformer, that he felt all was lost when he found himself in the middle of a life-and-death struggle between the workers and the reactionary forces; that in a lightning flash of messianic inspiration he was able to find, at last, his true mission and finally fought back when it was too late.

And now I could see that Allende had always had a clear vision of his place in the socialist revolution. Since the thirties. A revolution that didn't follow a single peaceful path. It followed many, including those of personal sacrifice and violence.

Why not? The Allende in 1952 whom Tencha describes was one among several itinerant preachers of revolution in the likeness of Recabarren, Lafertte, and Matte Hurtado—complete with dark suit and straw hat, red banner in hand, marching through solitary landscapes in an impoverished, rebellious country, ready to fight but also to gain votes, to win, and to raise a flag that could one day wave over La Moneda.

Hopeless campaigns had been the norm for workers' candidates since the beginning of the century—for don Reca in the nitrate-rich pampa, for Grove on Easter Island, but never for the professional parliamentarians. What moved Allende then to be the standard-bearer for the proletariat and engage in a struggle doomed to defeat from the start? What moved him to join up with a group of socialists and communists in a Popular Front sure to be persecuted by state-sponsored terrorism?

"González Videla was like a forgetful magician," Allende would say. "Since he was racing through a labyrinth that he never understood, he went along pushing buttons and opening doors that always led to the same dead end."

With the presidential samba winding down, González Videla couldn't help registering the futility of his hatred for

Neruda. He had persecuted the poet with zeal, obliging him to flee from house to house and city to city, on horseback through mountain passes, all the way to Argentina. Later, with a passport lent him by the Guatemalan Nobel laureate Miguel Angel Asturias, Neruda flew on to Europe.

"One could say that Salvador experienced that persecution as though it were his own," Tencha says, "and in living it, he identified with those working men and women who risked their lives protecting Neruda. Salvador and Grove constantly defended Neruda and helped the poet get the support of the leaders of other parties."

Arturo Alessandri, who at the time was president of the Senate, granted Neruda an official permit to leave the country without losing his senate seat.

Some phony socialists who had sold out for a small fee stayed in the González Videla government, provoking a split in the party. Allende, together with Raúl Ampuero, Aniceto Rodríguez, and a group of young militants, founded the Popular Socialist party. In 1952, when this party supported Ibáñez, Allende returned to the Socialist party of Chile.

Chapter Fourteen

The Proletariat's Banner

A good father? Yes. Good, affectionate, considerate. A good-natured companion to his daughters. A good husband? That's a relative question. A man who gives himself body and soul to the struggles of his party is not, and cannot be, the kind of husband one would expect in a typical bourgeois home. Yet Salvador did his part."

Summer for the Santiaguinos is an intricate migration to the beaches, lakes, countryside, and mountains. The morning trains rumble out of the city on shaky tracks, cross rivers on ghostly bridges, and lean screaming and rattling into the curves; the engine is knocking itself out and lets fly a blast on the whistle when you least expect it, as if to cheer itself on. Once over the crest of the hill, it goes freewheeling down at a modest but scary speed. The train drops families off on narrow, rocky beaches steaming in the sun, where the children will eat sweet, sandy bread. Sunday afternoons the Santiaguinos run by: heavy and out of breath they stagger on, dragging their feet in the wet sand. They hurl themselves into the waves and disappear to the applause of relatives and the dismay of lifeguards. Later, the sun sits like any ordinary plate on the shelf of the horizon, the little buckets and shovels of the children are gathered up, goodbyes to the drowned relatives resound, and the tired, puffing train drags itself off once again toward the capital.

The family dreams of a little house by the sea. The day will come. But for the moment family excursions are brief. When there isn't enough time to go to the beach, Salvador drives the girls to the foothills of San Cristóbal, and they walk on foot to the Pyramid. A big, sleek Afghan, with head held high and an elegant tail, goes with them.

The girls play. Salvador runs, followed by his dog. Along the path can be heard the roars of Julia, the lioness in the zoo. Cable cars pass overhead in silence, loaded with people who bid adieu to the present century. Foot travelers move off the path. The dog has stopped and is barking angrily. Salvador calls him. The dog continues to bark menacingly at the Christ of Elqui, a skinny little man with a happy face and long hair hanging loosely, who plants flowers and sows the plot given him by the man in charge of San Cristóbal Hill. This is where the saint lives and writes his sermons and whispers his prophecies in a lisping voice. From here he sallies forth to convert sinners and sell his oracles and breviaries among stevedores along the Mapocho River. Salvador says hello to the hermit and buys a history of his pilgrimage from the Andes, complete with an account of his little miracles and his innocent parodies of the New Testament.

They get back on the path. The dog frolics, wagging his golden tail. The girls go off and Salvador calls to them. They don't pay attention. It is a hot day, and a haze hovers over Santiago, extending all the way to Manquehue and Conchalí. Carmen Paz, la Tati, and Isabel are laughing. A girl whose big eyes smile from her little face is running with them. Her name is Isabel too; she is the daughter of a cousin of Salvador's and will become a novelist.

The doorbell rang and Salvador got up to answer it. He was alone in the house. Tencha and the girls were visiting relatives in Valparaíso. Salvador opened the door and a silhouette loomed imposingly in the summer dusk. The man was dressed in black; his hat threw a shadow across his face. He was taller than Salvador, and his frame filled the doorway. They shook hands and Salvador led him into his study. The visitor did not sit down right away, but first walked around the room observing the books and paintings. He stopped next to the window and looked absently over the groves of trees dotting Santa Lucía. Salvador settled himself into a chair and waited for the man to speak. The silence was a long one.

"Eugenio," Salvador said at last, "let's get right to the point.

There's no sense in beating around the bush. You and I are beyond the game of tactical silences."

"Right," Eugenio González responded. "Let's talk calmly, we've got all the time in the world. At least tonight we have. Even though, as you know, the ship has started to leak."

He sat down and took a silver cigarette case out of his breast pocket. He tamped the cigarette slowly against the case, placed it between his lips and lit it, enjoying the first deep pull. He made himself comfortable on the sofa and smoked with concentration, as if that in itself were the purpose of his visit. That's why he had come, to smoke the peace pipe. But his attitude was remote, almost indifferent; he was thinking and speaking from some point above the scene. González was a pale man whose big, sleepy eyes seemed distant yet smiling. Meticulously dressed in mourning clothes, he cut a Picasso-like figure in the Santiago of the fifties. He was the theoretician of the Socialist party, an academic, a novelist, a melancholy and eloquent orator who did not fit into the style of everyday politics. Allende treated him attentively, gently nudging him to start his business. But Eugenio González wasn't in a hurry. He never was.

"My motives are simple," said Salvador. "I just don't respond to political ambitions . . ."

"We all have them," Eugenio González interrupted. "Just scratch the surface, and there they are. Of course they are not the only thing that moves us. On that we can agree."

"The party is breaking apart," said Salvador. "Possibly the break is inevitable, maybe it's necessary and healthy. Why not?"

"That's right, I can accept that it might be inevitable. The important thing is to understand clearly why it is and what is pushing us to act. My position is simple, and responds to convictions I have maintained since the party was founded. We're not a group of politicians for sale to the highest bidder. We founded a revolutionary party to make revolution, not to postpone it, much less to slack off under the protection of an opportunist government. That much is clear. You and I have nothing to wrangle over on that account. But . . ."

Salvador had gotten to his feet and was serving whiskey from a heavy decanter.

". . . but it is one thing to split the party on matters of principle, and another to split it for strategic motives involving the presidency of the country."

Salvador remained standing with the glasses in his hand.

"I have said it again and again. I don't want to be president to crown a political career; right now what I want is to stop Ibáñez, and I want to do that because at present no one in the party seems disposed to do it except me."

He gave the glass to González and sat down again. It seemed as though the conversation were over. The silence became heavy, and neither of the men made a move to break it. Eugenio González was smoking and revolving his glass between thick white fingers. Following with hooded eyes the clouds of smoke as they ascended toward the ceiling, he seemed to savor the long pause.

"You," he said emphatically, "want to be president; the question is whether this is the opportune moment or whether you should wait. Why in 1952, at this precise moment, and not in 1958? Since your days in the Senate, your career has been well mapped out. Don Arturo," he added with a smile, "would have given you the same advice."

"You are advising me, then?"

"No, of course not," González said, looking at him placidly. In an affectionate tone of voice, yet with some detachment, he observed, "We were never pupils of don Arturo's school. And the difference between us, Salvador, is that you are breaking your own trail, whereas it's my role to watch and occasionally comment. In this case I think you may be headed wrong."

"Ibáñez comes on the scene in a uniform that doesn't fit him."

"Why not cut him a little slack? Isn't it possible that he has changed during his discreet exile in Argentina? Or that he learned something? His Alliance for Freedom . . ."

"Eugenio," Salvador interjected, "that 'alliance' is a borrowed slogan. What Ibáñez learned in exile can be summed up as follows: in order to get to power all he thinks he needs is Prestes's halo over his head."

Eugenio González kept silent, allowing Salvador to blow off some steam. After sipping a bit of whiskey, he rejoined, "You are talking about the political stage, not about the personal destiny of someone who wants the presidency. No one in Chile, in these times, can sweep out the garbage left by González Videla better than Ibáñez. He's got the broom and the strength and boldness required for the job. No one's saying that he's a revolutionary leader. To clean up the country and open new roads, it's enough to have ambition and courage. If he's wrong, we'll be the beneficiaries. That's the opportunity of '58 that's waiting for you."

Salvador adjusted his glasses and responded somewhat impatiently.

"Ibáñez is coming on like an old demagogue, full of talk about Prestes and hiding behind the image of Perón. To be Prestes, Ibáñez would have to be born again and wait for the Almighty to grant him the vision of a real social fighter. In order to be Perón . . . well, Ibáñez wants to start a populist campaign at the age of 74. We Chileans have a lousy memory, but he simply has no memory whatsoever. He'll snare himself in his own promises. He'll not deliver on anything. His government will be chaos and it won't take him long to surrender to the right wing. With age he's lost his dictator's claws. At this moment Ibáñez is a worse danger than González Videla, who turned the country into a clown show. Ibáñez can destroy it with a cannon shot."

"The Party is going to split again."

"You know why it's already divided. The ones who collaborated with González Videla were responsible. Now we have the chance to save it. Let's reject the populism without ideology that Ibáñez represents, and join the People's Front, the path of socialist revolution. Let's give battle in the polls, which will at least bring us together on common turf. José Tohá is with me, and Aniceto Rodríguez, and Astolfo Tapia, and . . ."

Eugenio González began pacing back and forth, wrapped in

the smoke of his cigarette. Once again he became the wise philosophy professor, the inspired storyteller of the Santiago barrios. He pulled away from the topic of Ibáñez and began making references to the steps Salvador was taking personally, maybe a bit too quickly, too unsteadily.

"Your candidacy will be a salute to the flag," he said. "The party flag. You'll come in on the Recabarren-Lafertte express through the northern pampas, you'll join the marches night and day, the proclamations delivered in ghost towns and in the plazas by torchlight, surrounded by a leaden circle of soldiers and carabineros, in the bewildering solitude of the voteless candidate, enjoying the sunrise through the bars of the local jailhouse. How many votes will you get, Salvador? Enough to mourn for? This campaign of yours has no name and no date. You're going to lose knowing that you could never have won."

"Win, lose? What are we talking about, Eugenio? An election is no price to pay for a revolution as it's taking off. I know you understand that. You've told me so yourself. I start on a path and the path widens. We grow with it. If the only result is the unity of the workers and some of the middle groups with a program of social liberation and economic justice, I'll settle for that. In the last analysis we will know that we're saving our party and our allies from raising a white flag or getting hit below the belt."

August is the wintry month when old Chileans give up the ghost. One August, in 1950 to be exact, don Arturo Alessandri Palma died. All of a sudden General Ibáñez felt very lonely, lonelier than he had ever felt in his life. How could he go on and on as an eternal candidate without the Lion, the old Lion of 1920, and his repertoire of exiles, triumphant returns, campaigns, and rhetoric? How could he keep going without this grand illusionist of Chilean history? Who would he perform his coups upon now?

"Chile is dying," it is said that he remarked to his father-in-law. "Without don Arturo this country will be lost, just another nation without an epic tradition. We'll regress to colonial times.

How I loved kicking him out of government and sending him into exile! But, you know something? I was never able to send him to Easter Island!"

Something was ending; the general was right. But it wasn't Chile. The final withdrawal of the big patrician families and the disappearance of their great mansions was part of a process in motion; the doors of La Moneda were banging open and shut in the breezes of chance. Don Arturo was making his final exit, and taking with him his canes, bowler hats, opera divas, thugs, and beloved rabble.

"What in God's name awaits us now?"

"The Era of the Technocrats and, if you're not careful, the Era of the Communist Rascals," the father-in-law responded evenly. "You have the cue for one group to disappear and the other to stay on stage."

Don Arturo had gotten out of his car one day, sending his chauffeur off with these words: "You go on, then. It does me good to walk. I'll come back on foot. Around teatime." And he went down a lonely street heading right for a place he knew. Once there, the old courtier and swordsman unsheathed his romantic weapon, attacked, and died of heart failure in full virile splendor. At eighty-some years of age.

General Ibáñez stirred his favorite royal jelly with a little spoon, and took the news as best he could. From then on he would have to do battle alone, and he would be no less a man than don Arturo. If necessary, he too would die with his boots on, weapon in hand.

The campaign was transparent from the start. Ibáñez was a "liberator" without much of a program, but with plenty of stilted, grandiose promises.

"I will repeal the Damned Law," he said. "The Communist party will be legalized again, and I'll bolster up the finances of the country and divvy up the land."

Salvador embarked on the campaign that Eugenio González had foreseen. Surrounded by young communists and socialists, he took to the stump in the capital, the barrios, the suburbs, and the factories, favoring the outskirts of cities and neighboring towns, wherever he sensed the concentration of the masses. He went to Barrancas, Conchalí, Til-Til, Batuco. Later he took a plane and carried his campaign north, to La Serena, and from there to Copiapó, Antofagasta, Iquique, Arica. He came back through Chuquicamata, Calama, Pisagua. Allende covered Chile, uttering the revolutionary slogans of the old guard—nationalization of the mines, agrarian reform, control of inflation. His campaign, supported by the labor unions, had the fighting spirit of the shantytown communist cells particularly odious to González Videla in his last days of government.

Ibáñez, who had announced his candidacy a year in advance, attacked the People's Front like the shrewd demagogue that he was.

He accused Allende of causing the split in the Left, and of favoring Arturo Matte, the conservative candidate. He was able to create a poisonous rivalry between the popular socialists and the militants of the Socialist party. Supported by the Democrats, the Popular Socialists, and the Agrarian Workers, as well as by the large mass of government employees from his previous regimes, and favored by a split in the Right, Ibáñez triumphed decisively.

Allende appeared neither surprised nor dejected. The day of the election he had lunch at home in mid-afternoon and called his inner circle of friends and supporters, telling them simply, "It's time to get ready for '58." A good ear could have detected a slight anxiety in his voice, not because he had lost the election, but rather because he sensed a hidden defeat in his young supporters, those in the fray for the first time. Perhaps they had thought that even in politics miracles can happen, and that with good luck a modest revolution such as theirs could actually take place during a presidential election.

"What do we do now?" Puccio, his private secretary, asked him.

Allende looked at him somewhat doubtfully. He was about to say, "Let's throw in the towel and go home," but instead he replied, "Get everyone together, Osvaldo. We're going to the Casa del Pueblo. We're going to see if there's a moral to this story."

And young students, union leaders, socialist and communist cell groups all went to the big, shabby house on Serrano Street, near the Alameda, in order to regain their spirit. It was getting dark, and the radios announced the election results without commentary: Ibáñez, 466,000 votes; the conservative Arturo Matte, 265,000; the radical Pedro Enrique Alfonso, 190,000; and Allende, 52,000.

The house had a huge front door with thick, grooved planks and a bolt lock. The front hallway, with its old floorboards, led down a long, poorly lit corridor to an interior patio. Under the weak, yellowish light, Allende appeared uncomfortable. He greeted José Tohá with an embrace. The tall and thin Tohá looked like an apostle, as though at one time he must have sported a tunic and a white, flowing beard. He looked down on you with big, kind eyes. But those eyes reflected not inner peace but some undefined alarm. He spoke in a slow, deep voice. At his side Allende regained his composure. Responding to the call of his comrades, he leaped onto a table and started speaking.

There was nothing to celebrate, nothing to explain. Quietly, without gestures, he began to sum up the campaign. Little by little his words took form, not the form of discourse, but rather of an activity expanding out into time, an activity whose meaning would come in its full extension, but not now, not yet, not in whatever promises or messages were being offered politically. Allende was a fighter, a leader in that big, dark house, amid the silence of his young comrades, at the threshold of a luminous September that was radiating the heat of battle down from the Alameda de las Delicias of the liberator Bernardo O'Higgins. "We haven't lost," Allende repeated. "We have taken one more step toward the unity of workers and intellectuals, on the straight path to power. Those who dismiss us today will march with us soon, and together we will create the first socialist nation in the Americas."

Puccio says that he saw tears in the eyes of the listeners.

Night had fallen and the rumor circulated that a mob was coming to the Casa del Pueblo to attack the group for not accepting Ibáñez's rule, and for having split the Left.

Allende saw his friends close the windows and doors and take up clubs and stones to defend themselves and their leader. Dissuade them? Nothing he could say would make sense. He already knew how it would turn out. And he was right.

The day would come when the differences between them and Allende's followers would appear with cruel clarity. But not now. Now there was nothing to do except wait in this dark house, wait for the fools to come shouting threats and hollow slogans, tossing a few rocks that would bounce off the metal roof. Best to wait for them to let off steam and then go eat and drink thinking they had won, when in fact both attackers and defenders had lost, and the defeat was already settling for all of them at the bottom of the great wine bottle emptied that night.

González Videla left his legacy, a painful economic crisis followed by strikes in the copper mines, on the docks, even in the banks. A deficit of two billion pesos. Jail terms for the leaders of the telephone and electric workers' union. Concentration camps for the opposition. New loans signed in Washington. Agreements with North American companies to fix the price of copper. The cost of living spiraled, and government spending exceeded 30 percent of the national budget. Military treaties with the U. S.

Months later, in March 1953, Allende once again takes the flag of the party into his hands. But now it isn't simply a gesture but a strong campaign and a great victory. He runs for senator from Tarapacá and Antofagasta. He is the only senator elected from the Socialist party.

There is a sudden crisis in the Allende household: Tencha has become seriously ill, and the diagnosis is painful for Salvador. Tencha has tuberculosis. Doctors prescribe complete rest. This is a serious blow to Tencha, who has been working closely with Salvador, traveling with him during his campaigns in addition to pursuing her own work as a librarian. The social demands of a senator require that they leave 191 Victoria Subercaseaux and move to a bigger house. They pick a street not far from the center of town, yet quite protected by the labyrinth of surrounding streets. They are isolated but inside the dynamic barrio of Providencia, an oasis consisting of a few sleepy blocks with unfenced gardens and leafy trees. The address is 392 Guardia Vieja, and it will become legendary. It is a two-story house. The hall leads to Salvador's study, then the living room, on one side of the dining room. French doors open onto a sunny terrace that is being invaded by a flower garden, where the long-tailed dog with the rambling gait reigns. On the second floor are the bedrooms. From the terrace one has the impression that the street continues behind— like a secret passageway—and continues on through neighboring gardens.

Tencha can no longer accompany Salvador on his political campaigns. She reads and receives visitors and friends. She talks with writers and artists, who begin to call on her as though it were a ritual. They discover her, striking friendships that would last a lifetime. Those who had defeated tuberculosis themselves were the most assiduous—young veterans of the San José de Maipo sanitarium, who no longer showed their scars to each other, nor discussed a recent pneumothorax, but instead spoke with a kind of educated solidarity, bringing Tencha into a circle, a circle that in the thirties had united more than one generation in the ambiguous atmosphere of Mann's *Magic Mountain*. Some remarkable people filed down this mountain: José Santos González Vera, a humorous storyteller of the old Santiago; Manuel Rojas, a delicate and gentle giant, carrying his book *The Thief's Son* under his arm, a poetic probing of the malaise of the twentieth century; and Dr. César Cecchi, a strange figure in the Chilean artistic world, a doctor in medicine and a musician, fascinating conversationalist, and master of the epistolary form, whose letters flew and still fly around the world, from hand to hand, from university to university, from academies to the European courts, from Santiago to Hollywood, to Rome, to Paris, Berlin, and Mexico. He was a virtuoso of an art not yet defined, in love with the hidden turmoils of his own sickness, arbiter of his own death. Cecchi drew close to Tencha and would never leave her side; he was loyal to the Allendes and simply didn't notice that they were making revolutionary politics, for he was a Renaissance courtier mistakenly dropped on today's calendar.

"I remember," Cecchi once said to me, "in those years, long before Tencha got the illness, the great novelists who contracted it—Manuel Rojas, Ciro Alegría—and the painters and poets, like José Venturelli and Gustavo Ossorio. Ours was a strange family tree, with pulmonary branches reaching out to each other, before Aureomycin came down on the wings of the Holy Ghost."

By the summer of 1954, Tencha had recovered sufficiently to accompany Salvador on a long trip through Europe that ended with a visit to the Soviet Union. They made the prescribed rounds of scientific and cultural academies, factories, and unions. They were received in the Supreme Soviet and visited Lenin's mausoleum and the Kremlin. But the true significance of the trip was not in the official tour but in the content of a document that Salvador wrote between visits and social functions, and which *Pravda* published that August.

The paper is a surprising analysis of the political and economic conditions of Chile, in which Allende, perhaps without intending it, establishes the foundations of what will be the program for a democratic route to socialism, and thus for his candidacies of 1958, 1964, and 1970. Allende reaches conclusions that defy the traditional slogans of the Chilean Left while at the same time proposing unexpected solutions to the social crisis that had been growing since the nineteenth century, and which by the fifties seemed ready to explode in a violent confrontation between Left and Right.

Curiously, Allende doesn't touch on the role that the armed

forces will continue to play and the responsibility that they will have to bear for their acts at the moment of truth. How strange that having the most implacable judge of his acts right at his side Allende did not see him! At attention, right hand in military salute, surrounded by a cloud of gunpowder, and Allende still does not see him.

In Moscow Salvador shuts himself in the hotel room and dashes off his brief on Chile while Tencha and her guides go to the Bolshoi Ballet. Defining the People's Front, he writes, "It is a permanent organization in which each party, while keeping its independence, enters into a serious commitment to the Chilean people. The program of the Front is broad enough so that progressive farm laborers, women and young people, employees and artisans, teachers and intellectuals, businessmen and traders who have the national interest at heart can group themselves around the core formed by the working class. The Front is struggling to make structural changes in the economy that will allow the tapping of our natural resources and an extensive industrialization of the country. And it promotes an agrarian reform that will bring about dramatic changes in the system of land tenure and in the living conditions of those who work the land."

Allende goes beyond the problem of socialist-communist discrepancies to suggest an amplification of the old Popular Front through agreements with the political center and even the traditional Right. His is a project of national coalition against all attempts to establish a dictatorship, and against the growing offensive of imperialism.

At first glance the Allende strategy would seem to be making reference only to the electoral process: the victory of Rafael Luis Gumucio, for example, who was elected representative by a coalition of communists, socialists, and Christian Democrats.

What was happening in Chile? What force would be capable of uniting all the political factions? Could it be Ibáñez, in the shadows of old age, his past as military dictator forgotten?

Ibáñez shakes his head and says no, forget it, leave me alone. The economic crisis is worsening. The cost of living goes up 70 percent. Two general strikes have been called in one year. One thousand workers go off to jail. General Ibáñez, depressed, is feeling the weight of his years. He appears on the balcony of La Moneda and observes the crowd of students who would relive the events of 1931. Frowning, he wipes his forehead with a large handkerchief and says in a quiet voice, "Hit them." No one listens. His ministers tell him that the Right and Left have joined forces to remove him from power. He looks at them and attempts a smile.

"No," he says, "it's not against me. They are just getting together because they are afraid. The Lion will come to set them straight."

"Excellency," his minister of the interior observes, "don Arturo is dead."

"Don Arturo is dead?"

"He died a long time ago."

"How ungrateful! He never informed me. What year are we in? No, you don't have to tell me, it's almost 1958. Year of rest. Right and Left united? Don't make me laugh.

"Allende again? Who is Allende?"

Part Two

The Victory Train

At the age of fifty, Salvador, you'll be the youngest president in the history of Chile."

"Fifty-one," corrected Salvador, "and I'm not there yet."

He was standing near the fireplace, wearing a sport shirt, a leather jacket, and a dark gray pair of pants. He smiled contentedly. On the mantelpiece was a picture of Alessandri Palma, with a long dedication written in bold strokes. Paintings by famous Chilean artists hung on the walls, and Chinese ivory sculptures and Indian artifacts were scattered about the library.

One of his daughters comes in. Tati, with her amiable expression and smiling eyes, often asks unpredictable questions and calmly delivers well-thought-out opinions. She is about to start medical school.

From outside comes the sound of clinking glasses brimming with heady *pisco*.

In a couple of hours the guests will arrive for an intimate dinner. Allende is celebrating his birthday. But true to his habit, he has invited some people early and retired with them to the library for conversation.

"Fifty years," he repeated, "is not the midpoint on the road of life, as you know, but a bend, maybe the next-to-last, maybe the last. My grandfather used to say that between twenty and thirty years of age a man prepares himself to be something, anything. Between thirty and forty, he will be that thing, if he can manage. Between forty and fifty, already established, he does what he came to do. Then the demons of the fifties and sixties mix everything up. You are in the most inspired time of life, the most intense and aimless, and the only time that has a really concrete present, because the future has vanished."

Later, in the living room, the conversation flowed into current events. Allende's friends felt that conditions were ripe for a victory in the '58 elections. Allende savored their enthusiasm.

The house on Guardia Vieja Street had become a meeting place for union leaders, professionals, writers, and artists. There was something in the name Guardia Vieja—actually the name of a tango—that seemed to change the atmosphere of the neighborhood. The big trees seemed older, the creepers more luxuriant, the dusk lengthier, the night balmier.

The Allendes received their guests with the affectionate cordiality customary to old Chilean families. Dinner parties were rich in anecdotes and conversation, news and memories.

Tencha presided on the little terrace. She carried the conversation skillfully; her deliberate, smiling manner could be disturbing at first, but soon won you over. Even in her solemn moments, a jovial, youthful spirit shone through.

Vigorous and flashy, Allende had always raised some eyebrows during his campaigns. Just recently, as he was walking out of the Viña del Mar Casino, where he had been chatting with the employees, a group of upper-class youths harassed him. He turned to face them. One of the youths mockingly accused him of begging from the Mafia. Allende grabbed him by the lapels, shook him violently against a wall, and threw him on top of a large flowerpot. The others didn't move an inch. Why did he do it? Arrogance, self-respect, too big a sense of his own importance?

"Look, my friend, these fops love to ride roughshod over authority. They have always considered it inferior, ergo fair game. When a rich punk fails to respect the people's candidate, you have to grab him by the short hairs."

He said it laughing. That was his style.

"You remember on the campaign tour, down at the docks, when we went to the slaughterhouse? In spite of the fact that a thousand workers were waiting there for our delegation, a police officer intercepted us at the door of the local union headquarters.

I immediately challenged him and asked if he knew me. 'Yes, Senator Allende,' he said. And then I shouted at him, 'Then how dare you block my way as I carry out my duties as candidate? You are disturbing the electoral process.' At that moment a tough-guy colonel appeared on the scene, and shouted at me, 'And what's the matter with you? What's this mess all about?' As if it were a fight between drunks. I kept cool and asked him how he dared speak to me in that tone of voice. 'First,' I said, 'come to attention and salute me, as it befits you to honor a senator and the next president of the republic. And then move on and open the way for me.' That character looked at me wide-eyed as a cow, backed away, and disappeared with all his troops."

What Allende didn't tell was that the slaughterhouse workers had received him while in the middle of their work, with a steer ready for sacrifice.

Allende waited at a discreet distance. The foreman approached the steer with an enormous knife and plunged it into his neck without batting an eye. An assistant came forward with a jar and collected the steaming, bubbling blood. He proceeded to add onions, garlic, and salt. After stirring it with a stick, he offered it to Allende. An incredulous smile moved through the crowd. Allende took the jar to his lips and drank without flinching. Then he wiped his mouth with the back of his hand to clean off the foam clinging to his mustache. That's how *ñachi* is imbibed. The leader could handle it.

Behind his observant, intelligent look, there was plenty of heart; but there was also a spark that could become a bright, lethal flame.

Allende was capable of being tough and cutting. Those who worked with him knew his anger and feared it. He never bore a grudge, however, and he was quick to beg pardon and return to his normal benevolent attitude.

In the living room the fire was crackling. It was a time of elation, and the place shone, not with luxuries or phony splendor, but rather with the radiant warmth of the Chilean middle class, well dressed and cordial, of ready wit. One could argue, make allegations in a loud voice and punctuate them with a bang on the table, but all was well received and there were no hard feelings.

Salvador felt very much at home with these people. The women, elegant and beautiful, enjoyed laughing with him the way he liked, without false modesty or deferential treatment. He talked with Moy Tohá and Isabel Letelier, with Mireya Latorre and Paula Silva. On the other side of the living room, sitting on a sofa surrounded by admiring youths, was a man who looked like a retired fakir, dark and prophetic—Salomón Corbalán. Standing with glass in hand was Carlos Briones, small and dapper, his prowlike profile jutting toward Hernán Santa Cruz, whose sentences flowed slowly and ceremonially. Augusto Olivares, very young but already a prestigious newsman, entertained them all. He was big and affectionate, like a pampered child. Manuel Rojas listened with a bored expression on his face, seemingly worried about his thin, pale friend, González Vera, who would suddenly explode in high-pitched laughter as though he were from outer space.

That night they covered all the topics. The butt of the jokes was the roller coaster government that repentant Ibáñez followers were rapidly deserting, still carrying the last emblem of power— a now-scraggly old broom. New ideas were proposed for the campaign of '58. Allende listened with attention. Corbalán explained how September's presidential convention would be a clear demonstration of unity and an effort that would surpass the convention of '38. Allende wanted an assembly, not only of political parties, but also of writers' and artists' associations, even of sporting clubs. "We're not going to champion a candidate," he said. "We're going to define a program to propose to the country."

They spoke about raising funds. Thirty, forty million pesos? Too little. We're up against a bunch of financial sharks. Our rival plays multinational poker.

Little by little, proposals for an innovative campaign emerged. The idea was to generate popular power, to pull in contributions not only from the workers but from the middle class—professionals, merchants, industrialists—even from the inner circles of capitalism that had become disillusioned with Ibáñez. Corbalán listed the names of those who should preside over important committees. Pablo Neruda for the propaganda committee, he said. A hoarse voice shot up. "We'll have a fund-raiser in the Bim Bam Bum." "What's that?" Allende asked. "Yes, sir. Just where I said, with the best strippers and my favorite comedians." The speaker was Gabriel Araya, president of the actors' union. "A benefit in the Bim Bam Bum. I'll set it up, and it'll make history!" Allende gave him a concerned look.

And the fact is that one night in August, after a performance, the dancers, singers, and musicians of the Bim Bam Bum got together to plan the benefit. They agreed that it should be held in the Caupolicán Arena and that all stage performers in Santiago should be called on to participate. "They'll never fill the theater," was Puccio's dry opinion. But they pulled it off, and the fund-raiser lasted until 3:00 A.M., with dozens of performers yet to go on stage.

From this group of burlesque artists came the motto "A day's salary for the campaign." The main idea was to attract workers and employees. But the organizers were surprised to find that even retirees responded. And with the hope of surpassing the queens of the Bim Bam Bum, a confederacy from the local brothels offered its support, calling itself the Belles de Nuit Command.

This, according to Puccio, was the way it happened.

One day, as Allende was working in his office in the Senate, a young woman appeared, requesting an interview. Allende asked her to wait while he finished a dictation to Puccio. Then he asked her in. Puccio rose to leave them alone, but Allende stopped him. He looked at the young woman and waited for her to speak. Embarrassed, she stuttered, unable to express herself. She took a pack of cigarettes from her purse. Puccio extended a lighter. The woman's hands trembled. Salvador noticed that despite her nervous state she displayed a certain hard stubbornness, bordering on disdain, especially around the mouth.

He tried to put her at ease with trivial questions. Suddenly she sat back in her chair, expelled a mouthful of smoke, and said, "Doctor, I've come to give you a message from my partners."

Allende thought that she represented a group of office workers, maybe a political cell in the neighborhood.

"Yes," he said. "Tell me then, what is your message?"

"Well," she said, her stammer resuming, "I don't know how to tell you, but we'd like to contribute to your candidacy with one day of our earnings."

"Ah," said Allende, relieved. "You are very generous and I . . ."

"Excuse me," she interrupted. "It's not—how can I put it?—so simple as that."

"Ah, no?"

"No. It's a little complicated."

Salvador observed her keenly. Her dyed hair hung loosely over a narrow forehead. Now he noticed that her toilette looked professional. Another dancer? The benefit had been a success, but to play the same number again, so soon, no way. Puccio remained quiet, a slight smile on his face. The woman looked at Allende and said in a low voice, "We work in a house, doctor."

Allende looked at her astonishedly.

"A house?"

"Yes, a house."

He was about to ask, "What kind of house?" but he looked at Puccio and finally understood the smile.

"We want to present to you in person, and in our house, the checks we have gotten together for your campaign. All of us will be there. Women from other houses will be there too. And street walkers . . ."

Allende adjusted his glasses. He looked at her very seriously.

"You understand," he said, "how much I appreciate this . . . courageous gesture of solidarity . . . but you also understand that . . ."

How to tell her? The young woman leaned over his desk, hanging on to his words.

". . . my party, the socialist ideology . . . you understand . . . no, it just can't happen."

She raised her eyebrows, and her expression lost its toughness.

"Although I understand and the compañeros will understand. I ask you to send these words to your colleagues. . . . I am moved and accept your contribution to our cause. I can't, of course, attend your gathering to accept it in person."

Then Puccio intervened.

"Compañera, the doctor cannot put himself in the position of having reporters follow him and take photographs. It would be a scandal."

The word "scandal" sounded too strong, so Puccio tried to back away.

"I mean, his enemies would stop at nothing to discredit him. No, I don't mean that you girls would discredit him. But for the doctor himself to go would be impossible . . ."

There was an uncomfortable silence. Allende toyed with a paperweight. The telephone rang. Puccio answered.

"It's compañero Tohá," he said.

Salvador thought for a minute and smiled. He took the phone.

"José, I'll call you in five minutes. Yes. Without fail."

"Compañera," he said, "I accept your support and that of your compañeras wholeheartedly. I won't be able to go in person, but two compañeros in whom I place total confidence will go instead, and it will be as if I were there myself."

And that is how the strange meeting in a whorehouse on San Martín Street was arranged.

The doors opened, and a serious-looking young woman greeted the two representatives, signaling them to come in. They entered stiffly and went into the living room, where the chairs were arranged in theater-like rows. The piano had been placed in a corner, and a table with a pitcher of water and a glass sat in the center. The room was cold, and a faint smell of mothballs came from the curtains. There were more than one hundred women there. But no frills. Most had put their hair up in handkerchiefs and were wearing overcoats. The madame invited the representatives to sit with her behind the table. She began to speak, her delivery plain and measured.

"We are professionals," she said. "And who's to say that we're not workers just like so many other women who earn their bread as maids, or in stores, offices, and factories? In our work there's no retirement and we die with our boots on. That's why today we're investing in the future—the one that belongs to us, the one we dream about. For those who despise us, we are just a cheap source of labor. But we won't be forever. Someday we will be free."

One by one the women got up and spoke of the closed world of their sufferings and persecutions; they spoke of infamous public health tests, of injections and medics, pimps and madams, of beautiful and murderous thugs, of their sons and daughters in the summer houses of the wealthy bosses. They complained, not whiningly, but with resistance and anger. Then they read the names of those who had brought checks and cash, applauding with pride. Even so, the event never lost the haunting quality of a brothel stage, with its empty punch bowls and lonely cots, quilts, and cretonnes, the lingering remains of a sad pantomime.

Finally, the refined and poised José Tohá, dressed in a dark suit with a white shirt and a blue tie, broke the silence. He looked at the women and said, "Compañeras, in the name of Salvador Allende and the people's party, we thank you."

Then Tohá and Puccio gathered the combined victory offerings, said goodbye, and went out into the rainy, freezing alley. They hailed a cab. One of them dabbed at the corner of his eyes as the other coughed self-consciously.

And one morning, in August 1958, the Victory Train left Central Station in Santiago.

In his second presidential campaign, Allende played all his political cards. He departed with his best team of counselors, activists, youth brigade members, and union leaders—men and women determined to wage a battle at the polls such as Chile had never witnessed before.

The idea of a train grew out of a birthday party on Guardia

Vieja Street. Someone proposed it as a reincarnation of the springtime carnivals in which costumed youths would take to the streets in flower-filled wagons and wake up the frozen Santiaguinos, coaxing them out into the sun and the splendor of the snowy cordillera. But whoever proposed the idea didn't take into account Salomón Corbalán. In his mind the allegorical wagon of the students metamorphosed into a locomotive, the flowers into flags, the costumes into the caps and overalls of railroad workers.

The day after the Allendes' party, Corbalán went to the state railroad offices, where the project took shape in a confidential parley with the head of the railway workers' union. The plan was to rent a train, equip it, and cover the central and southern zones of Chile in ten days, making 136 whistle-stops along the way. The union leader designed the itinerary in an impeccable drawing showing all the stops and junctions, branch lines, little towns and villages where Allende would give his speeches. A minimum budget was set; railroad workers would pitch in in the kitchen and the dining car. The conductors who volunteered would lead the journey like a revolutionary march.

The railroad people were opposed to either an electrically run train or a diesel. The Victory Train is the people's train, they said, run with coal, a lot of smoke, a lot of stops, and bells and whistles. They got an old locomotive and painted it shiny black, polished its wheels and bronze pistons, and gave it some bright red touches on the cowcatcher and the stack. The Chilean national emblem stretched across the front. One side read "Victory Train," and the other "A todo vapor con Salvador," "Full steam ahead with Salvador."

Puccio was named to head the expedition. They were to steam out of the station at 9 A.M.

Allende was happy. He got to the station early, surrounded by secretaries, speakers, and assistants. With him was Luis Corvalán, the secretary general of the Communist party, who was making his first public appearance since the party's legalization.

With a plume of smoke, the train moved out slowly from under the high glass and iron dome of Central Station, its wheels glittering. The bells clanged spiritedly as it found its way through the labyrinth of rails and switches, heading for San Bernardo. But the engineer quickly realized how difficult it would be to leave the station, much less to follow the chosen route. Hundreds of people accompanied the train as it departed, and hundreds more ran with it along the neighboring streets, invading the tracks and trotting next to the train as they brandished their workers' tools and banners in support.

Allende ordered the engineer to stop, and he got on the platform of the caboose to speak to his followers. Puccio convinced him not to try it, saying, "We'll never get out of here."

The train began its slow progress once again, and Allende went from window to window waving to the crowds.

At the San Bernardo depot, Allende and Corvalán spoke. Later, at Rancagua, Allende left the train and spoke in the plaza, where he was cheered by thousands of workers from the copper mines of El Teniente. The train passed through vineyards and pasturelands, through the pristine solitudes of Requinoa, Rosario, and Rengo—quiet little towns with closed doors. Along the tree-lined avenues, next to the rails, families of farmers raised their arms in greeting.

Allende decided to stop in Pelequén, a little town of five hundred inhabitants. A young campesino in a Castilian poncho stepped out to greet him in front of the assembled people. With his hat in hand, he welcomed Allende. He spoke haltingly, with emotion, until he came to what seemed a suitable, eloquent ending. "We will not rest," he said, "until compañero Allende is in the thalamus of the presidents." Allende's entourage had to work to hold in their laughter, but the candidate moved forward and embraced the man, thanking him for his efforts. He took the fellow aside and explained the malapropism to him. Then he spoke to the crowd and headed back to the train.

In Curicó, as Allende was giving a speech, a woman approached him from the wings of the stage area. When Allende finished his discourse, she tried to kiss his hands. Allende reacted brusquely.

"Compañeros," he said, addressing everyone, "I am no Messiah, nor do I wish to be one. I am a militant of the revolution. We'll never reach the presidency with people who believe in miracles. We have to strive for political clarity. We have to arrive at La Moneda supported by a fully conscious people. Tough years are ahead, and establishing socialism is no easy job. To change this country takes more than a few hours. The people will have to do it, not me alone."

The train traveled all the way to the southern end of the country, through thick forests and desolate wastelands, through driving, interminable rainstorms, along grand rivers, by a turbulent ocean. The dawn rose among slowly moving smoke signals from log cabins. Concepción responded strongly to Allende's expedition. The people waited for him in the station and went with him to the university, to the steel plants, to the coal mines. At dusk, the train stopped at Lota. Allende walked down to the mine entrances. With a miner's helmet on and a lantern in his hand, he spoke before the hidden doors of that black hell, the subterranean abyss where miners worked their whole lives, and sometimes to their deaths, following the fatidic hoofbeats of the blind cart horse.

On reaching Valdivia, Allende and his followers received the news that Jorge Alessandri, their conservative rival, had been the victim of a terrorist attack. A lunatic had thrown acid on him in the Osorno train station, lightly injuring him. Allende condemned the attack, refusing to change his itinerary. When they arrived in Osorno, Salvador and his delegation were surprised to see that the station was empty. A police officer approached Allende and told him that he had barred the crowds from the station and that the senator could count on his men for protection. Allende answered that if he had to defend himself from the people, he didn't deserve to be president.

Then, he and his delegation left the train and walked to a gathering of supporters waiting in the street. Allende stopped at the doors of city hall to watch them march. He commented that the crowds along the sidewalks appeared indifferent, even hostile.

The train completed its tour at Puerto Montt, after more than a thousand kilometers of arduous campaigning. In less than a month, Allende had spoken on 148 occasions. But the train was overdue and it was time to hurry back. Puccio and the other leaders changed the routing and dropped many of the scheduled stops. As they went through towns that had been eliminated from the itinerary, groups of workers lay down on the rails. The train would stop, and Allende would disembark to speak to them.

Finally, one night in late August, the Victory Train returned to Santiago. The parties of the Popular Front had mobilized their militants to welcome it home. More than 100,000 people surrounded Central Station. When the grunting, puffing train pulled into the station, enveloped in smoke and steam, its banners fluttering in the wind, the crowds flocked around it. All semblance of order disappeared, and Allende found himself borne aloft by the crowd all the way to the Alameda. From there, at the head of a gigantic crowd, he walked twenty-five blocks to Plaza Bulnes, where he gave a vibrant speech.

That night, escorted by a personal guard of friends, Allende stopped to eat in a restaurant before returning home to Guardia Vieja Street.

His friend Tohá studied him and in a low voice said, "Salvador, this is an apotheosis. It looks like you're really going to win, right?"

Allende remained silent. He remembered the campesino in Pelequén, the compañera in Curicó, the miners of Lota. He was going to say something, but refrained. He remembered that in one gathering he had asked the participants how many were registered to vote September 4. No more than 30 percent had raised their hands.

"Who knows?" he said with a smile to Tohá. "It seems that way."

It seemed that way. But that's not how it turned out. Allende's enemies had other ideas. They were saying that the coalition of the middle class and the workers had dissolved, that the Partido Radical was running on its own track, and that the Christian Democrats had mobilized a grass-roots movement that was restless and ready to fight, stirred to action by the bad times under Ibáñez.

But they didn't mention another factor, the decisive one. From the heart of Chile's old Manchester-style liberalism, which was supported by an impressive technocracy and powered by willing capital, came a strong man of few words, rigid principles, and imposing presence—Jorge Alessandri Rodríguez. This tall, austere man, always dressed in somber clothing, dragged the long shadow of his father behind him.

The Right put its confidence in don Jorge, the big boss at the paper company, the reliable, fearless manager who would set the financial situation of the country straight without recourse to magic or even computers. The renewed confidence of the international banks would be enough.

And which way did the winds blow from the U. S.? Would you take it for granted? Ah? . . .

In 1961 a Renaissance man, young, bold, and brilliant, would begin to govern that country. He would surround himself with intellectuals, brighten the White House with the fires of art and history, and move his scouts through the European courts and the barracks of the Third World. They wouldn't carry clubs as in the past, instead conduct themselves with muted elegance, sizing up their adversaries with a new yardstick with no dollar signs on it. John F. Kennedy believed that in order to calm things in the Latin American backyard, it was enough to launch some ringing reforms and create an atmosphere of respectful collaboration within the dream of an America without poverty or Marxism. The fate of those countries, he believed, was in the hands of Christian Democracy. The Alliance for Progress was born.

Allende smiled from his side of the court. He knew that the

duel between Alessandri and the Christian Democrat, Frei, sig-nified a major split in the Chilean Right. Kennedy never quite understood these subtleties of Latin American politics. For him the solution was simple: flex some international credit. Take a bit of the church from here, a touch of the middle class from there, add a few technocrats and some generals, and the pie was ready for baking.

When the Victory Train arrived in Santiago, Allende thought that the campaign was already won. Maybe not totally. "Just a little push," he said, "and we'll be there."

I remember him in his house, drawing out the after-dinner conversation at the table, directing questions that he felt would bring the answers that spelled victory. Dr. Benjamín Viel came from Magallanes bringing figures with him; he laid them out for Salvador without emphasis or conclusions. Salvador had already listened to debriefings from the north. Santiago and Valparaíso were no mystery to him. With data in hand, he thought for a long while. I sensed that the numbers had not convinced him that he was going to win. The statistics could add up to a mountain, but the end result could equal castles in Spain. Allende was not sure.

Painters gave us works of art, poets gave us poetry, magicians organized raffles and huge parties, queens prepared succulent banquets, vintners manufactured sweet, strong wines; and there were magnates, discreet philanthropists, who opened their wal-lets. In the homes of the iconoclastic and wealthy liberal bourgeoi-sie, in their luxurious apartments with wide balconies and views of the cordillera, in gardens bordering the Japanese and British parks, victory fêtes were in full swing. There was a current of af-fection for Allende. These people with good names, well traveled and progressive in their views, were rebelling against Alessandri the manager. They were defending an unwritten right to tear down the protective fence around the bureaucrats and big land-owners of the Club de la Unión. They would vote Left. They wanted to win.

"If you were to ask me," an architect says from his elegant

tower in Forestal Park, "the reason is very simple. It's about time to shake the yacht. Let the wheeler-dealers fall in the water and meet their equals, the piranhas, face-to-face. They'll get along just fine. Ah, you'll say, what about the Reign of Terror and the reprisals à la Stalin to follow? That scare tactic doesn't trick anyone. The Chicho River doesn't turn red over night. How could it? These brainless mummies would like to identify this new attitude with some brand of extremism and dismiss it as frivolous."

His wife's bracelets clink together in the air as she says, forming a sweet oh! with her delicate lips, "El Chicho, red? What a joke. True, the 'comrades' support him, and they must have their reasons. But in this country there aren't any tropical-style carnivals. Chileans are not fond of making noise. People dress in dark clothes and are horrified at the notion of making fools of themselves. Salvador has a head on his shoulders. He's not about to go overboard. He needs help. I don't like don Jorge. What sort of a figure does he think he is cutting here? Do you know what don Arturo used to say about that son of his? That he was God's understudy. How's that for a full-length portrait?"

In the victory parties the guests drank a cocktail called a Chicho sour, made with vodka donated by the millionaire who produced it. After the toasts and before the fund raising, Humberto Martones spoke. He was a specialist in playing upon those hidden heartstrings of partisan generosity. With a Merlinesque flourish he produced a desk and a chair, and the checkbooks and pens to go with them.

Roberto Parada raised his voice and recited my poem "Long Live Chile, for Shitsake!" Violeta Parra sang "The Lion's Cueca," and then the parade of financial angels started in motion up to the desk.

The election on September 4 was close. In the early hours of the afternoon, the radio began to broadcast partial results that looked good for Allende. At the voting polls you could sense a growing euphoria among the FRAP supporters. Allende voted and then shut himself off in the general campaign headquarters to receive bulletins from the Ministry of the Interior.

While his followers were writing down the figures on blackboards and work sheets, in the hubbub of telephone calls and the shouting of the crowds who had started to take to the streets Allende thought for the first time that he really could win, that he would be president. And the resulting tension he felt worried him. No one else would notice this tension at the time, but in a few hours the uncertainty of the situation would produce a crisis.

Allende should have won, there's no doubt. But the Right saved itself thanks to a last-minute trick. It invented and financed a stalking-horse candidate in a cheap circus act. The Left had not reckoned with such a grotesque possibility. This "popular" candidate, whose function it was to take votes away from Allende, was a defrocked priest known as the Curate of Catapilco. A biblical travesty, he paraded every day down the streets of Santiago riding an ass, with a coterie of ragged, undernourished followers who waved red flags and sang revolutionary hymns and slogans.

Allende's mother said that days before the election she went to confession in her church in Valparaíso. The priest heard her and during a pause, asked her for whom she would vote.

"For Salvador Allende," responded the señora.

"For that bad apple?" exclaimed the priest. "How could you? That man is a communist. He's going to burn convents and send our children to Russia. Do you know what you're saying?"

"Nothing of the sort is going to happen. Salvador Allende is a good man and a good son. He couldn't do such things."

"Ah, no? How do you know?"

"He's my son."

Allende visited Cardinal José María Caro and told him what had happened. The Cardinal informed him that the church would not intervene in the elections, but that if FRAP won, he wanted certain guarantees. Allende assured him that under his presidency no one would ever suffer persecution. They parted amicably.

And the Curate of Catapilco paraded on with his mob, riding the ass and accumulating votes.

At nightfall the minister of the interior announced victory for Jorge Alessandri, with 390,000 votes against Allende's 356,000, Frei's 192,000, and the Curate's 41,000.

The Curate had performed his miracle: he took the 41,000 votes that Allende needed to win the election.

After the official announcement of Alessandri's victory, the old house that served as the headquarters for FRAP became quiet as a tomb. No telephones rang, no typewriter keys clicked. Behind closed doors the debriefing was to commence, but no one wanted to be the one to break the silence. Finally, someone exclaimed, in a sigh, "They robbed us!"

The phrase resounded like a parting shot, not a lament. It was a call to action that puzzled Allende.

A representative of the Workers' party said, "They robbed us of the election. We should simply not accept the verdict of the Ministry of the Interior. Let's fight them in the streets."

"Yes, compañeros, it's time to get our people together and hit the streets," a socialist leader repeated. "Everyone in FRAP should follow the example of my party. The militants have taken to the streets. Let's take our posts."

Immediate and direct confrontation! Taking to the streets! Allende listened in silence.

From outside the echoes of the slogans shouted by the socialists could be heard. There were those who reasoned and those who shouted, but the verdict was the same: the Right had stolen crucial votes.

All of a sudden a tremendous subterranean rumbling shook the old house. Allende, who had a great fear of earthquakes, reacted immediately. To run out of that monument of adobe and large wooden beams, with its tile roof and cornices, was to invite disaster. He leapt to his feet and shouted to everyone to remain calm. After the initial shock, the radios and telephones regained their voices. The epicenter had been scarcely 50 kilometers from the capital.

"Can't you imagine what's happening now, compañeros?

They're stealing the ballot boxes and substituting votes. That's how they want to beat us."

The tone of the meeting became tough. The majority supported the idea of direct confrontation. Messages began flooding in from revolutionary groups congregated in Plaza Bulnes.

Allende directed FRAP members to head for the plaza and said that he was ready to address the people. Permission for a meeting was requested from the Ministry of the Interior and granted. Allende, bringing with him FRAP's top leaders, went on foot to the Alameda.

He seemed to be provoking a confrontation. The radios announced that the candidate of the Left was advancing toward the palace with a crowd.

It had been decided that Allende would speak from the apartment of Pedro Foncea, which faced the Ministry of Defense. The microphones and speakers were already installed. The crowds filled the streets up to a few blocks from the palace.

And from that tiny podium, Allende tossed out his surprise. He disappointed some, bolstered others, and disconcerted everyone.

Very few people knew that, in the late hours of the afternoon, Allende had received a delegation of miners from El Teniente. They brought the following message: "We've got 50 chests full of dynamite, enough for us to take over." It could have been the beginning of a national uprising.

"To send masses of workers, men and women, into the street to fight with stones and clubs against professionally trained troops is not only insane, but criminal as well," Allende said. "We cannot begin a civil war that would be the emblem of political and historical irresponsibility. We have never advocated the use of arms in the conquest of political power. We have elected to use the democratic process and we will stick to that decision. We have been despoiled of our legitimate victory, we all know that, but we're going to live with it and accept this indignity calmly. Our confidence comes from knowing that nothing will block our way.

In this struggle we represent the voice of justice and the will to triumph of the Chilean people."

And the crowds dispersed.

Congress took a vote, as the Constitution requires. With the support of conservatives and centrist parties, Jorge Alessandri was proclaimed president of Chile.

"Allende stops a mass movement," screamed the followers of the Trotskyite Fourth International.

"Allende shows again that he's a responsible leader," the Popular Front leaders concluded.

The Curate of Catapilco, smiling ostentatiously, gave his benediction to the new president, waited for the shot of the noontime cannon, and then proceeded to disappear into the dust and the fallen leaves of Santa Lucía Hill.

The Man with the Beard

The man with the bushy dark beard and the wavy hair was lying on his back on the cot. With his upper body naked and his arms outstretched, he looked as though he had been crucified. The slow-moving shadows of the leaves and clouds that filtered through the window created imaginary wounds on his chest and side. His eyes were half-closed, and his gaze was unfocused and opaque, as though he had been smiling piously before dying.

But he wasn't dead, and those weren't really wounds. Still, he scarcely breathed as he survived another asthma attack.

Allende looked at him without saying anything. He stood, waiting, in a corner of the room. The bearded man moved his head and looked at him.

"Sit down," he said. "I know you well. I tried to see you the last time I came through Chile. Impossible. I waited for hours, you know? Sit down, Allende, it's good that you came."

Salvador smiled and drew near, trying to help the man sit upright.

"No, don't bother, this will pass. I've got the miracle worker," he said, holding up an inhaler.

And then they spoke, Allende sitting on a brass bed and the bearded man on his cot. The window was open, but no breezes stirred.

"I was about to leave without meeting you. What a mistake that would have been! Did they tell you that I had arrived, Ernesto?"

"I heard something."

"That's the way it goes. The day I got to Havana, I walked along the avenue by the ocean to enjoy the bath of light and sea spray that comes with the air down there. All of a sudden a parade appeared that made my eyes pop out. It was about two hundred yanqui cops, marching in full uniform! I had to pinch myself to be sure I wasn't dreaming. What kind of revolution is this that begins with a display of walking refrigerators armed with clubs and pistols? Or had these cowboys knocked off their own government, too? Or had they started the counterinsurgency already? I bumped into Carlos Rafael Rodríguez and told him the story. He had a good laugh. No way, chico, he told me. It turns out that these cops were not able to cancel their trip. They come every year, march around, party it up, and go back to Miami. This year the revolution caught them in the middle of things. Carlos Rafael promised to put me in contact with Fidel, with Raúl, with you, Ernesto, and with Camilo."

"Don't call me Ernesto, call me Che."

"In Chile we'd say, 'Let's drink on that.'"

"Ah, yes, Chile and the wines!" Che exclaimed. "I remember Concón. On the plate a lobster, and next to it that golden wine which cools you off while lighting up your soul with the taste of sun and mountains."

"Someday we're going to celebrate the victory of a socialist revolution in Chile. It won't be like your revolution in Cuba, but believe me we'll be celebrating the same thing."

Che Guevara, breathing easier now, opened wide his sad eyes and observed Salvador. Che was sitting up in the cot, his arms hanging down. With his bare feet and white ankles, he looked like a man marooned in a shipwreck.

"How was Caracas?" he asked.

"A party, but closely watched by the CIA. I traveled with Frei."

"With Frei?"

"Betancourt had invited us both. Frei was cracking jokes as we boarded the plane in Santiago. He was saying that we'd unbalance the plane with the hundreds of thousands of votes that I beat him by. Then I told Puccio, my secretary, to take seventy thousand votes or so from my briefcase and stuff them in Frei's pocket, so the plane would right itself."

"Will Betancourt last?" asked Che.

"It depends on the yanquis. If he's a 'good boy,' they'll leave him alone. If not, the military will come back in."

They spoke in low voices, without urgency. The traffic moved slowly through the streets below. Che let his gaze float through the silhouettes of the jacaranda trees and out to the sky, with its disappearing clouds. Evenings in Havana belong to a time surpassing reality; the flush of colors seems to hide a memory of past years, of people constantly improvising their destiny.

"Our critics seem to ask us for what we can't give," Allende said. "Our revolution won't be through the use of arms, I'm sure. Are we an exception? Maybe. In Chile it's not crazy to think that socialism could be achieved through a presidential election. A socialist victory would be respected. A revolution like yours happens once in a long, long while. To try and repeat it now would be more than a miracle. The imperialists don't forget Sandino, even though Sandino didn't come to power. They stopped Arbenz in Guatemala. Now you people have come along. Watch out, my friend. Us? We'll take the electoral route. That's Chile's road. We have never had violence ingrained in us. We've used it solely to counter reactionary violence. Each of our presidential campaigns has been a step toward victory. The day will come."

Che rested with his back against the wall. He would ask something and then think about Allende's answer. He said he had heard two Allende speeches in the 1952 campaign.

"I liked one very much. The other struck me as very bad."

Allende resisted the temptation to ask what it was that Che had not liked. He said only that that campaign had been a show of strength.

"Chile is still a country capable of surprises. Deeply political, well-informed, and resolved, Chileans are cautious, methodical, and reserved."

"Reserved?" Che asked.

"Just an expression. To the rightists in power, that means 'conservative.' If you listen to them, Chileans are conservative by nature. That's the way they want us. Submissive. But what the reactionaries don't recognize is the tiger that every Chilean carries inside. And when provoked he springs—his fighting instinct knows no bounds. There's a big reserve of revolutionary potential in our countryside. Ranquil was an example."

Allende stopped talking. Maybe he guessed the question in Che's mind, because he added, "I can't conceive of a guerrilla war like yours in Chile."

Che looked at him with curiosity.

"I doubt that we'd have the support, the solidarity, that you had. Our countryside is a feudal patriarchy."

Then Che spoke about how conditions are not only inherited but also created, and about how solidarity sometimes flowers little by little but can also blossom suddenly overnight, surprising us with its strength.

"I know the parliamentary tradition of Chile and the strength of its union movement. I understand that the perfect political coordination of events could occur that would enable you to win an election. But it would be a tough road, filled with pits."

"We don't entertain illusions," Allende replied convincingly. Almost twice the age of Che and his bearded associates, he was imposing in his role as senator. Conscious of it, he used it to add weight and substance to his arguments.

Incapacitated as he was, Che was surrounded by the exaltation of triumphant guerrilla warfare and a mission accomplished. Would the bearded ones dismiss Allende as a political reformer? A social redeemer, liberal, and pacifist?

"I understand the Chilean situation," Che insisted, "and the effectiveness of alliances at the polls with the bourgeoisie to aid the working class's ascent to power. The Cuban revolution is with you, Allende."

"I hope so," Allende answered, smiling as he rose to say goodbye.

Che picked up a book, wrote in it with a firm hand, and gave it to Allende. It was his own book *Guerrilla Warfare*, and the dedication read, "To Salvador Allende, who is trying to obtain the same results by other means. Affectionately, Che."

They shook hands, and Allende went out into the street and got into a car that had been reserved for him. As he drove away from the Cabaña Barracks in the intense dusk of Havana, breathing the salt air mixed with the fragrance of leaves and lemongrass, Allende held the book in his hands and thought about the man with the beard—his naked torso, his wounds, his look that seemed to anticipate the open road.

Chapter Three

The March

The bay seems embraced by the white arm of the coastal avenue. Wagons come, pulled by small, hairy ponies. The descent to the beach is steep and muddy. The ponies slip, the wheels get stuck in the mud, the whips crack in the fresh morning air. The wagoners often have to put their shoulders to the load. Shouts from the sea mix with shouts from the coast and the noise of motors. The island business begins—the unloading of bags and packages, the mysterious exchange of shiny, dripping sea urchins, pulpy clams, iodine-smelling *piures*, thick abalone. The fishing boats are like floating huts that during the day navigate the waters between the islands of Chiloé and at night moor off the beach that fronts the port. The fishermen arrive and draw near the charcoal fire. With big sheets of canvas, they improvise a shantytown by the sea. Roofs and walls seem just another invention of the fog.

On the beach the merchandise is transferred quickly from hand to hand. With his knife the fisherman opens the brilliant black diadem that is the spiny sea urchin. He cleans it in rapid strokes, sprinkles lemon juice onto it from a dirty bottle, and hands over the little silky wet tongues to the thick eager tongue of the customer. It's one way to swallow the sea, to suck it and dissolve it in one's mouth, absorbing juices that quicken the pulse and make the fingers tremble.

Other beaches not so far away border the coal mines, the wet underground alleyways, somber tenements. There is something about these miners who survive in the deep caves of the ocean that reminds one of masked players—something in their gestures, pale faces, and dark, brilliant expressions. The miners go down as far as six hundred meters below sea level in the little rattraps called elevators. They walk for kilometers to get to the digs, where they spend the whole day scratching out coal with pickaxes. They struggle in their own way to better their conditions. But the government and its agents are far away and don't hear their complaints. So the miners declare a strike. This work stoppage has lasted for three months already. And since Allende is their senator, the miners appeal to him for help.

One day Allende arrives in Lota and organizes a march into Concepción. Wearing a leather jacket, a miner's helmet, and heavy boots, he walks in the front lines. "We're going to knock on the managers' doors," he says. The miners are not asking for much: that they be paid from the moment they descend into the mines until the moment they emerge on the earth's surface at dusk; that their medical services be improved, these miners whose life span averages 40 years of age.

They march 40 kilometers, with their wives and children. In Talcahuano dockworkers join them. They cross the Bío-Bío on the old bridge, with their headlamps lit. They gather in the main square of the city. From an improvised podium Allende addresses the crowd. Heavily armed soldiers wait along the side streets. It will be the customary rumble—the army against the workers. But this time something interrupts the ritual.

A strong quake hits Concepción. On the heels of the first shock follows another and yet another, each more violent than the preceding one. Houses and buildings crumble to the earth, and the settlements near the river are swept away by the current. The howl of sirens penetrates the smoke-filled air. From the darkness of the river comes the sound of alarms from drifting ships. The campus of the University of Concepción falls, and the municipal theater; the water mains break beneath the streets and there is flooding everywhere. On that day in May 1960, the south of Chile is destroyed.

And the seaport of the shellfish hunters and the fishermen, that friendly little bay of urchins and oysters, has its epiphany.

When the quakes subside, in the middle of a white, star-filled night, the ocean suddenly withdraws. It simply goes away. People run toward the hills of Puerto Saavaedra, and from there, in silence, they witness the return of the sea. In one single embrace, it strikes, scrambles, climbs, and takes houses, streets, churches, schools, plazas, belltowers, animals, furniture, and trees. It takes everything and then leaves behind a new ground, the dried bottom of the bay that appears shining for some moments. This centuries-old floor that was once a city is now shining with geological riches, shells and pearls, millenary mollusks, anemones, sponges, white coral and petrified algae, hidden reefs, and also copper-colored harpoons and greenish coffers, slowly opening on their rusted hinges.

Half of the town has disappeared.

On the following day the sand reveals its cataclysmic vacuum. Allende organizes the rescue. He commissions tents, mobile hospital units, and stew pots from family hearths. He gathers more than two thousand abandoned children and takes them in buses to neighboring cities, where they find refuge. Most go to Santiago, where they are received at the local socialist and communist party headquarters. Puccio recalls that two of them were taken to his house, where they were put up for a couple of months. When the time came for them to go back, one of the children thanked Puccio and asked that, if something similar were to occur in Santiago, his children not be sent to the houses of the miners. "Life down there is very hard," he said, "and your life is very beautiful."

In the Senate Allende pushes through legislation for long-term loans that the victims can use to reconstruct their homes and re-open industries. He procures government funds for public works to counteract unemployment caused by massive layoffs.

That's the way the coal miners' strike ended victoriously for the miners. With a cataclysm.

Chapter   Four

It's No Better
the Third Time Around

It appears to me now, so many years after these events occurred, that between 1960 and 1970 Salvador Allende defined his political career at last. He did it in terms so peculiar that in a certain way they explain the final mysterious ambiguity of 1973. You'll probably say, 'Ah, so you mean Allende was just another product of the sixties, of the young people's revolt, you know, the dropping out of the bourgeois establishment, the uprising against all the sacred cows—family, the big house, and so on.' OK. And why not? The Cuban revolution changed our political history and the whole program of insurgency against imperialism. But then you'll say, and you'll be right, that the U.S. itself changed its counterinsurgency strategies and the terms of its official approach to the semicolonies of Latin America. Thanks, that's perfectly OK. To your health, then! So, in two shakes of a lamb's tail, a socialist, nationalist leader of Allende's stature is caught between a Chilean rock and a yanqui hard place. The trip to Cuba changed Allende. It was as though after contact with the boys with the beards, his white mustache, his strong chin, his heavy eyelids, his whole presence took on a certain granitelike weight. Let me explain. Like a statue—have you noticed that his portrait is beginning to appear side by side with those of Bolívar, Juárez, Martí, and Sandino? I'm not exaggerating. It was hard for his friends to recognize him. I saw a photo of him next to Brezhnev. That man had a pair of imposing eyebrows. The touches added by the photographer in the printing process had a surprising effect. There is in Allende's image an air of defiance, a mustache,

155

an iron look that you associate with the gallery of faces in Red Square. Optical illusions. You're laughing of course, and thinking that it's just a photographer's trick for propaganda purposes."

Augusto Olivares touches a handkerchief to his lips and looks at me with smiling kindness. A bright intelligence beams forth through his thick glasses. His big hands handle his glass and cigarette gracefully. He speaks in long, rounded phrases, as though he were reading from a book.

And then later I am face-to-face with Allende, and I am persuaded that Olivares is right.

Allende—the loser of '58—surprises partisans and opponents alike with a well-considered and solidly executed tactical twist: little by little he is giving shape to the program that will characterize his future government. His future government! He, a two-time loser in the grand arena of presidential elections. Slowly, the idea is sinking in that this man does not really live by the normal political code, with its yardstick of electoral victories and defeats. Without great fanfare Allende has been preparing the leaders and professionals who will flesh out his program. In the sixties he founded a Work Institute with some of the most brilliant young Chilean economists. Max Nolff was director, and Jaime Barrios, José Cademartori, Pedro Vuscovic, and Sergio Aranda, among others, participated from the beginning. This research group not only helped develop the basis for the fundamental reforms of Allende's government, but also the guidelines and legislation for Chile's new deal for industrial and agricultural workers.

What blind faith, what brand of rock-hard determination moved Allende during the sixties? He turned fifty a while ago. He appears robust but not fat. His brow is lined and his penetrating look is a bit ironic. He speaks calmly, but his consonants explode, detonating his well-structured sentences. He is always pumping questions. He wants details on all significant political currents, within and outside the country. He doesn't pronounce judgments, seeming instead to warehouse his information for the future. His thick, strong hands with their reddish hair catch your attention. He raises an eyebrow, observes amusedly, and laughs explosively.

Salvador takes care of himself. At the table it's one glass of wine, nothing more. He eats sparingly. Today I observe him entering the assembly room of the Chamber of Deputies, where parliamentarians and Latin American writers convene. Allende listens attentively to the eloquent Uruguayans, Mexicans, Peruvians, and Cubans. Martínez Moreno, Mario Benedetti, and Angel Rama denounce the abuses of human rights in their country. I see José María Arguedas, Carlos Fuentes, Mario Vargas Llosa, Alejo Carpentier, Augusto Roa Bastos. Allende's is a patriarchal presence here; you can feel his weight as an experienced statesman, with a bit of the old-school pol, tricolored sashes and all, thrown in for good measure. His hair is dark, but with a reddish glow, contrasting with his mustache, which is turning white. Next to his bench sits his sister Laura, a socialist representative, a woman of aristocratic beauty. After the session the writers surround him to ask questions. Soon there will be new elections for president. Will he be a candidate again? Will the fourth time be the charm?

One summer day in Santiago, during siesta time, my telephone rings. The concierge informs me that Senator Allende wants to come up to my room to speak with me. Surprised, I lay aside the book I am reading, tidy up the hotel room a bit, and prepare to receive him. I have closed the curtains because the sun is blinding. I open the door, and there is Salvador, smiling at me, with a straw hat in his hand. His elegant summer suit makes him look somewhat nonchalant. He sits down and seems relieved by the coolness of my room. In a relaxed voice, almost with indifference, he informs me that he intends to make a trip to the United States. He wants to know my opinion.

"The campaign of '64 is coming up. I will be a candidate," he explains without emphasis.

Again. And I realize that it's perfectly logical, since his defeat was by such a slim margin and under such unusual circumstances.

"Why do you think I should go to the United States?"

I never thought that Allende would consider the United States to be an immediate concern in the context of his plans for the presidency. Was he that sure of winning in '64? We spoke at length. I became aware that Allende's question was not aimed at setting strategy; on the contrary, I had the impression that something quite different was going on.

Allende was extremely perspicacious. Many times I was able to tap into his powerful intuition. On this occasion what intrigued Allende was not what the State Department might think of him, nor BID's attitude once it discovered the intent and extent of his reforms. Those matters would occupy his attention later, around 1970.

In the early sixties Allende wanted to know about JFK—who he was, the stuff he was made of, the forces that had pulled him onto the stage. But he also wanted to read the pulse of American public opinion, to know what the reaction would be to the nationalization measures fundamental to his future program. I explained how he might set up his tour of the U.S. In my opinion he should aim at the universities and the unions.

"That will give you the podium you need."

Allende listened to me attentively but didn't reveal his impressions one way or the other, although he appeared grateful for the information. As he was leaving he turned and said, as though suddenly remembering an errand, "Before I forget, I'd like to ask you a favor. I'd like you to get together with Klein to work on a draft of my speech on the Alliance for Progress that I'll give in Montevideo."

I accepted happily, and we shook hands. On the way out he extracted a fat Havana cigar—one of those wrapped in delicate, aromatic leaves—from his inside jacket pocket, and handed it to me.

"You have to smoke these as though you were firing a bazooka, stabilizing them on your shoulder," he said.

Then he put on his panama hat, pushed it back off his forehead, and walked slowly to the elevator.

Allende erased the trip from his calendar without
further thought. And he plunged—there's no other word for it—
into the campaign that his advisers, from the beginning, considered an act of insanity. The Senate was to have elections in 1961,
and Allende had to choose the electoral district from which to
run. He reasoned with Salomón Corbalán and Raúl Ampuero, his
greatest rival in the Socialist party.

"This might seem absurd," he said, looking at Ampuero, "but
it has been said that the two of us don't fit in the Socialist party.
Where we don't fit is in the first electoral district, Tarapacá and
Antofagasta, because that's where one of us could lose. And the
one who's going to lose is you, because I'm sure to win. And we
can't have you lose because you're a good socialist senator. Consequently, I won't be the candidate for the first district. I'll take
the third instead—Valparaíso and Aconcagua."

A silence followed. And then Corbalán replied between his
teeth, "You're nuts. You can't win, you have no chance."

"We'll see," Allende said, rocking back on his chair. "If I go
for the first district, Raúl Ampuero loses. If I go for the fifth,
O'Higgins and Colchagua, you'll lose, Corbalán. I can't go for the
seventh, because we have the obligation to support Tarud. If I go
for the ninth, Aniceto Rodríguez—a great socialist senator—will
lose. The only one left is the third, Valparaíso."

And that is how it was decided. To Puccio's sad comments,
Allende responded, "Osvaldo, your compass is off on this one. It
is true that I don't have a big chance of winning. We all know that.
But take a minute and look at the scenario. If I lose, nobody will
blame me for a thing. He sacrificed himself, they'll say; it was an
act of generosity for the party. And if I win? Do you see? Will
anyone be opposed to my running for president in 1964? Ah?"

What happened then was one more miracle of the Allende
brand. He relocated in Valparaíso and covered the district in a

nonstop campaign on foot, by car, by ship, even on horseback. He commandeered an old bus that had been relegated to the junk heap. He painted it and installed speakers and a movie projector. He even put in a bed and a bathroom, and he drove through the hills above the port city and the neighboring valleys, playing the latest records of Víctor Jara, Rolando Alarcón and El Indio Pavez, giving speeches, handing out pamphlets. This was the most energetic and resonant campaign of Allende's career.

Not only did he win the seat in the Senate, but he also gave Jaime Barros a leg up. Barros was the Communist party candidate who was on the same slate in that district.

Then his generalissimos began asking, "Will '64 be the big one?" Allende looked at them absentmindedly before speaking. "We'll weigh in for the fight," he said, thinking that '64 wasn't going to be his year of victory either.

According to the Church report, sponsored by the U.S. Senate, the CIA, in 1964, made a direct contribution of over two million dollars toward the candidacy of Eduardo Frei in order to prevent Allende's victory. This amounted to more than half of Frei's campaign costs. Through an agreement reached by the Committee of 40, the United States then invested more than eight million dollars for election propaganda and other forms of help.

Never before in Chile had there been a day at the polls like this one, designed, it seemed, on the drawing tables of Walt Disney's studios.

They even brought Juana Castro, Fidel's sister, into the melée! A modern incarnation of Juana la Loca, stubbornly grasping her microphone, vituperating against Allende and the Popular Front from Buenos Aires. La Juanita didn't beat around the bush. She told Chilean mothers that Allende was a communist and that communists always shipped their babies to the Russians for training in the art of parricide. Her agents would go to the homes of terrified neighbors, giving out phony forms requesting information about how many rooms and utensils would be available for the time when Allende would carry out his housing reform program.

Hype artists and masters of collusion invented ingenious political games: the Right lined up with Julio Durán, a heavy-handed senator, while the Center-Left entered the ranks of Eduardo Frei, knowing full well that, in the moment of truth, all of them would support the latter.

The following was said about the Radical party: *los radicales ricos* vote for Frei, *los radicales pobres* for Allende, and *los pobres radicales* for Durán.

But the lines blurred after the election of a representative in Curicó. Faced with the surprise victory of Dr. Oscar Naranjo, a socialist, the Right became alarmed, withdrew support from Durán, and backed Frei. The Naranjo caper, as this election was called, produced the reaction and climate that would stop Allende.

Once installed in Temuco Allende began to extend his campaign through Mapuche Indian territories. He got chiefs and reservation heads together on Ñielol Hill in Temuco and signed a solemn pact with them, promising to respect the property rights of indigenous peoples and help them fight to recover what they had lost.

Those weren't empty words. That signature represented an act of conscience that neither Allende nor the Mapuches forgot. In 1970 Allende made every one of his promises to the Mapuches a reality. They then joined the front lines and battled to the end, until their resistance was smashed by bullets.

Chapter Five

Tati and the Nephews

When I first met her, Tati was a calm, sweet child with big eyes and an intelligent expression. Her smiling eyes were light brown, Chilean eyes, as they say. She looked like the compañera in Neruda's poems of 1920. That expression, so open in adolescence, matured over the years, but never lost the gleam of intelligence and kindness. She was a medical student and moved easily in her father's circles. People would say that she was the "son that Allende never had." She appreciated her father's sharp humor and would laugh gently at his remarks. I remember her sitting on the rug near his desk in the house on Guardia Vieja Street; she was plying me with difficult questions, occasionally delivering parries and thrusts that could become quite lethal. Under her father's tutelage her singular nature blossomed, including those strong features unique to her—her aplomb, a certain impatience with bores, a detachment that could be mistaken for arrogance.

Allende needed Tati. She became not only his personal doctor but his political gadfly as well, always trying to nudge him into a militant stance and a more rigorous ideological position. Tati was moving toward the intransigent Left. But oddly enough, she was indifferent to the cult of violence advocated by political hotheads. What appealed to her was the pure analytical tradition of orthodox Marxism. The homegrown sweetness of the schoolgirl was replaced by the sharp edge of the revolutionary sixties.

One could easily recognize in her Salvador's explosive temperament and his innate composure under stress. The way she could handle the unexpected was impressive. In truth she depended on Tencha. Tati, like her sisters Isabel and Carmen Paz, often challenged their mother's authority. They were capable of irritating Tencha, but beneath their rebelliousness and adolescent impatience, they sought her support and shared her deep sense of responsibility.

Toward the end of 1967, Allende took Tati on a trip through the Soviet Union, a trip with much personal meaning for both of them, although they didn't discuss it at the time. In addition to the confidence that she knew how to bolster in him, Salvador felt that through her it was easier for him to understand the rebellious youth of the far Left.

Salvador insisted with increasing urgency that the women of Chile be brought into the socialist cause.

"Our duty is to bring our compañeras into political and social consciousness," he had said in the campaign of '61. "Once again they have voted the reactionary ticket."

And he wasn't referring to just one sector of Chilean society. He was speaking in part about the working woman who, burdened with children and enslaved in her home—an underground of prostitution, sickness, and misery—entered the back door of the bourgeoisie, washed their clothes, cared for their children, and cooked their meals, all the while absorbing a bizarre sense of conservative stability through her bosses' paternalistic treatment. She voted as they did. But Salvador spoke too of the large numbers of middle-class and small-town women converted by the mirage of liberalism and peaceful reformism preached by Frei.

These women, Allende insisted, now gaining independence within an aggressively macho society, which up until the fifties had denied them the most elemental of civil rights, should join the socialist cause.

Salvador knew instinctively how to surround himself with militants who understood the uniqueness of his non-authoritarian political style; he was not fond of imposing himself, seeking to inspire rather than command.

He attracted women who identified with him and who, in working closely with him, became an essential part of his life. He was a man of burning ideals, but he was not sentimental by nature. He formed and destroyed many passionate alliances. He pursued a personal utopia with the unexpected pragmatism of a man who believed he would go all the way, when in fact he would never reach his final destination.

A totally unexpected incident shook up Allende's routine. When Puccio called to advise that he was housing a spur-of-the-moment guest in danger, Allende's immediate response was, "I don't want any part of it. . . . But we can't roll over on this one. Tell Pascal that I'll be over to talk with him this afternoon. Tell him not to move a damn inch. If they grab him, there's no way that he'll get out of it alive."

Andrés Pascal was Laura Allende's son. It was her responsibility to guide the difficult and potentially explosive relations between the militants of the Movement of the Revolutionary Left (MIR) and the cautiously moving Socialist party. Salvador had brought his sister into the political fray, and she went from the upper-middle-class salons of Viña del Mar to revolutionary activism without a misstep. He entrusted her with forming the Independent Committee of Women for Allende. Laura organized efficiently and directed seminars and conferences; in time she became a brilliant representative of the Socialist party and a firm source of support for Salvador in his final campaigns.

"What my nephew has to get through his head," Salvador said to his secretary, "is that the old days of beatings and electric shocks are over. These days they want to destroy us at the root. Watch it, compañero, the spring festival is over."

Later on, sitting in the Puccios' dining room, the young Mirista listened to Salvador with an incredulous, ironic look in his eye.

"Uncle," he said, "there's no reason to fly off the handle. The things that are happening were expected and we understand the risk. Whoever told you that we don't listen or discuss matters? On the contrary. What we most want is to discuss with you and clarify our differences. Do you know something? You folks got off the path some time ago. How many more times will you be a candidate, uncle? The years and months and days have crept up on you.

Our secretary general, Miguel Enríquez, has said it plain and clear. There is a way to get to socialism, but it's not the one with a long wait and a narrow door at the end. How many times have you told us to grab the bull by the horns? What were you saying after you got back from Cuba? The electoral system is an expensive delay, uncle, and you can measure it in light-years. Like Enríquez said it: Forget about elections. We want to change the country now. Come and join us. We can do it if we consolidate worker power, if we follow the steps of the workers in the street and in the factories. With an armed revolution, uncle. Agrarian reform means taking the land, and not through real-estate titles.

Allende listened to him seriously. He seemed to know the measure of Pascal's anger and impatience. Pascal and Miguel Enríquez were ready to shoot it out with DINA. They didn't give a damn about who and how many would be killed in the melee.

"We need to talk about the matter at hand," he responded. "You're safe for a couple of days here. Who knows. Of course no one is going to abandon you, but you should have consulted me. You people should know that assaults and takeovers seem more like a plot by the ultra-Right to divide and sabotage us than a revolution. Wake up and understand that our road to socialism is legitimate and will be effective. The Cubans see that, and you should too. So get off your high horse, and once and for all let's understand each other."

The boy stared at Allende, amused by the volley.

"Don't worry, uncle, I won't mess up your life."

"Puccio knows what has to be done," Allende interrupted. "And the next time, consult with me first."

That night Allende had to attend a dinner sponsored by the radical freemasons. The event was touted as a grand occasion. Allende insisted on going alone, on foot.

"Take my car," he said to Puccio on his way out the door. He wanted to walk because the conversation with his nephew weighed on him. It wasn't so much the boy's ideas that bothered him, but the wordless hostility, as though Andrés and his group wished to insult him by isolating him with silence. They dismissed him as a reformer and, on top of that, as an old fool. They rejected out of hand the mere suggestion that they might support him in his methodical march to power. Their stiff-necked dogma offended him, but he understood their impatience. All throughout Latin America presidents were falling like dominoes. These young people wanted arms. They dreamed of a network of guerrillas descending from the Andes to liberate the great cities. They wanted action now, not elections tomorrow.

Walking through the streets of Santiago's business district, Allende suddenly felt uncomfortable, suffocated. People were pushing and shoving, and the buses hurtled along seemingly out of control, shaking and rattling in clouds of dust and smoke. He had a choking sensation and felt disoriented. He thought about stopping for a moment to rest but dropped the idea. It was getting late. He could walk a few more blocks, go by the Senate. Then he thought of his mother, and decided to visit her. He stopped a taxi. When he got in he looked at his watch. It was after 10 P.M.

"Where to?" the driver asked.

"To the Italian Club," he said, thinking that he would visit her the next morning.

When he got to the club he realized that all of Santiago's freemasons were there. But he also noticed that the atmosphere seemed more tentative than triumphant. His socialist compañeros led him to the head of the main table.

"There are more than five hundred people," Puccio said to him, "but the big cheese got out of it. He sent you this letter."

Allende stuck it in his inside pocket.

"His excuse is not even funny. He says his wife is sick. But at any rate he expresses his solidarity with you, not in the political sense, but in the name of the masonic brotherhood. You will have to read it aloud after your speech."

Allende said nothing. He was going to sit down when Puccio stopped him.

"There's one more thing," he said. "The union leadership of

the waiters who are on shift tonight has told me that the garçons want to present you with a check for their campaign contribution. In other words, doctor, they're giving us their whole night's wages."

"We'll have to announce it. I'll do it myself. I'll start with that."

The banquet and the speeches began. Slowly, tortuously, the hour of the final test drew near. The freemasons declared themselves behind Allende, but not without certain reservations and caveats. The excuse of the gran maestro was symptomatic. From behind his big, solid desk, surrounded by leather and plush, in the soft serenity of his comfortable throne, don Aristóteles wished to glean the interpretations of his wisest brothers. This Salvador comes from out of the blue. Whom is he serving? What powers? God Almighty himself? He is in with the Marxists. That was the grave and frightened verdict emanating from ministries, law offices, barracks, banks, and businesses. Watch out!

When it was his turn to speak, Allende was slow in getting to his feet. He began by referring to the waiters' gesture of solidarity, but when he gave emphasis to his words his voice broke audibly. The silence seemed to hang on him. Puccio held out a glass of water. Allende drank it, followed by a sip of wine. He kept speaking. His speech was concise and technical in nature, with abundant statistics and quotes. The crowd listened attentively but without enthusiasm.

"I've never seen Allende so lackluster," Puccio said to his neighbor. "Something's wrong." He thought Allende should consult a doctor, but when he later tried to tell him so, the leader interrupted.

"No, my friend, nothing's wrong. Just tired. Forget about it."

In the car, as they were leaving the club, Allende told Puccio about his conversation with his nephew, the young revolutionary, and about the sadness that Andrés's words had caused him.

"Compañero," he said, "you know that we're not going to win this election. It's hard to admit it. But they're tightening the nets of hatred and terror around us. You feel it and I feel it. We have seen it in the reluctance of our friends who hide their faces from me as they retreat. They won't let us win, but even if we did, they'd hit us with every weapon at their disposal. The image of Allende that they've been concocting has finally taken form. We should expect coups from right and left."

Later he would recount that he had felt sick that night, that he was thinking about his mother, and that the gesture of the waiters had moved him more than it should have.

"Let's go see her," he said suddenly.

And the car headed toward the hills overlooking the city.

Two days after that visit, doña Laura Gossens de Allende died.

Salvador Allende's 1964 campaign was one of symbols, both big and small. The socialist front fought CIA involvement in a one-sided, ill-fated duel; the voices of liberation were counterbalanced by heavy sacks of dollars. And the bucks were flying, as Guillermo Atías would say.

"We arrived at the town of Nueva Imperial," Osvaldo Puccio recalls. "The construction of the hotel was not yet completed, but that's where we ended up after a hard day's work and an exhausting trip filled with meetings. They had only one room to rent, with one double bed, which compañero Allende and I had to share."

In the fishing village of San Vicente, near Talcahuano, on a bright sunny day, I shared a stage with Pablo Neruda and Manuel Rojas. Before us were thousands of men, women, and children cheering for Allende. Later, we ate at the union hall. The fishermen opened the mussels and clams with their knives and blessed the sea, the sun, the lemons, and the white wine. Neruda handled the fragrant shells with his thick, slow fingers. Manuel Rojas, self-absorbed as always, ate slowly, as though alone on a craggy, frosted peak.

A guitar was heard, rhythmically strumming. Víctor Jara laughed with his eyes and his sensual mouth, singing:

De ti depende,
de ti depende
que el presidente
sea Allende, sea Allende

We all moved with the Cuban rhythm of that *son*, sent to Salvador by Juan Puebla, the composer, especially for this campaign. A *son* consecrated with revolutionary rum from the island itself.

Yet the Popular Front lost, and Frei won with his promise of a revolution "in liberty."

Juana Castro assembled her paraphernalia and her bag of tricks, folded her tent, and happily flew off for the Miami circus.

After Frei's crushing victory, people began speaking of Allende in the past tense. "He's down for the count, he won't get off the canvas this time" was the general verdict. And Allende did nothing to contradict it. He gathered his personal papers, took them to Guardia Vieja, and announced to his family that he was going to Algarrobo to rest. With a touch of irony, he advised them that he would now have the whole beach to himself, since his neighbor of many years would be busy at La Moneda. Frei had indeed been that very neighbor, a loyal companion at the table, a friendly adversary in endless domino games, a real compadre in enjoying the sun and the sea.

On his second day at the seashore, Allende received a call from Santiago. His campaign headquarters had been torched, and nothing was left except for a few charred sticks.

"Search for the documents in the basement," he responded. "They must be OK. I stored them there with Puccio."

And a little while later, another piece of news put an end to the summer's jaunt. Salomón Corbalán, the young leader and main strategist of the Socialist party, had been killed in an automobile accident. In a homage in the Senate, Allende said, "The very best is dead." Corbalán had been the man who could soothe

the hatreds and feuds in the party, the one who always had the words to resolve the leaders' doubts.

Corbalán's death occurred at the worst possible moment, just when the Socialist party was splitting once more. Allende appeared back on the scene, patching holes in his old alliances, reining in extremism, and coaxing the Left branch of the Partido Radical into the socialist fold.

The split was heralded by symptoms quite familiar to Allende, who had seen them in times of defeat as well as victory. It was expected that the Socialist party would rethink its strategy after losing the presidential election. And it was equally logical, according to Allende, that the Christian Democrats would become mired in the quicksand of their recent victory. A powerful leftist faction under the leadership of Rafael Gumucio, a staunch ideologue of progressive Christian socialism, reconstituted itself as a new party, the Movement for Unified Action of the People (MAPU). A little later another splinter group rebelled against Frei—the Christian Left.

Soon Frei found himself under attack by both Left and Right, as he tried to maintain a political power base that was by then a mirage. The National party of Onofre Jarpa let loose its heavy artillery, calling Frei a sellout and accusing him of paving the way for communism in Chile. A group of military officers, on hearing these words, began rattling their sabers and demanding economic rewards. Just in case, they wanted to know if it was OK to warm up the motors on the big tanks. The answer was affirmative. They launched a slow, spiritless attack. Frei blew the whistle. A fleet of municipal buses surrounded La Moneda to defend the government.

The Frei model that LBJ defended for Latin America—the revolution in liberty and the nationalization of copper with due compensation for American companies—was destroyed. What had happened to the abundant majority of votes from the '64 election?

Frei would have liked to find his compadre Allende along the gentle beaches of Algarrobo and to renew the eternal duel at the afternoon domino board; he would have liked to forget the roar of tanks and the soured voices of his former followers. But that was no longer possible. He became more distant and dried-up with each passing day, and his face took on a funereal pallor. His hacking laugh began to resemble a death rattle.

In his desire to recapture power, he reached out to the Right, toward the barracks. Once again, Allende had the beaches of Algarrobo to himself.

Chapter   Six

Waves

They start far out to sea, in silence, forming powerful swells that gradually gain volume to loom
up where least expected, flooding a nation that secretly treasures
the rumbling and treacherous crosstides.

It is said that a conspiracy has begun and that Chile is the target of lances poised to attack from over the cordillera, up and
down the coast—lances that once hurled will land as prison bars.
It's being rumored that the democratic tradition in Chile is a trap-
door, its unions and professional institutes, academies and student federations infiltrated by the implacable, fanatical red menace.

Violence will soon explode in the big cities—people say—and
the ensuing flames will reduce the tried-and-true system of the
good old wise men to charred rubble. Nothing will escape this
devastation. The red wind blows from the north, from the mountains and jungles of the highlands. It feeds the flames of destruction as it rises from hot seas and tumultuous islands. It is said that
people without souls or beliefs have planned the surrender of the
country and that they nourish a secret ambition to have us executed by firing squads—us, the fathers and mothers, together with
our heroes consecrated in the holy prayers of the Te Deum, our
patriarchs, judges and generalissimos, our decorated sailors, our
volunteer firemen, and our awesome aviators. The reds will fall
upon our fertile fields and innocent campesinos like locusts, they
will burn and ransack our industries . . .

This man with a blue suit and a gray vest lifts an eyebrow,
looks at me with a smile and exclaims, "Republican militia? National police? Rubbish! All of that belongs to the past, the romantic era when the carabineros called themselves guardians of

the people and charged after thieves blowing on their tin whistles."

He raises his glass of *pisco* and takes another little cheese pie as he speaks. The top dog of the Club de la Unión sighs and nestles into his leather easy chair.

"We are, my dear friend," he continues, "in the age of science and technology, when secret agents are not just secret anymore but invisible. Just like the torturers and the well-equipped army popping out of the sky from inside a flock of tin birds. The spies coming back from the fog. The supermen who erase revolutions from the map. Do you know what happened to Che Guevara? Do you want to know the real truth?"

But I have mentioned the name of Salvador Allende, and he interrupts me.

"That name is beginning to be heard in a loud, uncouth voice. Don't you know? Allende the *red*, señor. Not the anticlerical, positivist red like his grandfather, a gentleman after all. This other Allende is a pinko without class. Did you know that 'El Chicho' is connected telepathically to Moscow and Castro? He's as crazy as a loon."

In July 1967 Allende, then president of the Senate, gets on a plane for Havana. He is presiding over a delegation of socialist and communist union leaders, all participating in the Tricontinental Conference for Solidarity. He sports a red carnation in his lapel.

The plane makes a stop in Mexico, and Allende makes his way quickly down the ramp. He notices that a man in uniform is aiming a camera at him. Allende asks the man's identity and is informed that in Mexico's international airport every passenger headed for Cuba must be photographed.

"I don't accept that!" he shouts. "As a Chilean senator, I refuse to be photographed like a common criminal. Hand over that roll of film!"

"What's eating this guy?" the sleepy-eyed airport functionaries ask themselves as they look at this loud-mouthed señor with a red carnation who is raising such a ruckus. "What's up?" Little by little people start waking up and moving about. Allende doesn't let up. Telephones are ringing off the hook. Officers are calling. Allende is dialing a public phone.

"Who? The president? What president? . . ."

"You heard me—yes, I want the president, in Chapultepec, at the Zócalo, wherever he is. I want to speak to the president."

They try to calm him down, but his voice grows louder. The appointed crowd begins to arrive: important figures in Mexican politics, Chilean diplomats, newsmen, tv people. They want to know what's going on and why this gentleman is so perturbed.

"Angry, am I? But don't you see that this airport is invaded by the CIA? Do you think these photos are for the society page? They are for the CIA, señorita, for the Pentagon."

His voice reaches its most powerful register and resounds throughout the domes of plastic and metal.

When Allende returns to the plane he is carrying an envelope in his hand. It contains a roll of film. He springs up the ramp and from the door of the plane turns briefly to salute the mixed crowd with a raised fist. The carnation droops from his lapel.

The delegates, rather intrigued with this performance, observe him curiously. What has gotten into the compañero?

Allende arrives in Havana wired for action, and he floods the microphones with unexpected fury: never were his attacks against imperialism more heated, his solidarity with North Vietnam more firm, and his evocation of Che Guevara more fervent. He has hit the ground in combat gear.

In the grand assemblies of the Tricontinental Conference, Allende appears for the first time as a leader of international stature. His speech is a well-documented analysis of the political panorama of Latin America, with allusions to the violent changes in Brazil, Venezuela, Bolivia, Peru, and Santo Domingo. It is in this speech that he proposes the formation of the Organization for Latin American Solidarity. He is elected president of OLAS, and back in Chile he becomes the target of vitriolic attacks for having "sold out unconditionally" to Fidel and the communist conspiracy.

On the last day of the conference, Allende was feted in La Bodeguita del Medio. As was his custom he took a walk along the beachfront toward Old Havana. Sea spray flecked the warm sidewalk, and from the big fort that had kept vigil over the ocean for centuries, the light of day seemed whiter and ever more burning.

Between the rocks and the gigantic cement fortifications, the sea snakes in and out, making little whirlpools of seaweed. Sky and stone. A monument that defies the sea, green with moss and surrounded by dark cannons, waiting for an invasion that never comes. It is said that no matter where you are in the maze of narrow streets surrounding the cathedral, your steps always lead you to La Bodeguita.

Allende had split away from the group and was walking with a compañera who jokingly described the pilgrim's route from the darkened lobby of the Hotel Ambos Mundos, where Hemingway lived out the creative angst of his Cuban short stories, down to La Floridita, where he still presides over the abundantly stocked bar in the form of a bronze bust complete with saucerwide eyes and scraggly beard. This is where he downed many a daiquiri, the compañera said, always standing up, with paper and pencil in hand for writing his rum-soaked dialogues.

The long, narrow counter in La Bodeguita received them with its gauntlet of *mojitos*, little glasses of rum and mint. There was a slow, rocking motion to the hubbub of voices reminiscent of a ship nodding its way into the gentle waves of a safe port. Later, the twilight-boleros of dusk were heard, mixed with the occasional quarrel erupting on the rim of the next-to-last *mojito*, for there is never a last one.

In the cavelike dining room, Salvador evoked the memory of friends who had passed through but lingered on in photos and autographs on the wall. He toasted the Cuban revolution, then moved on to more sentimental toasts charged with amorous emotions. A Chilean voice was reciting Neruda's poems to an improvised guitar accompaniment. "I heard this tune at the Casino de la Playa," said Allende. The drinking continued until dawn.

Glass in hand, the ice tinkling, Salvador wrote his message on the back of a big menu that will hang forever next to La Bodeguita's bar: "Viva Cuba libre, Chile espera . . ."

Several illegible words follow, seeming to move with the tilt of La Bodeguita toward the sea. Travelers from all over the world, clinking their glasses and shouting "Salud!" will forever try to decipher Allende's handwriting.

Dawn breaks, and the salt-and-spray breeze from the turbulent ocean bathes the faces of the revelers. There are still couples leaning dangerously over the seawall.

"What did the rum say to the mint?" Allende asks all of a sudden. "We'll get together in La Bodeguita."

Allende saw Ernesto Guevara five times after that first occasion at his bedside. Those meetings left a lasting impression on Allende, like messages engraved in the bark of a tree.

Guevara and Allende both grew up in moderately affluent environments, went to good schools, had distinguished university records, and received their medical licenses as practicing surgeons. They were both intelligent, committed activists in their youth. But there the parallels end.

Because of Guevara's sickly constitution, his family had to move from Rosario, where he was born, to Alta Gracia. In 1953 he successfully dodged military service and set out to travel around the world. He became an anonymous revolutionary throughout Latin America. He made a stop in Guatemala to serve in the anti-imperialist revolution of Jacobo Arbenz. He went to Mexico City, where he met Fidel Castro, Camilo Cienfuegos, Raúl Roa, and the team that would embark on the Granma to take Batista's Cuba. He fought in the Sierra Maestra and took care of the wounded and the sick. After the victory, when revolutionary power had been established, Guevara said goodbye to Fidel, to Cuba, to his wife and children. He first traveled to Africa and Asia, finally arriving in Bolivia in November 1966.

He died at age 39, ambushed by a fierce squad of rangers. The world was moved by the strange significance of his sacrifice, and even more by the miracle of his resurrection. Che Guevara was described by the press as "the liveliest corpse ever seen." Indeed, on the cement slab where they laid him to rest, with his bullet-ridden torso, throat, and pelvis, his legs nearly severed by machine-gun fire, Che Guevara smiled placidly, a sweet expression in his half-shut eyes, his hair like a dark halo over the pale face, his hands ready to give benediction.

His executioners, of course, could not allow this Jesus to mock them, and so they proceeded to cut off his hands, put them in a jar, and send them airmail to forensic wizards abroad for fingerprints.

In Chile, Allende, president of the Senate, got to his feet in a plenary session to pay tribute to the fallen leader. But beneath Allende's emotional recounting of Che's life, and his references to Che's speeches, letters, and diary, some could detect yet another story and another homage—and, too, an intimate, unfinished confession.

Allende would have liked to be that young doctor, a dreamer and fighter who abandoned his career, his family, his golden cage and went off to fight in the cities, plazas, and mountains of America. Yet this had been impossible for him. Of greater weight than his desire was a whole tradition of assemblies, parliaments, and national history. Visions of jungle warfare and military campaigns seduced him, and he would pack his bags for Cuba and Vietnam. He would return more eloquent than ever, with renewed vigor and courage to face congressional debates, to lead strikes and parades, to defy tyrants with bold gestures and legendary proclamations.

Allende didn't know how to play the role that history proffered him with one hand and took from him with the other: he wanted to make revolution, but with the unanimous consent of all involved. He asked for calm in the midst of the melee, he asked for respect for his office, justice and moderation before the muzzles of machine guns. He needed more than one life to learn to live and die like Che Guevara. And he wasn't given that kind of time.

That's why Allende was beside himself when he received the news of the massacre in Higueras and saw the laid-out corpse, smiling and bullet-ridden, on the front pages of newspapers throughout the world. Indignant, he shouted in the Senate, shouted to the four winds, demanding that they deliver Che's body to him, in the name of the revolutionaries of Chile and America, so that he could carry him in his arms to Cuba. And they laughed at him. Regaining his composure, he announced that he was going to find the four survivors of Che's jungle war and accompany them to Tahiti, stopping off at Easter Island, continuing on to France and then Cuba, in a voyage symbolic of resurrection and the return of Che Guevara.

And he did what he said he would do, despite the attacks of his political enemies in Chile.

Allende came back from that trip a quiet man, redeemed and with renewed fighting spirit. Puccio, who greeted him at the airport, describes his arrival: "When he got off the plane from Tahiti, he was wearing a *guayabera*—the national garb of the Cubans— and a straw hat on his head. He held a Tahitian walking stick in his hand."

Chapter Seven

The Angelic Smile of Ho Chi Minh

A dinner with army officers?" Allende asked.

"There will be about twelve all together, doctor. Young people who can be trusted," a secretary informed him.

Allende pondered a moment, adjusted his glasses and said firmly, "I have an important session at the Senate, and I have no idea when we'll finish. Tell them that I could be very late."

"There's no problem. They insist on meeting with you tonight."

"Do they know that tonight the Senate will discuss Viaux's demands?"

"Surely. That's why they want to talk with you and explain their position."

"Where will the meeting be? I don't intend to go to an army officer's house."

"Don't worry. The meeting is at Puccio's house. Nine-thirty."

"It will be a miracle if I can get there before eleven."

Allende got up, adjusted his tie and silk handkerchief, and looked at the woman before leaving. She was totally trustworthy and always maintained a discreet distance. She had accompanied him in the campaign of '64 and would again in others, without ever punching a time clock, not really at his side, but close by, part of the inner circle. Allende gave a quick glance at the memo in the typewriter and on his way out touched her lightly on the shoulder.

"I'll get there very late, compañera. I hope they'll wait for me," he said.

The Santiago winter was coming to an end. A cold, persistent drizzle soaked the pavement and the houses. People cursed the potholes and streams of water running through the streets. Cars splattered the sidewalks with mud. September once again became the month of the military.

The general-of-the-year was named Roberto Viaux. With a curious display of political instinct, he had decided to provoke the government a bit. Well, perhaps actually rock it a little, but without overturning or sinking it. Something like Ibáñez's performance in the twenties: raise a ruckus with drawn sabers, demand better wages, protest the ill-treatment of the poor defenders of the country. "Our wages, in addition to being miserable to start with, are paid out late and sometimes not at all," Viaux said. "We are not striking out against democracy or established order. Let's get that straight. Let Frei come to negotiate with us at the Tacna regiment. Here we can speak like true compatriots."

But President Frei wasn't in the mood for negotiations at the cannon's mouth—not with Viaux or anyone like him.

"Put down your arms," he ordered, "and return to your barracks. In good time we will see about bettering your situation."

Some officers of the new breed then thought about Allende. Why not? Allende could possibly be elected president in 1970. No guarantee, of course, but it was possible.

In fact Allende had made a clear decision at the beginning of the Viaux saber-rattling contest.

Well-informed about the Tacna uprising, he had an extensive interview at his home with Benjamín Prado and Enrique Krauss, leaders of the Christian Democrat party, after which he went to La Moneda to offer his firm support to Frei in facing down a coup.

"My party and the forces of the Left," Allende said, "will defend Chilean democracy against the forces of fascism. Do not doubt our resolve. But this is not to say that I have lost faith in the Chilean armed forces. They respect our constitution."

Meanwhile, the guests at Puccio's were becoming impatient. The pisco sours, the pickled-fish hors d'oeuvres, and the little *empanadas* were all circulating for the fourth time. People were smoking and talking, and still Allende did not appear. An awk-ward silence was growing.

"Let's serve dinner, sweetheart," the host said to his wife. "The doctor will join us when he arrives."

It was almost midnight when they heard the sound of tires slid-ing to a stop on the wet pavement. The bell rang and Allende popped into the dining room. The officers got to their feet. Allen-de apologized for his late arrival. Bright faces turned to him, and he felt their camaraderie.

The conversation quickly turned to politics. A blond, red-faced major, waving his napkin elegantly, as though he were danc-ing a *cueca*, gave his opinion in a quiet voice.

"Please understand, doctor, that we oppose communism, but not socialism. And we know where the line is that divides them. I would go further and say that after so many years of conservative and centralist political administrations, socialism might be a breath of fresh air, might even give a new foundation to our econ-omy, or at least push us out of the crisis."

"The major is right," said a captain at the far end of the table. "Socialism doesn't advocate dictatorships of any stripe. As far as I'm concerned, an Allende victory at the polls would be just fine. And I mean that." Then looking around the table with a cold eye, he added, "Let it be understood and repeated over and over, for the benefit of fence sitters, that with Salvador Allende as president, democracy will remain in Chile—the kind of democracy that de-fines us as a country and honors our middle-class tradition."

There was a warm silence, punctuated only by the light sound of silverware, while those present savored the opinions just deliv-ered by the two officers.

"Cheers!" exclaimed the major, smiling broadly.

"Cheers!" was the response.

Allende barely sipped his glass. He still hadn't said a word.

"A program like yours," said a gray-haired man on the other side of the table, "emulates Count Tolstoy's kind of humanism, and by that I mean Christian sentiment mixed with a true democratic mystique." Then, warming to the task, he added, "I have faith in your victory. But please, do watch the 'comrades.' They're oh so sharp, they like to take the chestnuts out of the fire with someone else's paw. Opportunists is what they are. Yes, go ahead and convert the state into a great planning center. That is modern and plausible. But leave industrial production in private hands, and above all don't muddle up foreign trade. My dear doctor, you are on the right road. Why look for problems?"

Allende peered at him from behind his thick glasses.

"We have not stirred up a revolt," the gray-haired man said, "nor have we conspired or mobilized troops. No sir, our work stoppage, and that is what it has been, is along professional lines. What we ask for is justified. We ask for better pay, more respect for the professional soldier and for the army—this glorious Chilean army that is falling behind, doctor, dangerously behind, if you compare our budget with those of the armed forces of our neighbors and traditional rivals."

"General Viaux," someone started to say, "is a man of impeccable record, a man . . ."

Puccio's wife had served coffee. It was 2:00 A.M.

Allende's imposing voice cut through the sleepy, complacent atmosphere, heavy with tobacco smoke and the bouquet of cognac. He had gotten to his feet and, pushing a chair away from him, he took his stand. The military men were also standing, and they listened carefully. But Allende paced up and down, gesturing them to take their seats again.

"Gentlemen," he said, "I appreciate the frank expression of your concerns with respect to your social and economic conditions. And I must be frank too, and tell you that you have risen up in arms against a democratically elected government. And you have made your demands for change while supported by firepower. That I cannot accept. You tell me that you have declared a strike and that you have not revolted. What kind of a strike is that, with dead and wounded? Who have the victims been? Innocent, ordinary people off the street. And those tanks that Viaux would have out on the street? No, gentlemen. I support the economic justice you demand, and I will make my position known to the government. I guarantee that if you put down your arms there will be no retribution. We will be united in our respect for the constitution, but never in armed conspiracy."

Allende took leave of his hosts and, with a crisp salute, walked past the officers, who looked at him with embarrassment.

Several days later, President Frei reached a compromise with Viaux. He agreed to study the request for higher wages, get rid of his minister of defense, and appoint a new chief of staff for the army.

General René Schneider came from the south. He was 54 years old and vigorous, his facial expression frank and intelligent. Some of his attitudes were bound to cause consternation in the army. The general was a painter. He painted in a studio that he had built in the garden behind his house, next to his son Raúl's, an artist known for his abstract oils. The general liked music and studied philosophy and the social sciences. He was able to expound convincingly on his concept of law and social structure, supporting himself with the ideology of Teilhard de Chardin. The general hit it off with the young priests, the self-sacrificing worker-priests who had moved into the tough barrios to spread the word of Christ. Soon René Schneider became known as the hippie general.

Surprised by the behavior and the communiqués of Viaux, who in the wink of an eye had gone from self-proclaimed leader of the military brotherhood to plotter of coups, the new chief of staff delivered a message to the country that soon became known as the Schneider Doctrine, a message that provided a constitutionalist basis for the relationship between the state and the military. Schneider said, "the military academy, and to a greater degree the army itself, have participated in all the alternatives to political and social development in the country; those first stormy, anarchic years were a rigorous test as the foundations of authority were being set. Moreover, the military academy, through its graduates, proceeded to establish clearly the basic concept of deliberate subordination and collaboration within the structure of the state. To think that taking over a barracks, ignoring legitimate military authority, and inciting subordinates to rebellion, all constitutes a *legitimate act*, and that such an act is just *an extreme measure but invariably accepted*, represents an aberration never really embraced by our army, and constitutes a disgrace to our tradition of discipline."

Schneider's forthright behavior moved Allende, the candidate, and calmed the hand of Frei, the president.

It was even said that the Tacna uprising was a product of Frei's own apprehensive nature, that recognizing the possibility of an Allende victory in 1970, and the subsequent intrusion of Marxist rabble into La Moneda, he decided to convert Viaux's little affair into a strategic political ruse, a self-coup. From then on, the Left looked at him with suspicion. He would appear suddenly in his big black limo, burning rubber down Grecia Avenue to the accompaniment of rocks hurled by students from the Pedagogical Institute.

Allende had to change gears. What had happened? At the beginning of 1969, facing the hazards of a tough election—this time for the Senate seat from the districts of Aysén, Magallanes, and Chiloé—Allende learned two things: that he could still win at the polls, even under the least favorable conditions, and that in his party a certain resistance was growing to what was termed his "presidential complex."

Allende astutely stepped back, looked over the battlefield of rivals and followers, and decided to remove himself temporarily from the struggle. He confided his plans to Tencha and discussed the details with Tati. They both supported his decision, and he left on a trip to the Far East.

As he flew in a Soviet jet toward Korea and Vietnam, Allende looked away for a moment from the tug-of-war in Chile and felt more clearly than ever that the fate of his country was decided not only in political conventions, but also in the hard-fought battles for liberation of faraway lands shrouded in mythic haze.

Allende was going to visit Ho Chi Minh.

Neruda wrote that this sweet, mysterious man was a poet "with long taproots in the Oriental tradition" who had come to manhood between "the bleakness of the colonial East and a harsh life in Paris." Freed from prison, Ho Chi Minh lived the life of a poor university student, a restaurant waiter, who kept his faith in the revolution and, when the right moment came, "returned to his country to fulfill his destiny."

Aged and infirm, Ho Chi Minh welcomed Salvador.

"I had the privilege of being received by that venerable old man," Salvador said in a lecture at the University of Concepción. "I will never forget the clearness of his look and the kindness of his words. When he greeted Eduardo Paredes and me, he thanked us for having come so far to lend his nation the moral support of our people. He was already gravely ill. I believe that I was the last politician from the West to be received by Ho. He died 25 days after I left Vietnam. Ho had deep faith in young people. He often wrote letters to his ex-students. It must have been a great stimulus for them to receive lines by the father of Vietnam, son of the revolution, writer and statesman, liberator of his people—this man who had attained, because of his exemplary life, the recognition not only of his own nation, but of all the people of the world. Those minutes with Ho Chi Minh taught me a great deal."

Years later, in 1973, Allende told his press aide Carlos Jorquera that "if the man exists with whom I would like to be identified after I'm gone, it would be, without a doubt, Ho Chi Minh."

The old man listened attentively to Allende. He made no comments, gave no special advice. Smiling affectionately, he walked him to the door. Salvador was heading toward a battle of uncertain result. Ho Chi Minh, the proven hero, stood outside for a moment. Then he went back into the house. One more test awaited him, and he knew how he would face it. He thought about Allende, and his smile faded away. He hoped his Chilean comrade would also know how to meet the end.

On his return Allende made a stop in Cuba, where he received a phone call. Puccio told him that some political groups had stepped forward to proclaim him the presidential candidate for 1970. Allende made no comment.

In Chile the rumor circulated that Allende had sent a cable to the wire services saying that he had respectfully declined any such nominations.

On his return Allende listened to several versions of the incident. Apparently he was not thinking about the angelic smile of Ho Chi Minh when he said, "The best hound grabs the fox! We're all on the same scent, the cleverest will be elected."

Uncle Ho would have smiled, because only he knew, walking toward the sunset, that the fourth attempt would signal victory, but also death.

Chapter Eight

"Habemus Candidatus," Said Condorito

Allende quickly picked up on the political changes that had occurred during his trip. It wasn't a domestic explosion, as one might surmise, but rather the crumbling of a world system. A young parliamentarian, who was a member of MAPU, told Allende, "You have to realize, Salvador, that your thirty-some years as a statesman have classified you. The young people believe they are watching a battle of titans. But it's no longer a contest between the big ideologies. Instead it's a squabble between leaders who are tangled up in the traps of outmoded capitalism and socialism. Your prissy parliamentarian style, the Masonic affiliation, are signs of decadence and compromise to these kids today. They just don't understand you. They look up to you as a father, but they end up walking away."

With an elegant, youthful gesture, Senator Alberto Jerez pushed back a lock of gray hair. Allende, catlike, was ready to respond. But other voices could be heard, more direct, more crushing in their force.

"Why should we keep believing in this electoral sleight of hand that compañero Allende uses to lull us? If he's so fond of the ballot box, let him have one to stuff his memories in. Times have changed. The road to socialism in Chile is armed revolution."

"Stay cool, compañero," a young leader said. "I don't support the reformism of the eternal candidate either, nor do I support his wooing of social democracy. But—and this is a major but—if the plank of my party tilts toward the legalist position, in that case, compañero, there's no other candidate besides Allende. He's the only one who can take us to power within the rules of a bourgeois democracy."

Senator Jerez, without mincing words, went right to the point. "Salvador," he said, "excuse me for saying it, but in our terms you are not the ideal person to represent the Left in 1970. It will be necessary to open the door for a new leader."

Allende, biting the tip of his mustache, lightning flashing through his glasses, responded with an argument that was no longer valid.

"The Chilean youth knows me and always has. It's not for nothing that I have years of revolutionary experience under my belt at the vanguard of my generation. How could they forget the years when I fought at the head of the Group Avance? My prison terms and banishments under the Ibáñez dictatorships? You people forget that I have a working capital of one million votes to start with. In 1970 that will add up to 1.4 million if the Popular Unity parties support me."

His listeners smiled, but Allende insisted.

"What's more, I'm the only candidate who can unite the Left. With me there will be unity, without me . . ."

His associates were no longer listening.

In the white-blossom evenings of Santiago, the trees around the house on Guardia Vieja Street were laden with flowers and dust. Their branches touched the sidewalks and covered neighboring houses, hiding the gates used by families to crisscross from one house to another. The street seemed narrower and more isolated. Everyone in that small world knew each other well, and there was often a kind of inner traffic from garden to garden, through gates left unlatched.

Those who had begun to doubt Allende's power were inclined to look on him as another neighbor, now a well-established senator resting on his laurels, distinguished-looking with his white mustache. He was someone you acknowledge with a polite gesture, but from a respectful distance. Allende didn't particularly mind those anonymous days because he knew they wouldn't last long.

The summer skies would soon light up the barrios, and Allende would again find himself center stage, but with new means to fortify his role in this drama, now at the start of the final act.

One night he received a visit from a group of young socialists who had come to consult him about the new currents within the party since the Socialist Congress of 1967. Among them was Miria Contreras, la Payita, who had become close to Salvador during his campaigns and was now his private secretary and confidante.

Allende invited the group onto the terrace to sit near the garden. The conversation quickly turned to the elections, and Allende confessed that he wasn't particularly interested in delivering an opinion about possible names for 1970 since he had decided to run himself, and whatever opposition there might be from within the party did not concern him. Someone in the group exclaimed, with youthful enthusiasm, "Then we'll push you to the top!"

Allende responded, "No, it's not a question of that. The word is out that my speeches have gone stale, that the same old record has been going round and round since the fifties; it's said that the young people don't understand me and vice versa. The people saying these things are wrong. In '70 we'll have a program and a message. The message is very simple. There's no road to power other than unity—not the unity of slogans and symbols, but the deeper sort that comes from shared convictions and agreements when ideology becomes action. FRAP was our battle horse, and we rode into the fray on it in '58. Our strength has always been the unity of the workers' parties and the support of the middle class through the Partido Radical. This time we'll go further. We'll form a national front, unifying all of the anti-imperialist and anti-oligarchical forces. We'll tie in the leftist independents with the socialists and communists and with CUT and the farmers' federations. This national front will be the most powerful revolutionary movement in our history, and with it we'll make a socialist revolution right here in Chile. Only when we have a clearly structured program will we choose a candidate. We're not fighting for a president, we're fighting for a program."

Listening to Allende could have been simply the ritual of visiting Guardia Vieja Street. But it wasn't a question of rituals now. Allende was making it clear that he was returning to the battle with new weapons.

When did the relationship between la Payita and Allende become intimate? It began to grow without taking any particular shape at first. At times they would see each other after a packed work schedule, sometimes after weeks or months. At the outset Payita drew close to Allende in order to carry out her professional chores—screening visitors, juggling his political agenda. Soon she was spending a few hours each day in his library.

She could type with at least twice as many fingers as Allende. She knew how to listen, and would smile when he became wordy and grave. She disarmed him, giving him confidence, yet sowing doubts when it was necessary. Her beauty was placid and insinuating at the same time.

This was a passion kept invisible and difficult to define. It arrived with utmost simplicity, during pauses on the job. And one day, or one night, a garden gate is left open allowing someone in, noiselessly, like a vine growing undetected over a neighbor's fence. It keeps growing, sprouts buds and flowers, and advances a little more until it fills a space that hadn't even seemed to exist before. And there it stays, offending some and giving pleasure to others. Can't do anything about it now. The wall has been crossed, this time in silence, and without the slightest flurry within the families concerned.

She was an exuberant woman, charming and intelligent, a companion of endless resource, competent and capable of vision. She gave herself with passion to Allende's work. She took her place next to him with a certain naturalness and adapted to his routine with enthusiasm, her energy unflagging. Soon she was indispensable. Allende depended on her organizational instinct, and she was infallible at unraveling the skeins of vested interests and party intrigues.

I remember her at Guardia Vieja, her youthful smile, her delicate cheekbones, the bright eyes that could be cordial, tender, but cutting, too.

Salvador could not resist her.

From the embers of the scandal, a chorus of rebukes rose in the air, from militants, friends, and relatives.

"Nothing new," was the stock response. "Chicho is fond of women and full of fire. He doesn't care what anyone says."

Then the whole beehive cracked open, and out flew the rejected ones, the abandoned ones, the forgotten ones, the presently-in-love ones. The buzzing became overpowering. There were comments on lovers of varied ages and talents, in the political, literary, and even the sports arena.

And with all this, could he still be the candidate?

"No," she said. "It doesn't mean what you think it does. In the first place it's nothing new. It has happened many times. In the second place it's already been decided. There will be no changes. Everything—do you understand?—everything will remain the same."

But what did "the same" mean? And did I have the right to ask that question? Gossip ran rampant through the political corridors, the editing rooms of newspapers and magazines, and the newsrooms of radio and television stations.

There is no doubt that someone used the scandal as a strategic breach in the campaign. Someone who deepened it, sharpened it, and sent it out on the air. The afternoon dailies took care of the rest.

We were in a gallery with large windows. Tencha was sitting on a white rattan chair. I was standing, a glass of whiskey in my hand. I had been looking at some old photos: a snapshot of her dressed in the style of the thirties with a hairdo that emphasized the oval of her face and the light in her eyes. Why was he waiting to come down? All the guests were there. Through the window I could see the darkening water of the pool, and in the distance the shadows of large trees and the movement of indistinguishable shapes, perhaps night watchmen on duty.

I felt the temptation to refocus the lens on this meeting of friends in the summer dusk. I spoke to Tencha about the university years, the soirées thrown by Bellas Artes in Forestal Park, a clownish all-nighter that ended with a *bal masqué* at the Club Hípico, the sad, dark pianist who was playing Vanidad, the big hit that spring.

"And you went and disappeared on us all of a sudden. But the adventures of our own little street band—Los Afónicos—continued anyway, in and out of the crummy little theaters in the sticks."

We came back to the same theme after dinner, at the coffee hour, separating ourselves from the crowd. And I started to speak to her in a low voice, trying to reconnect the loose ends of a family circle that someone had unwittingly broken.

"I think about the loyalty of this man who puts himself on the line, ignoring his past for a risky future. The path leads in directions I don't understand and would like to ignore."

She observes me, first casually, then fixedly. I feel an implacable rejection of what I am about to say. Then she talks of wounds that I know nothing about, omitting names. The two of them had come together after living years in a kind of dignified intellectual bohemia. They were young revolutionaries, optimistic about coming changes, changes that perhaps were little more than slogans and student protest songs. Their banners streamed out over the slums in futile marches, later to be furled by disillusioned hands, only to appear again in another ephemeral springtime rally.

"This woman . . . ," I managed to say before she cut me off with her hand.

The terms of the pact were clear. It was a question of a whole life. The life of a militant leader who would be president. For certain. No one could change anything. The little garden gate had been opened and had stayed open. Tencha went and closed it with a slow, firm movement of her hand. No wavering, no doubts.

I said nothing.

"The shape of our life will be the same. You will never have seen such unity in our family as in this campaign. Never more dignity."

That is how it would be.

Salvador had invented a retreat, a place of intimacy hidden among trees and rocks. It was a solitude that was perhaps never comfortable, and that at times was painful and compromising. Yet it was filled with passion. How long would it last? Not long. The days were numbered.

"The doctor is retiring now," the servant announced.

We got up. She went to his side, and it appeared to me that an invisible ring surrounded her waist, like the subtle rings on a sequoia marking the passage of years of inconceivable length.

In August 1969 the Committee of the United Left was formed. It seemed like a routine act: the leaders got together in a room of the National Congress, made speeches, and tried out new alliances and tactical maneuvers, repeating the game of Chilean election years traditional since the dawn of time. But things really had changed, and those who presided over the electoral exercise of 1970 knew that procrastination was no longer possible and that Chilean democracy was approaching its hour of truth.

How to maintain the legalistic tradition that over more than thirty years had allowed peaceful rule in Chile? Every six years presidents had come and gone, the campaign had raised hopes and the people had been entertained for a time. The country would be covered with banners, graffiti, and posters. In the rest of Latin America, governments fell like ripe mangoes. Tricolored sashes flew in the air like kites, while military hats popped up on balconies above the crowds. Sent on a mission by Nixon, Nelson Rockefeller had returned from an excursion through the U.S.

embassies in Latin America with the political strategy for a new era—more generals and new manuals on counterinsurgency. Where there were no generals, a colonel would do. For Chile, however, Ambassador Korry recommended some Christian Democrats, but also that the door be left open a crack for any kind of military person to enter, regardless of rank. Just in case.

But in Chile a different kind of alarm had been sounding since 1958. Watch out for Allende. That buck can do some damage. Only the Right, if it gets angry enough, can stop the commies.

Luis Corvalán, secretary general of the Communist party, had said that in 1964 the country was offered a government by two parties—the socialists and the communists—and that such a formula had to be replaced in 1970 by an alliance of workers' parties with independent groups.

To counter that strategy the Right responded by electing a single flag bearer for the entire oligarchy.

It was then that the Christian Democrats had to defend their position as the majority party. Their road was clear, so clear that it became invisible: their only chance was to pick a candidate who could unite the far Right, the oligarchs, with the conservative elements of the bourgeoisie. But the Christian Democrats were divided during Frei's government. Temporarily dominated by a leftist faction, the party pushed the candidacy of Radomiro Tomic, a leader who could not attract the interest of voters to the right of center.

It became obvious that winning the election depended on who controlled the political pendulum oscillating between fascism and socialism.

"United," said Allende, "not behind a man, but behind a program that will change drastically the political and economic structure of the country, we shall win."

Then, as the players of presidential poker sat around the table, and the deck was cut for what seemed to be the final deal, a man grabbed the cards and exclaimed, "I don't care how many parties there are, I'll deal them all in."

That was Luis Corvalán, an ex-teacher, small and wiry. Condorito was his nickname, and he handled the selection of a candidate with the flair of a gambler who doesn't play the cards as they are printed, but invents them as he goes along.

There were five aces in the Popular Unity deck: a law professor, an agrarian reform specialist, an ex-senator of Ibáñez vintage, a poet, and Salvador Allende. The Partido Radical, which was behind law professor Alberto Baltra, recognized from the outset the need to give the socialists and communists priority. The party had already successfully promoted three candidates for the presidency with support from the Left—Aguirre Cerda, Ríos, and González Videla. It was time to give the others a turn.

The ex–Christian Democrat MAPU's couldn't gain a majority despite the fact that their candidate, the agrarian reform specialist Jacques Chonchol, could theoretically win the support of a youthful electorate.

Rafael Tarud, the ex-Ibáñez man, was the candidate for certain ghostly factions, extremely weak and vulnerable to the fiery attacks of Santiago's yellow press.

Naming Pablo Neruda as one of the candidates was a master stroke. In this way the party could pay homage to the loyal and disciplined militant while also saying that a communist could represent a larger spectrum of political forces in the democratic process. However, it was a known fact that the Communist party was not going to insist on Neruda. When the moment came they would withdraw his name in favor of another, were it deemed expedient. Did that bother don Pablo? He took it in stride, just as he reacted to all political matters—with restraint, humor, and patience.

Neruda's candidacy was proclaimed from the balcony of party headquarters by Senator Volodia Teitelboim. The reporters were drawn to Neruda like bears to honey. They followed him everywhere, ambushing him at every turn.

"What was that question, compañero?" Neruda was sitting in a comfortable rocking chair, observing with evident amusement the newspeople and photographers who surrounded him.

"Listen, don Pablo, now that you're a presidential candidate,

I can't help asking this. Let's suppose that you go to a restaurant and they offer you a choice of two tables. On one table the presidency of Chile is served up for you, and on the other the Nobel prize. Which table would you take?"

"Neither one. I'd go to another table."

"You got off easy on that one, don Pablo. Here's another. If you were elected president, would you keep taking those long siestas that you like so much, right in La Moneda?"

"Of course, compañero. I'll keep snoring away my siestas in peace, knowing that at least while I'm sleeping I won't be a threat to my compatriots."

Neruda laughed from the inside, shaking as though someone were tickling him.

A bizarre stream of pedestrian traffic began to flow through Santiago. At all hours of the day and night, people with briefcases scurried along the Alameda and Agustinas, Huérfanos, Teatinos, and San Martín streets. They streamed in and out of party headquarters, and into the less conspicuous canvas tents of Tarud's faction.

The secret meetings of the Popular Unity alliance were the scene of an endless in-house voting process: of the five candidates, three took the lead, each having received three votes. None of them could gain any distance over the others. Whoever got the fourth vote was the man. The voting continued from dawn to dusk. Steam from the reheated coffee floated over the balcony of the Partido Radical. The delegates kept an eye on the golden boys, checking their pulses and their general demeanor under the stress. One or another delegate seemed close to fainting. When, in a particularly boisterous meeting, the Tarud representative found his candidate losing the day, he took a deep breath and passed out. Emergency first-aid measures were applied, and, fully recovered, he asked for the floor. Everyone expected a biblical healing message urging peace and harmony for all. Instead, microphone in hand, he lambasted socialists and communists alike in a thunderous voice.

Condorito smiled innocently. He outfoxed the opposition at

every turn and sniffed out every trap. His goal was to knock off Tarud and then make a pact between the *radicales* and the socialists. Baltra should resign soon. Chonchol too. And with his strong arms and thick hands, his sad, ironic smile, from the heights of his Olympus, the poet Neruda would, in the final hour, open the narrow door for el Salvador.

But of course things got complicated. Allende—the perennial, losing candidate—had not been the majority candidate of his party's central committee, which had preferred Aniceto Rodríguez. If MAPU backed away from its candidates—and it had two strong ones, Chonchol and Rafael Gumucio, a possible substitute—it would probably support Neruda. Tarud's heavy artillery was planted squarely on the road, fiercely blocking it against all comers.

With the December 31, 1969, deadline already passed, and the rightist candidate firmly in place and campaigning, the Communist party played its big card. It called for a major assembly of all the forces of the Left on January 22. There it would announce the candidate who could unify them all, whoever that might be. And if there was no agreement among the Popular Unity parties the communists would stick with Neruda.

Surprisingly, Chonchol, Baltra, Allende, and Neruda resigned immediately in order to end the bottleneck. Only Tarud remained, a puzzling figure in the vast cement oasis of Plaza Bulnes, all alone, looking out at the empty, strange ocean like one of the stone gods of Easter Island.

The Communist party continued preparations for its big meeting, and the Popular Unity people, full of high spirits in the fine summer breezes, prepared for the ultimate showdown at Plaza Bulnes.

January 22 rolled around at last. The executive committee of the Popular Unity alliance stayed in session, arguing and voting, trying new magical formulas. In the afternoon the hopeful crowds moved toward Plaza Bulnes carrying flags and signs. The organizers were working frenetically. Uncertainty gave way to alarm. There's no candidate. Still? Still no candidate. What will we do?

And Neruda? Where is Neruda? No need to worry. He's very close, waiting for his turn. Will he accept? Are you crazy? You don't even ask that question. Neruda is the voice of the party, and the party is Neruda.

In the afternoon a hundred thousand people overflowed the space around La Moneda and spilled out toward Plaza Baquedano and Central Station.

Then the telephones rang in Teatinos and San Martín, the couriers ran with the news to the stage where the leaders had gathered. Standing on tiptoe, looking like a shipwrecked man in a sea of heads, Luis Corvalán silenced the shouting crowd by exclaiming, "The white smoke signal is up. The uncertainty is over! We have a candidate. It's Salvador Allende!"

Who could tell Allende that the long-awaited smoke signal, pale in color but hot with angry passions, would not rise up to the sky, but instead lie curled, heavy, and doomed around the neon lights and skyscrapers of Santiago?

The bard's house started as an elementary ode and was never finished. In the beginning it was a bedroom and a dining room, a living room and a fireplace, a little watchtower and an ocean kept at bay by a jumble of black rocks. But the ode required more space, corridors lined up like a four-line stanza, with grave and acute accents. Pablo and his master carpenter added beautiful, fragrant wood, stained glass, masts and beams, ships' figureheads, a locomotive in the garden, a giant shoe on one side of the house, and old hawsers and anchor chains. One room followed upon another, with ever more doors and windows. Few stairways. One night a bar appeared, and its brass railing rang with the echo of ancient storms; the chairs were round and friendly and were screwed to the wood of the deck. The poet-navigator raised his flag—a compass and a fish floating on a blue background—fluttering in the stiff, constant winds of the rocky coast. Isla Negra, Black Island, was the name of the place; but there never was an island, and the days and nights were shaded emerald green. The table became covered with cruets, glasses, and bottles. There the poet would sit with his companions and talk as in the old days, close to the sea, for the house had already become a ship with a port of call on the horizon, and its anchors strained and danced in the water and sand below.

Neruda would receive you in the early afternoon and walk you through corridors filled with globes, seashells, and venerable papyrus documents. Emerging from the end of the tunnel, you'd arrive at the bar. Sitting on a stool behind the bar, Neruda would display his aged wines for you.

Matilde's face seemed lit by a warm halo. That's the way Diego Rivera painted her. Her big, chestnut-colored eyes would shine with merriment as she presided over trips to the San Antonio market. Her baskets would fill with the treasures of the sea and the colors of the countryside. Neruda's famous odes to wonderful national dishes would materialize in the kitchen in her hands.

Allende went to visit them from his retreat at Algarrobo. Neruda had a tall glass ready with ice and whiskey when Allende came in. And a well-tuned ear. No complaints. On the contrary, he felt good about the outcome and relief that the presidential contest was over.

"I didn't want to be president," he said, "but my party handed me a serious mandate, and I'm happy to have performed well. Now you'll carry on, Salvador, and we won't give up, compañero. We won't even blink until it's all over and we've won. Salvador, we're going to win and you'll be president. Did you know? I'm telling you, I checked in with my own fortune-teller. We'll win. We have to get ready."

Allende listened, encouraged and smiling. But Pablo, who had quick intuitions, sensed a hint of anxiety behind the optimism.

"The campaign will be tough," he said, "and maybe even violent. Thankless days are ahead, and the enemy has sharp claws. They'll stop at nothing, and the heavies with sacks full of dollars and their instruments of terror will appear on the scene. From far away Nixon will command whole fleets of attackers. His reach is

long, and the packs of wild dogs are hungry here at home. But we'll know how to defend ourselves. You, Salvador, will have the cages to trap them with. Don't let them provoke you into anything rash. Just protect your flanks. The very best Chileans are with you."

"I'm not frightened, Pablo. In fact I'm not even worried. I know where we're going, and I think I know how to get there. If we win, and I think like you that we will, we'll have done the easiest part of the job. The tough part comes later. To be frank, I'm more worried about the enemy within than the ones outside. The inside enemy feels the rage of a cornered animal. When he sees that the game is up, all pretenses will disappear, and he'll attack from all sides. But from where first? At what precise moment?"

Pablo was fiddling with a toy, his latest novelty. It was a little glass ball that would change color according to the amorous vibrations of the person who held it. He didn't give it to Salvador yet. The time would come. He got up, walked over to the window and looked out on the beach. The words he spoke brought a smile to his lips, even as doubts furrowed his brow.

"This country has had presidents of every conceivable stripe—fat, bearded ones who governed very little, scarcely at all, obsessed as they were with their own physiology and the latest inventions on Place Pigalle. One of them died suddenly and didn't have time to destroy the erotic paraphernalia that he kept in his strongbox. His family had to call in an exorcist-priest before they could bury him. There was another president who used to take off with his secretary to samba in Copacabana. And another who took great delight in eating royal jelly with his fingers during cabinet sessions . . ."

Salvador recited the litany of their names in accompaniment to Pablo's descriptions.

". . . And another who used to drink wine out of a special cane during the Te Deum and break wind gustily, causing the archbishop to cough in a vain effort to mask the explosions."

Enjoying his whiskey, Pablo sighed and continued, "And there will be a president loved by his people, a president who won't know how to govern because his generous, good soul, free of malice, will not let him. And he will believe in justice as a natural condition of humankind, instead of as a paragraph in the constitution."

Walking out in the garden by the locomotive, they talked about the pact of the Popular Unity parties. How will it be possible to govern if one's actions are determined by the totality of the parties in the alliance, with decisions made by "a plurality"? How will it be possible if the "actions of the president and those of the parties will be coordinated by a political committee made up of all these forces"? When the going gets really tough, who will make the decisions? And after how many meetings? Then Salvador asked, "Won't we be presiding over the funeral of the saddest utopian bureaucracy? The order of chaos?"

Neruda answered, "We have so much faith in winning, Salvador, that we forget about chance. The more certain we are of winning, the more cautious we should be. The establishment press is already saying that the president of the Popular Unity alliance will be nothing but a puppet in the hands of the parties. Let's not allow a lack of trust to divide us. A little faith right now is worth a lot more than great wisdom. Let's give time some room to work in. We're a new movement and we're offering a program to the country that's never been conceived of before. We have to break the trail and erect the signposts as we go."

Matilde called them to supper. Pablo served his magical wines, for this occasion from festive flagons decorated with the roses of Bulgaria and the lavender of Hungary. The time came, as it often did on Isla Negra, for the siesta hour. Before he retired, Pablo put the little crystal ball into Salvador's hands, saying, "Squeeze it a little, let's see how your batteries are charging and discharging these days."

"El Pueblo Unido Jamás Será Vencido"

H is hands were freckled, and a slight breeze caused
an almost imperceptible movement in the hairs
that covered them. Actually, they weren't freckles, nor were they
old-age marks, but rather small rings of light that lent the reddish
complexion of his hands a mellow golden tint. He was alone at
his desk with the window slightly open. He took the fine glass in
his fingers and looked at the reflection of the ice cracking in the
honey-colored liquor. His hand was calm and strong. He settled
into the chair, and the smooth leather felt good—cool—against
the back of his neck. He drank slowly. That morning had seen the
nasty surprise of a heart attack. It had been a clear and simple
message—the sudden commotion of an accelerated heartbeat, the
confused feeling of emptiness, a vague queasiness in the stomach.
He had been walking in the center of the city with Hugo Miranda.
They went to a pharmacy and called Dr. Oscar Soto from there.

Once at home Tati took charge, without a fuss, calmly. Later
she reproached him gently, warning him bit by bit of his limitations.

Salvador raised the glass to his lips and the liquid spread its
warmth throughout his chest and down into his stomach.

He heard the big bells ring—2:00 P.M. He could hear strong
voices coming from the terrace, and laughter. No one would
know anything about what had happened this morning. The
party leaders were out there waiting for him. Oh, he had a long-
distance call? There was nothing unusual about it lasting a half-
hour or an hour even. Allende was the center of attention. Calls
came in from all over the country and abroad, at all hours.

Allende stood and put on his leather jacket. He looked at his reflection in the glass covering a painting, and walked decisively toward the door. He crossed through the living room and went onto the terrace, smiling. The circle opened to receive him. He radiated strength, cracked jokes, yet continued to monitor the reactions of those around him. That day he was going to discuss the Forty Measures of the Popular Unity parties with its leaders.

Aniceto Rodríguez, a veteran assemblyman, was talking. He looked strong, handled himself elegantly, and measured every word. He analyzed the electoral power of the Popular Unity alliance throughout the country, province by province. He interrupted himself to confirm some precise detail with the others. He would turn toward Allende, pointing to locations on an invisible map. Corvalán, gray haired and reserved, had a youthful, ironic air, and spoke in short, crisp phrases. Allende felt good. Here were the best, all together—leaders tested in the cross fire at the polls and in the tough years of repression and persecution.

"No one is trying to outfox anybody around here," said Allende. He was computing voting projections in his head, and numbers weren't the problem. For the first time Chile was engaged in a political struggle over whether to change the social order of the nation from the roots up. Two political programs were on a collision course, dramatizing a deeply explosive class struggle.

Tencha said something about the role women should play in the campaign.

"The working woman," she said, "gets a taste of the revolutionary spirit every day in her collision with women in rich neighborhoods who have already taken to the streets, beating on their pots and pans, in protest against our revolutionary movement."

Tencha had helped organize a wide intellectual base for Allende's campaigns, and she was by this time a totally engaged political militant. Together with Laura Allende, and other outstanding professional women, Tencha had assumed a fighting role in this campaign, speaking in plazas, theaters, and stadiums, revealing a surprising and powerful political style.

A new angle for this campaign was developing. The leaders weighed, one by one, the problems that Allende would face as he campaigned throughout the countryside.

"Obviously you can't cover it all, and there will have to be rallies without the candidate in person."

"Each local leader is the candidate, as long as what he presents to the people is our program," said Allende.

The Forty Measures, carefully elaborated by Allende in consultation with the leaders, and based on the charter of the Popular Unity alliance, was now the battle flag of his candidacy.

The leaders remained silent. They were counting on the arrival of a reporter from the *New York Times*. When he finally showed up, Allende summarized the program for him.

"According to the statistics," he said, "one-half of the children in Chile under the age of fifteen are undernourished; 700,000 children are mentally retarded because of a lack of protein, especially in the first months of their lives. There are 300,000 able-bodied people who lack employment, and 43 percent of the general population suffers from an inadequate diet. In 1970 and 1971, 500 million dollars will leave the country to pay interest and amortization on our foreign debt. . . . We are determined to form a pluralist, nationalist, democratic, revolutionary government that will lead the march toward socialism. We're not saying that we're going to establish a socialist regime overnight. Socialism doesn't happen by decree, it's a process of social development. Our program establishes three areas: the state sector, the mixed sector—that is, both state- and privately owned—and the private sector. This is the program that responds to our reality in Chile, and it is the basic step. First we must recover our natural resources—copper, iron, nitrates—that today are in the hands of foreign capital, especially North American capital. Then we must nationalize the monopolies that are so influential in the social and economic development of the country. And to all this we must add a far-reaching, well-planned agrarian reform, the nationalization of the banks, and state control of foreign trade."

Irritated by the tone of the reporter's questions, Allende stated,

"From your perspective to be a communist or a socialist is to be in favor of totalitarianism. For me that is not so. I believe that man is free only when he distances himself from alienation. Man is free when economic conditions can guarantee him work, nourishment, housing, health, rest, and recreation."

When requested to be more specific on the question of expropriation, Allende said, "We have stated that we will concentrate on the expropriation of those investments that fundamentally influence the development of the national economy. For example, copper is the basic wealth of Chile. We believe that our copper mines should be in the hands of Chileans."

Allende did not waver on the question of violence. "The right wing is an element linked to imperialist interests, and it is ready to use any means available to exercise and maintain its authority. It will use violence, economic chaos, and terrorist attacks against individuals. We will respond to reactionary violence with revolutionary violence, but we will respond only. We reject terrorism as a matter of principle, because of our ideology and our humanistic convictions."

With regard to foreign relations, Allende declared that his program proposed links with Cuba, North Vietnam, China, and other nations with revolutionary regimes, and that it would vigilantly counter all attempts at political, economic, or military intervention on the part of imperialist nations.

The campaign was brief, tough, and sinister.

Jorge Alessandri, big, unsteady, and emaciated, traveled around the Chilean countryside dragging the tails of an overcoat too long for him. He moved along his campaign trail cursing and threatening enemies of past centuries and defending his interests in a paper and cardboard mill. One ill-fated evening in front of the tv cameras, his hands trembled so violently that the inkwells and the pens on the fake desk danced together, the water jumped out of his glass, and the microphones buzzed in irritation. In a moment of improvisational oratory, it occurred to him to say, "Those who wish to have us submit to the kind of slavery that characterizes certain countries that will go nameless will not be successful in their attempts. In Chile we still have a public militia and the carabineros, who will not allow criminal doctrines to prevail. If necessary they would act, motivated by the highest patriotism, to save us even at the cost of our beloved liberty."

It was a call for a barracks uprising, and one that required some fast backpedaling on Alessandri's part.

Allende covered ground too. Instead of the Victory Train of years past, he now used a DC-3 of World War II vintage. Union leaders, intellectuals, singers, and bodyguards were his traveling companions. His speaking style had lost the old assemblyman's rhetoric and was now terse and economical, well-muscled with statistics. There was no place in this campaign for the Curate of Catapilco or for spur-of-the-moment coups d'état.

The Popular Unity parties mobilized a whole world of poets, painters, musicians, and actors. The call was direct: take the jam sessions to the street, go from the circus tents to the plazas and parks of Chile, from the imposing, patrician stage of the municipal theater to the makeshift bleachers of O'Higgins Park.

The campaign needed songs, so Sergio Ortega wrote "Venceremos" and "El pueblo unido." A mobile, ever-present concert of guitars, drums, panpipes, and *charangos* livened up the marches. In the midnight jam sessions, the "new song" movement was led by the Parras, Víctor Jara, Rolando Alarcón, El Indio Pavez, Nano Acevedo. Songs sung in chorus at the ends of rallies became vibrant hymns in the repertory of Quilapayún and Inti-Illimani.

A new history was emerging from the murals on the walls of the Ramona Parra Painting Brigade—a history of Chile never taught in classrooms, consecrating the memory of such revolutionary heroes as the Matta brothers, Recabarren, Lafertte, Aguirre Cerda, and Allende.

The Right, alarmed, defended itself with some masterly examples of terrorist propaganda. The radio and television stations, the press, and the rumor mills repeated day and night that Allende was opening the doors of Chile to Russian communism.

From the beginning of his campaign, Allende had smelled the new tactics of the enemy. Strange tourists popped up in Santiago—people who looked uncomfortable in their civilian clothing, accustomed as they were to presenting arms, giving orders, and marching in the remote outposts of counterinsurgency training. They came from the North, their pockets stuffed with dollars, mysterious little leather notebooks, and bank-account numbers.

An international net was being spread to stop Allende. Scruples to the winds. The Tigers of the North were about to initiate a bloody World Series.

"Allende?" President Nixon asked one day in a press conference. "Who is Allende? Those people down there were not born yesterday. They're not about to give over their beautiful country to a communist."

But the popular campaign rose to a fever pitch, and Kissinger's traveling agents and the members of his Committee of 40 evaporated from Chile, frightened by the disciplined, militant masses at the Popular Unity rallies. In Valparaíso, 100,000 people; in Santiago, 800,000.

The Right's reaction was totally unheard of in Chilean political history, although it had made various attempts in the past to respond with arms to the challenge of a popular wave. Now, a strange political group of unknown origin cropped up, with bizarre connections in the U.S. and mysterious agendas. Like clouds in a winter storm, they gathered and struck with unexpected force. They blew in from secret meetings, sudden trips abroad, and clandestine interviews in Miami, using laundered funds and contraband arms unloaded at dawn from makeshift hangars. Odd leaders captained these groups. The headquarters of the Fatherland and Freedom party had never been an authentic horror show; at its best it couldn't even inspire curiosity. Closed and forbidding, it had become an incongruous ruin. Nothing seemed to be going on. But the rank and file, when they spoke at all, made reference to a network of armed squads spread all the way from Providencia to the high-class neighborhoods.

Patrols of masked men carrying chains and clubs jumped participants in the Popular Unity marches. Swastikas were seen mixed with Chilean flags. Burning torches lit up nocturnal rallies, and violent speakers barked their message into the night from Forestal Park and the foothills of San Cristóbal Hill. Weird birds indeed.

Central headquarters for the sorcerers of ITT and Pepsi was an office in a public building in downtown Santiago. It was attacked one morning by a group of pistol-packing communist youths who made off with the complete confidential propaganda package of Andalién, the advertising company hired to perform subliminal terrorism through the media. The scaffolding of the fascist propaganda effort collapsed. The bullies headed for cover with their tails between their legs.

Anything is possible, the fortune-tellers were saying. And these were second-class fortune-tellers at best, sitting before their old typewriters in poorly lit editorial rooms under dense clouds of cigarette smoke. A slick reporter, writing the evening news, said, "Allende is dying. Cancer or a heart attack. Pick one. But one way or the other, for sure." He went on to say that the leaders of the Popular Unity alliance and the Christian Democrats were meeting in secret to prepare another of the headlines of the century: Allende and Tomic would be pulling out of the race. "Who will be the new candidate of the 'pueblo unido jamás será vencido' party? The answer—and keep this under your hat: Gabriel Valdés or Felipe Herrera. Don Jorge is sure to win."

Allende went on tv to demonstrate that, contrary to rumors, he was fit as a fiddle. "How about your little problem when you were down south?" "Just a little cold." "How about that time in downtown Santiago?" "Indigestion, ate too much."

Those guesswork reporters never knew that Tomic and Allende did meet five times in secret. They would throw off their pursuers by going in and out of buildings and getting in and out of cars.

Some points emerged from their conversations, which, without being revelations, at least served to clarify what the campaign would actually be like and what type of government would be established.

"You're wrong, Salvador, if you think that the U. S. will let you nationalize the copper mines just like that, without paying an indemnity."

Allende said that his nationalization program was based on the excessive earnings of the North American companies. Tomic warned him, "They'll ambush you."

Tomic had expressd his opinion on this and other matters in an interview with *Ercilla* magazine. "Without the Christian Democratic party there is no such thing as popular unity in Chile. . . . The choice facing Chile is clear: either a government with deep roots among the people, thoroughly engaged in a revolutionary and democratic effort of national scope, or the frustration, unhappiness, hunger, and excessive foreign dependency that will bring on yet another coup followed by a military dictatorship. . . . There is no way forward now for Chile within the context of capitalism, especially neo-capitalism."

Allende, on more than one occasion, tried to joke with Tomic but was stopped cold by that fiery smile of his.

It was clear that any leftist government would have to stare down two gun barrels: one belonging to Nixon, for whom Allende simply meant the red flag of communism and an imminent attack on the copper companies; and the other of the Chilean Right, for whom both Tomic and Allende represented the victory of the rabble, which needed to be kept in its place.

Before shaking hands after their last conversation, the candidates agreed that if neither one got an absolute majority—and the election had to be decided by a plenary session of Congress—there'd be no nasty tricks. Whoever got a plurality would have the support of the other in the final round.

And then, in 1970, something happened that intrigued me. A strong pressure in support of the Allende candidacy came from the provinces, sweeping away the opposition. The thrust of the campaign had been felt most in the north and in the mining zone of the south. A solid network of political bases grew fast, and when election day rolled around, Allende had become the sole hope of a nation that had always lived in crisis but that only now seemed aware of such a fact.

Another interesting thing happened. I was coming from Temuco on one of those milk-run flights that ferry congressional representatives back to Santiago on Sunday afternoons, after the weekend. The top brass of the conservative parties—the whole bloody establishment—was on that flight. With some misgivings I took a seat in the first row. An economics professor whom I had met at the University of Concepción sat next to me.

From behind us the bellowing of the big shots from the south could be heard—powerful, arrogant voices. No one was even talking politics, they were so sure of don Jorge's victory!

Then, in what I hoped was a moderate tone of voice, I asked my neighbor, the professor, "So who do you think will win after all?"

He answered me in a smooth, even voice. The odd thing is, that as he began talking, a silence grew in the cabin of the plane until finally all of the representatives were quiet and you could hear only the droning voice of my friend, recounting statistics, historical data, demographic observations, and some surprising predictions.

"Allende is going to win," he said finally, in a prophetic voice.

I had two sensations: first, that someone would get up and slug him; second, that his argument was indisputable. He could not be wrong. As said in a poem by Pezoa Véliz, "The last shovelful of dirt was tossed, and still no one spoke up."

I said goodbye to my fortune-telling friend and got off the plane feeling like one of the new apostles getting off St. Peter's boat—absolutely sure of carrying the Good News. Allende will win.

September 4, 1970, finally rolled around. The most famous public-polling wizards of the United States gathered in

Santiago and handed their predictions to *El Mercurio*. "The winner is Alessandri," they assured the newspaper. "Allende? Third place. That's it." Their "public opinion" survey had been carried out in Washington.

Throughout a quiet, sunny day, the Chileans voted in stadiums, schools, and railroad stations; then they retired to their houses to await the results. Early in the afternoon, honking caravans of cars drove down from the wealthy suburbs proclaiming Alessandri's victory. But as the hours passed, and the street lamps and neon signs lit up the dusk on that warm spring night, the caravans slowly began to peter out. Soon, what had begun as the departure of a few cars turned into a retreat of alarming dimensions. Allende was beginning to pull ahead, slowly and laboriously. The minister of the interior, hesitating and doubtful during the afternoon, revealed a surprising bit of information: Alessandri was losing ground.

In the Guardia Vieja house, Allende was following the results at his desk, along with Puccio, Humberto del Canto, and Miria Contreras. Tencha and the rest of the family were in the living room with a group of friends.

The hours went by. At 11 P.M. Allende called General Camilo Valenzuela, who was in charge of keeping order in Santiago, and requested authorization for a street rally. He added that he couldn't contain his supporters much longer. The general said that he would have to consult with the government. After a while the phone rang. Allende thanked the general. He stood and said, "We have won."

He quickly went to the living room and embraced Tencha and his daughters. He arranged for the rally to take place in front of the Federation of Chilean Students building on Bernardo O'Higgins Avenue. Aniceto Rodríguez spread the word to the people of Santiago.

That night GAP, the Grupo de Amigos del Presidente, made its debut in providing security for the new president. The guard was made up of militants of MIR, who had quickly assembled in Tati's room and prepared a plan of action to protect Allende.

My friends and relatives left Ñuñoa in a truck, waving big

Chilean flags. I went on foot from my house across from Forestal Park, and was able to get within a block of the Federation of Students building. As I walked along I met up with people in all stages of ecstasy, euphoric, hugging, sobbing, and shouting, "At last, at last! It's like a dream, we've won!" Previously confined to "moral victories," these people finally had a palpable triumph in their hands. What would happen to us now?

From that distance I could barely see the silhouette of Allende, who spoke quietly in short sentences. He asked for calm, and held out a conciliatory hand to his adversaries.

"I am only a man," he said, "with all of the weaknesses and failings of any man, and just as I was able to take the defeats of the past, I can now accept without reservation or vindictiveness today's victory, which is in no sense a personal one. I owe it to the *radicales*, the socialists, the communists, the members of API and MAPU, the thousands of independents. These are the people who will walk through the doors of La Moneda with me on the fourth of November. . . . If victory was tough, tougher yet will be the task of consolidating that victory and constructing a new society. My only desire is to be your compañero president. Chile is blazing a trail that other peoples of America can follow, each country according to its own history and reality. Revolution doesn't imply destruction, it means construction. It doesn't mean demolition, it means building, and the people are prepared for this task. . . . I want to point out that our adversaries in the Christian Democratic party have recognized the popular victory. . . . Workers of the nation: you and only you are the winners. . . . The people, on this weekend, will take the country by the waist and will dance from Arica to Magallanes, from the mountains to the sea, in an enormous *cueca*, symbol of the robust joy of our victory."

As he was winding up his talk, I looked around and suddenly felt a sense of panic. The crowd was jumping up and down. Allende had disappeared from the balcony. People kept on jumping. A few days earlier, what had seemed like a million people had performed the same ritual during the last rally of the campaign, shouting, "If you don't jump you're a stiff!"

All of the leaders were jumping, but what was Pablo Neruda

to do, with his phlebitis and enormous body? He did a little shuffle on the boards, and the crowd accepted that.

I started to make my way toward one side of the Alameda, in the direction of Santa Lucía Hill. It was like cutting through the center of a whole nation. Slowly and steadily I beat a retreat. Walking around the hill toward Forestal Park, I realized that as one-half of the country was jumping for joy in the early light of dawn, the other half was waiting to continue on a spree of terror that had been in full swing for years and that was not even its exclusive little party, but one hosted by generations of fearful citizens. Those who fled the center of the city that night to pull down their posters of don Jorge, their banners and crests, began to pack their bags, wrap their jewels and art objects, stuff their dollars into wine jugs. The other half slept, resting up for the task of transforming Chile.

The night enfolded us all. In the heart of the city, the illuminated image of the Virgin was like a gust of snow against the thick, dark buttress of the cordillera. We had always been divided and had always hid the fact with the tactics of those who learn how to live without living, feigning life. "We are a big family," we would say to each other. And so we would share the table, never realizing that the table was precisely what had separated us.

On a day like that, history becomes accelerated and there's no time to sit down and take minutes. The factors that would push us into the realm of confrontation were not totally clear or definable, nor were the identities of the people who, with their weapons, would spell doom for us. We had come from a great distance, a few centuries of huge stone heads left on islands, to bearded men on horseback, oarsmen and lancers, togas and robes, arrows, bushy sideburns, cannons and gunners, severe lords and pious doñas, altars reflecting our grandeur as a nation and our helpless state of alms-seeker, given to the quest for wealth and the ritual of escape, branded by the fear of seismic eruptions and fire.

An illustrious president, José Manuel Balmaceda, having observed how the assailants of the republic threw grand pianos from balconies in a wretched assault against his followers, lay down on a narrow, unfamiliar bed and meditated placidly on the sufferings of Chile. He decided that all of the events on earth happen as in a stampede, without granting the time needed to think. After shutting the windows he put a bullet in his brains.

On this day Allende, still without a revolver, was heading for Guardia Vieja Street, also thinking that we weren't going to have time. It would be best to squeeze every drop out of the remaining hours and minutes and quickly lay hands to the task ahead. It was not just a new beginning, but a matter of life and death. He would be one of the first to enter his office on that day. On his agenda he would find the following message: "Memo: R. Nixon has decided that the new administration of Chile is defined by copper-mine expropriation; thus, Allende will be eliminated, overthrown, or obstructed."

September 15, 1970, Nixon instructs his people. Richard Helms takes notes:

> One in 10 chance perhaps, but save Chile!
> worth spending
> not concerned risks involved
> no involvement of embassy
> $10,000,000 available, more if necessary
> full-time job—best men we have
> game plan
> make the economy scream
> 48 hours for plan of action (Davis, *The Last Two Years*, p. 8)

The days immediately preceding Congress's confirmation of Allende's election were decisive.

Early in the morning following election day, Tomic phoned Allende's house. But Allende had not slept there. A massive threat was buzzing across the telephone lines in Santiago. At the advice of his bodyguards, the president-elect had sought refuge in the house of Dr. Eduardo Paredes's father. The high-speed trips down

Santiago's avenues had begun, and the whispered exchange of secret messages. The armed defense network fell into place. Allende boasted about the security measures that his people took for him. "Come, come," his guards said. "It's not like it used to be—a mere question of taking precautions during daylight hours. Now it's a matter of ambushes and brutal assaults."

In the past, Chilean presidents would walk unguarded through the center of the city—as Allende wanted to do. Alessandri and Aguirre Cerda had done so. "Those aren't streets out there, compañero president," said the GAP forces, "but one great big target range, crawling with Sunday shooters just itching to be president."

Tomic announced that he would come by to say hello to Allende at 9 A.M. The rumor traveled over the wire services, and in a few minutes hundreds of newspeople and photographers had assembled at Guardia Vieja Street.

Allende headed home quickly. When he noticed the commotion, he changed direction and went down Jorge Isaacs Street. Detouring through the house of his neighbor, Miria Contreras, he arrived at his desk at precisely the moment that Tomic entered the house.

There was nothing to say. Tomic and Allende were walking onto a stage where the preestablished roles precluded actual dialogue. Tomic's visit simply meant that Allende was recognized as the president-elect by his adversary, and that the big doors of the plenary Congress were slowly opening to him.

In the early hours of October 22, on some street corner in Santiago, faceless agents finally had their rendezvous. They weren't after Allende. Their intended prey was General René Schneider.

The general's blue Mercedes-Benz advanced at normal speed along the wet pavement. His driver and bodyguard was at the wheel. It was after 8 A.M., and they were heading for the Ministry of Defense. At the corner of Martín de Zamora and Américo Vespucio, three cars blocked their way, while a red jeep hit the car from the rear. The terrorists, armed with machine guns and pistols, jumped out of their cars. One of them broke the windows of the Mercedes with a club. General Schneider tried to remove his pistol from his briefcase, but a burst of machine-gun fire crumpled him in his seat. The driver was also shot, and he died instantly.

The attackers had practiced the coup for weeks. They were acting under the orders of a sinister group of associates, among them businessmen, big landowners, and a foreigner who had made a special trip to try out his aim.

Once the crime was committed, the killers disappeared, fleeing so quickly and successfully that they didn't stop until they reached the other side of the Andes; the fact is, they didn't stop until they reached California.

General Schneider was kept alive for 48 hours. He died one day after the plenary session of Congress.

The Schneider Doctrine, and its implications—particularly the army's expected acceptance of the judgment of the plenary Congress—made the general the target of the terrorist act. His assassination had been geared to create panic in the nation and to provoke the armed forces. There was indeed a reaction, but not the one the terrorists had hoped for; the armed forces closed ranks to defend the government. The whole country, stirred by the crime, submitted to military command and joined the government in demanding respect for the constitution. The Workers' Federation declared a two-hour general work stoppage.

In Congress some national and international political players had been preparing a cruel farce. Among Washington's Committee of 40 and the executives of ITT, it was known as the "Rube Goldberg gambit," an ill-conceived, cockamamy scheme if there ever was one. The right-wing representatives were to vote for Alessandri in the plenary Congress and, with the votes of the Christian Democrats, elect him president. Alessandri would then resign, thus necessitating a new election. Frei, now legally eligible

for reelection, would be the candidate of the National party and the Christian Democrats, thanks to Tricky Dick, ITT, and Pepsi Cola.

It actually seemed that this farce might be pulled off, until the morning of the attack on General Schneider. Alessandri was shaken by the violence of the incident, and realizing that the Rube Goldberg gambit was a public scandal, asked his followers not to vote for him. The Christian Democratic leaders agreed to give their votes to Allende, demanding as a condition that he sign a statute of constitutional guarantees.

Schneider lay dying in the military hospital when the plenary Congress finally decided: 153 votes for Allende, 35 for Alessandri, and 7 abstentions. The next day, Sunday, October 25, General Schneider died. Frei, Allende, and all the Popular Unity parties attended the funeral. The insignias of the Chilean regiments flew together with the red flags of socialism.

On November 3, Allende was sworn in and received the presidential sash from Frei's hands in the great hall of the National Congress building. The ministers of the Christian Democratic party walked out, dressed in frock coats, their fancy duck-tail hairdos slicked down with brilliantine. The ministers of the Popular Unity parties walked in with tired steps, dressed in modest business suits. They were led by José Tohá, now minister of the interior, tall, thin, and distinguished. The old guard was leaving the venerable cloister, and the new team had come to surpass the moral victories of the past.

Allende had asked that the traditional Te Deum, presided over by Cardinal Raúl Silva Henríquez, be an ecumenical ceremony.

The carriages waited outside. The horses, nervous and sweating. The coachmen, sporting coats, top hats, and white spats, doing their best to enter the annals of history too.

The celebration at La Moneda was a public bash. And Mama Rosa, the nanny who had cared for Allende as a child, was stationed in the Patio of the Orange Trees, presiding over the scene from a big chair.

A squadron of air force planes streaked through the spring sky

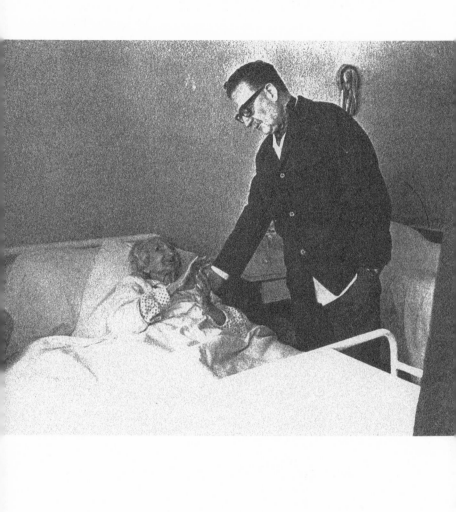

over Santiago. Little paper flags waved in the hands of the crowd. Allende walked out of Congress, and instead of getting into the presidential carriage, continued on foot, followed by his ministers. He walked all the way to the cathedral. Before entering, he stopped and greeted the crowds. One image remained with him from that victory day at noon: a clear blue sky and the combat planes practicing nosedives over the old rooftops of La Moneda.

Bye, Bye, Guardia Vieja

As the city of Santiago grows out toward the cordillera, its wealth becomes more ostentatious; the magnificent homes grow taller where the wood glistens and the cobblestones shine from the moisture of melted snow and rushing rivers. Wealth means country clubs, supermarkets, and a taste for blue jeans and polo shirts. The Mapocho River is forgotten. Indeed, here the rivers don't even come down from the hills: they evaporate in costly clouds of aerosol. The heads of families, faces shining in the morning sun, descend ill-humoredly into the heavy smog and soot of the old center of the city.

Smoke, mud, and potholes belong to another Santiago—the one paved with stones around the turn of the century—and to today's shantytowns, built from sticks, stones, and newspapers.

Allende intended someday to move the government from Santiago to Valparaíso. Later he thought of moving it further north, and then to the rainy, coal-mining south, and then to Aysén, to Tierra del Fuego, to Punta Arenas, and finally to the Antarctic. These ruminations may have been purely symbolic, but there was nothing symbolic about the move that Allende himself made from Guardia Vieja to Tomás Moro Avenue. Gossip columnists claimed that he was abandoning tradition for utopia. But Allende was not thinking about Sir Thomas More; he simply felt that his house was too small for the activities of a president. Eventually he bought El Cañaveral, a retreat made of beautiful stout logs, next to a river in the rocky solitude of El Arrayán.

The house on Tomás Moro Avenue was roomy and laid out in such a way that minor additions could be made easily. It was next to a convent, and the atmosphere had a calming effect on Allende. From then on he preferred to receive his closest friends and most-important visitors there. Traffic increased steadily as people came from all over to observe the birth of Chilean socialism.

One summer morning I got a call from Tencha's office in La Moneda. Her secretary advised me that I was invited to a private luncheon with her and a small group of friends, to welcome the great Argentinian writer Julio Cortázar. I had never met him. I went to the palace at the appointed time and waited for the writer in the company of Dr. César Cecchi. Cortázar arrived a little after 1:00. I was intrigued by this well-mannered, almost timid, giant with his French-sounding r's. Cortázar told the small group of luncheon guests that he had rented a car and gotten lost looking for beaches off the highways in the south, enjoying his trip over dirt roads and across trembling bridges. He appreciated the warmth of the people along the way. I liked hearing him, because without fanfare or pretense, he told us the birth of a magical story, such as the one he had written about the foundation, destruction, and rebirth of Solentiname in Nicaragua. We could sense his solidarity with Chile and his deep affection for it. He had come without notice on his way to Argentina, his purpose to salute the small miracle of our Popular Unity victory.

After lunch, walking down the corridor that led to the exit onto Morandé Street, we went by the president's office. A door opened and Allende appeared, accompanied by Foreign Relations Minister Clodomiro Almeyda. The president embraced Cortázar, saying, "This first visit requires a second one. How about tomorrow evening?"

Cortázar accepted, and we were to join Allende for dinner at his Tomás Moro Avenue residence.

Allende and Almeyda were buoyant. The first phase of the popular government was ending, and it had just won a solid victory in the municipal elections. Allende's work schedule was intense, his measures bold. He had confused his enemies by fearlessly plunging into the heart of the nation's most serious problems. His courage and political savvy would not take long to produce dramatic results.

The next day, on our way to Tomás Moro Avenue for dinner, Cortázar told me that on July 10, 1971, he had gotten together a group of Chilean friends in Paris to celebrate the Day of National Dignity, which signaled the nationalization of the copper mines.

A lady friend of mine was driving. She would leave us at the door, since she had not been invited. A reactionary through and through, deserving of the current epithet in Chile—a "mummy" —she nonetheless found some good things to say about Salvador. We were heading at normal speed down Bilbao Street when we heard the screaming sirens of the president's escort. Rocketing forward, changing lanes and taking curves at high speed, the Fiats zoomed by us. My friend, a neighbor of the Allendes, complained about the noise.

"Why can't they drive like everyone else?" she said. "Who do they think they are?"

And then she spoke of the scarcity of everything and the ignorance of the ministers, about how pushy the communists were, and how it would be better if Allende would muzzle his bodyguards and keep them in line. Cortázar kept quiet. We drove up to the entrance, where a carabinero asked for identification. My friend didn't show any documents, saying she was bringing us for dinner. Then she left us, still surrounded by the cloud of innocence that seems to accompany people who have never left the *barrio alto*. She made a U-turn, and disappeared in the elegance of her late-model Mercedes.

Tencha received us, and a little later Allende came down. They poured us a whiskey, and Tencha took me to a sitting room, where we talked about her international campaign to fund and create the Museum of Solidarity with Chile. As we spoke I looked at the paintings and art objects that had been lost in the tight space of the Guardia Vieja Street home, but that here stood out magnificently. Tencha, in her light dress, was again the very figure of fragile, mysterious beauty whom I had known at the Pedagogical Institute. I sensed her happiness and enthusiasm as she chatted about her many projects.

The walls were ablaze with the bold brush strokes of David Alfaro Siqueiros, the wide planes of Guayasamín, the placid Indian symbols of Diego Rivera, and the solitary landscapes, magically aquatic, of Julio Escámez. Nature offered a timid contrast to the Latin American masters, as a pale light filtered through the windows, mixed with green reflections from the garden.

When we moved into the dining room, I noticed that Cortázar was asking Allende questions. Among other things he wanted to know how the president was going to defend himself from the Nixon siege.

"We are facing a two-headed enemy. Nixon is the simpler of the two, just out to trick and liquidate us," said Allende, "but our local enemy is a bloodthirsty hound."

Tencha had taken pains to invite young guests, sons and daughters of diplomats. They too asked questions, expressed doubts and fears.

At the other end of the table, Joan Garcés, political advisor to Allende, followed the conversation in silence. But then he spoke up in a gentle voice that I seemed to recognize. I wondered which university he had attended, where he had acquired the strong background in political science that was obvious in his conversation, and where he had developed such a firm sense of revolutionary purpose. I was intrigued by his way of raising the level of the discussion without a hint of impatience, directing the argument above mundane conflicts to the social realm in which the destiny of the popular government would be determined.

Some months later, during an intimate dinner with the president and Tencha, the Mexican ambassador, and Garcés, I had another opportunity to admire the serene composure and astute judgment of this adviser. On that occasion the party chiefs were about to arrive to discuss the terms of solving a strike at the copper mines. Allende asked Garcés in a relaxed voice, "What are our limitations here?" And Garcés gave a figure, a percentage, offhandedly, like someone who is telling you what the temperature is outside; but that piece of data happened to contain the key to resolving the strike.

Cortázar wanted an update on the state of affairs, and so he was told about the far-reaching revolution of 1971 and how the president, with his militant cabinet, had proceeded to nationalize the copper mines, raise the salaries of workers and government employees, stabilize the cost of gasoline, electricity, and transportation, and plan the construction of low-cost housing on a grand scale.

More details of the offensive were provided by Allende: how the government had created a National Economic Council to nullify decrees used by the previous government to increase prices; how the government was able to expropriate the powerful textile factory Bellavista Tomé by taking out of mothballs an old decree of the socialist republic of 1932; how the government had been able to gain control over large chemical, cement, and steel industries, as well as hydroelectric plants, by buying stocks through the offices of CORFO, founded in 1939 by the Aguirre Cerda administration.

Paying no attention to the "screams" of the economy that Nixon had prophesied, the people's government applied articles of the Work Code to intervene in companies that were sabotaging production by citing labor disputes as an excuse for low output. The Telephone Company of Chile was snared in this way, allowing the government to enter into its affairs to combat the abusive monopoly of the parent company, ITT, which controlled the national telephone wires through a mammoth contract.

"Nor are we hesitating," Allende stated, "to nationalize the Lota Schwager Coal Mine, the Chilean holdings of the Pacific Steel Company, and the Bethlehem Mining Corporation. Who is screaming now?"

It wasn't possible to tell our visitor of all the accomplishments making the Popular Unity parties so proud at that time. But I had cut out a news article for him on the Second Message to Congress, on May 21, 1972, in which Allende had described the impressive growth of copper production and of the Chilean economy in general.

"In 1971 we produced about 730,000 tons of copper, a production level never reached before. We also broke a record in steel production with 640,000 tons, 10 percent more than in 1970. The output of electricity increased 16 percent. All in all, our national industries have reached the highest rate of growth since 1930."

One of the young people at the dinner mentioned the agrarian reform issue. He was told that the program had been initiated under Frei's Christian Democratic administration, but that it had been a timid effort. In 1971 Allende expropriated 1,300 large land-holdings—latifundios—totaling more than three million hectares.

Decrees had thundered out like cannon shots, brutal replies to the conservatives' wily efforts to reach an understanding with Allende. It would be so easy to give in just a little, the emissaries would say, to follow González Videla's example and close the door and lock it, for the sake of public well-being. Allende had been intransigent, carrying out his reforms with the accumulated fire and passion of decades spent scrapping his way to the presidency. At that moment Allende had full control of the government, and he was moving ahead of the leaders of the Popular Unity parties, who had not yet begun to sabotage him. Joan Garcés's thesis, which fascinated all of us that night, particularly Cortázar, was complex. According to him, the right wing's escalation of sabotage and terrorism was a form of suicide, which could finish off not only the Popular Unity government, but the state as a democratic institution. About the future, Garcés said, "A major coup capable of defeating us would also mean the definitive political defeat of the Chilean bourgeoisie as a competitive social force. The coup would be followed by a cycle of dictatorships making impossible a return to a democratic system of free competition. Everyone would be fully aware of the futility of democratic activity."

Allende made it clear that, judging from the recent municipal elections, the government had not lost favor with the middle classes. On the contrary, their support was more solid than ever. But Garcés struck a cautionary note. "In Chile," he said, "the government's conflicts with the majority of the lower middle class and the middle class are happening before the working class has consolidated its power. In other words, the state apparatus has not yet been able to change in either its civil or military dimensions."

We talked about other things, about the need to integrate the armed forces with the workers' militia, about international alliances that would be helpful in a moment of violent crisis. Allende became reserved. He would have preferred to continue the exchange with the young people around the table.

After dessert we went into the library, and for a few moments I spoke with Allende alone. We talked about his biography, which I was to write for a Spanish publishing house, and about the interviews, documents, and conversations that I would need to pull together. Allende mentioned that at any given moment he would be traveling to New York to speak before the United Nations. I spoke to him about Manuel Rojas, the old novelist, who was dying of cancer in a little house not far from Tomás Moro Avenue. I had just paid him a visit that afternoon, and he had asked me to give a message to the president.

"What is it? What can I do for Manuel?"

"He wants to be appointed consul to Bulgaria," I responded. Allende looked at me in disbelief.

"He said everybody gets a crack at a diplomatic post except him, and that he's got a long way to go before he's dead. The truth is, though, that his daughter, the doctor, says he won't last more than a couple of days."

Allende called Dr. Cecchi over and gave him some instructions.

"This is in your hands, César, don't let me down. This appointment is to be confirmed first thing tomorrow, and you expedite the matter at the comptroller's office."

After this interlude I noticed that Cortázar had been observing us from across the library. He had a sad but affectionate look on his face. There was also a question in that gaze. What did the wise and gentle master see? What truth, what dream, what enigmatic form of desolation?

Manuel Rojas never knew that President Allende had appointed him consul to Sofia. He died quickly, and Allende attended his funeral that weekend.

I never spoke with Cortázar about that friendly evening on Tomás Moro Avenue. When we said goodnight, Allende gave us some fragrant, gigantic Cuban cigars.

The next day the Argentinian writer flew to his country. That leg of the trip didn't go so well for him. They didn't like his living in Paris and that he made of his exile a joyous adventure, that he lived, loved, and did battle with a youthful and smiling spirit. They wanted him suffering down there in Buenos Aires. We wanted him to come to Chile, even if it was only to get lost on some dirt roads and meet a few people, and later write a beautiful, magical story about it.

Glowing with the strength and self-confidence of a long-distance front-runner, Allende had completed the first round of his anticapitalist offensive. And in the same way, he faced the aftershock—the high-level counteroffensive launched by the financial oligarchy of the United States.

I am sure that Allende was the first, if not the only, person to comprehend the true nature of the two-pronged conspiracy organized against his government—one from within Chile, and the other a multinational plot.

"We are not looking at a 'palace intrigue' or a barracks revolt," Garcés would write some time later, "nor at a military intervention along the lines of the 'hit the beach' invasion of Santo Domingo in 1965, or the overthrow of Makarios in Cyprus in 1974 by Greek officers" (Garcés, *Allende y la experiencia*, p. 65).

It wasn't like a right to the jaw, he meant to say. It was more like a net that commercial fishermen sew together, knot by knot, using patience and imagination, with blood and large fish on their minds.

In his memoirs Ambassador Davis reveals the amounts of the investments made by the Committee of 40 to destabilize the Allende government: "The U.S. government," he says, "spent, in rough figures, a little more than $6 million for covert action in Chile during Allende's three years in power, about $2 million a year" (Davis, *The Last Two Years*, p. 308).

Kissinger had created an ad hoc committee to seal the fate of the Popular Unity government, bringing in representatives of U.S. civilian and military institutions. Following his lead, the most powerful of the companies that still had investments in Chile founded their own committee: Anaconda, Kennecott Copper, Bethlehem Steel, Ford, Bank of America, First National City Bank, Ralston Purina, ITT, Firestone, W. R. Grace, Pfizer, and Dow Chemical.

Allende had named Orlando Letelier ambassador to the United States. They had been friends for years. Letelier was a man of imposing stature, tall and athletic, red haired, with a cautious, gentle nature. Although he had been a longtime militant of the Socialist party, he wasn't a professional politician. His field was economics. He came to the Allende government after serving for some years as an executive with the Inter-American Bank in Washington. But he couldn't be mistaken for one of the new breed of bureaucrats. Educated in Chile's Military Academy, Letelier ran the embassy as a very tight ship, and he kept his distance from his U.S. diplomatic counterparts. He would appear to see deeply into people as he scrutinized them. His conclusions were usually valid, but he exhibited some puzzling qualities. When it came to the moment of action he would hesitate, his modesty and good nature inducing him to wait.

In an embassy of more than fifty officers, there were only five who were sympathetic to the Popular Unity government, mixed in with the lukewarm, the undecided, and the declared enemies. Letelier tried to get along with all of them. Isabel Margarita, his wife, whom I had met at Allende's house when she was a literature professor, was quick at finding solutions to most any problem. She had big, green eyes and a smile that could seduce you or freeze you solid. She presided with wisdom over the cultural and social life in the embassy. When enemies showed their claws, the Leteliers would take out their guitars and sing like pros.

In his first cabinet appointments, Allende would have liked to fill each position with exactly the right person. He would say, "What better minister could we appoint than Felipe Herrera? And Hernán Santa Cruz, tempered by so many international missions, or Carlos Briones, an expert in social legislation? Aniceto Rodríguez or Luis Herrera? And Hugo Miranda?" Some, because they had seats in the Senate, others because they were indispensable in other positions, couldn't form part of the team. And Moy Morales de Tohá? Carmen Gloria Aguayo? Both were candidates to the Ministry of Family Care, an Allende project shot down by Congress. The compañero president surely must have considered Letelier for a cabinet position. He couldn't appoint him, however, because the "by party" quota system wouldn't permit it. Those who made up that first cabinet were José Tohá, interior; Clodomiro Almeyda, foreign relations; Américo Zorrilla, finance; Pedro Vuscovic, economy; Jacques Chonchol, agriculture; Orlando Cantuarias, mining; Ríos Valdivia, defense; Juan Carlos Concha, health; Carlos Cortez, housing; Manuel Astorga, education; José Oyarce, labor; and Jaime Suárez, secretary general.

In Washington Kissinger had been full of praise for Letelier's elegant, handsome bearing. And as he beamed at Letelier, flattering him about his brilliant background in economics and his flair for diplomacy, Kissinger was secretly meeting with the most hardened conspirators against the Chilean government.

I recall that during a work session it was proposed that Kissinger be invited to the embassy for a gala dinner. Knowing Letelier, and realizing that he would understand, I expressed my doubts on the matter. I said it would be infinitely more valuable to invite John Lennon and Yoko Ono, his magical Japanese companion. All were invited. On separate occasions.

And from out of thin air, a general appeared at one of the parties. He lasted through a whole evening of Orlando's tangos, with a pained and nervous expression on his face. We all knew that he had come from the conspiratorial underworld, and that the party was robbing him of precious hours for plot hatching. Orlando, oblivious and serene, sang, "Little duck, preening your feathers, quack, quack, quack . . ."

Allende knew Orlando well and had great affection for him. Once he sensed danger, and the coup attempts and countercoups began, he called his friend back to Chile to serve as secretary of state, and finally as minister of defense.

But long before then ITT had begun lighting up the night skies of the international banking world with a multicolored display of flares. The company sent out eighteen urgent messages and one desperate order: depose Allende before April 1972. Some of the specific recommendations: cancel all loans and trade with Chile; draw from U.S. copper reserves; take all dollars out of the country; share strategies with the CIA; sabotage the meeting of UNCTAD in Santiago and the renegotiation of Chile's external debt.

Why was ITT screaming so loudly over Allende's reform program? The testimony given before the Church committee of the U.S. Senate made the historical evidence public. ITT was the owner of 70 percent of Chiltelco, the telephone monopoly of the country, and its lion's share was worth about 150 million dollars. In June 1970 the directors of ITT asked John A. McCone, ex-director of the CIA, to make contact with Richard Helms, then director of the counterintelligence agency. William Broe, another of the CIA top brass, in charge of operations in the Western Hemisphere, was also called in. Together they were to take immediate measures against the Chilean government. Harold S. Geneen, a high-ranking executive of ITT, offered millions in support.

All of a sudden the doors in Washington began shutting, and Letelier had to face the specter of empty desks at the State Department. He acquired a new elegance in his role as representative of an invisible nation—a nation never openly affronted, but systematically ignored day in and day out. He was no longer recognized in the international banks. Then the embargo on Chilean copper shipments throughout the world was announced. Midnight couriers flew from the U.S. to Chile with sleeping bags stuffed with dollars. Those dollars were earmarked for buying truckers, taxicab drivers, and newspeople. Phantom accounts popped up in the banks of Santiago under the names of budding new consortiums.

ITT and the CIA had set some flawless traps for the takeover of Chile. Someone ordered the redesigning of the Chilean chancellery in Washington. The spooks had a grand time bugging every phone they could find in the old building on Massachusetts Avenue. One night they slipped through a window and ransacked the offices of Fernando Bachelet, our political adviser, and Andrés Rojas Weiner, our press attaché. "Everything's ready to go," the conspirators said. But they weren't counting on some nasty end-of-the-year surprises. Fidel Castro came to Santiago for a visit. The CIA road show had to change its plan.

The right-wing press maintained the position that, in Chile, Fidel Castro could only convince those who were already convinced. They forgot one thing: Fidel could, and did, get the fence sitters hopping.

That giant with the piercing eyes, bushy beard, and keen voice set out to do what had never been done in the history of Chile. In three weeks of intense travel, he opened a dialogue with a whole people, defining principles, asking questions, debating, attacking, defending himself, in an uninterrupted flow of speech that left him totally hoarse. He defied and unraveled political agendas, surprised and disconcerted followers and enemies alike, and like an olive-drab tornado, blew away all of the weather predictions, causing rains in Valparaíso, showers in the northern desert, springlike mornings in the Central Valley, quakes, avalanches, and canal divertings in the extreme south. Until finally one day *El Mercurio*, in a frenzy, demanded that he leave Chile, the country couldn't take it anymore, the year 1971 was never going to end, and it was all his fault.

Fidel would laugh and stop talking to gargle in the middle of a speech. He would banter with the hecklers in the balcony and dazzle the faithful in the pit. He started by addressing the president in the formal "usted" manner in a telegram sent as he crossed the border, but ended up calling Chile "tú," as he invited the people to "Keep on talking till the candles burn out."

He shocked all of mummydom to the core. They leapt from their coffins and began to attack Fidel because he ate meat pies with red wine, because he played basketball, because he would banish Coca-Cola ads from tv. "Why doesn't he stop talking?" they would ask. "Who is providing him with those gargles that seem to cure his throat?" "What is this guy, a vampire or something who doesn't need to sleep at night?"

President Allende answered for him: "Compañeros," he said at Puerto Montt, "I beg you not to push, because you will make things difficult for the carabineros. Give a hand in making things orderly. If you don't, the photographers won't be able to do their job either. . . . Compañero Fidel Castro has accused me of various things, and I must refute the charges; but I can tell you that a few years back, when I was in Havana, Fidel Castro came to get me in the hotel at 7:00 in the evening. We started talking at 7:30, and at 7:30 the following morning he dropped me off at my hotel door. I was exhausted, and as I walked up the stairs, I heard Fidel's voice below saying, 'Salvador, let's go fishing.' I told him I had a date with Morpheus and had to get to bed."

In reference to Fidel's health problems, he added, "Listen, Fidel, I implore you as a friend, I order you as a doctor, and I beg you as president—take care of yourself. There will be a rally. You'll talk longer than me, and then you'll go off and play basketball. And then you'll talk until 5 A.M., and then . . . Don't even think about swimming in the ocean. The ocean in Cuba is warm, but the Chilean sea is another matter. . . . Well, now that that's over with, you'll all be glad to know that I won't bill him for the medical advice."

Allende and Fidel enjoyed themselves together. Others choked. Cracking jokes all the while, stroking his beard, Fidel plumbed some real depths. He would suddenly get serious and ponder the content of the hoarse anti-reformist shouting coming from some University of Concepción students: "OK," he said. "If you were to ask me what's going on in Chile, I would say, in all sincerity, that a revolutionary process is developing. And we, too, call our revolution a process, a process that is not yet even a revolution, still merely a road. Yours is a revolutionary phase that is just beginning. You have your own conditions under which this process will unfold, with your own means, resources, forces, and alliance of forces. It is not the same as our process."

Allende took the floor then, and defended himself against the hecklers: "You compañeros who shout 'revolution' so much, have the courtesy to listen a moment. Revolution is not accomplished only by shouting the word 'revolution.' It is a conscious action by an organized people who know the risks of the game. And I want to tell those compañeros who shout 'revolution' all the time that Fidel Castro wouldn't be in Chile if a revolutionary government had not been victorious. Fidel Castro would not have come all this way to visit a country of opportunists with a faltering government. He knows that we are creating a revolution in accordance with our particular reality. . . . We have struggled, consciously, over many years. Before some of you kids who are gurgling the word 'revolution' were born—and I don't mean politically, I mean physically—I was already facing down the imperialists. I had already been expelled from the university and taken up the fight at the side of my people."

In between departures and arrivals, on the way from an airport to a train station, or from a meeting spot in an open field to a fancily decorated plaza, in factory courtyards and on rodeo grounds, in theaters, union halls, and universities, Fidel spelled out the difference between the Cuban revolution and the Chilean path to socialism. He denounced the new tactical violence of the reactionaries and the forces of imperialism; he denounced the manipulation of the external debt. And finally, he left us with a succinct warning that we were facing imminent attack. He expressed astonishment upon hearing Allende's spontaneous testimony of his own faith and courage in the shadow of a foreseen death, during a speech Allende delivered in the National Stadium.

Allende had said, in his speech on December 2, 1971, "I can tell you, compañeros of so many years, without the slightest qualm, that I don't have an ounce of the blood of the apostle or messiah in my veins. Nor am I a martyr of any sort. I am just a fighter in the social cause who is carrying out a job, the job given me by the people. But hear me now those who want to roll back history and the will of the national majority: I will not take a single step backward. Hear me now when I say that I won't leave La Moneda until I have fulfilled the mandate that the people gave me. Let it be engraved in their minds: I will defend this Chilean revolution and the people's government, because it is the mandate that the people gave me. I have no alternative. Only by cutting me down with bullets will they be able to block the fulfillment of the people's program."

What transpired between Allende and Fidel during those legendary weeks in the annals of the Chilean revolution? What was left unsaid, but nonetheless foreseen? Augusto Olivares taped a farewell dialogue between the two men. This conversation, as in the memoirs and commentaries that would follow, was in essence not really a question of words being recorded, but rather a wave of tacit, mutual revelations: the future that Allende had not yet lived and that Fidel saw with clear premonitions, but discreetly avoided discussing.

Allende appeared changed. As though he had been a figure waiting in the jumbled pieces of a puzzle and had all of a sudden assembled himself. As though the patrician shield of an old inherited, respected liberalism had suddenly fallen from his hands, and the fighter stood alone, with new arms, against a shrouded enemy who waited in ambush.

It was not that Fidel had delivered a sermon and that Allende had received it. The roads to revolution are many and varied. They had both said so and repeated it. But in the last analysis they found themselves at the crossroads of an ancient truth: if the people who make a revolution know how to defend it, and the leaders make such a defense a reality, the enemy will not pass beyond the gate.

With his eyes sparkling and his beard dusty, in shirtsleeves and wearing borrowed shoes, Fidel leapt into the middle of a hotly contested basketball game at the María Elena nitrate plant one afternoon. It was newsmen on one side and the Cuban visitors on the other, with a carabinero as referee. Fidel played all out. He had the crowd in his hand. In the heat of battle, he fell and rolled to the ground with an opponent as they vied for the elusive ball. The fans were howling.

But it wasn't just a question of winning basketball games. Fidel began to make some statements that the Chilean people would not forget. On violence: "Above all, you shouldn't forget that those who have used violence throughout history are not the revolutionaries but the counterrevolutionaries. And the historical reality of social class has been violence and repression, which have not been sought or invented by revolutionaries."

On the forces of unity: "And that is why we as revolutionaries have developed and articulated a notion of strategy that is valid for our people, but also for any people in the struggle: the need to close ranks, the need to unite, the need to coordinate, and the need to decide upon common methods. We have talked with many Chileans, and we are impressed by their patriotism and intelligence. Unite! Patriots, unite! Men of honor, unite! All who feel the Chilean cause deep in their hearts, and who know that this is zero hour in the history of Chile, in its dignity and sovereignty as a nation—unite!"

Defining the particular nature of the Chilean revolution, he added: "In Chile a totally unique process is occurring, a process wherein the revolutionaries are trying to bring about change in a peaceful manner. Now, the question is whether the historical axiom predicting the resistance and violence of the exploiters will hold true here as well. Because we have said that there is not in the annals of history a single case in which the reactionaries, the exploiters, the privileged members of a social system resigned themselves passively to change."

In 1971, with the government of President Allende sailing full speed ahead, the historical period of expropriations came to an end. Allende had been elected decisively, and the government was preparing to face its increasingly aggressive adversaries at home and abroad.

Fidel Castro called upon the Chileans to recognize clearly the true nature of the enemy who stalked: "What do the exploiters do when they lose control of institutions? What is their reaction when the mechanisms they have counted on throughout history to maintain their control begin to fail? They simply destroy them. Fascism in its violence eliminates all in front of it. It strikes against the universities, crushing them and closing them; it strikes against the intellectuals, oppressing and persecuting them; it strikes against the broad-based organizations and the unions and cultural groups. So there is nothing more violent, more retrograde, more illegal, than fascism. . . . And we say to you with all frankness that we have had the opportunity to learn and to see fascism in action, and there is nothing that could teach us more about fascism than this visit."

Who was aware of these things in Chile in 1971? Who expected a fascist assault instead of the traditional duel between the executive branch and parliament? Fidel had touched a sore spot. He had not known the tiger hidden in every Chilean worker. Now he began to recognize it.

"What has impressed us so much is the passionate nature of the Chilean character, its courage and decisiveness. We've seen men, and women with babies in their arms, risk their lives at a moment's notice. We've seen qualities in the Chileans that our own people did not possess at the beginning of our revolution: a higher cultural level, more of a political heritage."

But then, too, he warned that the enemy would not come by traditional means—a barracks revolt—but with the tactics of vengeance learned from the entrenched technocrats of death.

"You also have another thing we did not have. In our country the oligarchs, the landowners, the reactionaries, had not had the experience of their counterparts here. In our country they didn't worry about the problem of social change, because they would say, 'The Americans,'—they call the North Americans 'Americans'—'will take care of such problems. There can't be a revolution here.' In Chile it's not like that. The oligarchy is much better equipped to resist ideological change. They have the weapons to battle you on every front opened by the revolutionary process: whether ideological, political, or military—mark my words— they know how to do battle right in the street and get the help they need to do it."

At last the mystery of Fidel's trip had been clarified. Invited by workers, intellectuals, students, government employees, men and women embarked upon a peaceful revolution, Fidel left his hosts a message as valid for those constructive years as for the ruinous ones to follow: learn to recognize the enemy, and prepare. He was full of hope and support for Allende, and he predicted the political unity that was the key to the narrow door.

"If you want my opinion, the battle to assure the success of this extraordinary process will be won or lost on the ideological front, as you struggle for the backing of the masses. It will depend on the revolutionaries' ability to win over the middle class. Because in our modestly developed countries, the large middle groups are often vulnerable to lies and deceit. . . . How have we been able to resist in Cuba? Through the unity of our people, through the strength that it generates. . . . We have an unbreakable bond between the people and the armed forces, and that is why we can say that our defense system is strong. . . . When one looks for similarities between the objectives of Marxism and the most beautiful precepts of Christianity, one can see how many points of confluence there are. And it is easy to see what the humble priest who knows hunger, sickness, and death firsthand, and those who work among poor peasant families, and those who give their life in taking care of the sick all have in common. Then we realize how it is possible to have a strategic alliance between Marxist and Christian revolutionaries."

Chapter Eleven

Allende
in New York

Allende is 64 and a bit thicker around the middle. He observes his surroundings with mistrust.

The presidency that a year ago had been characterized by romantic, proletarian slogans has become increasingly distant. As if living the dream of a Tolstoyan colony, Allende had dared to occupy an office at the Sumar Textile Company in order to explain to the workers the subtleties of expropriating and of becoming, overnight, the director of a big industry, responsible for plowing industrial income back into the community and the socialist nation.

"You are the chosen people in our proletarian world," he had told the copper miners in Chuqui, El Salvador, and El Teniente when they went on strike earlier in 1972. "Your conflict is not with the Popular Unity government, but with North American imperialism, which denies us machinery, parts, and credit, embargoes our copper exports, and lowers Chilean wages by manipulating the international markets."

MIR called a Popular Assembly, in an effort to steal the political initiative from the government or, as MIR put it, to rescue the revolution, which was "sinking in the process of using merely defensive tactics against the bloody attacks of the fascist reactionary forces."

Explosions, fires, sabotage of electrical plants, tv stations, and refineries, sinister movements of uniformed and civilian groups out in the provinces, rumors, threats, calumnies. What kind of a presidency is this, in 1972? It would be more apt to call it a trap, a blind labyrinth with closed doors and false walls.

One morning the big city awakens to discover that it has been plastered with signs that say JAKARTA. On another day the signs say "Operation Sack." The whole country is a sack on the back of mobile spies, who are opening manholes to bury meat rations, chicken, milk, and liquid gas. Now it's on the back of the farmers, who have become pyromaniac foresters, truckers without wheels, smugglers with dollar bills, and diplomats addicted to machine guns.

In Congress the opposition declares the expropriations made by the government after October 14, 1971, to be illegal, and it demands the return of the industries to their former owners. The moment will come when Congress will systematically reject every piece of legislation proposed by the Popular Unity government. It is as though Allende's defenseless ministers were standing accused and the verbal firing squad proceeded to blow them away. The compañero president has to reorganize his cabinet twelve times. The opposition controls the Supreme Court and the Office of the Comptroller. Brandishing arms, the conspirators call for an uprising, provoke the armed forces, walk into the High Court with gangs of lawyers, make their press statements, and demand Allende's head.

One warm afternoon in December, a column of elegant ladies files down Providencia Avenue in what appears to be a fashion parade. But wait, they have pots and pans, and yes, they are beating on them and shouting that the government is not feeding these high-life women properly. They are graceful even as they clown, with the self-confidence of the well-established woman in society. Actually, they are copping a scene from a 1964 carnival in Rio, but they improve on it by adding Elvis's gyrating hips. They put so much pizzazz into it that working people join in, until finally an enormous rumpus is in full swing. No one ever dared to strike out at the elegant ladies from the *barrio alto*. Until that night when Fidel Castro bade farewell to Santiago.

In March 1972 the rightist leader Onofre Jarpa raises a hue and cry for the ouster of the Allende government. He goes to a séance of the warlocks of subversion at Chiñigüe, the headquarters for all such matters. The warlocks are indignant at the timid behavior of the militants and send them symbolic fetishes in the mail—a chicken feather here, a photo of a lamb there. The ladies of the *barrio alto* leave their pots and pans and go to the doors of the Military Academy. There they form a circle and make like chickens. Later, they throw kernels of corn at the cadets on guard duty.

The circle is closing around Allende, his enemies play hide-and-seek. One day at dawn they appear in Mendoza; the next day hecklers are attending mass in La Viñita in Santiago. Through remote Andean trails the saboteurs take more than two hundred thousand head of cattle away with them, thus contributing to the meat shortage in Santiago.

The country becomes a gigantic food line, waiting impatiently for meat, gas, and detergent.

Supply and Price Control Groups appear in support of the government. Volunteer work programs spring up to replace the strikers.

Nothing that the Popular Unity government can do is enough to stem the tide. A rumor spreads that the country is on its knees, the Treasury has disappeared. The government, paralyzed by the chaos, awaits civil war with resignation.

Then the truckers' strike begins. The authorities are puzzled. This isn't a traditional weapon in the history of Chilean union battles. In past showdowns, when the workers' movement wanted to throw a knockout punch, it used railway, mail, telegraph, coal, or copper strikes to do the job. Where did this strategy come from, which mixes unionism with the hidden powers of small proprietors? The truckers have suddenly and inexplicably joined ranks with the oligarchy to knock down the people's government. They want spare parts for their trucks, and they say they will die fighting "government plans to requisition their vehicles." But no one has said anything about government requisition of trucks. Allende's arguments don't budge them. They call for a fight to the death, and they unleash a brand of highway terrorism. They park in barbed-wire encampments, they block all the entrances to Santiago and the bridges and tunnels. They flex their biceps in the corridors of the Palace of Justice.

The truckers are enjoying the benefits of hard currency in this strike, very hard currency, since they are being paid off in U.S. dollars. "We can hold out until Judgment Day," they say. They defend the reign of the almighty dollar. Next, the opposition will gain the support of small retail businesses and bank employees. The Popular Unity government loses new sectors of the middle class daily. The truckers' strike lasts 26 days, and the loss to the national economy adds up to more than 100 million dollars. Those truckers loyal to the cause of socialism risk their lives strike breaking. Two million men and women—workers, employees, students, artists, intellectuals—perform volunteer work during this critical time.

"How is Allende?" I ask Perro Olivares. "Can I see him? Is it true that he is thinking about resigning?"

I had just been on television in Santiago, on the program of Mireya Latorre, Olivares's wife. Everyone saw it. People called me to ask whether Allende's government was living on borrowed time.

"False, one-hundred percent bogus information," said Olivares. "Allende is vigorous and strong despite the pressure. Let's go see him, and you can judge for yourself."

We have arrived at El Cañaveral, Allende's retreat. Springtime, poplars and willows down near the river, white boulders, the echoes of beating wings and songs. Venturelli, the painter, is there, tall and pale in a gray suit, looking like a Chinese official. He has brought Allende a painting of some trees covered with yellow birds brightly reflecting the sunset.

Salvador is eating a peach as he tells us of his next trip.

"Mexico is the way station before the United Nations."

I had never felt so convinced of Allende's clarity and sense of purpose as in that moment, even as the Right was honing its weapons of revenge and barking about sinking the Ship of Fools.

As Allende describes his speech at the United Nations, I notice that he seems older and that he has become gray around the temples. But his look is bright and sharp.

He has some aces up his sleeve, I think, along with an irrefutable argument and the confidence of a fighter in his prime.

The fact is that wherever he was—on Tomás Moro Avenue, Castillo Hill, or El Cañaveral, at party headquarters, or in the factories—compañeros were working on his United Nations speech: the language itself expressed a battle for economic liberation fought day by day, within and beyond national borders, at the side of a people massed together to defend their revolution and assume the offensive once again.

There must be a moment in the life of a fighter like Allende when a long-held vision suddenly comes clearly into focus and is dazzling in its simplicity; an instant of revelation, an understanding of limitations, even as the vision is materializing. I had that impression as I listened to Allende revealing the form of his speech, because in describing it, he was revealing the secret of the Chilean people's own evolving consciousness of their dynamic truth—not only through action but through the signs and words that translate it.

December 3 started off cold and cloudy in New York. Steam from grates and ducts floated on the streets, as though an invisible population were breathing in the basement of the city. We were in a long line at JFK Airport, waiting for Allende at the arrival gate reserved for the presidential plane. Orlando Letelier, hatless, his red hair slicked back, was looking on worriedly, his hands clasped behind him. Next to him was Humberto Díaz Casanueva, our ambassador to the United Nations, who was talking to the Chilean officials of CORFO. In front of us, on the other side of the barrier, were men working among giant cranes and trucks. The New York police were not in evidence. Then, from an invisible landing strip, the white LAN-CHILE jet, with its huge national shield and smoke-stained motors, came into view, advancing slowly toward the gate. The plane stopped and the door opened. President Allende appeared and descended the ramp, followed by Tencha and their retinue. He greeted our group. Next to me was Ramón Astorga, of old socialist vintage, now our agricultural attaché. Allende spoke briefly with us. Everything went very quickly. Where a few minutes ago I had noticed the absence of police, I could now detect the presence of secret agents with walkie-talkies. Allende drove off in an official car, followed by some unmarked black limousines.

That night Allende decided to take a walk. He threw on an overcoat and a fur cap, and left the towers of the Waldorf Astoria Hotel. The security police were annoyed and mobilized an ambulance and dozens of agents and patrol cars. The squadron guards on foot and in cars moved slowly down the avenue, while Allende, his stride long and rapid, walked along, cracking jokes and stopping in front of display windows, saying that he was going to buy this and that because he had to bring some Christmas presents back to Chile.

Then suddenly, as though by magic, through the snow that had begun to fall lightly, a ghostly building with huge red neon letters loomed out of the dark in front of Allende: ITT. He couldn't believe it. Had they put him on this street on purpose? Was it trick photography? A hologram? Thunderstruck, he looked at the building with its gigantic letters. "Let's shoot it," he said, "bring the cameras." The reporters ran over, and Allende strode away laughing, saying, "What more do you want now? Wait for tomorrow, the photos will be better."

At that moment two young people approached, walking in the opposite direction. One of them turned to Allende and asked, in an obvious Chilean accent, "Are you the president, the compañero president?"

"And what are you two doing in New York?"

They told him they were students.

"Go back to Chile when you're finished studying," Allende told them. "We need you there. Don't stay here to work for ITT."

He went back to the hotel around midnight and closed himself off in a meeting with Letelier and Díaz Casanueva.

When Allende appeared on December 4 in the huge auditorium of the United Nations, there was a mild diplomatic impasse. The rules allowed only the speaker at the podium. Allende wished to have his military aides next to him. It was agreed that they would remain standing toward the rear of the speaking platform.

The auditorium was filled to capacity, and the atmosphere had an edge to it. It was quite possible that reactionary elements would try to create a disturbance. But Allende took command from the outset. Little by little he emerged as a combatant willing to challenge capitalist expansion at the international level. And in a reasonable tone of voice. "The respectable rebel" is what the *San Francisco Chronicle* called him on the following day.

"I come from Chile, a small country . . ." were his first words.

It was the opening statement of a political speech that grew slowly, stage by stage, and spread out in many directions. He fascinated his listeners with his restrained style and the power of his political suggestions.

The form of the speech suggested to me an avant-garde building with multiple levels and dimensions, glass walls and steel columns, and a feeling of open space.

His second theme: the image of an underdeveloped Latin American Third World that had been minted abroad and circulated on the international exchange, combining with a colonial legacy to transform us into "second-class citizens."

"We had to do away with a situation in which we Chileans, floundering in a stagnant pool of poverty, were sending huge sums of capital out of the country for the benefit of the most powerful market economy in the world. The nationalization of basic resources constituted a process of justifiable historical restoration. Our economy could no longer tolerate seeing 80 percent of our exports in the hands of a small group of large foreign companies that always placed their own interests and needs ahead of those of the countries in which they prospered. Neither could we continue to accept the scourge of feudalism, the industrial and commercial monopolies, credit rates for the benefit of a few, and the brutal inequities in the distribution of our GNP.

"As a result of the planned restructuring of the economic and social structure of Chile, a pluralistic movement is recovering the natural resources of the country, nationalizing its industries and public utilities, and gaining control over foreign commerce and credit.

"We have nationalized our basic resources. We have nationalized copper. We have done this through the unanimous decision of parliament, where the government parties are in a minority. We want the world to understand clearly: we have not simply confiscated grand-scale copper-mining companies without paying indemnity. But in accordance with constitutional guidelines, we have partially repaired a historical injustice by deducting all profits in excess of 12 percent made after the year 1955 from these indemnity payments. . . . Such is the case, for example, with a branch of the Anaconda Mining Company, which between 1955 and 1970 obtained a 21.5 percent yearly return on its book value, while the profits of the same company in other countries received only 3.6 percent per annum. Or the case of a branch of the Kennecott Copper Corporation, which in the same period earned a 52 percent annual return, reaching profits as incredible as 106 percent in 1967, 113 percent in 1968, and more than 205 percent in 1969. . . . These very companies, which exploited Chilean copper resources over a period of many years, took out more than four billion dollars in profits in the years under discussion, after an initial investment that did not surpass thirty million dollars. One simple and painful contrast: in my country there are 700,000 children who will never be able to enjoy life in terms we can understand, because during their first eight months in this world they never received basic levels of protein."

Allende then laid bare the mechanisms of the multinational

companies and the local oligarchy in their aggressions against Chile. He made reference to "forces that operate in the shadows, without flags, with sophisticated weapons handed out in power centers.

"We are the victims," he added, "of subtle activities, often disguised as declarations of respect for the sovereignty and dignity of our country."

Allende described the illegal tactics of certain financial agencies and referred to attempts at embargoing Chilean copper earmarked for the European markets, and to the open warfare waged against Chile by ITT and Kennecott.

"The world discovered with disbelief last July," he said, "the various elements of a new plan of action presented by ITT to the U.S. government. The overt purpose of this plan was the overthrow of my government within a period of six months. I have the document, dated October 1971, which contains the eighteen points that constitute the aforementioned plan."

ITT looms like an animated rubbery monster in an old movie. But in this case King Kong is not clawing at a skyscraper where a beautiful blonde in a scanty gown helplessly defends herself on a balcony. He's attacking a little republic of cupriferous deserts and vaults brimming with black diamonds beneath the sea.

"Distinguished delegates," Allende exclaimed, as he ended one chapter and began another, full of unexpected twists and turns, "we are witnessing a direct confrontation between the great transnational corporations and the sovereign nations themselves. The latter are being meddled with in their basic political, economic, and military functions by global organizations that do not depend upon any state, and which do not answer to, or present financial records to, any parliament, or for that matter, to any organization representative of the collective commonwealth. In other words the political infrastructure of the world is being undermined. 'Merchants have no country. The mere spot they stand on does not constitute so strong an attachment as that from which they draw their gains.' That quote is not mine, it is Jefferson's."

Finally, Allende described the recent campaigns waged by nations subjected to the sadistic whims of the Pentagon, and asked, "Where do the genuine freedom fighters of America take up arms, struggle, and overcome? Not in the paper jungles of the Miami banking establishment, nor in the orthopedic torture chambers presided over by the counterinsurgency experts. No, they are in the ports, the mountains, and the shantytowns of our workers' republics."

Allende exalted the liberation movements of Central and South America, and paid homage to Cuba and its revolution, to General Juan Velasco Alvarado in Peru, to Mexico—"so far from God, and so close to the United States"—and to the Chilean people, who were digging in for the decisive battle against fascism.

" 'Those who make a peaceful revolution impossible will make violent revolution inevitable.' That one's not mine either. I share it with John F. Kennedy! Chile is not alone, and no one could isolate it from Latin America, or from the rest of the world. . . . The abuse of power demoralizes those who use it and sows deep doubts into their own conscience. The convictions of a people defending their independence breed heroism and make them capable of resisting the violence of even the very largest military-economic machine. . . . When one feels the passion of hundreds of thousands of hopeful men and women crowding the streets and saying, 'We are with you, don't give up, you will win out in the end,' all doubts disappear. Those are the people, all the people to the south of the Rio Grande, who stand up and say, 'Enough! Enough of being dependent! Enough pressures! Enough interventions!' They stand up to affirm the sovereign right of all of the developing countries to dispose freely of their natural resources."

Allende was neither received by Nixon nor listened to by Kissinger, occupied as they were with maps of Vietnam and bombs in Chile.

The compañero president never did buy any Christmas presents. He put on his coat and hat, got on his snow-covered plane with the smoke-stained red star emblazoned on it, and flew off, taking a last look down at Manhattan, where, as the poet Parra once said, "Liberty is a statue."

Chapter Twelve

The Butcher's Thumb

"August is the month when old people die off," says this relative of mine, a well-known fascist who owns a trucking company.

"Quite right," I respond, "and it's also the month of the cat."

"What does that have to do with what I said?" he asks, his blue eyes wide open, his lower lip trembling.

"Cats always land on their feet, no matter where you toss them. And speaking of throwing things, how much do you weigh, shorty?"

He's as mad as a hornet, his blond locks plastered to his head, and he shouts wildly, "They're going to kick the shit out of you commies, go on, go tell that to your buddy Allende."

I look at my watch and tell him, "I'm late. Don't get too choked up now, dear, and watch out for the GAP's."

I get in the car and head to a service station. It occurs to me that there are thousands of Chileans who, like my entrepreneurial cousin, are checking off items one by one on sordid little agendas on this very day. They know just where to surface with their trucks at the appointed time. Their hands tremble as they feel their pistols in their pockets and hide their rifles under the front seats of their trucks.

On this twenty-ninth of June, a Santiago daily reports that some units of the army have risen up against the government and are surrounding La Moneda, and that Allende has resigned and arranged to flee the country. A few weeks earlier, on June 6, in a meeting with government leaders, Allende had predicted that a fascist coup attempt would surface within three months. September 1973. The leaders looked at him as though he'd stepped off a spaceship. They kept mum. It was lunchtime. "Yes, yes, yes," they said. They had siesta on their minds. Allende tightened the screws. In a foreboding voice, he asked for the authority to conduct a plebiscite. His political fate was at stake. If he was victorious in a plebiscite, the danger of a coup would subside and better times would come to the land. He would dissolve Congress and seek an alliance with the Christian Democrats, order the generals and admirals with plans for a coup into retirement. A little peace in order to regroup. "That's all I mean, compañeros."

Tired and impatient, the leaders said no. A big, fat NO. One of them ventured an opinion: "We'd get slaughtered."

Still waiting for my turn at the gas pump, I hear a loud thumping and creaking of huge chains behind me. A tank pulls up beside me next to a pump, a turret hatch opens, and out pops a red-faced officer in battle dress, madly shouting orders.

The other customers and I stand there agape. Two more tanks are waiting out in the street, and others are crawling slowly along like giant caterpillars toward the center of Santiago.

The officer wants diesel fuel. I have a ridiculous notion. Will he ask the kid to clean his windshield, or check the oil? Will he pay or won't he?

The man acts as though he were the victim of a flea attack. Maybe he suffers from various odd tics. He finally calms down enough to crawl into his tin can and clank off toward the palace.

Who is he? Where is he going? And his mates?

But on thinking it over, there is nothing new about this scene. At the end of 1972, in the midst of strikes called by professional people, truckers, and bank clerks, some generals were nudged into retirement. General Arellano Stark said later, in an interview with the *Miami Herald* on February 18, 1974, that five army generals, and an identical number of air force generals and admirals, had been ready to deliver the coup de grace.

General Pinochet, interviewed by the *Los Angeles Times* on December 29, 1973, stated that in March he had already signed a document declaring the impossibility of a constitutional solution to the Chilean crisis. What the general meant was that since the opposition could not win the two-thirds vote in the March congressional elections necessary to toss Allende out legally, a peaceful solution was not in the cards.

"There were eight of us officers who made the plans and followed them to the letter," he declared.

In May 1973, while General Prats was in Europe on an official mission, and President Allende was out of the country attending the inauguration of Héctor Cámpora's government, the coup-happy team of generals decided to go for it. But someone, a lawyer linked to the Fatherland and Freedom party, ran off at the mouth. The government discovered that some divisions in the provinces were planning a coup for June 27, and that the navy, the air force, and the carabineros were involved. General Prats returned and arrested a group of officers, thus thwarting the coup.

For a few days.

In order to finish the story, an incident right out of an opera buffa must be mentioned: the adventure of Lady Maceteada and the commander in chief of the army.

On June 27, during rush hour on Costanera Avenue, a car pulls up alongside General Prats's as he is waiting at a light in heavy traffic. A strange-looking person is at the wheel. The general observes this person unconcernedly, but his driver, fearful of some sort of violent act, grabs his pistol. The person in question—big and strong, with short hair and a heavy ski sweater—starts insulting the general. No reaction. All of a sudden a large mouth opens like a missile hatch, and out pops a long, aggressive tongue, aimed directly at the general himself!

The light changes, and the two cars speed off. Horns and shouts are heard. The general believes he is being set up in grand style. He gives orders to pursue the owner of the offending tongue, and outdoing his driver he unholsters his pistol and shoots out the tires of the fugitive.

Traffic stops. Prats hops out. The driver of the other car follows suit. A hundred or so people have already gathered around them. Photographers and newspeople arrive as though conjured up by a magician. How great must be his surprise when the general realizes that his antagonist is not a man, but actually a gigantic woman. He is crestfallen. Now it is the crowd's turn, and they shout at the top of their lungs, "Woman beater! Chicken! Murderer!" and other choice epithets. Others of a bolder nature surround the general's car and begin to let the air out of the tires. For a few moments the chief of the army and vice-president of Chile finds himself totally forsaken and helpless at the mercy of a potentially violent crowd. At that moment a taxi stops and the general gets in and heads for the Ministry of Defense. The next day the opposition press reports that the general "had retreated from the field of battle when routed by the patriotic attack of a lady of high society."

Meanwhile, back at the filling station, with the gas-guzzling tank under the command of a coup-happy colonel apparently suffering from St. Vitus's dance on the morning of June 29 . . .

The colonel was Roberto Souper, and he had commandeered eight tanks in an effort to spring his jailed fellow officers from the Ministry of Defense. Next stop would be La Moneda. He was counting on the support of snipers entrenched in the Ministry of the Interior and the Bank of South America.

A little later, with Souper and his tanks in combat position, the palace guard unit of the carabineros opened fire on the attackers in defense of the government.

As Radio Nacional de Agricultura and the Associated Press transmitted their versions of the coup attempt, insisting that Allende had been overthrown, the president was planning his defense strategy and a counteroffensive from the house on Tomás Moro Avenue.

Allende himself narrated the events in the following manner: "At 8:55 in the morning I was called by the undersecretary of the interior, compañero Daniel Vergara, who told the whole story in a single phrase: 'Compañero president, we have some tanks out here facing La Moneda, in Constitution Square. They are firing and I am informed that there are other tanks actually surrounding the palace.' I told Vergara that I would take immediate measures to crush the revolt. Then I called General Prats and gave him the necessary instructions. Minutes later Vergara called me again and said, 'President, we have received an order from the rebels to surrender. Our decision is not to capitulate. Here is Lieutenant Pérez in command of the palace guard.' I told the lieutenant that history herself knew the appropriate response for the occasion: 'The guard may be flesh and bones, goddammit to hell, but it never surrenders!' While this was going on, the commander in chief of the army, together with Generals Pinochet, Pickering, Urbina, and Sepúlveda, mapped out a plan to crush the revolt."

General Prats sent Bonilla, in command of the Tacna regiment, to take over the barracks of the armored division, while he himself took command of the historic Buin regiment and went off to defend La Moneda.

The battle was brief and flashy, with fewer shots than words exchanged. The Chilean people watched General Prats on their television screens, as he skirted the city center and arrived at the Alameda in a cluster of reporters and onlookers; several steps away, his helmet and combat boots on, machine gun in hand, General Pinochet was sniffing out potential enemies to put out of commission. Prats, in his regular uniform, approached the tanks in front of La Moneda and spoke to the leaders of the rebels.

"It is imperative to avoid bloodshed."

All surrendered, except one officer who whipped out his pistol and tried to fire on the general. He was quickly disarmed. The Cantankerous Tank-coup was over.

Allende and his guard approached the palace in armored vehicles provided by the chief of the carabineros. That same afternoon the president addressed 200,000 workers assembled in

Constitution Square. He expressed himself charitably, as befits a victor.

"I am going to say something that some of you will not like, but I must, because I have always spoken plainly to the workers; I am not going to commit the absurdity of dismissing Congress. We have said that we will carry out our program, and we will continue, within the framework of the constitution and the law. If it is necessary, I will call on the people to declare their position in a plebiscite."

How many of those gathered were thinking that time had run out for such magnanimous gestures? Perhaps many, but no one said a word.

General Prats, still smarting from the outrage of Our Lady of the Tongue, handed in his resignation. With great difficulty Allende was able to dissuade him.

The aborted tank revolt, called El Tancazo, with 12 dead and many wounded, was not even a dress rehearsal. It was scarcely a puff of smoke from a dragon running out of diesel fuel.

One coup had failed, another was coming. The consensus was that the constitutional and peaceful road to socialism had come to an end. The two enemies were about to take up arms in a decisive civil war. One of them did. The other asked for calm. Some people noticed an apparent oversight—while the government was asking for calm, the civil war had already begun.

On the night of July 27, a squad of terrorists surrounds Captain Arturo Araya's house. He is the president's naval aide-de-camp. The terrorists open fire from a plaza. Araya comes out on the balcony armed with a machine gun and attempts to defend himself alone. A bullet hits him and he dies instantly. Allende, who holds his fallen adviser in high esteem as a staunch defender of the people's government, is outraged and declares the funeral as an occasion for national mourning. The country wears black. In a few days detectives arrest the murderers. The rightist press publishes misleading articles about the circumstances of the shoot-out, and spreads rumors of vendettas. The Justice Department drags its feet and tries to bury the case.

The cocktail hour went quickly. Allende seemed worried. Not about the dinner occasion that brought together ten of the highest-ranking generals, but about some threats he had heard that afternoon. With his head thrown back, he was only half listening to a general who had chimed in on the conversation. He made an attempt to be courteous, but his vague smile indicated that his interest was flagging.

The generals at the table, dressed in civilian clothes, tried their best to stick to small talk, but you could have cut the tension with a knife. It wasn't long before some inopportune remarks were made. Allende remained silent.

What was it that his adviser had said? The words hovered around him but soon vanished in the fragmented reflections from the glassware, drowned in the amber highlights of the wine glasses. The adviser had said something about the mistrustful people around him. Something like, "These are the hours in which the needle on the delicate scale of military power edges over a bit toward the opposition."

Allende smiled. That was it, that was exactly what he had said. Of course he hadn't imagined its precise effect on the president, and the particular associations it would awaken for him. Yes, the president was thinking about that needle. But not exactly about the needle itself. He was thinking of what forces the needle over —the butcher's thumb. When he leans on the scale with that fat thumb to cheat the customer as he weighs the meat, compañeros, the butcher's thumb on the scale. Whose fat, hairy thumb is it?

Allende looked around the table. There was total silence. The generals were not comfortable before the spectacle of a president smiling to himself. Then, to his right, General Pinochet began speaking. They had gotten together to express themselves on the subject of General Prats's fate. In Pinochet's mind there was no doubt about the outcome. In an obsequious, folksy voice, he was saying, "My respect and friendship for Prats are not something recent. They are long-standing facts, and there are no limits . . ."

There was a murmur of approval, punctuated by the sound of knives and forks.

". . . And just as deep and strong is my loyalty to the president, and my need to affirm the constitutional function of the armed forces."

Bang! At that very instant a blond general attacked his chicken with a fork. The victim flew through the air in a shower of peas and gravy and caromed down the table, landing at last in the lap of a fat, dark general, who gave it a baleful look.

Allende had to suppress a laugh. If only he could explain. Because he wasn't laughing at the general's runaway chicken, or at the pea-and-gravy medals now decorating the chest of the other. He was laughing at the phrase that kept flashing through his head like a lightning bolt. Who was tipping that needle-cum-sword at this "last supper" of chicken with peas and french-fried potatoes?

He became serious. With crisp sentences and ringing consonants, he began describing the chaos in the country and the evil alliance between the enemies abroad and the terrorists from within.

"Our responsibility is historical," he said. "I have never felt it so squarely on my shoulders and been so conscious of its gravity. . . . More than a daunting burden, I regard it as something we bear equally. In your hands is the scale. But let it tip naturally in the proper direction, toward the legitimate destiny of our nation and away from sinister collaborations with the enemy."

There was a respectful silence.

Now there was the matter of General Prats to attend to. The general had wanted an expression of support and loyalty from his colleagues. Some of them had denied him that. Among those who defended him in the matter of the Costanera Avenue incident, six were present that night: Pinochet, Urbina, González, Brady, Pickering, and Sepúlveda. Four others had listed themselves among his perennial friends.

Had Joan Garcés been present at that moment, he would have been able to add his angle on the story, for the erudition of the guests.

"As surprising as it may be at this stage," he would write later, "I can attest to the fact that Salvador Allende never chided or reproached the armed forces. On the contrary, he had formed his own idea about the nature of their role, and he aimed to establish a harmonious relationship between them and the government with its policies" (Garcés, *Allende y la experiencia*, p. 149).

Allende listened to the generals' opinions, which, in the end, carved out a sort of monument to the absent general. González and Brady declared that for the good of the armed forces, its unity and sense of discipline, and to prevent civil war, General Prats should retire. General Pinochet reiterated his protest against the abuse heaped upon his colleague, and declared that taking into consideration all of the circumstances . . . General Prats really should not remain in the army after all.

At that moment a chair fell over backward. Making a great effort first to speak, and then to get up, General Pickering seemed himself to be on the verge of tottering over. His comrades-in-arms came to his aid and carried him to a sofa. Seriously ill, he was taken home. The next day Pickering presented his request for retirement.

The president's dinner with the ten generals had ended abruptly.

Much later, alone, Allende remembered some unpublished verses that his friend Neruda had read to him once:

> All war long I spent my peace
> figuring accounts,
> but not of corpses,
> but not of flowers, no.
> . . .
> and if I came out losing
> or if I came out winning
> I just don't know, the earth
> doesn't know . . .
>
> Et cetera.

The big terrace behind the house on Tomás Moro Avenue seemed deserted, and the pool reflected the shadows of old trees and slow-moving clouds that were pulling apart in the approaching darkness. Faceless guards carried weapons along invisible paths.

Tomorrow, the president thinks to himself, I will accept Prats's resignation. Prats, the admirable tactician and keen intellect, whose role in the peaceful revolution had never crystallized. Events had seemed to rush past or lag behind him, veering away from his heroic vocation and humanistic principles, making it impossible for him to fulfill his mission of saving Chile.

One week later, at the end of August, in a kind of visionary outburst, Allende uttered the words that still hang in mystery over the ruins of a vanishing dream: "No one seems to understand what has been done to Prats, despite the fact that in a few months he will be the most important man in Chile."

"In a few months" that never happened.

Chapter Thirteen

The Bull
by the Horns

Tati had married Luis Fernández Oña, on the staff
of the Cuban embassy in Santiago. She was still
the apple of Allende's eye, and as the years went by he sought her
company more and more, not to nourish his confidence, as in the
past, but simply for the pleasure this loyal relationship gave him.
Perhaps he had more time now. Perhaps too, as in the Violeta
Parra song, "the flames of autumn" were turning to embers, and
the amorous flings that had once singed him before burning themselves out no longer claimed him. Carlos Jorquera, one of his closest confidants, tells me, "Allende said, in one of those solitary moments that seemed to drain him toward the end, that after all was
said and done, he loved and respected Tencha more and more, and
that his feelings were even stronger toward his daughters and
grandchildren."

That's why Allende told Jorquera and Augusto Olivares, on
the eve of Tati's birthday in 1973, that despite her pregnancy,
"We'll have a party at El Cañaveral."

And there he brought his people together, the most intimate
of them. But in the very midst of partying, he suddenly felt sad,
very sad.

"I saw him like that, feeling down," said Jorquera, "and talked
with Perro. We decided that it couldn't be so, we had to raise his
spirits. We asked him whether he would like to listen to music,
and whether it would be OK to call Angel Parra. The president
said, 'Of course, let's lighten up the scene a bit.' And Orlando Letelier? 'Sure, get him to come if you can.' And the party got
going."

Angel Parra was at the time a small youth with a catlike face, large, dark eyes, and thick brows, who played the guitar with an ever-present cigarette butt between his fingers. His voice had an unexpected resonance. Where did he get his energy? You could ask the same about his uncle Roberto, composer of *cuecas choras*. Wiry, skinny, and nervous, both men had hidden reserves of strength. They seemed to be made of guitar strings tuned to a bright chord. Intense, like Chilean red wine, they had freewheeling imaginations and had mastered the galloping rhythm of the *cueca*, fast but sad, too. Both were disciples of Violeta Parra, Roberto's sister, Angel's mother. Workers on the timeless night shift, they tied together a country shaking apart, and they did it with ribbons of light, carnations, strings, and pegs. All at once they would hit a jazz vein and improvise under the benevolent shadow of Django Reinhardt, the gypsy. Their jam sessions didn't last all night, they lasted for weeks. After a party they would take a guitar inventory and head for La Reina, Nicanor Parra's parcel of land.

Orlando Letelier was something else again. No one was ever ready for his musical transfigurations. Radiating with a sort of lunar glow, like Doctor Caligari, he would grab a guitar and sing with everything he had. His was the typical voice of a barrio singer, and his tangos weren't the kind to make you jump up and dance. No, Orlando's tangos threw kindling on the fires of romance, nostalgia, bravura—all in due time and in their proper place, of course.

So Allende had the party that he wanted for Tati, and after the candles had burned out he stayed up chatting with his young friends. From time to time he would throw in the sort of thing said at dawn after an all-nighter: "One should expect public figures to possess public virtues, which can all be summed up as this—remaining true to one's own mask."

"Is that line yours, president?"

"Like don Arturo, eminent shoplifter of other people's witticisms, I could answer, 'Yes, my friends.' But, ah, no. It's Antonio Machado's. Probably a bit modified by a bad memory, as is another that goes something like this: God did nothing at first because there was nothing to be done. Then He saw chaos all around Him, and He liked it, so He said, 'We will call you world.' That's all there was to it."

"You mean you don't think He said, 'We will call you Chile'?"

"And would that be the end of everything, compañero? The end of the world, of Chile, of a dream that we may have lost already? It can't be. Doors that never existed have been closed to us. The witch doctor said they would squeeze us till we screamed, and then squeeze some more. Where are we, in what age are we living?"

Angel Parra sang "La señora araña."

Wandering over to a window, Allende remained lost in thought. Then he began to ask questions that would float in the air unanswered. The night had turned cold. Olivares weighed the changes he observed in Allende. Had he lost his edge? No, but he kept himself in check now. He no longer trusted intuitive, spontaneous relationships. He had not lost a fraction of his fighting spirit, but the battlefield was elusive, hidden from him. He hadn't lost his courage, but the world itself had crumbled around him. Impotence pained him intensely. Political ropes tied him down and his own party kept him from untying them. A wall of bureaucracy and mistrust loomed between him and the principles he was dedicated to. Plenty of people pretended to act responsibly, but when the moment came they hid and left him alone. He felt carried away by a black undertow, rolled over by the threatening waves of days and nights. He wanted to fight. Olivares argued with him, no longer about political strategy, but in an attempt to untangle the web of circumstances that was starting to tighten around them inexorably.

Get tough? Yes, with fighting words, curses, and hard-earned lessons, bitterly repeated. Names were shuffled like cards, and fell quickly on the hearth. Memories of offending words, stubbornly held and wrong-headed attitudes, warlike gestures of defiance, a daily litany of threats against him, his family, his compañeros, all returned to gnaw at him.

In the fireplace a huge log lies dormant among flying sparks from the other, noisily burning, logs. It seems unscathed by the flames and won't catch fire; yet ever-thickening streams of smoke pour out of it from all over. Then all of a sudden, a little flame appears, a little tongue of fire that lights up the bark and hides again. It peeks out from behind the log, then from underneath. Inside, the hard old heart is burning intensely. But the log remains intact. It will explode in luminous flames, not now, but later, in the night waiting beyond. Meanwhile it stores its powers and its fires.

Allende listened to Angel's songs, to the rough wisdom of Violeta Parra's poems. The strumming of the guitar recalled the hoof-beats heard in summer, way out beyond the little pond, among the deadfall of fragrant woods, past where the tracks disappear and the smoke ascends toward the tops of the hills.

The sounds of the city floated up to us, ever more distant and muted. The vision that had once shot forth as a fiery and urgent gaze upon the world was consuming itself from inside, blinking near the end.

What had gone wrong? Was the game lost? And for whom? Allende was certainly not going to give up the ghost. When the moment came he would still be fighting, improvising strategies, using new weapons.

In the twilight, as the songs brought back snatches and echoes of old battles, he felt the same surge of willpower as in his early campaigns. He had come to power riding a dream. A dream?

"We came in with a program and the right team to carry it out, and the organization, and the support of the masses, and . . ."

A song ended. The final chord echoed in the darkness, and then silence fell heavily. Allende said, "How did we fail?"

No, it's not failure, just another skirmish, a huge ambush, but we'll save the day.

"The country is paralyzed," Allende continued. "Everyone expects the coup. Nothing else. No one is doing anything, and I'm thinking that maybe we never understood the basic rhythms of our history. We moved ahead without first establishing ourselves. That's the tune we've sung, Angel. And we allotted mere days for the work of years."

The clock struck midnight, and there was no more talk of the nonexistent army, or of the land that had never belonged to us, or of the National Treasury that had shut its doors in our faces.

Someone poked at the fire. A few logs fell onto the hearth. Sparks flew, smoke invaded the room. We opened all the windows. It was freezing.

What else was said? We talked of death, our own. It mustn't catch us unaware. We must know how to face it.

Pablo Neruda, bedridden at Isla Negra with the cancer that is eating away at him, writes a message to his friends scattered over the globe. He warns them that the little socialist republic, squeezed between the mountains and the sea, is about to be sacrificed.

Electrical towers are falling, oil pipelines are blown to bits, trains grind to a halt in the middle of nowhere, bombs go off in tunnels and under bridges. The truckers are on strike again, provoking bloody skirmishes, ambushes, and lawsuits. Political maneuvering results in accusations against Carlos Briones, the minister of the interior. The secretary of state, Daniel Vergara, denounces the two hundred terrorist attacks that have occurred thus far and the extensive highway and railroad damage. Allende insists that the truckers respect the laws of the land. They respond with sticks of dynamite, causing a power outage while the president is speaking on television. General Ruiz is out, General Leigh is in. Seventy attacks in Santiago precede the bombing of the monument to Che Guevara in the commune of San Miguel. Three hundred terrorist acts overall in the month of August. The Cabinet falls.

Fidel Castro has sent a letter to President Allende.

"I see that that you are caught up in the delicate matter of opening a dialogue with the Christian Democrats in the midst of such grave events as the assassination of your naval aide-de-camp and the latest truckers' strike. I can imagine the tension of the moment and your need to gain time to strengthen your coalition in case things blow up. And I imagine that you are identifying a course that allows you to continue the revolutionary process without civil disorder, at the same time making preparations for what might occur. Those are good goals. But if the other side, whose intentions we are not in a position to evaluate, commits itself to a policy of treason and sabotage at great cost to the Popular Unity government and the revolution, don't forget for a single minute the formidable strength of the Chilean working class and the strong support it has always given you in your most difficult moments; that strength is at your beck and call if the revolution is in danger. You must call on the workers to paralyze the coup makers, to keep the fence sitters leaning toward you, to impose their own conditions and decide, if necessary, the destiny of Chile. The enemy must realize that the workers are aware and ready for action. Their strength and willingness to fight can tip the scales in your favor, even when other circumstances are unfavorable.

"Your decision to defend the process honorably, risking your life, an act of which everyone knows you are capable, brings all the fighting forces in Chile to your side. Your courage and firm leadership in this historical hour provide the key to the dilemma."

Was Castro able to see the political reality that Allende was facing? Was the working class in Chile in any condition to resist a massive attack by the armed forces? Was it feasible to think in terms of a mass worker mobilization and counteroffensive that would give Allende and his loyal generals time to organize a resistance movement with some chance of success?

The workers would occupy their stations. And then? To hit the streets with flags and picket signs was easy. To surround the palace while it was under tank and air attack? That was something else again.

Carlos Briones declares the truckers' union to be in violation of the law.

A complex and well-oiled fascist machine is operating secretly at full capacity. One can only guess at what is really happening through news flashes on tv or over the radio. But a chain of key events is actually beginning to take place.

On September 3, General Pinochet, in a confidential session with Minister Letelier, makes surprising revelations, later revealed by Joan Garcés: "We have a bunch of nuts here, going around maintaining that the armed forces should take a stand now, even if it costs one hundred thousand lives, because it's better than losing one million later, after a civil war. I'm doing whatever is possible to stop them, in accordance with instructions given me by General Prats before resigning and repeated by the president. I am visiting the regiments now for that purpose. The atmosphere is difficult there. . . . To send the generals who are grumbling into immediate forced retirement could complicate things. I need a certain amount of time to secure my loyal contingents in the armed forces. . . . If there is an uprising now we run the risk of seeing all the armed forces involved, and not just a unit as in the attempted coup of June 29" (Garcés, *Allende y la experiencia*, p. 332).

In a meeting of the political committee of the Popular Unity parties, at which Letelier reports on the military situation, the president urgently proposes a plan with four points of action: consult the citizenry via plebiscite; reach an agreement with the Christian Democrats; form a defense and national security cabinet made up strictly of military people; grant the president emergency powers for a three-month period. The parties are to give an answer the next day. Several days go by. No answer.

On September 4 General Pinochet calls La Moneda to ask what time the president will receive the heads of the armed forces, who wish to congratulate him on the third anniversary of the government.

That night about a million people parade in front of the palace shouting:

> ¡Allende, Allende
> el pueblo te defiende!

On September 7 Ambassador Nathaniel Davis leaves Santiago for Washington.

The admirals pressure Letelier to demand that Admiral Raúl Montero, head of the Chilean navy, be replaced by Admiral José Toribio Merino. They go all the way to the president. They want more: they want Carlos Altamirano, secretary general of the Socialist party, drummed out of the Senate, in order to try him in the civilian courts for inciting the navy's rank and file to revolt. Merino keeps a constant pressure on his officers in Valparaíso.

Searching for arms, the air force launches a surprise mission to the Madeco and Mademsa industries. The workers resist. The soldiers retreat.

General Pinochet informs Minister Letelier that the rehearsal for the military parade on September 19 will take place on the fourteenth, and that only the troops stationed in Santiago will participate, in order to "save gasoline."

Nathaniel Davis, painstaking chronicler of the ins and outs of the military coup, observes: "But Pinochet said after the coup that his real reason was that he intended to mount a coup on the fourteenth. Concerned that the workers in the industrial belts would trap his units in the center of the city, Pinochet wanted to maintain an outer, concentric ring of forces that could move against the *cordones* from outside Santiago" (Davis, *The Last Two Years*, p. 213).

Prats reveals these plans to Allende and to Letelier, suggesting that five or six generals be retired immediately.

Merino secures his people with a decisive agreement: the fleet will not take part in a rendezvous with the North American ships from Operation Unitas. It will instead give only the appearance of departing from the port.

Meanwhile the strikes increase: doctors, nurses, pharmacists, dentists, pilots, merchant marines, all close ranks with the truckers, taxicab drivers, and merchants. Is this a strike of the middle class against the workers' government?

Allende meets behind closed doors with General Prats on the afternoon of September 8.

They put their cards on the table. "The coup will take place within ten days," Prats says.

"And Pinochet?" Allende asks.

"Yesterday I received a letter from him," the general responds, "in which he assures me that the army will continue to fulfill its institutional duty to support the government."

Allende mentions the possibility of calling a plebiscite.

"President," says Prats, "there's no time left for that sort of thing."

"What do you propose, then?"

"A truce. Ask for authorization from the Senate and leave the country for a year."

What times are these, general? The twenties, when the Lion would sail over to the Old World? Allende doesn't actually say these words. On the contrary, he says something that he may regret later: "Me, abandon the country? Never . . . there will always be some regiment loyal to the government."

Next Allende asks in Miria Contreras to arrange an appointment with Generals Pinochet and Urbina for the following afternoon at Tomás Moro Avenue.

That night the expected reply comes from the political committee of the Popular Unity alliance. Allende opens it and reads it immediately. Garcés reveals the contents: "Agreement with the Christian Democrats, rejected; plebiscite, rejected; formation of a security and defense cabinet, rejected; vote of confidence for the president's authority to adopt emergency measures, rejected. Recommendations of the political committee: none" (Garcés, *Allende y la experiencia*, p. 338).

Allende requests a meeting with the political commission of the communist party for Sunday morning. In that meeting it will be agreed to announce the plebiscite during the president's speech at the State Technological University.

Sunday, September 9, started off as a warm and brilliant day; the trees swayed lazily, the flowers opened, the bees

buzzed away; the generals put on battle dress and opened their windows. Time to fly. It's so quiet. Stretch a bit, and relax. No more nervous waiting around. Now the real thing is here for sure. Now? Well, it won't be today, Sunday, or Monday either. Allende has put off his speech until Tuesday. Tuesday at dawn. Everyone in the barracks. When the clock strikes 6:00 A.M., we hit.

The Christian Democrats called in their best gurus for consultation. Party leaders from the provinces descended on the capital to hear the oracles. Patricio Aylwin, president of the Christian Democratic party, presided over the ceremony and counted the informal vote. Unanimity: President Allende and all of Congress should resign. Let there be a plebiscite and new elections. Clean the slate and start over again.

The sun was high as the city grew increasingly absorbed by speculation. People stood on the streets pumping each other with questions. All was quiet, like the silent wick attached to a keg of dynamite. Then Carlos Altamirano walked up to the podium in Chile Stadium and provided the match.

What did Altamirano say in his speech? Just that the coup should be fought with a countercoup. What do you mean? I mean, with armed defense posts manned by workers and farmers, that is, with people power. Admiral Merino immediately sent two emissaries to General Pinochet to ask one last time that he bring the forces under his command into the conspiracy. Once in Santiago, Admiral Sergio Huidobro and Captain Ariel González spoke with Admiral Carvajal, who then called General Gustavo Leigh. An appointment was confirmed for that evening at Pinochet's house, where a birthday party was taking place.

Merino's message was terse: the coup is set for Tuesday, September 11, at 6:00 A.M. Pressured by the presence of the emissaries and General Leigh, Pinochet finally signed and placed his seal on the document.

That Sunday, Ambassador Davis returned from Washington.

And that same Sunday, the officers from the coast headed for Santiago with the good news, the codes, the countersigns, and the holy oil for extreme unction. Following suit, the couriers sped off

to unite the troops at Antofagasta, Iquique, Concepción, Valdivia, and Magallanes.

General Pinochet called a meeting of high brass in his office for Monday at noon. Generals Bonilla, Brady, Benavides, Arellano, Palacios, Leigh, and Viveros were present, the latter two from the air force. Colonel Geiger was also present. Pinochet gave a detailed account of the coup.

A communications network began to grow like a spider web, encompassing radio stations, offices, planes, and ships. Radio Nacional de Agricultura became a mouthpiece for the Fatherland and Freedom party. A flying saucer–fortress of sorts, bristling with wires and electronic ears, floated amidst the snowy solitude of the Andes. It was not from outer space but made in the USA.

In Valparaíso the fleet went out to sea in the early afternoon and waited patiently in the blinding sunset; at the appointed time it sailed back to port full steam ahead. It was 10 P.M.

The generals of the carabineros, undecided until that moment, threw their hats in with the insurgents at the urging of Arturo Yovane and César Mendoza. General José María Sepúlveda remained loyal to the government.

The conspiracy was at last definitively set: Tuesday at dawn, the eleventh of September.

And President Allende? He called together his ministers, had lunch with some of them, and held them in conversation until 3:00. They spoke of the latest arms searches and about the speech to be given at noon on Tuesday. In the evening the ministers and party leaders attended a gala reception at the Bulgarian embassy. After the party Briones and Letelier headed for Tomás Moro Avenue. The vigil began.

Wide and open in the starry night, the house on Tomás Moro Avenue echoed with the murmur of voices until after midnight. A vague sense of alarm hovered over the greenish darkness of the olive trees; a heavy calm, a dream already lived out and now dreaming itself back, furrowed the brow of the tired man as he thought and listened. His hands will not remain calm, and sweat, like blood, traces a sad face in the air of the ancient Chilean spring.

Briones, Letelier, Olivares, and Garcés lingered with Allende at the table, after dinner. Nothing to be alarmed about: advice from Briones resulting from his conversations with the Christian Democrats, Letelier's suggestions about neutralizing the coup, Garcés's opinions, questions by the president. The telephone rings. One of the guards takes it, passes the phone to Olivares.

"René Largo Farías is calling from the palace," Olivares says. "He has information to the effect that military trucks are mobilizing from Los Andes and San Felipe and heading toward Santiago. The word is coming from road workers paving the highways."

The president asks Letelier to call General Brady.

"There's nothing new," the latter responds. "Everything is normal. If something pops up, I'll call you." Largo Farías keeps calling. He's in the Press Office, with Miria Contreras, Carlos Jorquera, and a group of reporters.

"Tell Brady about the trucks," suggests Briones.

A little later, at 2:00 A.M., Largo Farías leaves the palace and notices some unusual activity as he walks by the Ministry of Defense.

Carlos Briones and Orlando Letelier say goodnight to Allende.

From his house Briones calls different locations in the country to monitor truck movements. Letelier goes to bed at 3:00 A.M., after confiding to Isabel Margarita that Allende will not only announce the plebiscite in a few hours, but also the retirement of several trigger-happy generals.

Garcés and Olivares spend the night at Tomás Moro Avenue.

Meanwhile, a call is received at Tati and Fernández Oña's house: "The coup starts at 7:45 A.M. The central committee of the

Communist party assembled before midnight when it received news of fleet movements. The headlines of *El Siglo* have changed. Now they're calling on the workers to take combat positions."

A little before midnight General Pinochet takes a leisurely stroll next to his house. His hands are behind his back, and he breathes deeply of the intense fragrance of jasmine in the night breeze. A car goes by slowly. He is not alarmed and keeps walking. Just agents of the Bureau of Investigation making their evening rounds. They continue on.

The city of Santiago is a tremendous silent arsenal with a tri-colored wick, soon to catch fire.

Why worry, why hurry? There's plenty of time, let's give time some time, let the speed freaks burn themselves out. Me? I'll wait till the last moment. He goes back home, gets ready for bed, looks at his watch, smiles. What do you suppose the other fellow is doing?

The general sleeps well. Without dreams. When dawn breaks, and dreams begin, it will be time to get up and step out shooting. He wakes, rested, at the normal hour, 5:30 A.M. He walks to the bathroom without hurrying, takes a shower, dresses, has a modest breakfast. He leaves without making a sound. He hears the telephone ringing behind him.

Why listen to calls of alarm, complaints, and reproaches? Let them ring off the hook, he thinks to himself. Allende must be glued to the phone right now. He'd be better off with a document in his hand—with a signature, a seal, a quick, crisp, patriotic resignation. I wonder if the plane is ready in Los Cerrillos. That's the important thing.

From his house he goes to his daughter's place.

"You say the coup has begun?"

"Of course it's begun. What do you think, I'm running away from it?"

"It's just that they're asking about you in Peñalolén. Station number 1."

What is the general waiting for? What does he have up his sleeve?

The Popular Unity staff is still arriving at La Moneda. Allende watches them calmly. He has a phone in his hand. He calls Tencha and recommends that she stay at the house. He is surprised to see Tati and Isabel. He argues with them, insisting that they leave the palace. He says to Tati, who is pregnant: "Your duty is to protect the life that you are carrying and not sacrifice it. You must leave now, before it's too late."

Someone mentions Letelier.

"Where is he?" Allende asks. "Call him at the Ministry of Defense."

But Letelier can't respond to calls anymore. Early that morning he had called the ministry and spoken to an evasive Admiral Carvajal. He decided to see for himself what was going on. Once in the street he discovered that his bodyguard had disappeared. When he got to the ministry, the guard on duty stopped him. From inside an officer gave the order to let him pass. All of a sudden Letelier found himself surrounded by soldiers with machine guns. He felt a sharp blow to the back of his head and lost consciousness among the gun butts and barrels.

Allende decides to address the country through a chain of radio stations. Corporación is the only station that responds. Radio Nacional de Agricultura is playing military marches. Matter-of-factly, without emphasis, he describes the situation he is facing. He asks for calm. "I will handle the crisis," he says.

Puccio, observing from one of the balconies, warns that the palace guard is starting to fall out. Allende looks. The guard is moving toward city hall in a little quickstep that looks bizarre, given the enormous size of the carabineros. General Sepúlveda tries to stop them, but they don't obey him. Now they are taking orders from General Mendoza, their self-designated chief.

Radio Nacional de Agricultura announces that La Moneda will be bombed. From his desk Allende watches the first bombing flights approach. He tries to get through to Carvajal. Puccio speaks to the admiral: "All the women, the secretaries, and service personnel must be evacuated from the palace."

"No problem," Carvajal answers. "You have ten minutes of truce."

Allende says goodbye to his daughters and assures Tati that he is fine and confident of his actions.

"The days of uncertainty and waiting, while the net drew tight around me, are over. It's a relief. Tati, the worst is over. Worry about your son and your compañero. Take care of Tencha. Find her. What has happened at Tomás Moro Avenue?"

A military campaign was unfolding mysteriously throughout the city. Taken by surprise, the local party headquarters, unions, and shantytowns felt its iron claws tighten around them. The bloody vendettas had started, but now there was no need for the assailants to hide in trees and spring down on their victims; they could just step out of big luxury cars, machine guns in hand and fire at will, with impunity. Hatches of ships opened up to swallow workers, students, professors, and doctors, all headed for the torture chambers and death.

There was no time left, president. But where was the force of the workers' movement, the thunderous power of its will to resist and counterattack?

"Faced with these facts, it only remains for me to say to the workers: I will not resign. Placed in this moment of historical crisis, I will pay for the loyalty of my people with my life. And I say to them that I am confident that the seed which we have sown in the noble conscience of thousands of Chileans cannot be cut down forever. In the name of the sacred interests of the people, in the name of the country, I call on you to have faith. History does not stop because of the existence of repression or crime. This is an impasse that will be crossed. It is possible that we will be crushed, but tomorrow will still belong to the people,

it will be for the workers. Humanity advances toward a better life."

Allende never learned that the house on Tomás Moro Avenue had been bombed. Tencha's life was saved by Allende's personal guard.

"I address, above all, the modest women of our land, the campesina who believed in us, the women who worked overtime, the mother who understood our concern for children. I address the professionals of the country . . . the youth, those who sang and gave their joy and fighting spirit to the movement. I address the men of Chile, the worker, the campesino, the intellectual, and those who will be persecuted."

Time is playing an absurd chess game, which Allende interprets as a singular challenge—he against everyone else on Judgment Day. Circumstances simply get in his way; he is anxious to face the outcome.

Allende joins the group that begins the armed resistance. In his hands he cradles an AKA machine gun, a gift from Fidel Castro. He speaks once more into the microphone of Radio Corporación. His message: defend yourselves in the workplace, don't provoke massacres. He gathers all of his people in the Toesca Room. He asks those without weapons to leave the palace.

"It is not a dishonor," he says. "It is a revolutionary duty. The resistance must go on outside, not for a day, not for weeks, but permanently and to the death."

Garcés gives an account of those who stayed until the bitter end: "By that time less than fifty civilians were left inside the palace. Of them there were some fifteen militants of the Socialist party, and six agents from the Bureau of Investigation who belonged to the president's escort guard. Twenty-one armed men made up the entire defense against infantry, tanks, and Hawker-

Hunter jets" (Garcés, *Allende y la experiencia,* pp. 394–95).

One way or another these people sealed their own fate on that day: Arsenio Pupin, Augusto Olivares, Jaime Barrios, Claudio Gimeno, Jorge Klein, Eduardo Paredes, Ricardo Pincheira, Enrique París, Enrique Huerta, Carlos Jorquera, Osvaldo Puccio and his son, Daniel Vergara, Lautaro Ojeda, Fernando Flores, and Miria Contreras. And the doctors serving the presidency: Danilo Bartulín, Arturo Jirón, Patricio Arroyo, Oscar Soto, and Arturo Guijón.

Surprisingly, Allende called Joan Garcés and asked him to leave La Moneda: "Someone has to tell what happened here, and you're the only man to do it."

Moments earlier he had released his aides-de-camp from any obligation to stay in the palace.

The phone rings. Commandant Badiola asks to speak with Allende. Negative. Puccio takes the call. He transmits a message from Pinochet: "Immediate surrender. The president must go to the Ministry of Defense."

Allende responds: "Tell him that a president of Chile does not surrender, that it is he who must come to La Moneda."

The rest becomes garbled with insults. A few minutes later Badiola calls again and asks the president to get in touch with General Baeza. Allende accepts. The dialogue is hair-raisingly eccentric: "Good evening, general," Allende says at 10:00 A.M. "How is the señora?"

"She is fine, thank you, excellency."

"And you, how is your health? You must take care of yourself, general. Did you recover from your heart attack? These are not things to take lightly. You must avoid excitement."

"Thank you, president. As a matter of fact, I wanted to repeat General Pinochet's request. He says for you to surrender, and that the plane is ready for you, your family, and whomever you would like to accompany you."

Allende is silent for a few moments and then says, "I won't

surrender, and I don't need any plane. The responsibility is yours. You will go down in history as the murderers of the president of the republic. . . . You don't stop history and a social process with bullets."

Badiola calls again to say that the bombing of the palace will be delayed an hour, and that there is still time to avoid a tragedy.

Even as he is speaking, however, the firing intensifies: the palace is under attack from artillery, machine guns, and automatic weapons. Allende, lying on the floor, covers one window and is firing next to his personal guard.

A new attempt at a truce is made a few minutes later. Minister Flores establishes direct contact with Admiral Carvajal, and both discuss the possibility of a parley. Allende rejects the idea.

A messenger from snipers who are defending the palace from the nearby Ministry of Public Works arrives unexpectedly with a plan to rescue the president. They want to take him out through Morandé Street and then to the ministry; from there, they are to cross the rooftops to Bandera Street. The messenger traces the plan in great detail. Allende refuses to participate, saying that his place is in La Moneda, right to the end.

At that moment two Hawker-Hunter jets fly over Santiago.

There is something beastly in the astute, unexpected movements of the jets as they buzz San Cristóbal Hill. They fly the length of the valley of Santiago just above the rooftops of Mapocho and San Pablo. They draw close to the center of the city, along a line of fire between the cathedral and Congress. They fire their first rockets. The explosions shake the city. Afterward the echo of small-arms fire lingers. The planes come back. A loud whistle and a halo of fire follow the collapse of the colonial walls of La Moneda. The glass roof over an inner patio crashes to the ground. The building is burning on all sides. Clouds of black and yellow smoke engulf a Chilean flag flying outside the palace.

"To be sure, Radio Magallanes will be silenced, and my voice will no longer reach you. It doesn't matter, you will con-

tinue to hear me. I will always be next to you, and at least in your memory I will be a worthy man who was loyal to his country. The people must defend themselves. . . . Workers of my country, I have faith in Chile and its destiny. Others will take on the struggle and surpass this gray and bitter day that the forces of treason claim to have won. Know that sooner than later the great avenues will open to free men who will pass down them on their way to constructing a better society.

"Long live Chile, long live the people, long live the workers! These are my last words, spoken in the knowledge that the sacrifice is not in vain . . . and that at least there will be a moral punishment of the thieves, cowards, and traitors."

The tear-gas attack begins. Allende is not able to put the gas mask on over his glasses. The Ministry of Defense responds to a request by Flores that the planes cease bombing the workers' living areas. Allende consents to a parley, and Flores, Vergara, Puccio, and Puccio's son go out to negotiate in an open jeep. They move under the crossfire of snipers and soldiers.

Artillery is firing at the president's office. A Puma helicopter comes and goes, spitting its fury at the defenders of the Ministry of Public Works. Allende has the doors to the armory blown up with grenades. Four machine guns, Sik rifles, ammunition, masks, and helmets are found.

"Perro Olivares gestured to me," says Carlos Jorquera, "and showed me the white cloth he was wearing, as many others were, on his left arm, to help identify him. Luckily, I had a white handkerchief. Then he signaled to me very quietly, inviting me to walk with him out of the presidential office. In the little anteroom belonging to the president's private secretary, he talked about a tacit agreement between us, one we had never dared to speak aloud. He said, 'Brother, the last bullet in this weapon is for you. And I want you to agree that your last one is for me.' We embraced, and Perro, with his left arm around my shoulder, led me back to the president's office."

Later, looking for water, Jorquera went down to the basement, where he suddenly heard a strange noise: "The funny thing was that all of our little world was just one big noise. But now I heard a kind of hoarse moaning sound, soft but deep; it was a noise that, in spite of coming from down below, could be heard above the others. It was coming from one of the rooms that looked out onto Morandé Street, which is where most of the firing was taking place. It was a room in shadows. It had only one window, half open, and a ray of sunlight was shining through. In a chair, holding his machine gun on his lap, was Perro, dying.

Jorquera made himself heard by shouting at the top of his lungs; doctors Soto and Jirón ran down. Allende would come down himself a little later. Jorquera cried, and the president embraced him, repeating, "My poor kid . . . my son, my little son!" They went back to the corridor where the president's security guard was firing on infantry commandos who were trying to break through resistance at the Morandé Street entrance. The commandos were repulsed by machine-gun fire.

Allende organized a group, the last one, to try to leave the palace.

"In single file," he said. "Leave your weapons over here."

Miria Contreras describes the departure: "The president gathered us all together in the corridor. He told us to go down calmly and leave all our weapons, helmets, and masks behind. . . . He would stay, with a group of compañeros from his private guard. He ordered Soto to proceed first, carrying a white rag. Before we left he said, 'I want you to be calm, and before you go I want a minute of silent homage to the first martyr of the Chilean revolution, compañero Augusto Olivares.' After having surrendered, out in the street, I wondered what happened to Olivares's body. Someone told me that they gave it to his compañera, Mireya Latorre."

Later, much later, in exile, I look at the face of a woman on a movie screen. A voice asks, "What did you lose on September 11, 1973?"

Other people have already answered the same question. This woman looks up and keeps silent. The camera closes in on her face. Seconds pass. The silence becomes unbearable. I have the feeling that she has stopped time. In the woman's eyes I see a world I know and a story that is almost forgotten. Time passes. I know that she will never answer. Silence fills the screen.

No one has said that on the day of the coup she arrived at La Moneda in a car driven by her oldest son, that there was no time to say goodbye, that as she entered the palace her son was held by soldiers, taken to the basement of a nearby building, pushed against a wall, and shot along with other prisoners.

As I listen to her silence, I see her face. Fragile shadows seem to move across her eyes. She says nothing. Nothing. Entering the palace she stopped for a second, framed by fire and smoke. She was wearing a black blouse with green polka dots, and black slacks. She walked in, fast. Now I see her face and all her sorrow fading like a soft sun disappearing heavily behind the horizon.

Jorquera ended up in the Ministry of Defense building, his collarbone broken. He was shut in a room with Puccio and Vergara. Observing his state, Puccio had the presence of mind to pass him some pills.

"I thought I understood," said Jorquera, "and with a farewell gesture I swallowed them down. I was committing suicide. But the pills weren't poison, they were aspirin."

While Jorquera was being held prisoner, he saw Dr. Edgardo Enríquez being taken down to the basement of the building for interrogation. According to Dr. Jirón, don Edgardo was told to lie face down on the floor. After about an hour the soldiers ordered him to stand up and undress. Tall, calm but defiant, don Edgardo refused. He had already been lined up against a wall when a general came in, recognized him, and took him back upstairs to his own office.

Allende and his compañeros have been fighting for two hours.

The infantry advances. Toxic gases surround and invade the

palace. A violent explosion knocks the president down. He is wounded, with pieces of glass stuck in his neck and back. The Aide-de-camps' Room is in flames. All the water faucets are open.

The soldiers are at the Morandé entrance. They start up the stairs.

Allende and his men file singly along a nonexistent path, a trail of smoke and scorched stucco, while stray bullets ricochet through the rooms, sending pieces of furniture flying before the bullets bite into the walls. Shrill whistles follow the tails of fire streaking through the air. A coffered ceiling caves in, and along with the beautiful wood of the wainscoting, curtains, picture frames, and tapestries are now burning. The busts of Chile's presidents are blasted and charred.

A door, like a flame, seems to leap up in front of them, and Allende shouts that it is the way out. Now they run, stumbling, coughing, covering their mouths with handkerchiefs. It is impossible to distinguish faces, no one can recognize anyone else. His daughters are out in the street. His compañeros are disappearing quickly. Someone hesitates and for a few seconds is silhouetted in the door of fire. A voice calls his name, but the crash of a piece of roof buries the sound. He thinks he has responded, moving his lips, but he only thought her name.

Then Allende returns to combat. This time he is alone, groping his way blindly in the darkness, pursuing distant flashes, surrounded by explosions and bullets. His glasses are now useless. He is unable to distinguish between the landing of the stairs and the hall that leads to the office of Chile's presidents. The building has been burning furiously for some time. Now there is nothing but mud, ashes, and smoke. Armed men are searching for his body in the corridors, under the desks, behind the curtains, shooting relentlessly at phantoms.

Their bullets can't find the man in his infinite solitude, the man who refuses to fall, who moves through shadows and ruin, looking for the door of the Red Room, which has disappeared in flames.

Allende can hear voices behind him, coming from invisible

hallways. The first patrol advances toward him. Wounded and suffocating, alone, deafened by strafing helicopters, the wild dog pack of soldiers ever closing in, he sees his own face in a broken mirror, shining with sweat and blood. Two officers appear in the mirror and shoot. Allende, looking into his own eyes for the last time, squeezes the trigger.

It was a few minutes before 2 P.M. My neighbor, the president, had just died.

Postscript: After the Coup

Jorge Alessandri Rodríguez, former president of Chile (1958–64), gave his firm support to the military during and after the coup. After a long illness he died at the Military Hospital in 1986.

Hortensia Bussi v. de Allende and her daughter Carmen Paz flew to exile in Mexico under the protection of the Mexican government. They are now living in Chile. Daughters Beatriz (Tati) and Isabel went to Cuba. Tati committed suicide in October 1977. Isabel is back in Chile directing the Salvador Allende Foundation.

Laura Allende, President Allende's youngest sister and a socialist representative in Congress, went to Cuba, where she took charge of Tati's children. Fatally ill with cancer, she tried to return to Chile. Pinochet would not allow it. John Paul II and Queen Elizabeth of England interceded, to no avail. Laura Allende committed suicide on May 23, 1981, and is buried in Havana.

Isabel Allende, novelist, second cousin of Salvador Allende, lived in exile in Venezuela. She now resides in San Rafael, California.

Clodomiro Almeyda, minister of foreign relations and vice-president of Chile, was exiled for a time in East Germany. He has since returned to Chile and was until recently ambassador to Russia.

Carlos Altamirano, secretary-general of the Socialist party during

Allende's government, managed to evade the secret police and go into exile in France.

Alberto Bachelet, air force general, remained loyal to the Allende government. He was imprisoned and tortured. He died in Santiago's public jail in 1974.

Fernando Bachelet, first secretary at the Chilean embassy in Washington, D.C., returned to Chile and is now consul general in Buenos Aires.

Jaime Barrios, director of the Central Bank, died fighting in La Moneda.

Danilo Bartulín, President Allende's personal physician, survived the battle of La Moneda, and went into exile in Mexico.

Carlos Briones, minister of the interior, was imprisoned by the Junta. He was later set free and is now living in Santiago.

César Cecchi, physician, was the victim of an accident and died on the operating table.

Luis Corvalán, secretary-general of the Communist party, was taken prisoner, then allowed to live in exile in the Soviet Union. He has since returned to Chile.

Miguel Enríquez, physician and secretary-general of MIR, and his wife, Carmen Castillo, were ambushed by DINA. Miguel died fighting. Carmen, who was expecting a child, was wounded; she was later allowed to travel to France.

Edgardo Enríquez, physician and minister of education, Miguel's father, was imprisoned on Dawson Island, then exiled to Mexico.

Fernando Flores, minister of the economy, was taken prisoner and sent to Dawson Island. He and his family now reside in Berkeley, California.

Eduardo Frei Montalva, former president of Chile (1964–70), remained in Chile after the coup. He died in 1982.

Joan Garcés, political adviser to President Allende, returned

to Europe and became a university professor in
France.

Carlos Jorquera, journalist, was sent to Dawson Island, then exiled to Mexico. He now lives in Chile.

Gustavo Leigh, air force general, was thrown out of the Junta by
General Pinochet. He survived an attempt against
his life and now lives in Santiago.

Bernardo Leighton, Christian Democratic leader, went into exile
in Italy, survived an attempt against his life, and returned to Chile.

Orlando Letelier, minister of defense, was sent to Dawson Island.
After being freed by the Junta, he traveled to Venezuela and then to Washington, D.C., where he was
murdered by agents of DINA, the Junta's secret
police, and by anti-Castro Cuban exiles. The legal
process against his killers is still open. His wife,
Isabel Margarita Letelier, and her sons lived in exile
in Washington, D.C. They are now in Chile.

César Mendoza, general of the carabineros and member of the
Junta, was fired by General Pinochet and lives in
Santiago.

Pablo Neruda, suffering from cancer, died of a heart attack soon
after the coup, on September 29, 1973.

Eduardo "Coco" Paredes, director of police investigations in the
Allende government and physician, was taken prisoner in La Moneda and brutally killed by soldiers.

Payita, Miria Contreras, left Chile for exile in Cuba. She later
moved to Paris, where she works for the Cuban
Travel Agency.

Carlos Prats, army general loyal to Allende, was allowed to leave
Chile and to settle in Buenos Aires. His friend General Juan Perón, president of Argentina, warned
him of a possible attempt against his life. In 1975
a commando, believed to be in connivance with the
assassins of Letelier, ambushed him and his wife in
front of their house and killed them.

Osvaldo Puccio, President Allende's secretary, was imprisoned for two years. Until his death he lived in East Germany, where he wrote and published a book of memoirs. His son Osvaldo Puccio Huidobro returned to Chile and is now a leader of the Socialist party.

Aniceto Rodríguez, socialist senator, was imprisoned on Dawson Island and then allowed to leave Chile and to settle in Caracas. He is now Chilean ambassador to Venezuela.

Andrés Rojas Weiner, press attaché at the Chilean embassy in Washington, D.C., now lives in Sausalito, California.

José María Sepúlveda, general of the carabineros, remained loyal to President Allende and fought in La Moneda. He lives in Santiago.

Oscar Soto, personal physician to President Allende, was taken prisoner in La Moneda. He lives in Santiago.

Volodia Teitelboim, communist senator, went into exile in the Soviet Union. He now lives in Chile and is secretary-general of the Chilean Communist party.

José Tohá, minister of defense, was imprisoned on Dawson Island and then brought back to Santiago gravely ill. His wife visited him the day before he died. He had been the victim of sadistic interrogations. According to hospital administrators he hanged himself. He was probably strangled by his guards.

Moy de Tohá, widow of José Tohá, lived in exile in Mexico. She returned to Chile and entered the diplomatic service.

Radomiro Tomic remained in Chile after the coup. He died in 1991 in Santiago.

Daniel Vergara, undersecretary of the interior, was wounded en route to Dawson Island. He died later in exile.

Chronology:
1920-1989

1920–24   During his first administration, Arturo Alessandri
Palma is unable to secure congressional approval
for his liberal reforms. General unrest increases as
a result of unemployment and economic depression. In September 1924 Alessandri resigns. Congress refuses to accept his resignation, instead giving him a six-month leave. He travels to Europe. A
military junta led by General Luis Altamirano takes
over the government.

1925–31   Young officers, led by Carlos Ibáñez, rebel against
General Altamirano. At their invitation Alessandri
returns to Chile in March 1925. A new Constitution is approved. Following an impasse with Ibáñez, now the defense minister, Alessandri resigns
again in October 1925 and appoints Luis Barros
Borgoño to succeed him. In 1926 Emiliano Figueroa Larraín is elected president. He resigns in
March 1927. Ibáñez assumes dictatorial powers.
The stock market crash, economic depression, and
Ibáñez's ruthless political persecution of the opposition bring an end to his dictatorship.

1932–38   After the failure of interim governments such as
those under Dávila and Montero, and the socialist
republic led by Grove for one hundred days, Alessandri returns once again to the presidency. In
1932–33 the Socialist party of Chile is founded;
from 1935 to 1938 a dissident group of young mil-

itants from the Conservative party organizes Falange Nacional, which will eventually become the Christian Democratic party; and in 1936 Chilean leftist parties unite in a Popular Front, in preparation for the coming presidential elections. In 1938 Chilean führer Jorge González von Marées leads a Nazi attempt to overthrow Alessandri's government; his followers, mostly university students, are defeated and executed.

1938–41   Pedro Aguirre Cerda, the Popular Front candidate, wins the presidential election. His administration is seriously hurt by an earthquake that destroys much of the south, including Concepción and Chillán. Allende is appointed minister of public health. President Aguirre Cerda dies in 1941.

1942–46   Juan Antonio Ríos becomes president. The Popular Front is dissolved. Ríos visits the United States. Upon his return he is taken gravely ill, and he dies in 1946.

1946–52   Ríos's successor, Gabriel González Videla, is elected with the support of communists and socialists. González eventually turns against them and supports Truman's Cold War campaigns. His persecution of Pablo Neruda becomes international news.

1952–58   Ibáñez is once again elected president of Chile, this time as a reformist candidate. His administration is deeply hurt by economic problems.

1958–64   Conservative leader Jorge Alessandri Rodríguez, the son of Arturo Alessandri, is elected president. He narrowly defeats Allende, who runs as the FRAP candidate.

1964–70   Eduardo Frei Montalva, a Christian Democrat, is elected president as the leader of "Revolution in

Liberty," a nationalistic, anti-oligarchy movement. Frei places emphasis on rural reforms.

1970–73   Salvador Allende, the Popular Unity candidate, is elected president on a platform of drastic anti-imperialist measures, such as the nationalization of the copper industry. Allende defines his administration as a socialist revolution within a democratic framework. A military coup on September 11, 1973, overthrows Allende's government. Allende dies in La Moneda.

1973–89   A dictatorship of the armed forces rules Chile under the command of General Augusto Pinochet. In October 1988 Chileans reject the dictatorship in a national referendum. Presidential elections are held in December 1989. Patricio Aylwin Azócar, a Christian Democrat, is elected president.

Notes

The following acronyms are used in the text:

API	Acción Popular Independiente
APRA	Alianza Popular Revolucionaria de América
BID	Banco Interamericano de Desarrollo
CORFO	Corporación de Fomento
CUT	Central Unica de Trabajadores
DINA	Dirección de Inteligencia Nacional
FECH	Federación de Estudiantes de Chile
FOCH	Federación Obrera de Chile
FRAP	Frente Revolucionario de Acción Popular
GAP	Grupo de Amigos del Presidente
MAPU	Movimiento de Acción Popular Unitario
MIR	Movimiento Izquierdista Revolucionario
OLAS	Organización Latinoamericana de Solidaridad
UNCTAD	United Nations Conference on Trade and Development

4 September flags: Chilean flags displayed in celebration of the day of national independence, September 18, 1810.

5 Puerto Montt: A city in southern Chile and the center of German colonization, famous for its seaport Angelmó and its fish markets.

6 Operation Unitas: Joint naval maneuvers held yearly by the United States and Chile.

6 massacre of Santa María: A bloody repression by military forces, on December 21, 1907, of protesting workers in Chile's nitrate fields. Workers and their families were held prisoner in the main courtyard of the Domingo Santa María School in Iquique. The soldiers opened fire, killing several hundred people.

7 Gastón Pascal Lyon: A businessman and member of an aristocratic family in Valparaíso, he and Laura Allende Gossens were the parents of Andrés Pascal Allende, one of the leaders of MIR.

7 Partido Radical: A middle-of-the-road party geared toward the liberal ideas of professionals, intellectuals, and public employees. Its equivalent in the United States would be the Democratic party. The Partido

Radical was founded in 1863 by such political figures as the Matta brothers—Manuel Antonio (1826–92) and Guillermo (1829–99)—and Enrique MacIver (1845–1922).

7 Recabarren: Luis Emilio Recabarren (1876–1924), one of the founders of the Workers' Federation of Chile (FOCH) in 1909. In 1912 he started the Socialist Workers' party, forerunner of the Chilean Communist party. Recabarren committed suicide in 1924. See my book *Como un árbol rojo* (1968).

14 Pablo Iglesias (1850–1925): Founder and president of the Spanish Workers' Socialist party. Iglesias's ideas had a powerful influence on Recabarren and other Chilean labor leaders.

14 Bilbao: Francisco Bilbao (1823–65), author of *La sociabilidad chilena*, a book representing anticlerical, liberal ideology, which was bitterly attacked by conservative forces. Bilbao suffered prison and exile. In 1850 he founded the Sociedad de la Igualdad together with Santiago Arcos, to defend his revolutionary ideas. Bilbao died in Buenos Aires.

17 *rotos*: The name applied to Chileans of the working class; also, an epithet to indicate national character, as in, *roto muy valiente*.

19 he was the only Chilean military leader in those years who had actually fought in a war: Carlos Ibáñez del Campo led the first military mission sent by Chile to El Salvador in 1903. Ibáñez founded the Military School of El Salvador and led a Salvadoran regiment in a war against Guatemala.

20 the Lion of Tarapacá: A nickname applied to Alessandri during his presidential campaign in the northern provinces of Chile.

21 *"What could that noise be . . . ?"*: The words to a popular song referring to the political activities of university students.

35 *medio pelo*: A derogatory term for the "middle class."

51 the magazine *Topaze*: A weekly, satirical magazine, directed by Jorge (Coke) Délano. It reached high popularity during the Ibáñez and Alessandri governments.

71 Chaco War (1932–35): A lengthy and bloody conflict between Bolivia and Paraguay, motivated by the oil interests of these countries and multinational companies. See Oscar Cerruto's novel *Aluvión de fuego* (1936).

71 *Claridad*: A Chilean literary magazine founded by Pablo Neruda, Pablo de Rokha, and Domingo Gómez Rojas, among others. It followed the antifascist, antiwar beliefs of the European movement Clarté led by Romain Rolland, Albert Einstein, Georges Nicolai, and Henri Barbusse.

71 *"Para la noche buena . . ."*: "On Christmas eve / on Christmas eve / mamita, mamita / they'll be hanged."

74 the granting of a seaport to Bolivia: A reference to a conflict between Chile and Bolivia in regard to Bolivia's plea for a seaport.

76 *pisco*: An alcoholic beverage produced in Chile and Peru.

79 Prestes: Luis Carlos Prestes (1898–1990), a revolutionary military leader in Brazil, who led a legendary march against the government in an attempt to establish a Soviet regime.

102 the polemics of Proudhon: Mariátegui (see below, note to p. 106) participated directly in these polemics regarding Marxist ideology.

102 the Spanish Marxist Iglesias: See above, note to p. 14.

102 king of the Araucanians: A reference to a legend regarding the fabulous female warriors in the Marañón River. The City of the Caesars is a reference to the same legend.

104 "the people call him Gabriel": A reference to Neruda's poem for González Videla, at that time his personal hero, later on a hated personal enemy.

106 Mariátegui: José Carlos Mariátegui (1895–1930), Peruvian essayist, author of *Seven Interpretive Essays on Peruvian Reality* (1988; orig. pub. 1928). He represents Marxist tendencies opposed to the liberalism of Víctor Raúl Haya de la Torre, the leader of APRA. Rómulo Betancourt, the Venezuelan leftist leader, was president from 1945 to 1948 and from 1959 to 1964.

109 Matte Hurtado: Eugenio Matte Hurtado (1896–1934) was cofounder of the Socialist party and a close friend of Allende. An attorney by profession, he became gran maestro of the Chilean masons in 1931. In this same year he founded a movement called Nueva Acción Pública (New Political Action), a forerunner of the Popular Front. Matte is the author of *Nuestra cuestión social*.

115 Prestes: See above, note to p. 79.

141 FRAP: A coalition of leftist and Center parties, including the Partido Radical, the Socialist party, and the Communist party, in support of Allende.

144 Workers' party: Partido del Trabajo was a small leftist group founded in order to influence the balance within FRAP.

152 *piure*: A mollusk considered a delicacy in southern Chile.

160 Committee of 40: "The 40 Committee was a sub-Cabinet-level body of the Executive Branch whose mandate was to review proposed major covert actions. The Committee has existed in similar form since the 1950s under a variety of names. Since 1969 it included among other officials, the Undersecretary of State for Political Affairs, the Deputy Secretary of Defense, the Chairman of the Joint Chiefs of Staff, and the Director of Central Intelligence. Heading the Committee at the time of the Allende election was Nixon's National Security Advisor, Henry Kissinger." (Chavkin, *Storm Over Chile*, p. 45.)

168 Guillermo Atías: Chilean novelist, author of *Tiempo banal* (1955), *A la sombra de los días* (1965), *Y corría el billete* (1972), and *Le sang dans la rue* (1978).
216 Eduardo Paredes's father: Eduardo "Coco" Paredes served for a time as director of police investigations in the Allende government.

Selected Bibliography

Aguilar, Alonso, et al. *El gobierno de Allende y la lucha por el socialismo en Chile*. Puebla, Mexico: Universidad Nacional Autónoma de México, Instituto de Investigaciones Sociales, 1976.

Alegría, Fernando. *El Evangelio según Cristián, el fotógrafo*. Buenos Aires: Ediciones de la Flor, 1988.

————. *El paso de los gansos*. New York: Ediciones Puelche, 1975.

————. *Salvador Allende*. São Paulo: Brasiliense, 1983.

Almeyda, Clodomiro. *Liberación y fascismo*. Mexico City: Editorial Nuestro Tiempo–Casa de Chile, 1979.

Allende, Salvador. *Salvador Allende y la América Latina, 12 discursos y 2 conferencias de prensa*. Mexico City: Casa de Chile, 1978.

Allende, Salvador, et al. *La vía chilena al socialismo*. Mexico City: Siglo Veintiuno Editores, 1973.

El alma de Alessandri. Santiago: Editorial Nascimento, 1925.

Archivo Salvador Allende. *América Latina: Un pueblo continente*. Puebla, Mexico: Universidad Nacional Autónoma de México, 1986.

Bitar, Sergio. *Transición, socialismo y democracia: La experiencia chilena*. Mexico City: Siglo Veintiuno Editores, 1979.

Boorstein, Edward. *Allende's Chile: An Inside View*. New York: International Publishers, 1977.

Buhrer-Solal, Jean Claude. *Allende: Un Itinéraire sans détours*. Paris: Editions L'Age de l'Homme, 1974.

Cárdenas, Cuauhtemoc, et al. *Imágenes de Salvador Allende*. Morelia, Michoacán, Mexico: Centro de Estudios del Movimiento Obrero Salvador Allende, 1981.

Castro, Fidel. *El más alto ejemplo de heroísmo*. Havana: Instituto Cubano del Libro, Editorial de Ciencias Sociales, 1973.

Charlín, Carlos. *Del avión rojo a la República Socialista*. Santiago: Empresa Editora Nacional Quimantú Ltda., 1972.

Chavkin, Samuel. *Storm over Chile: The Junta Under Siege*. Westport, Conn.: Lawrence Hill & Co., 1985.

Correa Prieto, Luis. *El presidente Ibáñez, la política y los partidos*. Santiago: Editorial Orbe, 1962.

Davis, Nathaniel. *The Last Two Years of Salvador Allende*. Ithaca, N.Y.: Cornell University Press, 1985.

Debray, Régis. *Conversación con Allende*. Mexico City: Siglo Veintiuno Editores, 1971.

Dinamarca, Manuel. *La República Socialista Chilena, orígenes legítimos del Partido Socialista*. 2d ed. Santiago: Ediciones Documentas, 1985.

Donoso, Ricardo. *Alessandri, agitador y demoledor*. 2 vols. Mexico City: Fondo de Cultura Económica, 1954.

Durand, Luis. *Don Arturo*. Santiago: Zig-Zag, 1952.

Feinber, Richard E. *Chile's Legal Revolution*. New York: New American Library, 1972.

Fidel en Chile, textos completos de su diálogo con el pueblo. Santiago: Empresa Editora Nacional Quimantú Ltda., 1972.

Garcés, Joan E. *Allende y la experiencia chilena: Las armas de la política*. Barcelona: Ariel, 1976.

————. *El Estado y los problemas tácticos en el gobierno de Allende*. Madrid: Siglo Veintiuno Editores, 1974.

————, ed. *Nuestro camino al socialismo: La vía chilena*. Buenos Aires: Editorial Papiro, 1976.

González Camus, Ignacio. *El día en que murió Allende*. Santiago: Cesoc, Ediciones Chile y América, 1988.

Hersh, Seymour M. "The Price of Power: Kissinger, Nixon, and Chile." *The Atlantic Monthly*, 250, no. 6 (1982): 31–58.

House of Representatives. *United States and Chile During the Allende Years, 1970–1973*. Washington, D.C.: Government Printing Office, 1975.

Kelley, Ken. "Mrs. Hortensia Bussi de Allende." *Penthouse*, 7, no. 2 (1975): 71–90.

Kirberg, Enrique. *Los nuevos profesionales: Educación universitaria de trabajadores. Chile: UTE, 1968–1973*. Mexico City: EDUG/Universidad de Guadalajara, 1981.

Labarca Goddard, Eduardo. *Chile al rojo*. Santiago: Ediciones de la Universidad Técnica del Estado, 1971.

Ladrón de Guevara, Matilde. *Destierro*. Barcelona: Editorial Fontamara, S.A., 1983.

Lafertte, Elías. *Vida de un comunista (páginas autobiográficas)*. Santiago, 1961.

Lavretski, J. *Salvador Allende*. Moscow: Editorial Progreso, 1978.

Loveman, Brian. *Chile: The Legacy of Hispanic Capitalism*. New York: Oxford University Press, 1979.

Martner, Gonzalo. *El pensamiento económico del gobierno de Allende*. Santiago: Editorial Universitaria, 1971.

————. *El gobierno del presidente Salvador Allende, 1970–1973: Una evaluación*. Santiago: LAR, 1988.

Méndez Arceo, Sergio. *Homilía por Salvador Allende.* Mexico City: Catedral de Cuernavaca, 1973.

Mendoza, María Luisa y Edmundo Domínguez Aragonés. *Allende, el Bravo: Los días mexicanos.* Mexico City: Diana, 1973.

Novoa, Eduardo. *La batalla del cobre.* Santiago: Empresa Editora Nacional Quimantú Ltda., 1972.

Ortúzar, Ximena. *México y Pinochet, la ruptura.* Mexico City: Editorial Nueva Imagen, 1986.

Pinochet de la Barra, Oscar. *El Cardenal Silva Henríquez, luchador por la justicia.* Santiago: Editorial Salesiana, 1987.

Pinochet U., Augusto. *El día decisivo, 11 de septiembre de 1973.* 3d ed. Santiago: Editorial Andrés Bello, 1980.

Politzer, Patricia. *Altamirano.* Buenos Aires: Grupo Editorial Zeta, 1989.

Prats González, Carlos. *Memorias, testimonio de un soldado.* Santiago: Pehuén, 1985.

Puccio, Osvaldo. *Un cuarto de siglo con Allende, recuerdos de su secretario privado.* Santiago: Editorial Emisión, 1985.

Rojas, Robinson. *Estos mataron a Allende: Reportaje a la masacre de un pueblo.* Barcelona: Editorial Martínez Roca, 1974.

Secretaría General de Gobierno Chile. *Documentos secretos de la ITT.* Santiago: Empresa Editora Nacional Quimantú Ltda., 1972.

Selser, Gregorio. *Chile para recordar.* Buenos Aires: Crisis, 1974.

Timossi, Jorge. *Grandes alamedas: El combate del presidente Allende.* Havana: Editorial de Ciencias Sociales, 1974.

Taufic, Camilo. *Chile en la hoguera, crónica de la represión militar.* Buenos Aires: Ediciones Corregidor, 1974.

Tohá, Moy de, and Isabel de Letelier. *Allende, demócrata intransigente.* Santiago: Amerinda Ediciones, 1986.

Uribe, Armando. *El libro negro de la intervención norteamericana en Chile.* Mexico City: Siglo Veintiuno Editores, 1974.

Vuskovic, Pedro. *Una sola lucha.* Mexico City: Editorial Nuestro Tiempo, S.A., 1978.

Witker, Alejandro. *El compañero Tohá: Esbozo biográfico, testimonios y documentos.* Mexico City: Casa de Chile, 1977.

———. *Salvador Allende, 1908–1973: Prócer de la liberación nacional.* Puebla, Mexico: Universidad Nacional Autónoma de México, 1980.

Zemelman, Hugo. *El proceso de transformación y los problemas de dirección política, 1970–1973.* Mexico City: El Colegio de México, 1974.

Library of Congress
Cataloging-in-Publication Data

Alegría, Fernando, 1918–
[Allende.   English]
Allende : a novel / Fernando Alegría ;
translated by Frank Janney.
p.   cm.
Includes bibliographical
references (p.   ).
ISBN 0-8047-1998-5 (acid-free paper) :
1. Allende Gossens, Salvador,
1908–1973—Fiction.
I. Title.
PQ8097.A734A7813
1993
863—dc20
92-441